Dying for LA

Ian Jones

Clink
Street

Published by Clink Street Publishing 2021

Copyright © 2021

First edition.

ISBN:
978-1-913962-28-9 - paperback
978-1-913962-29-6 - ebook

Chapter One

Late Sunday; February, in Downtown Los Angeles.

John Smith wandered along slowly on his way to 7th Street Metro Station. All around him huge buildings towered up, normally this would be a bustling area but now the streets were quiet, it had just gone ten in the evening and the city was winding down, getting ready for the week to start all over again the next day. He had enjoyed a good meal in an expensive Chinese restaurant, courtesy of a grateful customer. His work in the city was complete and he was considering staying a couple of nights extra to have a good look around. He had never spent a great deal of time in LA so he was interested to see what it had to offer, then he could get on a plane and go and see his daughter in New York.

He had enjoyed dinner that evening, a restaurant that despite the day of the week had been busy. The food had been excellent and the service impeccable. Despite his initial reservations the evening had been worthwhile, it was likely there would be even more work as a result.

It took him a while to find the station, there was no signpost but eventually he found it, on a corner behind thick black pillars. He was still out of sync with LA time so he decided to stop by at an Irish bar just round the corner and sat down with a Miller Lite watching premiership football on the screen in front of him. West Ham were beating Liverpool. The guy sat next to him was watching NFL on the three other screens which were all in a line along one wall and they cheerfully criticised each other's choice of football to watch, until Liverpool scored an equaliser and his sparring partner decided that actually more was happening on John's screen and bought him another beer, and they sat watching until the final whistle blew.

John politely declined the offer of more to drink and then left. He walked down to the corner, entered into the station and went through the turnstiles and then down the steps to the right platform. It wasn't too busy, no more than twenty or so people waiting. He wandered about half way along and leant against the wall next to a staircase, waiting. There were stone seats in a square further along with an old drunk sitting at the other end smiling to himself and softly singing 'Dirty Old Town'. The other waiting passengers were spread out disparately along the platform, standing singly or in small groups. Close to John two women stopped to wait, one was repeatedly checking her watch. She twisted around to look down the tunnel and a mobile phone fell from the bulky handbag she was clutching. John bent forward and picked it up then handed it back to her. she took it and stared blankly at him.

'Thank you,' the other woman told him with a frown at her companion.

John nodded and went back to leaning on the wall.

The information message was unchanging, it seemed to have settled on the next train being two minutes away.

Everything was calm and serene, people were just waiting patiently for the train, it was the end of the weekend, time to be at home.

Suddenly there was a shout, followed by a shrill scream, then another, louder. More shouts. Sudden panic and yelling all coming from where a set of stairs descended. John turned to look and saw a man running fast down the platform toward him, his mouth wide open. Behind him were two men in pseudo-combat uniforms, moving stealthily forward and aiming assault rifles and he could see more similarly dressed figures visible behind. John didn't think twice; he didn't stop to wonder what was going on or if there was anything he could do, he instantly threw himself down against the wall he was leaning on, into the corner tight to against the floor just as the guns started firing single shots; repeatedly, deafeningly loud in the confined space, sounds of breaking glass and ricochets and then silence. Muffled sobs, footsteps, and then more shots, closer this time and then a loud thump.

Silence again. More footsteps, then another couple of single shots.

Silence.

Then rapid fire, a short burst, forward to where John was lying, two guns that were moving, bullets suddenly blasting and raking across the wall then into the floor. A chunk of thick tile shot up and struck him hard on the forehead. He screwed his eyes up in pain and could feel warm blood running down.

Footsteps moving cautiously close by. Short muffled conversation.

Slowly, carefully, John moved his head to look. He could see the body of the woman who had dropped her phone lying on her side, and another close by. Impossible to tell if they were alive or dead. Next to them there was a pair of scuffed combat boots, then another pair appeared, walking hesitantly, and stopped. Two men were standing there together. One of them put down an AK-47, leaning it against the wall right where John had been standing. John could see it in his peripheral vision. His instincts took over. It was an old original model, wooden stock. It looked well cared for, and fitted with a standard magazine. Thirty rounds. The gun had been placed with the selector lever facing him, he could see it was set to single. There was a carving in the stock near the shoulder rest; 1-Too. It rang a bell, but he couldn't place it. But there was only one important thing: and that was there was a gun. Right next to him.

So …

How many shots have been fired?

Would the magazine have been full in the first place?

Had this gun even been used at all?

If not, did it operate?

How many men were there in total? He could see the two for sure, and could hear at least one voice calling from further away.

He moved his eyes again, careful not to move his head. The two men were facing each other, side on to him. There was rattling, and then a bag dropped to the floor. It was the bag the woman had been holding.

'Nothing?' he heard one man ask with a heavy accent.

'Nothing there,' was the reply.

Then a shout from one of the men, a couple of words, in a language John had heard before but couldn't place. A shout in return from a distance, and then another from the same place but moving away. Then the bag was kicked hard, and it skittered away, scattering its contents across the floor.

'It's not here!' a shout, in English.

Muted conversation, and a different bag was kicked heavily.

One set of feet turned away slightly, then the other. More muttered conversation, then raised voices, cursing, not in English.

It was clear the men were annoyed about something, distracted.

John grabbed his chance. Do or die.

He tensed up and then rolled swiftly out from the corner, grabbing the gun and whirling round, yanking the operating handle as he did so. A round shot out the ejector port and still moving up on to his knees he fired twice, hitting both men; one in the chest and the other in the neck; the second man's gun dropping to the floor with a clatter and then he was moving, running fast and aiming toward the end of the platform to the exit, where he had heard the shouts. He could see one man moving up and he sprinted down the remainder of the platform and fired up, hitting the man near the top and he fell, rolling and then being carried upward on the escalator.

He moved steadily up following the body with the gun held out in front of him and reached the top then walked forward and cautiously turned the corner. He reached the next set of stairs and headed upward slowly, still keeping the gun trained forwards. At the top he saw the street, there was no sign of anyone there, then he heard shouting again from behind him so he ran back down to the platform, taking in the scene properly for the first time. Everyone was still on the floor. There was a man sitting slumped close to him who was calling out for help, over and over.

'Call 911. Right away,' John ordered.

The man closed his mouth with a snap and looked back at him, shocked, staring at the gun in his hand.

'Do it,' John told him. 'Now. And then get on up to the street to wait for them.'

The man nodded rapidly and pulled out a mobile phone.

John walked further down. All around him people were staring up at him, frightened, totally bewildered.

'If you are unhurt please stand up, there is no danger now. Head upstairs,' he called out.

Slowly, people began to stand, looking all around them, dazed. There was a body not moving close to him so John knelt down next to it, laying the gun down. It was a woman, she had been hit twice in the chest. Her eyes were staring at him but she had a weak pulse. John pulled his jacket off and balled it up and pressed it hard against her chest.

'Come here,' he ordered to a man who was standing watching. 'Look, keep the pressure on, hard, we have to try and limit the blood loss do you understand?'

The man nodded, bent down and did what he was told.

There was another woman lying further down. She was on her back by the edge of the platform, John went over to her but he knew she was dead immediately, there were gunshot wounds across her stomach and chest and a lot of blood. There was a third woman's body right next to her, lying on its side facing away from him. Also dead.

He returned back to where he had been on the platform. The drunk was looking wildly around, muttering. The two women that had been standing there were now lying on the floor. He couldn't see if they were alive or dead so needed to help. As he knelt down he heard the sirens and then within minutes the platform was crawling with LAPD and not long afterward the medics arrived.

Gratefully he stepped back and let the professionals get on with it. He looked up and down. People were moving, shocked and glad to be alive, trying not to look at the bodies prone on the platform, including the two attackers he had shot. LAPD officers were talking to people, and he could now see several were pointing at him, which was inevitable.

A young officer with cropped black hair walked over to him.

'Sir, can you raise your hands?' he asked as got close, one hand instinctively moving to the butt of the gun at his belt.

Obligingly John did so, laying his palms flat on his head. Another officer came over and searched his jeans pockets, but there was nothing to find other than a couple of hundred dollars in cash and a hotel key card.

'Er ... sir? We've been told ... I understand sir that you shot the two men that are over there, is that correct?' the first one asked, looking confused.

John nodded.

'Yeah, and there's another one. Upstairs.'

'So, sir is it correct to say that you attacked, the er ... the attackers? You used their own gun?' the same officer asked.

John nodded again.

'Sir, my name is Officer Rose, and this is Officer Macker. We need to move you to where somebody senior can talk to you. We have to ask you not to speak to anyone else here at this time. I hope that this is not a problem.'

'No problem,' John told him quietly.

'Sir, do you have any identification on you?'

John walked over to where the first woman was lying, now being worked on by paramedics. His blood-soaked jacket was lying discarded on the floor, he dug into the inside pocket and handed over his passport. Rose took it gratefully, flicked quickly through it and then pushed it into his breast pocket.

Officer Macker, who had been speechlessly staring at him spoke to first time.

'Jesus. You got their weapon and you turned it on them. I never heard nothing like that. In my mind, that makes you Superman. Sir.'

John shook his head.

The drunk, who was shuffling along behind them, called over as they led John down the platform, his voice shrill.

'I've seen some things in my life. Terrible fucking things make a man weep. But this man. You look after this man. He is a fucking hero. He saved all of us. You hear me!!! A fucking hero!!!'

John grimaced and Macker patted him heavily on the shoulder as they ascended the escalator, then went around the corner and back up to street level.

Upstairs was a hive of activity. All that could be seen was a sea of flashing red and blue lights. There were TV crews already at the location and people being held back by a police cordon. Rose and Macker led John over to one side and he sat down heavily on the floor, suddenly very tired.

Macker looked closely at the wound on John's head.

'That's going to need sutures. I'll get a medic. Can I get you a drink, some water?'

'Please,' John replied gratefully and the officer moved away, returning with a paramedic and a plastic bottle, unscrewing the cap as he passed it over. John drank deeply.

The medic worked on John's head.

'It's deep, but there's not a lot of flesh here. Just thin skin and thick bone. That's why it always bleeds a lot and looks bad,' he commented conversationally as he worked.

Macker stiffened and nodded to Rose. Two men were walking toward them, both with a distinct air of authority. One was tall, late fifties maybe, smartly dressed with a bewildered look on his face as he turned his head from side to side while he walked. In front of him was another man, a few years younger, short and stocky with a red face and a tie done up tight around his neck. He was wearing an LAPD vest over his shirt and carried a radio. He stopped close to the stairs and looked around, and then walked quickly over to where John was sitting. Macker moved over to meet him but he was pushed brusquely aside.

'You the man?' he barked at John, then looked at Rose. 'Is this the man?'

'Yes sir. This is the man. John Smith sir. He saved nearly everyone in the station. Sir.'

The man looked stonily back at him and then down at John again.

'Mr Smith? My name is Captain Truman. I'm sure you appreciate that we have a lot of questions. There has been a terrorist incident and we need to ensure the safety of the vicinity and let the public know the situation. We can't speak here for obvious reasons, so I am going to get you taken down to the precinct. I will get there as soon as I can. Meantime, please don't talk to anyone.'

With that he glared at Rose and pulled him away barking instructions to him and then swept away down the stairs. Rose walked back over looking very uneasy and sat down silently next to John. For a few minutes they watched all the activity, the people from the platform were now slowly being led out of the station into the media circus, flashlights popping and a scrum at the cordon.

With a heavy sigh Rose stood up.

'Come on John, we need to get you out of here,' he said quietly.

John stood up and with Macker and Rose flanking him they headed out of the station. Immediately there was a surge forward and reporters with microphones held out began shouting to him. There was a flurry of bright blinding flashlights. John allowed himself to be steered through, police officers pushing back the crowd for them. The area was packed with people. They barged their way toward the line of police cars and as they got near a woman burst forcefully through, a man trailing behind and holding up a camera, a light shining.

'Hey, no,' Rose said and turned to face her but the woman was determined and pushed past holding a microphone.

'How bad was it, did you see anyone getting killed? Have you got anything to say to these people?' she asked loudly, the camera fixed on John.

He turned and held out his hands to Rose and Macker, and then looked at the camera.

'Yeah. I've got something to say. I'm going to find the arseholes that were responsible for this. And I'm going to make them pay, whoever and wherever they are. That's a promise.'

The woman looked back dumbfounded, probably speechless for the first time in her life.

Rose guided John into the back of a patrol car and slammed the door closed, and the two officers got in the front and with Macker driving eased through the crowd and were away.

Chapter Two

Yann Voorhees watched the footage from the scene at the Metro station on the TV and pressed the pause button on the TIVO remote when he heard a sound and the door opening into the apartment. Voorhees turned his head slowly and eyed the two men walking in, Rico in front. Behind him Sal nervously closed the door, staying back, out of the way.

Rico walked into the small room, which was an exact square with no windows, an unmade bed and the TV in it. The apartment was their temporary base, or so they had been told, but they had been there more than four months already. He glanced warily at Voorhees who was looking at him appraisingly.

Yann Voorhees was huge. Literally. He weighed over four hundred pounds and stood six three. His head was absolutely massive, with bizarrely tiny piggy eyes which stared out, unblinking from the fat fleshy round face. He always wore dark coloured gowns with baggy trousers and bright flip-flops. Rico absently wondered where he got his clothes from. They had been together here for some time now, and nobody really knew anything about Voorhees, not even Rico and he was Number One, basically a supervisor. A title bestowed upon him randomly by Voorhees while they ate yet another pizza in the tiny kitchen. Rico couldn't work the man out at all; he never left the apartment, not once. Without him, the men used to go to a bar some evenings, but this had been stopped a few weeks before following an incident which had brought attention to them and made Voorhees furious. Rico had sorted the problem out and done it very well but had felt the wrath even so. Occasionally they would return to the apartment after driving out past Barstow having spent hours shooting at targets in the desert and he wouldn't have moved, although there was often a pizza box empty on the kitchen table. And he really smelled, sour, unwashed. Plus, he never smiled; Rico had not seen him do it once.

Everyone was scared of him. That was a simple fact. Despite all the bravado and what was said when he wasn't with them the fear was tangible, absolute. He was in charge. They did what he told them. Nobody ever questioned. He made everyone nervous. There were rumours of what he had done in the past, unverified but believable.

This meant that right now Rico was conscious of getting too close to the big man, and he stood to one side, deferentially.

'So it went wrong,' Voorhees said calmly. Unnecessarily in Rico's opinion, not that he would ever say so.

'It did,' he agreed.

'You failed.'

Rico shook his head vigorously.

'No Yann. I didn't. We didn't. The intelligence was wrong. It wasn't there. I don't even know if she was there if I'm being real honest, we never saw a clear photo. I mean I guess it might have been her but the package wasn't. Definitely.'

'She was there. I have been told. She was seen going in. These people do not make mistakes.'

'Yann I don't know what she looks like. None of us did. We only had the description, the photo could have been anyone.'

'I just told you. I thought I made it clear. She walked in the station. They knew exactly where she was from when she arrived. She was being tailed, she was with the other woman. I explained this to you. This is why you were told to be Downtown, we knew where she would go, it was all set up.'

Rico sighed.

'Look Yann, we searched all the bags. it wasn't there. I don't know why it wasn't, and I sure as hell don't know what you were told but there was nothing. And they searched everyone, every bag.'

Yann glanced over to the back of the room at Sal then turned and gestured at the doorway.

'Come in here Rico.'

He led the way to the room he called his office. This would have been the living room. It was the biggest in the apartment and the only one with proper windows. There had been a lot of resentment that Voorhees had made it into his office considering the cramped conditions elsewhere, but of course nobody had said anything. There was a wide table in the middle of the room with an ancient laptop on it and an old beaten-up office chair. Voorhees spent most of his time here. Nobody knew what he did all day, or what the laptop was for. There was no Internet in the apartment as far as anyone knew, but again, nobody said a word.

Voorhees walked around the table and lowered himself into the chair which creaked alarmingly. He laid his forearms onto the table top with a heavy thump and leaned back.

There were no other chairs in the room, any time anybody had to talk to him they had to stand in front of the table feeling like a child. But Rico was defiant. This had not been his fuck up, whatever Voorhees said or did now. He had done exactly as he was told. He walked over to the side of the room and looked out of the window saying nothing. They were five floors up, he looked down in the darkness at a scruffy parking lot and a scruffier basketball court, and then the freeway, bright headlights sweeping in both directions. On the other side of that was a large construction site, a mall being built. The whole area felt depressed, the apartment block they were living in had sprung up with a bunch of others all round it back in the seventies, and they hadn't lasted well. There were a couple of blocks of cheap shops and bars, a few fast-food outlets, and that was it. Mount Pleasant, Los Angeles, USA. Mount Pleasant? Yeah, right.

He turned to look at Voorhees who was still staring at him.

'So, tell me then Rico. What happened? And where are the others?'

Voorhees had a high, mesmerising, sing-song voice, which was impossible to read. If he was berating someone's ineptitude or talking about the weather it always sounded the same.

'We did exactly as we planned. Exactly. We were there and waited till we got your call. All of us went in the station, OK? We did everything as you told us to. Once we were downstairs Pol and Sung went off down the platform, we were looking at all the women, just to be sure. Max stayed put at the bottom and me and Sal came back upstairs. Like I said, just as we planned it.'

'And?'

'And nothing. The place was real quiet, not many people there. Lot of screaming and yelling then we heard the shooting. Then Pol shouted out to Max, and he called up to us. It wasn't in any of the bags, there was nothing. It was a bust, right? I told Max to keep looking then me and Sal hustled back to the van and waited.'

'So where are the others?'

'I don't know Yann. I have no fucking idea. We were sitting there and like in minutes the place is filling with cops, all running in the station. It was crazy how quick they were there. Then we moved out the way, we could see the doors but nobody came out. So we bailed, there was no choice.'

'Lot of witnesses Rico. There's a guy who says he is going to hunt you down, he's on the TV.'

'What? Who? What guy?'

'I have no idea Rico, but it's what he said.'

Rico snorted.

'Right. Let him try. I'll deal with him.'

Voorhees pursed his lips.

'Rico, we are being paid to do something. We are very expensive to hire. There is lots of planning. This is our first job together am I right? And what happens? Five of you go out, and two come back. Lot of money has been spent but I am down three men and I don't have what they need. I've got to explain this. I have to make the phone call. Tell me Rico, what do I say?'

Rico shrugged, he wanted to be able to say something in his own defence but nothing would come to mind. This had not been his fuck up, whatever the fat man said. He needed a distraction, then remembered Voorhees was always going on about being connected.

'But you can find out right Yann? I mean, what happened to the others. You can find out.'

Voorhees picked up a cellphone from the desk. It looked impossibly tiny in his vast paw. He dropped it and spun it around on the table top.

'No doubt I will get a call Rico. Leave me in peace. I need to make some arrangements.'

It was a short journey, once they got clear of the scene they were pulling up in the police precinct car park within five minutes. Macker got out first and opened the door for John who climbed out and then stood looking around. This was obviously a police parking area, but it was practically deserted. He guessed everyone would be down at the Metro station. Rose joined him and led the way over to the building. Both policemen seemed awkward, embarrassed. Rose punched in a code and the door buzzed open. They walked into a rectangular room with a squared off section of bars down on the right with a couple of sorry looking individuals sitting inside and nothing else there other than a high desk at the back. John looked at Rose quizzically.

'I'm real sorry John. We gotta book you. It ain't our choice, but orders is orders.'

John froze. Macker stood looking at the floor. Rose held his hands out; gesturing toward the desk.

'Book me for what?' John asked.

'We just gotta book you in. Get you checked over. Truman wants to talk to you. We're at the bottom of the food chain here. We just do what we get told,' Rose replied, visibly bothered by what he had been told to do.

'Fuck this,' Macker growled and walked over to the desk. A tall sergeant moved over to talk to him. Macker's body language was clear; it wasn't just he wasn't happy, he was very angry. The sergeant calmed him down as best he could, looking over at John the whole time. Rose sighed loudly and then took John over.

John Smith stood in front of the desk, pissed off. His head hurt. He looked over at the cage.

'Drunk tank,' Rose told him. 'Don't worry, you ain't going in there.'

The sergeant smiled at him ruefully, and Rose passed over John's passport. The sergeant nodded his thanks and began typing on a keyboard. He also looked awkward with the situation now that Macker had spoken to him.

'So, if I'm being booked, what's the charge?' John asked.

The sergeant looked at him earnestly.

'There is no charge Mr Smith. As far as I can see we only need to talk to you regarding the terrorist incident you … er … witnessed. So we're just going to look after you here until Captain Truman gets back. He gives the orders, he wants you booked in. I'm sure you will be on your way real soon. I'm sorry, you need to empty your pockets.'

He shrugged. Macker tutted loudly.

John shook his head and did as he was asked. A few hundred dollars and the key card for his hotel room. The sergeant swept them carefully into a plastic bag along with the passport and printed John Smith and the date and time on the label then sealed the bag.

To John's left was a barred steel gate. The sergeant pressed a button under the desk and it clicked open.

'This way Mr Smith. You two stay out here,' the sergeant said with a look at Rose and Macker, and then guided John through the gate and pulled it closed behind them. There was a steep set of steps going down and then a double right turn so they ended up under where they started. Now they were in a long room, cells on either side. Simple bars and gates. Most were empty. They walked down to the end where there was a cell with a partition wall to the rest in its row and it had a toilet with a sink set in the top of the cistern. John looked at the sergeant.

'VIP?' he asked.

The sergeant grinned uncomfortably.

'Yeah, we get the occasional Hollywood someone or other in here, usually a DUI. We have to keep them comfortable.'

He turned and looked up at a camera set high on the wall and the gate to the cell opened. John walked in and sat down on the low bunk. He stared up at the sergeant.

'Mr Smith, I am real sorry about this. Way I hear it, you deserve a medal not all this bullshit. But I ain't taking your shoes or your watch OK? I got to put you in here but it don't mean I agree with it.'

'How long am I gonna be stuck in here?'

'I'm positive it won't be long. It sounds like they just want to clear a few things up. It's a really big deal, it would be in any city, something like that happening. The public and the press needs to be handled right, you know, there will be a lot of panic.'

John shook his head, saying nothing. The sergeant moved outside the cell and closed the door, then looked in through the bars.

'Look it gets a bit chilly down here, I'll dig out another blanket and find you a pillow. I'll get you a bottle of water too, but if you need anything there's a buzzer on the wall right there.'

'Maybe a couple of painkillers if you can find some.'

'Sure. Anything else, just buzz I'll be right down.'

John looked up at the red button and then back at the sergeant, who coughed awkwardly and walked away.

John went over to the tiny sink and ran the tap, and washed the worst of the blood from his face, using his watch glass as a mirror. There was a lot of blood on his polo shirt. His head hurt, what he really wanted was to get back to the hotel and lie down, but he guessed that was going to take some time yet.

The sergeant was back in a few minutes with the blanket and a pillow, a couple of ibuprofens and two bottles of water. John took them and made himself comfortable on the bunk, leaning back against the wall and drawing his knees up. Hopefully Truman wouldn't keep him hanging around too long.

In the end it was over an hour when the sergeant came sheepishly back. John looked at his watch, just after 1am, it felt like it should be a lot later. He stood up and waited for the door to open. The sergeant stepped back and allowed John through and then ushered him along between the two lines of cells, which didn't seem to have acquired any more residents.

'Quiet tonight right?' John commented.

'Thank Christ,' the sergeant replied. 'We got enough to do now we got terrorists on the loose. I gotta thank you personally for taking some of them out the game. Serious shit.'

They reached the top of the steps and then walked across the front of the desk to a set of doors on the opposite side of the room. It looked like there were a couple of newcomers in the drunk tank. The sergeant entered a code and then pushed the door open and they were in a corridor with numbered doors on either side. Everything was quiet and clean. He stopped outside number three and rapped on the door and then pushed it open. John walked through into a small square interview room with a large pane of mirrored glass on the far wall. There was a camera set up high and recording equipment in a corner. Truman and the older man who had arrived at the Metro station with him were sitting down at the table in the centre. Truman gestured for John to sit down and he did so. Silently the sergeant left the room and closed the door behind him.

John looked at the two men opposite. Truman was fussily fidgeting around his seat, the older man reached out a hand.

'Mr Smith, my name is Chief Brady. We need to discuss the events of tonight with you, anything you can tell us will be a great help.'

John nodded his head and shook the man's hand. He glanced at Truman who was still squirming around irritatingly. Truman scowled and spoke accusingly.

'And no more bullshit OK? No more; I've heard enough. Stick to the truth,' he growled glaring at John.

John was confused, bullshit? He hadn't actually said anything yet. He wanted to make the point but decided to stay patient.

'Fine, where do you want me to start?'

'At the beginning, and I have to tell you we are recording this conversation is this OK with you?' Brady asked, producing a thick well-used notepad and pen.

'No problem.'

So John relayed everything from his arrival at the Metro station, missing nothing out, speaking clearly and carefully. He even included picking up the woman's dropped phone. Brady made occasional notes, while Truman sat fidgeting, staring across the table and shaking his head. When he finished John sat back and looked steadily at the two men. He wondered who was watching on the other side of the mirror, if anyone was.

Truman was obviously desperate to speak but was restrained by Brady who was scanning through what he had written, which wasn't a great deal. He raised his head.

'So, Mr Smith …'

'John.'

'OK. John. So, John, just tell me what you are doing in LA, why were you in the Downtown area?'

'I'm over here doing some work for a client. I've been successful, so he took me out for dinner. I was just going back to my hotel.'

'Downtown?' growled Truman. 'Nothing there. There's more interesting places to be in this city.'

John glanced at him then back to Brady.

'Like I just said, my client invited me to dinner. His choice.'

'Right. And where are you staying?' Brady asked.

'Montage.'

Truman whistled. Brady raised his eyebrows.

'Expensive tastes. So what is it that you do, exactly?'

'I resolve problems.'

Brady looked unimpressed.

'Very vague explanation Mr Smith if you don't mind me saying so.'

John shrugged.

'You asked and that's what I do. Nothing else to say.'

'Well, that's a matter for further discussion. You said you are over here for business so who are you working for?'

John did work for many people, plenty of whom would prefer to stay under the radar, particularly when it came to police involvement. Fortunately in this case, there were no such problems.

'It's a guy called Simon Butler. You won't know him. He's British, but he spends quite a bit of time here. He is a property developer, a lot of international stuff.'

Brady scribbled the name down.

'OK, so what are you doing for him?'

'It's already done. He had a problem with a partner here. Deals had been done but he hadn't received any payments.'

Unable to contain himself any longer Truman butted into the conversation, leaning forward aggressively.

'Why couldn't he just have sorted that out for himself? It must have cost him a fortune to fly you all the way out here and put you up in the Montage, plus I expect you want paying for it. I assume this is a lot of money we are talking about.'

'He tried, but he was encouraged to forget about it. Threats were made. Mr Butler prefers to keep his hands clean, so to speak. And yes, it is a lot of money.'

Truman sneered

'This is bullshit.'

Brady tutted.

'Dennis, please. We're having a conversation, getting to the facts. And to be frank, at the moment you aren't helping. Mr Smith how long have you been in LA?'

'I arrived Friday evening, about seven. Simon picked me up and took me to the hotel. Then we met up in the morning and I went to see his business partner over here.'

'Right, and who is this partner?'

Again, John had no reason not to answer.

'His name is Randall Flanagan. He has some kind of property business here.'

Truman looked blank but Brady clapped his hands slowly.

'Randy Flanagan? Jesus. Been a few years since we heard from Mister Flanagan. No wonder your guy didn't have any luck with him, he is a solid gold crook that guy. Jesus, so he's in the property development game now. I can't recall the last time his name got mentioned. But he's got a fellow as big as a house looks out for him. Clarence I believe his name is from memory. So what did you do that changed his mind?'

'I just persuaded him that as plenty of money had been made the fairest solution would be to pay what he owed as he had originally agreed. And he decided I was right.'

Brady say back heavily in his chair and smiled despite himself.

'And he agreed just like that?'

John nodded.

'You know this Flanagan?' Truman asked Brady in a low voice leaning toward him.

Brady raised his eyebrows.

'Sure. Age-old scams in housing. Every trick in the book and obvious too. Rents on properties not his, selling vacant lots, you name it. He was at it for years. It finally caught up with him, he got five in Ironwood. I haven't heard his name in … has to be ten years.'

'Well, it's easy to check out then,' John commented.

Brady nodded.

'Oh yeah, but like I said, that's not why we're talking here. I'm just trying to get the backstory, we need to understand who you are and how you came to be there. I'm sure you understand the seriousness of the situation.'

John looked at both men. Truman stood up and leaned on the table next to John.

'You don't look very happy Mr Smith. Well let me say I'm not either. This is all too neat right? You just happened to be right there. Just happened to be in LA in the first place when we get a terrorist strike …'

'They weren't terrorists,' John interrupted, talking to Brady.

Truman's face got even redder.

25

'What? What crap is this? You're saying they're not terrorists? I knew you were up to your neck. What the fuck is your involvement with this?'

'Calm down Dennis,' Brady cut in. 'Sit down. What do you mean John? Explain.'

John turned away and spoke deliberately to Brady, ignoring the stewing Truman.

'It's simple chief. I was there. They didn't spray bullets. I hit the deck and it was all single shots. There was a short burst at the end but that's it. When I came back after chasing the guy up the escalator I looked, and all the cameras had been shot out, plus the assistance phone. It was targeted, the terrorists I've had dealings with don't shoot that well.'

'Bullshit,' muttered Truman. But Brady was looking at John. He was interested. There was something.

'Go on.'

'It was a hit. Tell me, anything at all in the victims? How many people were killed? Anyone stand out? Anything different or unusual?'

'Don't tell him anything!' Truman shouted.

Brady sighed.

'Dennis, please. Ok John. Yeah, there is something odd I suppose. There were twenty-one people on the platform including you. Sixteen men and five women. Five people killed, nobody else shot other than the three men that you took care of.'

John looked patiently at Brady who sighed and continued.

'It was all five women shot and killed. Just the women.'

John was shocked.

'All the women were killed?'

'Yeah. Of course, we don't know if that's the real story, you interrupted them. Maybe everyone would have been dead now, you included.'

'Yeah, well maybe. To me they seemed like it was done, they didn't get what they were looking for. But I didn't realise it was the women they were after. I can't believe I didn't notice.'

Brady rubbed his eyes.

'Yes. Four of them were standing in two pairs and one was on her own. Youngest thirty, oldest forty-eight. Four dead before the paramedics got to the scene and the fifth passed away on the journey to the hospital.'

'So, it was a hit,' John mused.

'How do you figure that smartass?' Truman asked.

John looked at him, his patience running out.

'Jesus, how the fuck did you make captain, you ignorant prick? Of course it was a fucking hit. One of the women at a guess. But they didn't know what she looked like I reckon, maybe they only had a vague description, and maybe didn't even have that so they killed the lot.'

'And you just happened to be there, in the right place.'

'No Truman, in the wrong place. At the wrong time. It was self-preservation, my instincts. The gun was there and they were standing right next to me. So I acted. You know what? Do me for murder. I'll make my phone call now.'

Brady stood up.

'Let's just calm down here OK? John, what you did tonight was heroic, to say the least. It's unheard of. Captain Truman wants to get the facts straight is all. There's gonna be a shitload of paperwork that's for damn sure. But right now we have a problem, with you.'

John shook his head sorrowfully.

'Really, you do surprise me. What now?'

Brady looked at Truman.

'Dennis, maybe you'd care to explain …'

'Right, well Mr Smith, we have your passport. Lots of trips in and out of the United States.'

'Yeah well, my daughter lives here. New York.'

'Right. So, we made your passport and guess what. All we can get is your name and date of birth. Nothing else. It's all locked down, we can't access any more information at all. So, we go to the CIA, they'll help us. Bur guess what? Soon as they know it's you they tell us it's gonna take some time. Now why the fuck would that be? It stinks. Who are you?'

27

'I used to work for the government. Maybe this is over your pay grade, captain Truman.'

Truman looked disgusted. Brady laid his hand on the other man's arm.

'Dennis, why don't you go see if we gotten a reply yet? Go on. We're done here anyways, it's getting late. I'll get Mr Smith comfortable again.'

Truman angrily stared at both men and then walked out, slamming the door behind him.

Brady looked at John.

'Dennis has a difficult job to do. He's quite new here, big shoes to fill. Captain Ryan ran it a long time, well liked, well respected. He was shot, some gangbanger up from South Central. He was lucky to survive, but he'll never walk again. So Dennis has a tough job replacing him.'

'I'm not interested chief. I don't care.'

Brady leaned forward earnestly, trying another tack, he needed John on side and they both knew it.

'John, you know what you're doing don't you. I heard what you said about the terrorists you have dealt with. Who says that? I got to say I never met anyone who deals with terrorists like you did. I'm looking at you and what happened tonight hasn't fazed you at all. You say you worked for the UK government, what was it you did?'

'It's not up for discussion chief.'

'Look, I've listened to what you have said and I have to admit it does make sense. But other departments are involved, obviously, we hit all the major action buttons. A bunch of guys loose with AKs in a Downtown Metro station, it's big news. Huge. We never had it before and it's bigger that I can deal with, that's for damn sure.'

'I get that chief. And I understand that something like this goes down and it just happens that a bloke with no business to decides to pick up a gun and shoots three of the men. So of course there is suspicion, maybe I'm even one of them in the first place. I get that.'

'Well Captain Truman is …'

John had heard enough, and interrupted.

'Truman is an arsehole. I know what he's thinking. He has had this land in his lap. Promotion written all over it if he nicks someone early. Don't deny it. Look chief I've seen his type before and I would bet my house you have too. But if he tries to do it at my expense than he's gonna regret it.'

Brady sighed. He looked like he was about to say something then changed his mind.

'Look John, I'm sorry about this but I need to keep you here until morning. I have to do it all properly. The CIA will get back to me and I've got a feeling it will be all clear. Of course we're not looking to charge you with homicide or anything. There's every chance you saved a lot of lives, including your own.'

He stood up, and resigned to his fate John did too and allowed himself to be led back down to the cell.

The sergeant came back down with him and fussed around making sure John was comfortable and then left. John took the easy option and removed his boots and jeans and lay down on the bunk. He wondered if he would be bothered again until morning and decided to wait and see. Sleep when you can, it had always worked well for him in the past and within a short time he was out.

Chapter Three

Surprisingly, and despite everything, in the end he slept really well, and was woken up when a different officer came in with some breakfast. Somebody had been out to pick something up for him, so John imagined there must have been some changes overnight. He ate everything and drank down the coffee and then stood up stretching and touching his toes several times. He felt refreshed and ready; it was just past seven in the morning.

He put on his jeans and boots and then settled down comfortably to wait, he was good at that.

After fifteen minutes a new uniform sergeant appeared and politely escorted him back up to the booking area and returned his belongings, he didn't speak very much while he was doing it so John wasn't sure if he was completely free to leave at last. He noticed a man watching who walked over as John was putting everything back in his pockets.

'Hi John,' the man said, 'Care to come with me?'

John looked at the newcomer. He was older, probably the same age as Brady, but was solid with a street fighter's face topped with unruly grey hair. He wore dark jeans, a plaid shirt and a persistent smile as he led John out the doors chatting affably about nothing in particular. To John's relief they passed by the interview rooms and up a couple of flights of stairs. The man stopped at the top by a set of doors.

'I should probably introduce myself, sorry I always forget that. My wife chews my ass off about it. Anyways, I'm Chief Keane, pleased to meet you. Call me Ron.'

He held out his hand and John shook it, a firm handshake.

Keane pushed open the doors and led the way into a large open-plan office.

'Say John, I think you've been stuck dealing with some assholes up to now, let's hope these next assholes ain't, well … assholes.'

'You say you're the chief?' John asked as they crossed the room.

'Yeah, but not here in glamour town. Real police. Special department.'

He gave John a wink and led the way into a conference room with a big table in the centre.

Chief Brady was already seated, as was Truman. There was a large black man wearing a sharp suit and a tie looking at him with interest who stood up when they came in and shook John's hand.

'Hi John, I'm Kyle Warner,' he told him passing over a business card.

'Thanks,' John said and flipped the card. CIA.

They all sat down and John looked around expectantly.

'We're waiting for one other,' Brady announced. 'We sent a car to the airport to get him.'

'It's a her. No need to hang around, we may as well get started,' Warner said.

They asked John to repeat exactly what had gone down at the Metro station and he did so, it was obvious they had already been briefed as nobody showed any reaction. Warner made a few notes but asked no questions.

'So John, you told Chief Brady that in your opinion it wasn't a terrorist attack?' Keane asked.

John nodded and explained his rationale based on the shots that were fired.

Warner also nodded. 'Yeah, and I agree with you. I got the full crime scene reports and it's just as you say. We are leaving it with the press that it's terrorists at the moment so you will be seeing it all over the news but I want to keep most of this quiet for now until we find out more. I have to say John; from our side I'm fucking grateful you were there. Every witness from the platform confirmed what you did. You're a hero.'

'John, what can you tell us about the men down in the Metro? We got three dead guys, but so far only one ID,' Keane asked.

'I'm not sure about their nationality. Two of them, and I was on the ground so I am guessing this was one of the men standing next to me; spoke to another at the far end, maybe the guy I shot on the escalator. I recognised it somehow, but I still can't place it. Eastern, maybe Arabic at a guess, but I can't be sure.'

Keane produced a photograph and placed it on the table. It was a young man, mid-twenties with short dark wiry hair and an expressionless face. He was standing on a flight of steps looking down at the camera, wearing a dark green coat done all the way up.

'This is Pol Ritorsky. Polish, of Russian descent. Twenty-seven. No record of immigration into the US, but we got a hit on Interpol. He is wanted in Lithuania for the murder of a doctor there. He disappeared almost a year ago, and we think he came in through Canada about six months back as it looks like he may have been on a boat that came into Quebec, we are doing all we can to track him.'

John looked at the photo. It could have been one of the men on the platform or the escalator. He hadn't heard anyone speaking Polish.

'But they did speak in English. One of them spoke, but it wasn't his native language, then another said; "It's not here," but he sounded clear as a bell,' he told them.

'Hmmm,' mused Keane, scratching his head. 'It's not here?'

'That's the thing. That's why it was a hit. They were looking for someone. Or more likely something judging by what John heard them say,' Warner said, reading from a sheet of paper. 'It's right here, John said it last night. We should have got going a lot earlier.' He looked accusingly across at Brady and Truman.

'No argument from me,' Keane agreed.

'But why make it look like a terrorist attack?' Brady asked, speaking for the first time. 'It makes no sense; they must know how we would react.'

'Yeah, and that's why they did it. Because they know the panic it will set in and know what we will throw at it. The fact it was a hit will never be picked up. There will be dozens of us on the plot, different agencies, huge amount of publicity. Perfect cover,' Warner stated.

'It just worked out, and lucky for us, Mr Smith here happened to be there. If he wasn't, we would be chasing our asses, and likely a whole lot more dead,' Keane said.

Warner nodded sombrely.

'For sure. Leave maybe a couple of survivors, no reliable witnesses, then nobody can really tell us anything. We have a bunch of armed terrorists on the loose and we got to protect the city. But we know different thanks to Mr Smith. We need to start at the beginning, Captain Truman did you get anything from the surrounding cameras?'

Truman stood up, then sat down again quickly.

'Well, we picked us up some footage. We got them arriving and leaving in a Ford Transit van, it's an old model, with fraudulent plates on it, so we got no hits anyplace. Five men got out, all wearing some kinda uniform it looks like. Footage ain't very clear but we sent it off for definition, we may get lucky.'

He placed several black and white photographs on the table, and they were passed around. They were all very similar, just taken from different angles and locations. Five men; getting out of a van, crossing the road, gathering outside the Metro station and finally entering. Then a couple of shots of two men getting back into the van.

'Nothing from inside the station,' Truman continued, 'They shot out all the cameras as they went through, must have checked it out beforehand.'

John picked up a picture. The men were all wearing basically the same clothing. All wore beanie hats, and all had their heads lowered. He looked through all the photos again, not a single face to be seen clearly at any point.

'Yeah, they are savvy to the cameras,' Warner said. 'I can't see definition helping any.'

'You said they spoke to one another in another language as well as English, you really can't think what it might be?' Keane asked.

John shook his head.

'No, and I know I should do. I've heard it before. It's frustrating. But they definitely said "Nothing there" and "It's not here" in English, plain as day. They were going through bags, maybe every one there for all I know.'

'Every bag?' Keane asked, looking at Truman.

'We don't know for sure, but we think it's likely,' Truman answered earnestly, keen to be involved.

'That's not good enough. These are the things we have to be definite about.'

Truman coloured and looked down.

'And we need to discuss the 1-Too that was carved on the guns, right?' Brady asked.

Warner sat back and tapped his fingers on the desk.

'I've seen it before,' John told them.

'Yeah, and me,' Warner said flatly. 'You go first Mr Smith.'

'It's just John. I worked for the government for a while, a case came in. I wasn't assigned to it, but other people were working on it. 1-Too was at the heart of it. It was a big deal, at least for a while.'

Keane looked around and produced a tatty notebook and a chewed pen. He looked all around the room.

'OK. Start again. We need to make an action list.'

***

Samantha King walked into the newsroom, aware that Frank Moran was glowering at her from his office but she ignored it. Nothing new there.

She dropped into her seat and threw her bag onto the desk with a loud sigh.

Opposite her Simon Gray gave her a shy smile.

'Want to see?' he asked.

'Definitely.'

They stood up and eagerly she followed him across to the editing suite. He sat down and pushed out a chair for her next to him, then started manipulating the controls along the desktop. The large monitor fizzed and blurred then replayed the scenes outside the Metro station the previous night. There was a lot of footage, neatly put together by Simon into a three-minute segment, Sammy would record an audio over the top of it for transmission.

'Perfect,' she said with a wide smile.

The previous night's events were big news. Huge. Exactly what the channel needed. Sammy King had only been working for LA Plus for four months, she had been approached by the CEO following her very public second divorce. She had been living in Indianapolis and been the anchor there for twelve years, so it was a fresh start for her at a time when she needed it. Sammy King was a petite and attractive forty-three-year-old woman, although her bio had her age at thirty-four. She had been a broadcaster since her late teens and married twice, first to a movie producer which lasted for six years, and then a second time to an ex-NFL running back, this time it ended after seven. But she wasn't unhappy, and so far was enjoying living and working in LA.

The problem was the viewing figures, which were dropping alarmingly. LA Plus was a box standard cable channel with news, current affairs, documentaries and in the evening the usual mix of comedy shows and a movie. Nothing ground-breaking. But the internet was killing cable, to be fair the problems had been there a long time before Sammy was on board, but recently had got a lot worse. There was a lot of finger pointing internally. Moran, who was head of news, was blaming her, she had not been his choice. Angelina Ball, the previous anchor had been doing a good job as far as he was concerned. Of course, the fact that Moran had been sleeping with Angelina was not lost on Sammy, hey if he had been nicer she would have even considered doing the same. He was not a bad looking guy. Angelina had been arrested for a DUI, and had a bag of coke in the glovebox in her car. No going back from that, however hard Moran fought her corner.

Simon set everything up and they carried on working, she drafted an audio and then recorded it. The clip would be part of her mid-morning show, the attack at the Metro station would be the prime focus of course. She would be interviewing Chief Brady, plus some other 'experts' the channel had lined up. They had wanted to speak to some of the survivors that had actually been there but been warned off by the police, they needed time to process all the statements, inform next of kin and so on. This was routine but frustrating.

The work done, they played it through one more time and she gave Simon a kiss on the cheek as a thank you, which produced a deep blush. He was nearly twenty years younger but she always noticed him checking her out, something she was well used to men doing. Today she was wearing a shorter dress than normal and he was clearly very pleased about it. He was good at his job and always helpful and just maybe he might get lucky. She could do a lot worse, she decided. Mr Right may as well live on the moon as far as she was concerned.

The recording ended with a scary British man staring at the camera, blood all over his face and shirt and calmly delivering the threat. He was serious, it was obvious, his eyes were like ice. Sammy tapped the screen with a long bright red fingernail.

'I won't forget him, he is interesting. I'd like to sit down with this guy,' she said.

'That's a good idea,' Moran was standing behind her scowling into the room. 'You should find him, before someone else snaps him up and we lose out. It's called journalism, in case you hadn't realised that's what we do here.'

She turned and smiled at him.

Asshole, she thought.

'OK, well, I'll ask Chief Brady when he comes in.'

Moran looked at her and stalked off.

Sammy turned back and stared at the screen.

'Now who the hell are you?' she asked quietly, and decided to talk to some of the others who had been working at the channel for years, she was sure that at least one would have an idea how to find him, just in case Chief Brady wasn't interested in being helpful.

Chapter Four

In the conference room Keane was holding forth. He was writing conscientiously in his notebook and painstakingly going through the chain of events the previous night. They had been joined by a woman called Judy Blake from the FBI.

She had ferociously burst into the room and introduced herself, and then wanted an immediate update, asking many questions as everything unfolded.

'So, you're the famous John Smith? Or should that be infamous?' she asked looking at him with a mischievous smile.

'Preferably neither,' John replied.

'You'll need to convince me. And Patrick says hi.'

Patrick Skelton, John's good friend in the FBI.

'That's good to hear. Tell him hi back.'

'We had a conference this morning, early. Patrick rang to give us the low down on you. He wasn't surprised you were caught up in this. At all.'

John shrugged.

'Yeah, he has witnessed this kind of stuff happening to me.'

'He said that. But he vouched for you, and from him, that means a hell of a lot.'

'We do have a history, I was with him in Texas just last year.'

'Yeah he told me about that. He told me to apologise again for dragging you into it. So, sorry!'

She reached into her bag and took out a file, and slid it across to Warner.

'It's all about him,' she said, with a sideways nod at John.

Warner opened the file, and Keane moved over to look over his shoulder.

'Let's go get a coffee,' Judy suggested, and she and John left the room.

There was a small kitchen just down a corridor, and John and Judy sat down with a coffee each.

Judy Blake was a homely looking woman in her forties. She was wearing a grey trouser suit and a red blouse and looked as if she had been rushing about all morning. He dark hair had tinges of grey she didn't bother to cover up. She was carrying a handbag with Paw Patrol stickers all over it and there were different colour stars on her mobile phone. She was a busy mum. John liked her.

'So you from Washington?' John asked.

Judy shook her head.

'No, but I do actually know Patrick. I worked with him some time ago now, he is a sharp guy alright. Now, I head up a unit out of Atlanta.'

'You do realise this isn't a terrorist attack, right?'

'I do yes. That's not the unit I run. I got alerted when the whole 1-Too thing got mentioned. They are on our radar, same as the CIA.'

'Right. I don't know much about them, but if I can use a phone I can get all the information we got.'

'Cool, let's go.'

Judy was clearly not someone who could stay still for long. She moved back into the big office and commandeered a phone. John thanked her and called Neil Wallace, his old boss back when he was in the department.

Neil was surprised, but pleased to hear from him, and was happy to give John all the information, offering to email across the relevant documentation. Judy gave the thumbs up and passed John her email address, and Neil promised to send it. With a loose arrangement to meet for a beer soon John hung up.

Keane walked across to them.

'Let's go sit down again,' he suggested.

They moved to a smaller meeting room. Brady and Truman were not there. Warner was already sitting at the table and passed the file back to Judy.

'That's interesting reading,' he said with a half-smile at John.

John desperately wanted to know what was in the file but knew better than to ask.

'Right,' Keane began, and then stopped. 'You want to do this Kyle?'

The big black man, who always appeared to be cheerful shook his head.

'No Ron, this is your city. You take the lead buddy.'

Keane cleared his throat.

'Right, well we have made a decision. Now Judy's here, I think we are all set. First thing, we are cutting the PD out.'

'I thought you were a policeman?' John asked.

'Sure I am, but not the running round busting heads kind. I don't do that no more. I'm more behind the scenes.'

'Ron here is our liaison,' Judy said, and Warner nodded in agreement.

'Now, we got to discuss this 1-Too thing,' Keane continued. 'What can you tell us John?'

'Well I just spoke to Neil, he was my old section head at the department. Like I said, I was never assigned to it but they were a big deal at the time. Basically, two city boys got murdered. Both shot in their own homes on the same night. They were oil and gas traders, both young, rich guys. The Met, as in the Metropolitan Police, found a fax to one of them warning that 1-Too were asking questions. It meant nothing to the Met, the guy's wife had never heard the name, and none of his colleagues had either. The fax was sent from a computer somewhere, untraceable. Both men worked for different companies and as far as we could work out had no connection other than they both did the same job. Eventually they realised that 1-Too had a connection to criminal organisations right round the world and in the end, it was passed to us, but this was several months afterward. We found out who and what they are, but it took some time. They 're not actually a terror group, they are a kind of revenge outfit, anyone can hire them. The two men that were murdered were part of a money laundering scheme which was financing a Lebanese syndicate. We found links to several governments all around the globe. We also discovered that they stayed around in London for a long time after the murders. But we couldn't get anyone to talk.'

Warner nodded his huge head.

'Yeah, well we are pretty much the same. We got involved after some witnesses under protection got murdered around the New York area. Four people in total, all under assumed names and hidden. It was a big case. But they were all killed in the space of maybe two months. Feds were working on it with the local PD and they find an email on various computers belonging to three of the victims. No text, just an attachment which was a photograph of an outline of a body like you see after a murder scene, you know on the ground. In the shape was the words 1-Too. We talk to the Feds, they start digging, and get a connection to a guy who flew in from Beirut. So, we get busy, and find out the same as you Brits did, it was a part of an operation but nothing else. Dead end.'

Judy picked up the story.

'I have been working on this ever since. In total we can put eleven deaths in the US down to 1-Too, make that sixteen with the five yesterday. Essentially, they were all assassinations. But I never could pin down any personnel, they are like smoke. We get a lead, and prepare, move in, but they are already gone. Every time.'

'And that is why, we have decided no PD,' Keane said.

John nodded in agreement.

'Basically, we had the same problem. Neil says we made too much noise in the investigation, we had the Met and MI-5 involved. The bad guys had connections, and were warned, so they always vanished.'

'It was exactly the same from our side,' Judy agreed.

John sat back, looking at the other three and wondering why they were telling him this.

'So … what we are thinking is that we run this as a small team. Just us. Kyle has spoken to his people, and Judy to hers, and well, this is why I'm here,' Keane said, almost apologetically.

They all looked at John expectantly, and he realised what they were saying.

'Hold on, hold on, look I don't work for the government anymore. I'm nobody. I'm self-employed, I just tidy things up for people.

Keane shrugged.

'Listen John, take a look. What do you see? None of us are, what you would call operational. Kyle, well he's a big man, but kinda outta shape if we're being honest. Sorry Kyle.'

Warner held up his hand.

'No sweat.'

'And Judy has been out for a long time. She's got other people beating down doors. And me, well I'm a year past sixty. And what you did last night, you know you just picked that gun up and started shooting. You dropped three just like that. Ballistics say you fired three rounds, three for three. That is good shooting.'

'I can't get involved in this. Seriously, I was in the wrong place at the wrong time. I don't have any right to be a part of anything,' John maintained.

'Yes, you do.' Judy told him.

'Oh yeah, you do.' Warner agreed.

'You're exactly what we need. Nobody knows who the hell you are. Anyone on the inside at the PD, or the FBI or the CIA won't be able to make a connection. You are exactly what we need right now. Your file is incredible reading, you are used to this shit. We need you John. We really do,' Keane told him earnestly.

John looked back at him, unsure. He lived a quiet life these days. Mostly. Apart from the confrontations, the frequent broken bones he inflicted and the overall threat of violence most of his work involved.

But this time all he had been doing was travelling back to his hotel. He hadn't been working, he was literally minding his own business.

Why not? The fuckers had fired a gun at him. Maybe unintentionally, but it had been very close. He had the wound to prove it.

The others in the room were all gazing at him.

He raised a hand.

'OK.'

This would be interesting. It could be a good morning after all.

Chapter Five

General Morgan was not having a great morning. He had a new driver, who picked him up late and then took a crazy route to the Pentagon, moaning about the traffic all the time and the general walked in more than fifteen minutes later than he normally did. The general didn't like that.

Normally, due to his rank and high level clearance he breezed through the complex and diligent security without any issues, but that morning there had been an alert increase which meant he had to queue like everyone else, so by the time he got up to his office after all the delays it was well over an hour later than normal, and he didn't like that either.

And then when he finally sat at his desk his secretary didn't come straight in with his coffee, and didn't answer the intercom when he wanted to know exactly the damned reason why not. So, he had to get up, and go out into the pool only to discover she had been moved to another position, hadn't been replaced yet and nobody had bothered to mention anything to him. So, he had to go and get his own coffee, and he really didn't like that.

He realised finally what everyone else around him already knew, that six months into his position and placement at the Pentagon he really didn't have the respect he believed he deserved and that was another thing he wasn't happy about.

Then to cap it all, he got a message on his personal mobile phone, which he absolutely did not need at all.

He looked at the calendar on his wall. The third of March circled in red. A little more than three weeks away.

Grand Marshal Yin looked out the window of his office high up in the Ministry of National Defence building.

A chilly Beijing spread out before him, a billion lights twinkling in the darkness.

He considered the message he had just received, and looked at the calendar next to the window. The third of March was not long now, and he would have to travel two days before.

He wondered if there was time. He hoped so.

He knew his options were limited now.

There was a light tap on his office door and one of his assistants walked in, bowing as he did so. He passed a sheet of paper over to Yin and then left again, bowing and closing the door quietly.

Yin read it and sighed.

As if he didn't have enough to do, he decided.

He picked up the phone.

***

In Moscow Colonel General Rostov sat in the back of his car watching the cold and wet streets glide by. Snow piled in high heaps everywhere. He had been to lunch at the Kremlin, which had eventually ended four hours later. Lots of the old men at the ministry eating way too much, getting drunk and morose and talking about the good old days. Rostov was young for his rank, just fifty-five. A tall, good-looking man with neat grey hair. He had been glad to make polite excuses and get away, and had been collected swiftly.

The building of the Ministry of Defence loomed into view. He leaned forward and tapped his driver on the shoulder.

'It's late, I won't go to the office now,' he said.

The driver nodded and turned at the next junction, heading north. It would be an hour and a half before Rostov got home. He settled back and dug out his mobile phone, checking his upcoming appointments.

March 3rd jumped out at him.

He had a call to make, things were not going as planned and Rostov was used to everything always going his way.

***

Sammy eventually found somewhere to park and walked back toward the bar. This wasn't an area of Los Angeles she had ever been in before, and it was a marked contrast to Downtown, where she spent most of her time when she wasn't at work or home.

MacArthur Park was beaten; tatty and tired, lines of discount shops, lots of people standing around, street corners all busy. All in all, it wasn't the most comfortable place she had ever been in.

'You're a long way from Indianapolis,' she told herself.

She pulled herself upright and marched forward, staring straight ahead, not meeting anyone's eye. It might be the middle of the afternoon but she knew all too well the crime statistics in some areas of the city.

The bar was an ugly, rundown rectangle on the corner of a block, plain grey painted walls and black window frames, the Flanagan's name on the sign above the door now read 'Flana ans'.

She walked in, inside it was gloomy and shabby. There were several drinkers sitting at the long bar, all male, and no doubt there for the duration. She had been told exactly where to go once she was there so she walked across and headed out through a door at the end of a short passage which had grim looking toilets on either side. Now she was in a foul-smelling covered outside area, which had a small bar in the back corner. Jimmy Frost was sitting at the end, exactly where she had been told he would be.

She moved a stool and sat down next to him and smiled.

Frost looked at her, taking in the short red dress, slender, shapely legs and the buttons undone at her chest. Sammy had taken advice and made sure her cleavage was on display beforehand. Let him see the goods, she had been told. Nothing she wasn't used to.

Now, she leaned forward, resting her breasts on her folded arms, just to reinforce the view.

Frost leered, and smiled, showing yellow-stained teeth. He took a drag of his cigarette and then had a long drink, without taking his eyes off her.

Maybe he would find a use for that Viagra he had bought after all. He'd had it long enough.

'Hello Jimmy,' Sammy said.

Frost raised his wild eyebrows. This really was his lucky day. There was no way this broad was a hooker, and she looked real familiar too.

'Hey,' he said.

She stuck out her hand, still keeping everything on display. 'I'm Sammy King,' she told him.

Sammy King? Shit. He knew who she was now.

'Ah. Ms King. And what brings you down here?'

'I came to see you Jimmy.'

This could only mean she wanted something. Jimmy was a drunk and a long way from what he had once been, and he knew all too well what he looked like. Stick thin, with a pot belly and what hair he had left all over the place. But if she wanted something, and really wanted it, he could turn it to his advantage. She was a looker alright, and there were worse ways to spend an afternoon. Well, five minutes of an afternoon in his experience, although it would be a great five minutes. But he had to play it cool.

Sammy was exuding confidence, but inside feeling pretty sick. When it had been suggested she go and find Jimmy Frost all the women had offered advice, as had the men, but both sides different. Now, sitting there, trying to look alluring she was wishing desperately she was wearing jeans and a jumper. She was used to being ogled by men, and often used it to her advantage but this guy was drooling over every inch of her, practically salivating. Simon had been concerned and offered to come with her, she wished she had accepted it now. Jimmy Frost was an ugly, unpleasant individual. Sammy was here because she was looking for the British guy from last night, she had asked Chief Brady a direct question about him and she had immediately seen the effect; Brady had instantly become evasive, he looked nervous. She had tried the usual tricks but nothing worked, Brady changed the subject time and again then off camera insisted he had nothing to say. Afterwards she had gone to the team and asked them the best way to get something from the police, and everyone had said the same thing. Jimmy Frost.

So she was here now, and desperately unsure. But she wanted to speak to the British guy before someone else did, if only she had grabbed hold of him last night, but there had been so much going on.

Frustrating. He could be big, big news.

'Oh yeah? And what can I do for you?' Jimmy asked, fiddling with his crotch.

'I'm looking for someone Jimmy. And I was told you were the man to come and see.'

'Maybe, but nothing is for free baby.'

'I'm happy to discuss that.'

'Hmmm. So you been working at that LA Plus a few months, right? How come you didn't come and look me up before?' Frost asked, a hint of bitterness in his voice.

Sammy looked around her. There were a million reasons why she wouldn't normally set foot in this dump, and another million to never speak to Jimmy Frost. But there had been a time when he was as good as it gets, a crime reporter second to none in the city, probably the whole of California. She had even heard his name back in Indianapolis. But ten years ago, at the very top of his game, Frost been following a story about a corrupt district attorney. It was a big deal, the main event for some years. And he had been warned off, repeatedly, CBS had told him outright to drop it, which he had ignored. But always overconfident he had been outfoxed, set up, discovered by police in a motel room with an underage prostitute, several packages of heroin and cocaine and the icing on the top; two Glock handguns.

Frost had been out of it, incoherently mumbling about being drugged, but it was no good.

Because there was no sexual activity, he was so wasted, and the toxicology report showed no cocaine or heroin in his system just a cocktail of other illegal substances Frost avoided a custodial sentence, but it was a close call.

The CBS news channel he worked for promptly got rid of him, they couldn't handle that kind of negative press, nobody could. And he had slid fast down the ladder, getting work when he could, which was becoming less and less.

He had done several stories for LA Plus, there was no doubt when he wanted to he still had the touch, and undoubtedly still had the contacts, but now he spent most of his days in Flanagan's. He had a crappy little apartment just round the corner, and enough dwindling savings left meant reality was somebody else's problem. For now.

'Sorry Jimmy, I've been busy, settling in, you know,' Sammy told him.

'Yeah, sure. I bet.' His mouth set in a firm line. 'Well, you're here now, and just maybe you found who you are looking for sweetheart, you and me, we could work out real well.'

Sammy shuddered inside, she was afraid she might really vomit. She sat back up straight, cleavage away as much as she could without being obvious and dug a photograph out her bag. A still of John Smith staring at the camera.

'I need to find this guy Jimmy. He was with the police all last night. I think he still is, but nobody is saying anything.'

Frost looked at the picture and shrugged.

'Don't know him.'

'Well, no I know you don't. I mean neither do I, he spoke to me last night after the attack at the Metro station and we're real keen to get his story.'

'Why?'

'Because he was there. And the police were very interested in him last night.'

'So what, he's the attacker? This guy is a terrorist?'

'No, I don't think so. The only person we've been able to talk to is a guy who was walking into the Metro, and he said it looked to him like this man chased them off. But when I mentioned this to Chief Brady he got real funny about it. We got told we're not allowed to interview any witnesses until they say so.'

'Yeah, well that's usual in things like this.'

'I know that. But I need to get out in front.'

Frost looked at her again.

'Well you certainly do that missy. You do that real good.'

'So can you help me? Please? Everybody says you got the connections, that someone in the police department will talk to you.'

Frost drained his glass and lit another cigarette, considering.

'Maybe. But what's in it for me?'

He placed a hand on her leg, filthy fingernails digging in.

She gave him a winning smile, and with an effort didn't move his hand away.

'Well let's just see Jimmy. Meantime, before we get to know each other better, have a drink on me.'

She laid two hundred-dollar bills on the bar, keeping her fingers on them. She had been advised that was the going rate.

Frost looked at the money, and then at her. He licked his lips, then sighed.

'Sure. Why the hell not. OK, I can make some calls I guess.'

She slid the notes across along with a business card, thankful but desperate. Now she could get the hell away from here.

'My cell's on that. I got to go, I'm sorry.'

She climbed off the stool.

He looked at her.

'You'll be seeing me again baby.'

'Oh yeah, you bet.'

With great difficulty she fixed on a smile again and walked back into the main bar, where she hurried straight across without looking anywhere and into the street, fighting the urge to run back to her car.

Chapter Six

Keane had advised John to get away from the Montage, he needed to get undercover, hide out of the way, and fast. The press was always hanging around the place. John could see his point, but it was shame as it was a beautiful hotel. Arrangements had been made for John, Judy and Kyle Warner to stay down in Santa Monica, which was a busy, transient location, lots of hotels and motels. Outside the police station Keane gave the address to Warner.

'Look, right now, we got nothing. Na-da. I got some clearing up to do here. I need to instruct these guys exactly what they can and can't do, and what the can and can't say. And if what I believe is right, I will be spreading some misinformation because if there is an inside man, or even men, it will right here in this building. I'll meet up with you there in a couple of hours. John, you look like shit. Get some sleep,' Keane told them, and disappeared back into the building.

They looked at each other and climbed into Warner's car, a dark blue Buick. They went to the Montage first so John could check out and get his stuff. Warner drove deftly, no problem with the traffic, constant lefts and rights and easily crossing the city toward Beverley Hills. John was impressed.

'So you live here then?' he asked.

To his surprise Warner shook his head.

'No. I'm based in San Diego now, Detroit originally. I'm the same as Judy, the 1-Too connection set off alarm bells right across the network and next thing I know I'm on the next plane. But I was here a long time right through to 2013.'

'You did the same job here?' Judy asked.

'No, I was just your box standard agent back then. I wanted to get up the ladder, but there weren't many opportunities, CIA in LA was low-key after 9–11. But we had a good life. My wife was a teacher, she became a drugs councillor, working with the kids, dealing with the young ones in the gangs. She put her heart in it, seriously, and then one day she gets shot in Inglewood.'

'Shit,' said John. 'Is she OK?'

'She survived. It was a close call, she's doing good now. But the agency took pity on me, and offered me a post down in San Diego, dealing with organised crime coming over the border mostly. It was a promotion, and we really had to get out of here so I took it. 1-Too kinda fell in my lap, nobody knew nothing about it. I picked it up from New York because originally they believed it was Mexican, and after that it kinda stayed with me.'

'You married John?' Judy asked.

'No. It was close. I got a daughter, lives in New York actually.'

'Two girls for me,' Judy said proudly. 'Oldest is twenty-four with a daughter of her own. Scary.'

'I got two boys,' Warner told them. 'Ten and eight.'

'Granny Judy,' John smiled.

'OK, OK,' Judy replied smiling back.

'Granny got a gun,' Warner said, and they all laughed.

The hotel was called Ocean Vista, and was a simple concrete three-storey block painted white, with all the rooms opening off of front landings which ran straight across on all the levels. It was barely a level up from the cheapest motel, but to John, it was perfect. There couldn't be anywhere more anonymous in the world, let alone LA. They had three rooms side by side on the top floor. John and Warner took the rooms at either side with Judy in the middle.

John dropped his bag on the bed then went and stood outside his door, hands on the railing. Right in front of the building was a tiny square pool with a few plastic chairs around it and a big 'Residents Only' sign. There was nobody there.

On the other side was a car park, and after that a bar with a Chinese restaurant next door. The main street was a four lane that ran along at right angles to the hotel on John's left, with a fair amount of traffic flowing. There was a big petrol station immediately opposite, and there were several shops, bars and restaurants along from that. Between the buildings he could see the sea, sparkling in the February sunshine and far away the pier was just visible.

He walked back inside, stripped off, had a shower and cleaned his teeth, then dressed and laid down on the bed. In a few minutes he was asleep.

***

Breakfast, in fact any meal time in the apartment, was depressing. There was a small kitchen, but nobody ever cooked anything. Normally at mealtimes Voorhees would pass over twenty or maybe even thirty bucks and depending on the time of day one of the men would go to McDonalds or KFC. If they were really fortunate, possibly Taco Bell or even Denny's, occasionally Chinese. That morning was slow to start. Rico and Sal had a more comfortable night, as it was now only the pair of them sharing the room, it had been five before that, all in sleeping bags on the floor. Voorhees had a proper bed in the other bedroom, which had the TV in it.

Sal had gone to McDonalds in the end, and paid for it with his own dollars as Voorhees hadn't got out of bed. He sat with Rico in the tiny kitchen as they ate.

Rico checked his watch.

'It's late. Reckon we should wake him?'

Sal prodded the brown paper bag on the table.

'Maybe. I got him breakfast, it will be cold probably. But I ain't fucking going near him.'

Rico rubbed his eyes. He wouldn't do it either. He sighed deeply and looked around. There was not much to see in the room, beer cans and crap on every work surface, a broken coffeemaker, a bin overflowing with takeaway wrappers. He wanted a shower more than anything but it made a lot of noise and Voorhees complained bitterly if anyone used it when he was in bed. He drank the last of his coffee and looked closely at Sal over the brim of the paper cup.

'This is all shit, right?' he spoke very quietly.

Immediately Sal looked around him, but Voorhees was nowhere, and he was not a man who could easily sneak up on someone in this tiny apartment.

'Well, it ain't what I was expecting,'; he replied, equally quietly.

'Right. I was told a team of six, with backup. Professional. But there's only ever been five, and no backup. And we don't never know what we are supposed to be doing. Four months we've been here. Four months in this shithole, and then out the blue we get told to go get a package? And that isn't even there when we finally do it. It's bullshit. I'm telling you.'

'So what are you going to do Rico?'

'I don't know man, I really don't. I'm here for the money, same as you. I don't believe in no cause or shit like that I just wanna get paid.'

Sal nodded glumly, with one eye permanently on the door to Voorhees' room.

Rico stood and looked out the tiny window, which gave out over a narrow alley between their block and its neighbour. There was a thin slice of a view if he looked painfully hard to his right. Beyond, he could see the city, the Hollywood hills in the distance.

'I never been to LA before you know,' he said ruefully.

There was a series of thumps, and then the bedroom door opened. Voorhees stood there, wearing the same gown as yesterday. Maybe he slept in it. Who the fuck knew. He looked in at the two men.

'What are you two talking about?' he asked.

'Nothing really, me and Sal want to see the Lakers. You know, while we are in the city.'

Voorhees scowled.

'This isn't a holiday camp. We're gonna be here longer, now you fucked it up last night.'

'I got you breakfast Yann,' Sal cut in quickly, and handed over the food.

Voorhees grabbed the bag, sniffed and peered inside, then disappeared into his office, slamming the door closed.

A minute later they could hear his voice on the phone.

Rico sighed again.

'Come on, let's clear this craphole up a bit. It fucking stinks in here.'

Rico doubted they could do anything about the place smelling like Voorhees but they busied themselves shoving rubbish into plastic sacks and dropping them into the big garbage bins at the back of the building. Neither man spoke much, they were just glad of something to do for a while. They rolled up the now unneeded sleeping bags and straightened their bedroom. Then Rico took a long shower, standing underneath the feeble spray until the water started to run cold.

Meanwhile Sal had been fiddling with the coffeemaker, and believed it would now work, so was attempting to make a cup.

The office door opened and Voorhees walked through, completely filling the small hallway. He looked in at the two men.

'Been busy then?' he asked.

Both men nodded silently. Sal handed him a mug of black coffee. Voorhees just stared at it, and eventually Sal put it down on the counter again. Voorhees crossed his fat arms.

'OK. Well, I got four new guys coming in, one tonight the rest tomorrow. We got to get this shit back on track, right? And Sal? You're now Number One. It ain't working out with Rico.'

He stared at them with his tiny eyes, then disappeared back into the office and closed the door.

'Rico …' Sal started but Rico raised his hand with a smile.

'Don't. You know what? It's fine, I wasn't enjoying that fucking job anyway. You'll be good at it. Good luck.'

He held his hand out and Sal shook it.

Chapter Seven

John was woken by a loud knock on his door. He sat up and looked at his watch, nearly 2pm. He had been asleep over three hours. He got off the bed and padded across to the door. It was Keane.

'Come on, we got news,' he said simply.

They got together in Judy's room, which was identical to John's apart from Judy had bothered to unpack.

Warner was in the only chair so Judy and Keane sat on the bed and John took the floor.

Warner spoke first, handing out some poorly printed sheets.

'We got some fresh intel on Ritorsky. He did his national service in Poland, and they wanted to keep him. Seems like he was a good soldier, and in line for a sniper position.'

Warner paused and looked around.

'But …' said Keane.

'Yeah, but. There was some kind of altercation with his commanding officer. Of course, we don't have all the information, this is the military. But Ritorsky was out, and that was that.'

'Sniper?' John asked.

'Yeah, and I bet we're both thinking the same. And the even better news is we have ID on the other two men that John took out. They are Korean and …'

'Korean! Of course. I knew it, I just couldn't place it,' John interrupted.

'Yeah, both Korean. One is Ji-hoon Kong. Thirty-three, and a US resident since he was six years old. Raised in Boston, last known address is in Seattle. Now he was a good student, but ran off the rails at sixteen, started running with a gang who were moving coke all over Boston. Arrested at seventeen, then went from bad to worse, ended up in Concord doing a five stretch for arson. Then disappears, to resurface in Seattle, where his gets arrested for holding up a drug store. He gets bail, and never shows up for the hearing, so there's a warrant out on him. Or was. Second man is Sung-min Byeon, thirty, no record of immigration into the US. We got as much as we can, which isn't a great deal. He was a long-term resident of Incheon and his record shows he spent some time in prison for assault and kidnap, but was recently held following a rape charge. I've not got much more on this other than he disappeared and the police there couldn't find him.'

'OK,' Keane said, 'so can we tie any of these three men together?'

'Not really,' Judy said, 'but we do think it's possible that Kong and Byeon knew each other. There is some footage that's been found at the Metro station two days ago, my guys have been working real hard on this. Kong is seen with another man, and take a look, I think that's Byeon. They were checking the place out, so we were right; this wasn't a chance thing last night.'

Printed photos were passed around, they all looked, and everyone agreed, there were two grainy pictures, in one the two men were looking down the stairs and in the other side by side on the platform, it was definitely Kong looking straight up at the camera and the other man wasn't clear but his build was like Byeon.

'There are more; we got these shots from Seattle PD.'

She passed round more prints, there was a mugshot of Kong, standard, and then two other photographs, one of him running down a street; the picture taken from high up and then another of him walking with two other men, taken from a patrol car camera. Kong was on the left, and the man in the centre looked similar to Byeon. It could be.

'Also, Byeon had an old greyhound ticket in the pocket of his jacket. From Sacramento, dated October,' Judy told them.

Warner whistled.

'So, he been here four months? Maybe all of them came in from out of town?'

'Plenty of time to start making friends,' Keane stated.

'For sure,' Warner added.

'And we got one more thing, which is again about Kong, indirectly. His record shows an associate in Seattle, one Rico Perez, Puerto Rican, thirty-two. He's got a record for armed robbery among other things. Now this is only interesting for one reason. The PD got called to a fight at a bar in Echo Park, five or six guys involved. Perez was detained but released. This was end of January.'

'So Perez is here in the city?' Keane asked.

'Seems so, well at least last month he was.'

They all looked at each other.

'We need to find this Perez,' John said.

'Four million people in the city, give or take,' Keane said ruefully.

John nodded.

'I get that, but it's a start. If he was detained, he would have given his details, right?' he looked at Judy, who triumphantly produced yet another sheet of paper.

Keane looked at it.

'Lynwood, that figures,' he said.

Warner stood up, chair creaking as his bulk moved out.

'What are we waiting for?'

Sammy kept looking at her mobile, but eventually gave it up. She would have to be patient, let Frost do his thing, whatever that was. She was tired, she had been working until three in the morning and back in the office at eight. She looked across at Simon who was busy tapping away on the keyboard of his PC.

'I'm clocking off for a while,' she told him.

He gave her a big smile.

'No problem.'

'If Moran asks, tell him to go fuck himself.'

He laughed.

'I won't be doing that, but I'll think of something.'

She blew him a kiss and walked out the newsroom, and across reception, anticipating the whole time that Moran would appear and start giving her a hard time. But he didn't, and she rode the lift down to the car park under the building. She climbed in her BMW and got going, heading home.

She was renting an apartment in Pomona, and she liked it well enough, apart from the journey. But today was pretty clear, the rush hour had not yet started so she made good time. Once inside she kicked off her shoes and went in to the bedroom, standing in front of the mirror, scrutinising herself, something which she had been doing every day for as long as she could remember. Her reflection looked back at her, well presented, perfectly made up.

She would never admit it but Moran's open hostility had shaken her badly. She had been well aware of her power over men since she was a teenager, and used it well, she was always confident and assured. Her second divorce had been difficult, not because of personal feelings or any sense of loss but because it had been so loudly played out in public. In fact, she had read about her impending divorce before anything had even been said between them. Of course, she and Jason had gone out and said all the right things, they loved each other but decided this was the only way forward, they would always be very good friends etc., but this was the best thing for both of them. Please could everyone respect their privacy during this difficult time, etc. The reality was they had nothing in common, the initial fire had quickly died away and they both had numerous affairs. She hadn't taken any of hers seriously at all, they had been a welcome distraction from her unhappy home life at the time, but Jason had decided he wanted a twenty-three-year-old pole dancer more than he wanted her. She had taken the LA Plus job because the timing was perfect and Indianapolis was suddenly way too small. Looking in the mirror she thought about Jason, the first time in forever, they had met when The Colts were flying high and he was the star, described in hushed terms as the best fullback in the NFL. She interviewed the team several times and it had seemed almost inevitable, the spark was obvious. When they got married, she was thirty-five and she had believed this was it, her life was mapped out. She had been happy, excited. A year in and everything was different already, but they made it work. Kind of. Publicly, anyway. Or so she thought.

But she realised too late that deep down she had known early on. They had both had.

She sighed and took off her dress and hung it up in the wardrobe carefully, then returned to stand in front of the mirror again, critically looking at her reflection, now in her underwear. Forty-three years old, and in the public eye for twenty-four of them. Body of an eighteen-year-old Jason used to tell her. No plastic surgery, and she didn't have to hit the gym much. But she wasn't feeling so good about herself anymore. She had moved here to start again, in a city where there was a long line of people just waiting for her to fail, and Moran was right at the front.

She needed to prove herself, that she wasn't just a pretty face. As that clearly wasn't working.

If she could find this British guy, that would do it. She wouldn't need to feel so second rate. They had done a great job in the aftermath of the Metro attack, she knew it. The other channels had barely turned up in comparison. If she could just track this man down and run a piece on him she could name her price, and the nationals would come calling. Moran would have no choice but to back her. She thought about Jimmy Frost and his blatant leering, knowing what he believed was on the table. She shook her head and looked away, she would have to toughen up.

Whatever it takes, she told herself. This was a fresh start, and could be the last one she would ever get. Whatever it takes.

***

They were driving down Alameda Street when Keane's mobile started to warble. Warner was driving with Judy next to him, John and Keane in the back. They all automatically checked their phones.

'Me!' Keane announced and held it to his ear.

'Hello.'

He listened for a while and then gestured for something to write with. Judy produced a pad and pen and Keane started writing, listening intently, grunting and nodding. It took a while but eventually he asked for everything to be emailed across and hung up the call, the notepad had a long list written on the page.

'OK, we got the IDs of the victims. The five women, and we know who they all are.'

He scrutinised the list.

'First look nothing of any real interest. The two that stand out are a Deanna Hayter and a Madeline White. Deanna was thirty-three and just married an army major three weeks ago. Madeline was forty and a high-class hooker. Of the other women, I got a doctor, a nurse and a restaurant manager.'

'Any records?' Judy asked.

'Well, that is interesting because both Deanna and Madeline do, but nothing on the others.'

'What for?' John asked.

'Madeline is straightforward, she worked Vegas for years, so she got a string of soliciting misdemeanours, no real prison time. Deanna was a stripper, again in Vegas. Her maiden name is Clark. She's also got priors for soliciting, but doesn't look serious. Seems like they were friends, from their final locations they were the two women close to John on the platform.'

'Deanna Hayter just married an army major?' Judy asked.

'Yeah. In Vegas. I don't have any real details, but he has been informed.'

'What about the other three women, Ron?' asked Warner.

'Right, Christa Vorchek, forty-eight, married, one daughter, she was a doctor. Fiona Bright, thirty-one, married, no kids, a nurse. Her and Christa were travelling together, they just ended a shift at USC hospital. Then there was Jane Elliot, thirty, unmarried, manages the Deluxe Grill. Staff there say she left before her shift ended, she wasn't feeling too good.'

'Hmmm, anything in that I wonder. You know, that she left early,' Judy wondered.

'Could be I guess,' Keane scribbled a note on the pad. 'So, assuming for now Christa and Fiona are in the clear we got Deanna, Madeline and Jane to look into, or have I missed something?'

'I don't think so, no,' Judy replied.

The rabbit warren of Imperial Courts slid past the windows of the car, and then further down Warner turned left and with several turns followed a couple of streets before pulling over to the kerb.

'Got to be careful here,' Warner said grimly. 'These motherfuckers always got a point to prove.'

John looked around. It was a street among several similar with low single storey houses on both sides, all of them identical. On several porches groups of young people were sitting, male and female, mostly black. They looked relaxed, but isolated in their respective groups. A motorbike came down the road from the opposite direction, and pulled a wheelie halfway along, the bike almost completely upright, rider with his head hanging off the side, no crash helmet. Several people whooped and cheered.

'What number you got?' asked Keane.

'I got 1163 ,' Judy replied, and Warner rolled slowly down the street as they checked the numbers, until he stopped dead. They were looking at two burnt-out houses, side by side.

'That's it,' Warner told them, pointing at the left-hand ruin.

They got out the car and walked over. It was obvious the fires had occurred a long time previously. Both sites were little more than burnt scattered bricks and remains of timbers, but there were weeds and long grass everywhere.

'Real clever right? Let's go,' Warner urged, aware they were attracting interest. He knew only too well how quickly the local residents could react, and most of them would be carrying guns.

They got back in the car and drove off.

'Well, I know Kong got arrested for arson, but I don't think we can make that work,' John said as they cruised back to Santa Monica.

Keane shook his head.

'No way, that's got to be five years old, probably more.'

'It shows how organised they are, Perez must have shown his ID, and that was what he had. Already set up and ready to go.' Judy said.

'Probably his passport, and he just gave that address. But yeah, it proves they know what they're doing, 1163 would have checked out through the system as valid, nothing on the PD computers to say the place is a pile of ash.' Warner told them.

'So, we got nothing,' Keane sullenly repeated what he had told them earlier but John shook his head.

'You're wrong. Let's focus on the women, got to be something there.'

Chapter Eight

By the time they had fought the traffic and they finally got back to the hotel it was past seven, so they decided to go straight out for dinner. They ate at the bar, and afterward Judy wanted to go back to her room. She had a case going to trial in a couple of days and wanted to make sure her team was fully briefed. Warner went with her, he wanted to Skype his family, which left John and Keane sitting at a table next to the window.

The bar had been done out with a supposedly tropical feel, the staff all wore Hawaiian shirts, there were lots of plastic palm leaves and coconuts everywhere with a simple seafood menu and a long cocktail list.

'This used to be my patch,' Keane told him. 'Back in the day, I was a detective here for twelve years and then came back again later as the chief.'

'You're the chief here? I didn't realise,' John replied.

'No, I took a sideways move about five years ago. I'm based in Long Beach now, but I guess that's why I thought it would be good to set up over here. This place is full of people coming and going, nobody notices a new face.'

John nodded.

'Yeah, I suppose you're right. Now I think the same thing.'

Keane looked at him shrewdly.

'You can look after yourself, right?' he asked.

'Not sure what you mean.'

'You know exactly what I mean. If it starts getting rough, you don't hide away. You get stuck in. It's written all over you.'

John touched the dressing on his head.

'I suppose so, but no more than anyone else.'

'I ain't sure about that I got to say. Well, I got an idea of someone we can go see. This guy knows what's going on, he ain't someone I trust, not at all, he is an evil motherfucker but he's always got an ear to the ground. Mostly because he is a sly son of a bitch who walks a fine line, always changing sides. But he could be useful. He's got slices of this and that all over the city and knows a lot of people, good and bad.'

'OK. Is he local?'

'Yeah, not far. Down near the ocean.'

They left the bar and walked along the street, the turned down another that led straight onto the beach, the sea was right there, in front of them. Keane stopped outside a bar that looked tiny from the front, just a door and a small window. Inside, it was long and thin, with the bar on the left. There were a few people in there. As John walked across the floor a woman uncurled herself from a stool and went over to him, but then she saw Keane and stopped with a scowl.

'Not tonight Candy, we ain't buying,' he told her, and she went back to her seat.

Keane led the way across to a doorway at the back, with a short narrow staircase leading steeply down.

'Mind your head,' he said, and went down the steps.

At the bottom, it was dark, and there was another door, which looked like an afterthought. It all looked very suspicious in John's view, but Keane didn't bother to take out his gun, he just pushed hard and walked straight into the room beyond, with John close behind.

Inside was a small room, with nothing in it but a desk and a two-seat sofa. One wall was covered in stacked cardboard boxes, and there was another small door in the far corner. Sitting at the desk was a squat, wide man in a suit with black hair gelled flat and a big square chin. Two other men were sitting on the sofa, one white and completely covered in tattoos and the other a lanky Mexican. The man behind the desk jumped up.

'What the FUCK?' he roared and heaved the desk over and grabbed at Keane's shirt front. The Mexican also leapt up and took a swing at John. Distracted by what was happening with Keane, John managed to duck and the blow landed on the top of his head, immediately he surged forward, grabbing the Mexican by the throat with his left hand and battering him hard in the face with his right, three, four punches, all solid blows, the Mexican flailing around ineffectively.

The Mexican fell to the floor and John whirled to face Tattoos.

But the man was standing up and smiling, hands raised. He glanced at John then nodded across the room.

Keane had his assailant in a headlock and ran toward the rear wall driving the man's face hard straight into it. He let the man go and pushed him over with his foot. John looked at Tattoos who was doing nothing, still smiling; no threat, and then turned to Keane, confused.

Keane had a hold of the man's collar and hauled him up, then dropped him into his seat.

The man looked around and scowled.

'Thanks for your fucking help Louie,' he spat at the tattooed man, blood running from his nose and dripping off his chin.

'Fuck that. Did you see what he did to Paolo? No fucking way, I like my face,' Louie replied and sat back down on the sofa again, grinning, unconcerned.

The Mexican was sitting up, head bowed.

'I can't fucking believe you would just bust in here like this Keane, you fuck,' the man in the suit said. His cheek was also swelling and his right eye starting to close.

'John, this is Billy Wheeler, commonly known as Billy Whizz, cos he does everything fast. Right Billy?'

'Fuck you.'

'That's not very nice. Me and Billy's dad go way back, John. But you ain't quite there yet Billy, are you?'

'Fuck you,' Billy said again, slowly.

'He's a witty guy, right?'

With an effort Keane righted the desk and pushed it back so Billy was effectively trapped against the wall behind, then leaned forward.

'Now Billy, I need your help with something. We got some shit going down in this town, you will have heard all about the terrorist attack on the Metro. Well I'm the man been sent to hunt them down, so what do you know?'

Keane turned and sat half on the desk, looking down at Billy, who shrugged, easing the desk away from himself.

'I don't know nothing. I'm not involved in any of that shit, you know that.'

'Sure, yeah I know that. But you do know a lot of things, and I thought maybe you can help us out.'

'Seriously Mr Keane, I never heard nothing. I don't know shit.'

'OK. So how about you?'

Keane turned his head and looked at Tattoos.

'Me? I haven't heard nothing neither. That shit took us all by surprise.'

Nobody said anything, Billy Whizz sat looking around uncomfortably. Keane produced the bio picture of Rico Perez and laid it on the desk.

'You need to keep this real quiet, but we would like to speak to this guy.'

Billy looked at it and shook his head, then slid it across the table to Tattoos, who picked it up.

'No idea, don't know him,' Billy told them adamantly.

But Tattoos was looking closely at the photo.

'I seen this guy, maybe a couple of times. Place called Miss Sin, in Hollywood. I got a girl that works there, he's been in. I'm in there a lot I guess. But I don't know him, never spoke to him. Sits on his own. Quiet. But I'd say it's this guy, for sure.'

The man in the suit thumped the desk and pointlessly shot him a warning glance.

'When was the last time you saw him?' John asked, ignoring it.

'I ain't sure. It's been a while since I seen him, ask the girls, they may be able to tell you something, they're paid to be friendly.'

'OK. Thanks, that's helpful,' Keane said. 'You see Billy, being an asshole isn't ingrained in everybody.'

Billy shrugged again.

'One more thing Billy, I need a gun. For my man here. No trace.'

'Come on Mr Keane don't try this shit,' Billy pleaded.

'I'm not trying anything, but John here isn't official. I can't arm him myself and things are going to get ugly at some point so I got to look out for him.'

'Mr Keane you gonna fit me up, I can't …'

'Fucking hell Billy, you ain't listening. This is not about popping a cap in some asshole and you taking the blame. It's bigger than that shit. Much bigger.'

'Jesus Mr Keane,' Billy whined.

'Listen to me. Your pal here just helped, which I'm very grateful for. Now it's your turn. I don't care what shit you got down here.'

He turned and pulled on one of the boxes stacked against the wall. It fell off the pile and burst open. Porn DVDs scattered all over the floor.

'Now, if you play nice it will mean I'm gonna ignore these. One good turn deserves another, but I ain't a patient man Billy, you know that.'

Billy looked up at John helplessly, and then with a deep sigh and muttering to himself, stood up and went over to the door in the corner.

'Make it a nine-mil please Billy, keep it straightforward,' Keane asked, pleasantly.

Billy grunted and nodded then unlocked and went inside, closing the door behind him, but John still saw a small room full of stuff. Billy returned a few minutes later with two cloth-wrapped bundles, which he laid on the desk, then stepped back. John moved forward and unwrapped them. There was a Browning Hi-Power and a SIG Sauer P226. Both guns were used but looked in good condition. He picked up the SIG, it was a gun he liked.

'Good choice,' Tattoos said, and Keane nodded.

John checked the clip and the chamber, which were both empty, then looked hard at Billy, who rolled his eyes.

'Fuck.'

He picked up the Browning and started wrapping it up again.

'I think we'll take that too Billy,' Keane told him holding out his hand.

'Fuck,' Billy said again and pursed his lips, then threw it back on the desk. Keane picked it up with a smile and put it in his jacket pocket.

'Ammo?' John asked, patiently, enjoying the game.

Billy threw his arms up, then disappeared behind the door, then came back and dropped two cartons on the desk. John picked one of them up. Good quality IMI rounds, twenty in a box.

'Thank you,' he said, and meticulously loaded the clip, snapped it back into the gun then racked it so there was a round in the chamber, dropped out the clip again and thumbed in an additional bullet, then clicked it back together and pushed it down the back of his trousers.

'Look Mr Keane, about the guns. You never got these fucking things from me OK? You never did, I don't know nothing about them OK? Billy said, still worried.

'I'm not interested in chasing down your homies Billy. Don't panic, I was never here. And you'll get them back,' Keane said with a smile.

'Yeah, yeah. Until your buddy here blows his own head off or gets it done for him.'

'I'm not too worried about that Billy. John here has proved he's more than a match for these scumbags.'

Keane bent down and picked up a DVD, which showed a naked woman tightly tied up while two men stood at either side of her. The title on the box was Real Rapes.

'I got the feeling a lot of people would be unhappy with these Billy, and I mean a lot. I guess if I got a team down here and went right through these I'd find a lot of things that would make me real sick and cause a lot of anger in certain places. What do you think?'

He produced his mobile phone and held it up.

'One call, they can be here in less than fifteen.'

'You got it wrong Mr Keane. These ain't mine.' Billy blustered.

Keane held up a hand.

'Just make sure you don't never say a word about our visit.' He looked keenly at Tattoos. 'Both of you. If I find someone is expecting us, I'm coming back here, and I won't be in such a good mood, am I clear?'

'Crystal,' Tattoos said.

'Good. Let's go John. I fancy a cold beer, get rid of this shitty taste in my mouth.'

Chapter Nine

Voorhees hadn't left his office all day apart from to receive a pizza that was delivered. He didn't offer to share it, just disappeared again. Rico and Sal eventually took a walk around just to get some air. It was common not to see a great deal of Voorhees during the day but normally they would have had an instruction however vague, whether it would be some kind of reconnaissance somewhere, getting information, shooting practice or an exercise of some sort. Since they first set up in LA they had spent time in the library researching LAPD response times and their options, and been sent all over the state collecting various items; guns, clothing, rucksacks, vehicles and always for cash. Always something to do. But today, nothing. In fact this had been the same for a while now.

Unsurprisingly Sal wasn't convinced of the benefits of his promotion, and had been attempting to persuade Rico not to do anything drastic. They had wandered around for a couple of hours before resignedly heading back to the apartment.

Voorhees was standing inside the door, waiting.

'Where the fuck have you been?' he snarled.

'Just walking Yann, just getting out.'

'You been in a bar? I told you, no more, not after last time. I fucking told you.'

'No, no way,' Sal told him.

Voorhees moved closer and looked closely at both men.

'I need you to be at Union Station for eight-thirty. I got a new guy called Karl Weiss coming in, I got no idea what he looks like so you'll have to be smart.'

Rico paled.

'Downtown? You sure that's a good idea, after last night I mean.'

Voorhees glowered at him.

'If it hadn't got fucked up I wouldn't have had to arrange this, would I? So just fucking do it.'

'Er ... where's he coming in from Yann?' Sal asked.

'Phoenix. And the word is he can be an asshole, so make sure you persuade him to leave any of that shit outside the door OK?'

Both men nodded.

They set off in an old Chevy Lumina just after seven, they didn't want to risk being late. Rico's obvious nervousness was rubbing off on Sal, and both men were fighting inner demons by the time they pulled up close to Union station. They sat in the car waiting for the time to pass, which it did slowly. They made small talk, watching a policeman drinking coffee from a stand along the street.

'Cops everywhere, man,' Rico said looking all around.

Sal was doing the same. He saw a patrol car at a junction further along past the station and two uniforms just inside the station doors.

'Yeah, but they ain't looking for us, right?' he said pensively.

'I guess so.'

They got out of the car and walked down to the station entrance, trying like all the world to look like a couple of regular guys come to meet a buddy. Both men just wore jeans and t-shirts, which they were now regretting as the night was chilly and inside the station was no warmer than outside. The police at the doors paid them no heed as they passed.

Sal had written 'Karl' on a sheet of paper and was holding it up lamely as people walked out from the platforms. Rico checked the arrivals board.

'Due in a few minutes I reckon,' he told Sal.

They sat down to wait on a bench, constantly looking everywhere, knowing there would be cameras in the station and there was nothing they could do about it but keep their heads down.

A train pulled in and eventually a line of people appeared walking away from the platform so they stood near the exit, Sal holding the sheet of paper in front of them.

A man walked out on his own, late twenties, tall and thin, long white hair shaved on one side, wearing sunglasses despite the fact it was night and a long black coat. He looked around, spotted them and headed over.

'Jesus Christ,' breathed Rico.

'You Karl?' Sal asked when the man stopped in front of them. He could not have stood out any more.

'Yep. Who the fuck are you?'

'Oh Jesus,' Rico whispered to himself, not really believing what he was seeing. Yann was going to go apeshit.

'I'm Sal, and this is Rico. Let's go.'

They led the way out the station and down the street to the car. Sal moved over and opened the boot.

'What the fuck is that?' Weiss asked, finally removing the sunglasses.

Both Sal and Rico turned to see what he was looking at.

'It's a car,' Sal told him,

'It's a piece of shit. Should be a fucking limo. Don't tell me I got amateur hour here.'

Rico lost his patience.

'Karl? Get in the fucking car. Or I swear to God I'm gonna start breaking some fucking bones. We do not need any more shit.'

He stood very still, right in front of Weiss, staring up into his eyes.

Weiss stared back insolently, then looked away and stepped back, throwing his bag into the boot.

'OK, OK, Jesus. What the fuck. I'm just saying.'

Rico clenched his fists, Sal led him gently away. The last thing they needed right now was any more trouble. Weiss sniggered and climbed in the back of the car.

They drove back to the apartment in silence, Weiss put in earphones while Rico fumed as he drove and Sal worried next to him. The walked into the apartment and Sal crossed the hallway and knocked on the office door. Weiss looked around the dismal surroundings and shook his head.

'No fucking way.'

Sal beckoned him over.

'Boss wants you,' he said, then pushed Weiss inside and shut the door.

Chapter Ten

John and Keane walked the short distance back to the hotel, climbed the stairs and then knocked on Warner's door.

The big man answered then went back to lying on the bed in his pyjamas, watching a movie on a laptop. Keane explained what he and John had done earlier without any real detail, and Warner looked impressed.

He stood up.

'So, trip to Hollywood?' he asked.

Keane looked at him carefully.

'I think just me and John should go. I'll tell you for why. I don't know this place the tattooed guy mentioned but they are all the same, if it looks like we are going in strong they will clam up. All sorts own these goddamn places, nobody wants to say the wrong thing. All we got to do is ask a couple of questions about some guy who has been in there a few times, just keep it casual, no big deal. You are a big black guy Kyle, no way we can change that. You look like muscle, that's how it is. On our own we can fumble around like a pair of assholes, nobody gonna look twice. You cool with this?'

John looked at Warner, wondering what he would say. He could be very pissed off, see it as a slight against the CIA, and worse maybe a slight against race. He looked like he was considering it, weighing up the pros and cons, then shrugged, much to John's relief.

'No problem. I guess that sounds about right. Just don't do nothing that's gonna bring down any heat OK?' He laid back down again and folded his hands behind his head.

'Got it,' Keane said, and the two men shook hands.

They left the hotel and climbed into Keane's car. He drove out into the evening traffic and headed south and east.

'So what's the deal with Billy? He could cause us a lot of problems if he starts running off at the mouth,' John asked.

'No, he ain't that stupid. His dad was the main man around Santa Monica, right from way before I was a detective and still going when I was the chief. Tony ran a tight ship, lot of rackets, but he was always real tidy about everything. We knew what was going on alright, but nothing stuck and the real truth was he never caused us any problems, in fact it was a two-way street. He gave us a lot of information, anyone he didn't like the look of came our way. If he got rid of somebody, we never found them and nobody complained. I knew some of the boys in the precinct were getting paid, but I never took a single cent. Billy started working for him, just being a gofer really. Anyway, one day, some other team starts trying to operate on their turf. A pair of Ukrainian brothers, real hard cases. And they were making life difficult, being real noisy and getting in people's faces, but we got nothing, they ain't breaking any laws we can see. So, Tony asks to see me, saying what am I going to do about it. What can I do I ask him? I tell him I'm sure they are up to their necks in shit but we can't find nothing. Of course, he ain't happy. We have this whole long conversation and I say; look if they commit a felony and we catch them that's that, but I can't do nothing if they're clean. He is real pissed about it, so tells me he's gonna get Billy to deal with it, about time he started doing some real work. So, I say fine, but any shit turns up, it don't matter that we had this conversation.'

'OK. So how did that go?'

'Suddenly we got a war. Guns going off all over the place. For about three months we had a lot of extra patrols on the ground permanently, it didn't let up. And people are scared, the phones are going crazy and the brass are all over us. So now I'm really pissed. I go speak to Tony but he just says he don't know nothing, but I can see he's getting upset. Then we get a body.

Eleven bullet holes. This guy, I don't recall his name but known to be an enforcer for the Ukrainian brothers. So, I go back to Tony and he's smiling and offering me whisky and still saying he knows nothing. Next, we got another one, and now it's the elder brother; Vladimir Cheskov his name was. He's got half a dozen holes in him, and then nothing. Nice and quiet. It all goes back to normal, so I'm thinking Billy must have done OK.'

'But?'

'But. Tony gets shot in the back getting in his car. Survives, he is a tough old man. Must be about six, seven years ago now. He can't walk, and has to pee in a bag but he's still going. He handed over to Billy soon after that, set him up under the bar we were at. Tony cleared up; sold off his clubs and his pawnshops and all the other bits and pieces, lives down in Orange County now, I never hear from him. Billy ain't so bad, he's learning, but he's only interested in the right now; make some dollars on this, make some doing that, while Tony was all about the long term. My guess now is there was another firm, probably more than one making life difficult back then.'

'I have to say going in the bar wasn't like the TV. I thought you'd have your gun out and be breaking down doors.'

'Nah, I don't do that. In fact, LAPD don't roll like that no more. Too many civil liberties. Whether that's for the good, I don't know. LA is famous for the gangs, the Crips and the Bloods, and they're there, they're real, and a whole bunch of others who wanna be just like them. Truth is, we got busy police in this city, real busy.'

'Do you mind me asking Ron, what exactly is your unit? I thought maybe counterterrorism but I'm guessing that's not it, you seem too streetwise to me.'

Keane grinned.

'Ha, no, not counterterrorism. Hell, I got no fucking clue about that stuff. We're kinda fortunate here, we seem to be escaping the worst of that. I sure hope that continues. It's a fair question John. Thing is, my unit doesn't really exist but I'm the chief. The chief of me.'

'You're on your own?'

'Yeah, in a nutshell. I mean, I got direct links to plenty of other departments and teams, I can get SWAT on the ground in minutes if I need to. Judy said I was the FBI liaison, which I guess is as good a way of saying it. I do that, and the CIA, plus Interpol, and a couple of others so far if needed. My job is to be the front line between the LAPD and all these other agencies. Before, it was the chief of whatever precinct or division was involved, now, they got to come to me first. I got the call on this even before we even got ID on that guy Ritorsky. The CIA were notified of course, which came back to me, and straight away it looked like a big deal. Meantime, they find out some English guy called John Smith is caught up in it, took out the bad fellas with their own gun and who the FBI of all people think is the golden boy, and it keeps on getting bigger. So, I'm here, for the duration.'

John nodded.

'Right. So how we doing so far chief?'

'Well, being honest, and I never like saying this, we ain't got much of nothing.'

They entered Hollywood and Keane drove down the boulevard, then turned off into a street which was a sea of neon, pulling up right outside a dark painted place with a big awning and Miss Sin glowing in big letters.

'I thought you said you didn't know this place,' John said as they got out the car.

'Yeah well, look, I like Kyle, and I trust him. But we got an operation going down here, people trafficking, these girls are turning up all the time. This is one of the places on the list. So, I didn't want to mention any names, just keep it casual OK? Last thing anyone needs is the CIA wielding the big stick if you know what I mean.'

'Yeah, I get it.'

***

Rico and Sal were drinking beer in the kitchen talking quietly.

'I ain't sure about this guy,' Sal said. 'We're supposed to be invisible, right? He ain't fucking hard to miss!'

Rico nodded.

'Yeah, and he got an attitude too. I bet Yann is going crazy on his ass in there.'

They listened, but apart from the low murmur of voices there was nothing. No sound of any excitement, then they heard Voorhees' mobile phone ringing.

Minutes later the door opened and Weiss sauntered out with Voorhees behind him looking pleased.

'Right. Get your asses in gear. Things are changing, we got work to do.'

He passed Sal a sheet of paper with some scribbled writing on it.

'Hollywood. Get up there and get it done. Full description, and where he'll be. Don't fuck this up, bring the briefcase straight back to me and then you can go celebrate. Relax. Take Karl for a beer or some shit.'

Sal took the paper and looked at Rico then Weiss.

'Really? OK thanks Yann, sure.'

***

John and Keane walked in, and were met by two curvaceous girls in tight red shorts and little else. They led them into a huge dark dimly lit room with red velvet curtains everywhere and small raised platforms dotted around. There was a stage with a runway on the left and a curved bar on the right. Tables scattered randomly everywhere and booths along a centre island and one wall. There was a skinny naked girl swinging around a pole on the stage while a dismal eighties song played loudly. The place was about a quarter full, more girls in red shorts and tiny bra tops running drinks everywhere on trays, while others wearing even less cavorted in front of men at a few of the tables. They ordered a couple of beers and sat down in a booth to one side.

John looked behind them at the bar, which ran along half the back wall in a semi-circle that jutted into the room. There were a couple of bartenders behind it, mixing drinks while some waitresses hovered. It wasn't particularly busy back there, he could see less than a handful of drinkers sat alongside, most in the room were at the tables or in the booths, and he knew that there were more behind the many curtains paying for a private dance.

John leaned into Keane.

'Can I have the picture?' he asked.

Keane nodded and passed it to him and John stood up and wandered back over to the bar. There were several security guys in place, and he had to deal with this carefully. He sat down on a stool, and casually waited for one of the bartenders to get close to him.

'Hey, can I ask you a question? I got to find this guy, he comes in here a lot, his name is Rico. I'm wondering if he's been in.'

The barman glanced at the picture.

'Not sure. Hey, Jonty!' he called out to other man working behind the bar, who walked across.

'Know this guy? He does look kinda familiar.'

Jonty picked the picture up.

'Yeah, he comes in here. Not been around in a while, mind.'

'Did you talk to him?' John asked.

Both men shook their heads.

'No. You need to go ask Sugar, she spent time with him. He was sure sweet on her.'

'OK, which one is Sugar?'

Jonty scanned the room.

'Must be doing a dance out back I guess. She's got long pink hair, can't miss her.'

He went back to working and John returned to sitting with Keane, and relayed the conversation. They sat there, sipping their beers, watching the room. A girl appeared, and began to gyrate in front of them. Keane slipped her twenty dollars and asked for privacy, she didn't look put out, just shimmied away to the next table.

'Let's make this quick, it's gonna cost a fortune to sit here,' John said, looking around for a girl with long pink hair.

They saw her five minutes later, emerging from a curtain with a wad of banknotes in her briefs. She was short with impossibly round breasts, tottering along in the highest heels John had ever seen. They got up and wandered across, intercepting her as she stalked her next victim.

She was good. A professional. She glanced at Keane, then fixed on John, he was younger.

'Hey, hey baby, you looking for me? I can get a friend for your dad if you like,' she smiled, all white teeth and breasts standing to attention.

'Er, yes I am looking for you, and my dad's fine right now thanks. Can we sit down?'

She pouted theatrically and looked slowly all around, then shrugged and followed them back to the booth. She perched on the very end, legs crossed, continuing with the wide smile, sticking with her persona. John could see she was a little older than he had first thought, probably late twenties, and had bruises just visible under the left eye on her heavily made up face.

'I drink champagne, as you're asking,' she told them, with a slow wink.

Keane shook his head and resignedly dug in his pockets.

'That figures. Sure.'

He gestured at a waitress who came over and stood next to Sugar.

'Champagne for the lady please,' Keane asked, passing over a twenty.

The waitress looked at it and didn't move, just stared back at him. Keane tutted and passed her another note, but she continued standing there.

'Jesus,' Keane murmured and passed one more.

The waitress smiled sweetly and walked off.

'Sixty bucks for a bottle of champagne!' Keane fumed shaking his head.

Sugar laughed delightedly.

'Bottle! That's for a glass you tight asshole!'

John decided to move it on so they could get out of there. He produced the photo and slid it across the table to Sugar who picked it up disinterestedly and then looked at him.

'We need to find this guy. Rico,' he told her.

She raised her eyebrows and looked at the photo again, then shrugged.

'Yeah? Why?'

'Because,' growled Keane, pissed off about how it was going, and especially the champagne.

'Look Sugar, we just really need to speak to him, that's all,' John cut in quickly.

'You cops? What's he done?'

'No, I'm not a cop. I don't know that he's done anything,' John told her truthfully.

Sugar's champagne arrived in a frosted glass and she delicately took a sip, spilling some of it down her front.

'Oh!' she said, wiping her impressive chest, 'I'm such a messy bitch. You would not believe how dirty I can get,' she breathed at John, big eyes fixed on his.

Keane rolled his eyes and John spoke fast before he could say anything.

'Sugar please, if you can help, it would be appreciated.'

'OK. I like appreciated. How much?'

John looked at Keane, who was about to speak when one of the security men appeared out of nowhere and loomed above them.

'It's ok Gary, I'm fine,' Sugar said, waving the man away.

The man looked closely at Keane and John and then moved on to another table.

'There's some cash in it. How much depends on what you can tell us,' John let her know.

Sugar looked hard at him, and drank some more champagne. Then she tapped a long bright pink fingernail on the table and looked around the room again. John sat waiting patiently while Keane squirmed in his seat. Finally, she turned back to face him again.

'Fine. Looking this good costs you know. Listen, I don't really know him OK? Rico comes in here, and he always gets a dance, sometimes two. He's sweet, he doesn't maul me or nothing, keeps his hands to himself. He ain't been in for a while though.'

'Always on his own?'

'Yeah, I think so. Actually, he was with another guy one time. Brown curly hair I think, I can't remember, I didn't do him.'

'Did Rico talk much?'

'Nah. Not really. Just he was working here for a while, and was bored. I think he was lonely.'

'Did he say where he lives?'

'Er, in the city for sure. He did say something … yeah, he said he was sharing an apartment. I remember now, he told me once it was real shitty. He said he couldn't take no one back there. Not that I was gonna do that,' she added hastily.

'He never talked about anyone else, his family?'

'No. Like I said, we didn't really talk that much. He didn't ask no one else for a dance, and he would just sit up at the bar. He seemed happy to be here, I guess it was good to get the fuck out of his apartment, right?'

'Did it look like he had a lot of cash on him?' Keane asked.

'He always looked after me, I mean, like sure I could get more, but often a lot less. He was OK. I wouldn't say he was rich.'

She was getting bored of the conversation, eyes constantly looking around, finding her next contributor.

John dug in his pocket, and pulled out a hundred-dollar bill, and then wrote his mobile number on a napkin and pushed them over to her. She immediately added the cash to the rest in her knickers and then looked at the number written down.

'We going out later honey?' she asked, smiling sweetly.

John smiled back.

'No, sorry. But if he comes in, maybe you can call me, ok?'

She considered.

'Ok.'

They stood up, and moved out. John bent down to Sugar as he passed.

'Keep that number, ok? I'm John by the way. You may want to call it, I can help stop whoever's doing that to your face,' he told her.

She raised a hand to the bruise and stared at him.

'I …'

'Think about it, I can help,' he interrupted, and they walked out the strip club.

'Let's get back to the hotel, get some sleep, tomorrow's a new day, right?' Keane said aggressively as they climbed in the car, still smarting about the damage to the contents of his wallet.

Chapter Eleven

General Morgan sat behind his desk, mouth open, looking up at Lieutenant Clay disbelievingly.

Clay returned the look impassively. Like the majority of staff in their section of the Pentagon he thought Morgan was an asshole, the man hadn't been here that long considering, and had managed to pretty much piss everyone off. Even that morning he had been stalking around complaining to anyone who couldn't get out of the way quick enough about his lacking a secretary. Like he really needed one anyway, she only made him coffee and passed over a whole bunch of bullshit memos anyway. He knew the history; Morgan was a relative, some in law or something of an assistant to the previous army chief of staff, who had retired a couple of years ago. Now, nobody seemed to know what to do with him so he had ended up here, which was their loss.

'When did you find this out? I mean, how am I only being told this now?' Morgan asked in a strangled voice.

'Because sir, I was only advised about the situation a couple of minutes ago. I came straight in to tell you, that's the first thing I did. Sir.'

Morgan's cheeks reddened.

'Well, who notified you?'

'It came direct from Fort Indigo sir.'

'Did it? But ...'

Morgan stopped, speechless. Indigo had been his, he had been CO there for over five years, right before he was moved to the Pentagon. He knew everyone on the base, well everyone that mattered. He couldn't believe that not one person there had thought to call him personally.

'Right. Well, find out who is dealing with it! I need to speak to them. And that is urgent lieutenant.'

'Sir, it will be the MP XO, and you …'

'I know that!'

In agitation Morgan picked up a pen and threw it down again. He couldn't remember the MP XO at Fort Indigo, he wasn't even sure where they were situated on the big base out in California.

Clay said nothing, just continued standing easy.

Morgan scratched his nose. What to do, what to do.

'Right lieutenant, please find me the officer I need to speak to. And get me Colonel Carter on the phone. That will be all.'

Clay snapped his heels together and wheeled out the room, smirking as he did so.

Morgan watched the door close and stood up, looking around aimlessly. Like most offices at the Pentagon, his had no windows, just grey walls all round. He looked down at his desk, breathing in and out slowly and deliberately.

Was this down to him? It couldn't just be coincidence surely. But he hadn't done anything to cause this. Anything that had happened was nothing to do with him, it couldn't be.

He stared at the calendar. March 3rd. Now it was way too soon.

He sat down heavily. He needed to think.

***

They met for breakfast in a diner just down the street from the hotel, John and Keane recounting the events of the previous evening. John kept quiet when Keane briefly talked about the meeting with Billy without mentioning the guns, and neither of them said the name of the strip club.

The plan for the day was to take an in-depth look at the three women; Deanna Hayter, Madeline White and Jane Elliot. Judy would see if she could find an apartment or in fact any building rented out to a Rico Perez, or if there was a credit card, mobile or anything in his name. Warner wanted more information on the two Koreans.

John couldn't help feeling dissatisfied, Keane was right; they had nothing, or next to nothing anyway. He had spoken to Keane about trying to find the van, but there didn't seem much hope. Keane believed it would have been left in Compton or Lynwood with the keys in, best way to get rid of an unwanted vehicle in LA apparently.

Judy's mobile began ringing shrilly, and when she got up to answer it Keane's started, leaving Warner and John sitting at the table finishing their coffee.

Keane came back over quickly, eyes alight.

'I got news, this could be something …' he began.

Judy appeared right next to him.

'A Major Hayter got shot dead last night in Hollywood. The husband of Deanna Hayter,' she finished for Keane who looked at her and nodded dumbly.

'What?' asked John.

Keane looked at Judy, but she smiled and waved at him.

'Over to you Ron, you tell a good story.'

'OK, well, here's what we know. Just before midnight last night two men walked into Steel's, which is a sports bar just off Hollywood boulevard. No more than two minutes' walk from where we were John. Major Hayter was in there at a table with a couple of other guys; one of them an army buddy from what we got so far. The men approach the table, one pulls a gun and shoots Hayter in the face, the other grabs his briefcase and they split the joint. The major's army buddy follows them out. There was an off-duty LAPD cop pulling some hours as a security guard at an all-night pharmacy and he hears the shot and runs into the street. One of the two men then starts shooting, and the cop plugs him. The other man jumps into an old Toyota Corolla, there is a third man waiting in that and they get away. The guy the cop shot dies at the scene. That's where we are.'

Keane looked around at everyone.

'Wow,' John said finally.

Keane nodded.

'You got any more on your side Judy?' he asked.

'Well, not really. They're running an ID on the guy that was killed in the street, and LAPD are doing all the usual, so we should get ballistics later today.'

'One more thing,' Keane said. 'The gun the shooter was holding; Walther P99. It was on the ground next to the body. With 1-Too stamped on the grip'

His mobile beeped, and he looked at the screen.

'OK, I just got the details of the MP dealing with this for the army, I'll give him a call.'

'So the link is Deanna, right?' Warner asked. 'Maybe the major was the target and supposed to be with her at the station. It still don't make a lot of sense though.'

John shook his head.

'No it doesn't, apart from they were after the briefcase. Maybe it was hers, and he just got in the way.'

'I'm surprised he was in a bar, he just got told his wife is dead,' Judy ventured. 'But I guess it takes all sorts.'

'We've got a body, and we've got a gun. There's a lot we can find out from them, I know it takes a bit of time but they're looking at the AKs from the Metro station right now too. So we could have a whole lot more this time tomorrow,' Warner told them.

'This is going to twist and turn, I can feel it,' Judy said morosely, and sat down again.

Keane walked in, bright and efficient.

'OK, the army want to help. Major Hayter was some kind of supply officer at Fort Indigo. I just spoke to an MP there called Captain Reed. He wants to meet, he's coming out here. He said he'll be about an hour.'

'Army helping?' Warner and Judy asked together, quizzically.

'Yeah. Sure this shit never happens but don't knock it, we need all we can get.'

***

Sammy and Simon sat together at the meeting table, Moran on the other side along with a couple of other people from the technical side of the news team. But at the top was Costas Blanic, the charismatic president of the channel, and rarely seen in the office. Blanic was an Albanian migrant who ended up in the US toward the middle of the sixties, an orphan who had been smuggled out when his entire family were murdered after speaking out against the ruling party at the time, at the height of the Marxist state. His mother, father, grandparents, two brothers and a sister all slain in one night. Costas had been staying the night with his cousin. The gunmen came for them too, but his aunt; his mother's youngest sister had some spirit and was able to get them away. She got to Greece, and then on a ship bound for New York. Once there she did everything she had to and made a home for Costas and her own daughter in Brooklyn, with just the vaguest knowledge of the English language and no understanding at all of life in the west. After a year that would have destroyed even the hardiest person the seven-year-old Costas did what he had to, and got on with it. He did well at school, and university, working all the time to put food on the table, as did his cousin, and his aunt.

When he was twenty-two he bade an emotional farewell to his aunt and his cousin and took an apartment close to Chelsea Village and went to work on Wall Street. He was a natural, numbers were his thing. He made his first million within three years, and grew from there. Happily he bought a beautiful house for his aunt in New Jersey and when he was twenty-eight started up his own trading fund, which took off immediately. By the time he was forty-five he was married with three children and was in the top hundred richest people in the USA.

He never, ever discussed his past. But he never forgot where he came from. He continued to strive, investing, manipulating, all the time. It took him nearly twenty years of trying, but finally, got a US passport.

They moved out to LA when his wife decided she wanted out of the rat race, find some sun and a beach and he agreed, so bought a big house across the other side of the country right on the ocean in Malibu. He didn't need to work, but he couldn't just do nothing, so bought into a cable network TV station called LA Plus, that was short of finances and a future. He moved them into new offices, brought in some people and built it up, brick by brick.

He became president simply because his fellow shareholders believed it would be easier for everyone if he had something to do. He accepted the position, having never done anything remotely similar in the past, but he had the Midas touch, suddenly the channel was profitable and even winning awards. Everybody at the station, in fact everyone in the industry knew he didn't have to work, that he could probably afford to practically buy the city if he wanted, but they listened to him, and if he got involved, then you took it seriously.

Sammy was nervous of him, like most people. She didn't know him at all and had spent very little time in his company, but had listened to all the stories from the team; rags to riches, who cared if they were true or false at least they all had jobs. He was short and plump, and sat there in tatty jeans wearing an old Billabong t-shirt, his hairy fingers playing with a stack of sheets of paper in front of him.

Behind them the footage from the previous night had finished playing on the wall-mounted TV screens, and was frozen with Sammy standing outside the bar where the major had been murdered; the location of the second terrorist action.

The big news was getting bigger, and so far, they were out in front.

'It's great work Sammy, you got to be very happy Frank,' Blanic said, knowing full well Moran had a big problem with her appointment at the station, nothing escaped him.

Moran pursed his lips and nodded.

'The thing is, nobody likes news like this. Nobody wants these animals on their doorstep, it's the worst news for the city and everyone in it. But we are handling it real well, we're on the ground, we're not sensationalising anything, it's great reporting, and that's down to you Sammy,' Blanic continued, and clapped his hands loudly.

Sammy blushed.

'Thank you, Costas.'

'Now, I got the numbers before we sat down. Incredible. From where we were, it's night and day. So we need to keep it moving, we've got to make sure that we are moving this along all the time. I'm listening to ideas.'

Sammy looked at Simon, who wielded a laptop and started clicking buttons. The picture of John Smith appeared.

'I caught hold of this guy after the Metro attack. He was down on the platform when it happened, a British guy,' explained Sammy.

Simon pressed another key.

'Yeah. I got something to say. I'm going to find the arseholes that were responsible for this. And I'm going to make them pay, whoever and wherever they are. That's a promise.'

Blanic watched the British man talking and staring into the camera, eyes ice cold, and couldn't help shivering inside, he believed what he was hearing.

'Ok,' he said slowly.

Sammy gave him a winning smile, but she was feeling the pressure.

'Please, bear with me. Now the LAPD sent us some CCTV footage they got from last night at Steel's, they are appealing for witnesses to come forward, they already found the car. And Simon was going through it so we can put something together, run it as part of the show, and look what he saw.

Even Moran was interested now. The screen changed, a grainy shot of a street, Hollywood Boulevard visible at the top of the screen running left to right. Steel's was on the right, there were a bunch of men standing outside smoking. Then a fast forward, and an early model Toyota Corolla came into view and pulled up on the opposite side of the road close to the junction with the boulevard. Time clock showed 23:07. Another fast forward to 23:13 and a man got out the car, head down, wearing a dark jacket and a beanie, no sign of his face and disappeared into Steel's. Fast forward to 23:38 and he emerged from the bar and got back into the Toyota. At the same time two men left a building on the corner at the top and crossed the street walking diagonally down toward the camera.

One of them was John Smith. He walked past with the other, an older man and disappeared.

Next up 23:43 and two men get out of the Toyota walking fast, and enter Steel's, running out again less than a minute later. Then the off-duty cop appears at the top coming down the street, gun drawn, one of the men, with long hair flying starts shooting, then gets hit and falls down, meanwhile the other jumps in the Toyota which disappears.

Blanic looks at Sammy in amazement.

'So, you think he is involved? What do the LAPD think?'

Sammy took a deep breath.

'Right, here's the thing. You saw my interview with Chief Brady, right? So, I ask him about witnesses, and survivors from the station, and about the British guy I spoke to. And he gets real evasive, changes the subject. Just won't answer. So, I think OK, ask him after. And I did, but he was even worse, ended up getting shitty with me for even talking about him. Straight away I think I need to speak to this British man, everyone agreed. Now, last night Simon worked on the footage for the show and spotted him, and told me to take a good look. So, I get Brady on the phone, and straight off I realise that it's news to him. He is all "You're wrong, you're wrong, leave it to us, just stay the hell away from this" and I can't get nothing out of him. Now yesterday I went to see Jimmy Frost to see if he can get any information for me, I haven't heard back yet. I don't know what this guy's part in all this is, but something is going on. For sure, this is not at all as it seems. I think this is big news, and the PD are covering it up. So there is a story here for sure. And I want to get there first.'

Blanic nodded, then smiled.

'This is very good. This is real journalism, you are doing great work. I am impressed Sammy, and Simon, and I want to thank you for your work. I'm sure Frank feels the same. I mean this is big. Real news. Whatever you need, I want to know.'

Chapter Twelve

It had been a bad night, and it didn't take long for Rico to realise that the day was likely to be even worse. He and Sal had followed everything to the letter; dumped the car, and then made it back in the most circuitous route possible. It had taken them well over two hours, finally getting back about half past two in the morning. Voorhees had been waiting, dutifully they checked in their unused weapons and had handed over the briefcase then reported exactly what had occurred.

Voorhees said nothing at all about Karl Weiss being shot, in fact he had barely spoken, he just walked into the office with the briefcase and closed the door. Rico and Sal had looked at each other then sat in the kitchen with a beer. All they could do was discuss what had happened in low voices and keep an eye on the door.

Weiss had been jumpy the whole time, right from when they set off in the car. Because there had been so little information Rico and Sal had to make plans as they drove while Weiss sat in the back hopping around and fidgeting with the Walther Voorhees had given him. They reached the bar and Rico had appealed to Weiss to just calm the fuck down. Then Sal walked across and went inside and had a beer, checking the place out. He came back and explained exactly where the target was sitting, the locations of everyone else inside along with exits and the camera locations he had seen. Rico listened then explained carefully how it would play; repeating it several times and then when the time was right got out the car with

Weiss who was still acting like a child and they went inside. This part went near enough to plan, the basic idea had been to do a quick scout of the room first in case anything had changed then confront the major but Weiss instantly produced the gun and pulled the trigger, so in the immediate panic and confusion Rico grabbed the briefcase and they got out fast. Outside the bar things rapidly got worse. As soon as they were heading quickly towards the car Weiss had suddenly started letting out loud whoops and parading along the street waving the gun around. A security guard appeared, and then Weiss just started shooting. There was no need at all, the guard was more than forty feet away, the car was close by, they were free and clear. But Weiss kept on shooting, emptying the clip, hitting nothing but buildings and the guard dropped him with a single shot. Rico didn't hang around just piled in the Toyota and Sal got the fuck out of there.

They had explained this carefully to Voorhees, with no response. He didn't say a word, just disappeared with the briefcase.

Afterward they sat pensively in the kitchen wondering what the hell was going to happen now.

After some time Voorhees had come out of the office and stood in the entrance.

'Nothing in the briefcase. Practically empty. So, not what we are looking for. It's not there. Go to bed.'

Then he disappeared, his bedroom door slammed shut.

Sal and Rico had done as they were told, but neither could sleep. With no windows, it was impossible to tell whether it was morning but in the end they drifted off, to be woken shortly afterward by Voorhees kicking them awake.

'Get up. We got to talk.'

He stomped out the room into the office, and wearily the two men climbed out their sleeping bags and pulled on jeans. Once dressed they walked through, to once again stand in front of the desk while Voorhees glowered up at them from his chair. He didn't say anything at first, Rico took a quick look around.

Nothing had changed in the room. This could be difficult now. Neither he or Sal were armed, they didn't have weapons of any sort. These were handed out by Voorhees from one of three large, locked trunks before any action. So he could have anything hidden in the ridiculous voluminous gown that he always wore, maybe even have a bazooka in there. And there was nothing in the office that Rico could see that would be of use if Voorhees decided he wanted some payback for whatever it was they were being blamed for.

His stomach sank further, and he knew Sal felt the same.

Voorhees sat back in his chair, and looked at them balefully.

'This is so fucked up. We're in a mess. It seems like everything is always going to shit. You can't do nothing right, you've lost four soldiers. I am getting crap like you would not believe.'

Rico said nothing, just looked back.

What could he say? It was clear that everything was to be laid at their door.

But it was Sal that surprised all of them, even himself. Quiet, emotionless Sal, who never said a word, never questioned, who always did what he was told.

He stepped back and crossed his arms, then stared down at Voorhees belligerently.

'Yeah Yann, we're in a mess. Look where the fuck we are living. Nearly four fucking months. When we set up here, you said it was temporary, not for long, blah blah blah. And yeah, things have gone wrong. We did nothing in all that time, and we didn't know what the fuck was going on, you never tell us nothing. Then we get the call on the station, and you know what? We did what we said, exactly as you told us. We checked it out, we knew where everything was. And we followed the plan, me and Rico, we followed the fucking plan, man. Soon as Pol and Sung were on the platform we went back out, check the street, that's what you said and what we did. And we have no fucking idea what went on down there. Nobody is saying nothing, but we know they got killed. And that fucking Karl yesterday? You said he was an asshole, and he was. Don't fucking call him a soldier. He was jumping about in the back of the car on the way to Hollywood like a kid going to Disneyland. Again, me and Rico did exactly what was in the script. I checked the bar out, and then we made a plan. We knew what to do, we covered everything. We knew all the people inside, where everyone was, and what the target was doing and who he was with. Weiss, he was a fucking asshole Yann. From start to finish. He said nothing when we put the plan together in the car, he was just fucking around with the gun he had then he went in with Rico and doesn't follow what we decided, just starts pulling the trigger. Which was the same in the end I guess, we got the briefcase. But he decided to go all Wyatt Earp in the street, and gets taken out by a security dude. But by nothing more than luck we got away, and we did everything right after.

He dug in his pocket and took out a black metal tube and threw it on the desk. It rolled across and came to a rest against Voorhees' gut.

'By the way, he took the silencer off the Walther. I found it in the car when I checked it over before we dumped it. So the whole of Hollywood probably heard the fucking shot. So, hey Yann, don't start giving us the usual shit. Yeah, we're down four guys. But me and Rico are still here, and what the fuck does that tell you Yann, eh? Maybe, just maybe, it's because we do it right.'

Mentally Rico clapped his hands together in his head. He looked at Sal with new respect. Voorhees was also looking at him, pink mouth open.

'Leave me,' he said finally, and gratefully Rico and Sal got the hell out and went for breakfast.

Chapter Thirteen

They were all back in the diner within an hour. Keane had more information on the shooting the previous night. They ordered coffee and made themselves comfortable.

'Before we start, we got the ballistic reports on the AKs from the Metro station, which is to say, there ain't much at all. No serial numbers, all filed off, nothing new there. All late 1960s models. The guns were well used, but so far no trace anywhere with the usual parties if they have seen any action in the US before. They believe the guns were fully loaded before the attack.'

Everyone nodded.

'Right, to last night. I spoke to the cop who was working the security shift. He was out on the boulevard when he heard the shot, and came around the corner. He saw two men running in the road and told them to stop. One was yelling and holding a gun then started shooting. Wild he said, bullets spraying all over, so he took him out. It's how we train; the guy was a danger to the public. Can't criticise him at all, he's got enough trouble explaining his second job. Nothing he could do about the car making off, there were civilians around and he couldn't risk a shot. We got some footage from the street and also the bar camera.'

He laid down some photographs. Usual black and white, showing the street. Two men, running. One wearing a dark jacket done right up, with a beanie hat, his head down. The other man was pulling his hat off, showing long, light hair, and holding out a gun. Inside the bar the two men could be seen, now both wearing beanie hats. One very careful to keep his head down, while the other man with the long hair didn't seem to care.

Keane produced a tablet and opened up a video, again from inside the bar. All is calm, then the door flies open and the two men come in. The long-haired guy is moving fast, holding a gun then shoots, hitting a man who is sitting between two others. The other man grabs a briefcase and then they leave. Total time less than ten seconds.

Keane played the recording a couple of times then looked up.

'So the guy who did the shooting is the one in the morgue. He is one Karl Weiss, age twenty-nine, lived in Tucson, and got a long record alright. He held up a liquor store in Phoenix two nights ago. Real chatty apparently, told the clerk he needed to raise a train fare. We're checking the stations now, see if we can find a trace on when he got into town.'

'So this Karl Weiss is part of 1-Too?' Warner asked disbelievingly.

'We're starting to have a rethink here,' Judy told them. 'We're going back through what we know and now we think it's likely that they operate in cells, and then recruit. Previously we believed that they were an army, fluid, going where they were needed. They probably got contacts who can find them people. Could be they do it when needed. This guy has a long record like Ron says, but nothing like this. Mostly second-rate assault and robbery with violence. No connection at all.'

'Major Hayter was in the bar with an army colleague, a Captain James Bryant, and also another man, one David Anthony Mays, and we know him. We have both of them in for questioning,' Keane explained, putting the tablet away.

'Who's this Mays?' John asked.

'He's a bookmaker. Ex-army, but a good few years ago now. Lot of shady shit with him, but nothing concrete.'

'So maybe the hit was on him?' Warner asked.

'It could be I guess, but they took the major's briefcase. And we got the connection to Deanna of course.'

'True.'

John looked at the photographs again and tapped the man with the head down.

'You know, we need to check these further. Can we get any extra detail on these photos? I reckon this is the same man we saw around the van by the Metro station.'

Keane took a long look.

'You sure?'

'Yeah, I am. I really think it's him.'

The door opened and two soldiers walked in. Two Military Police, a man and a woman. The man was the singularly most impressive person that John had ever seen. He was huge, had to duck down through the doorway and his head practically scraped the ceiling as he walked across. But he wasn't just tall, he was big. Really big. Massive shoulders, they were both wearing short sleeve shirts and his forearms were like John's thighs. The woman walking next to him was dark and petite, and looked tiny alongside the giant.

She looked across and spotted them, and tapped the big man on the hand and they headed over. Everyone made room and they sat down opposite each other on the ends. Even seated he still towered over everyone.

He smiled and introduced himself.

'Hi. I'm Captain Thomas Reed, and this is my sergeant, Louisa Gonzalez.'

Gonzalez nodded. She was pretty, and carefully made up, but had a pinched, mean expression, while his was open and friendly. He was no older than early thirties. John imagined that for the grunt caught stealing out the stores just the sight of him would immediately bring about a change of mind.

A waitress scurried over with more coffee, the two soldiers thanked her gratefully.

They all introduced themselves and Reed looked at John with interest.

'I just been reading some shit about you on the way here. You sure had a career,' he said with a grin.

John smiled back, but said nothing.

'So, you know what went down in the subway station on Sunday, and we got a strong connection from that to your man getting gunned down in Hollywood last night. Like very strong, and John here thinks we can maybe place at least one guy in both locations. So, I guess that's why we are all here, what can you tell us?' Keane asked.

Reed laid his massive hands on the table, fingers spread.

'Well, Major Donald Hayter was what we refer to as backroom. He was one of the senior guys in the supply division at Fort Indigo, been there seventeen years, made Major nearly eight of them ago. Now I'll be honest here, neither me or sergeant Gonzalez had much to do with him. Other than the odd theft occasionally, I never really had a need to go over there. None of us did. So, we don't really know him. I've only been at Indigo six months anyway. I used to see him in the officer's club, and at various meetings every now and then. But I couldn't really tell you nothing about him from a personal point of view.'

He passed over a slim folder.

'Here's his jacket, what I can tell you anyway, it's been censored, there ain't a whole lot in it now, like you'd expect. This is the army after all. But in truth, there ain't much else to report.'

John opened it and looked inside. Half a dozen photocopied sheets, top one with a photograph. He scanned through the contents, then looked up at Reed.

'No active service?' he asked.

'No. Never been in combat. He was fifty-one and the word is he made major because he was at West Point back in the day with General Morgan. Always been in supply, and slow to climb the ladder. He made first Lieutenant, it took him a while, then finally Captain. He was finished at Major, wasn't going anyplace upward.'

John continued reading then shuffled the sheets back together and passed the folder around to Judy.

'OK, thanks, but there's not a lot in there really Captain.'

'Please, call me Tom.'

'OK, Tom. Not a lot there, and I understand that. As you say, you're the army. But what's the real story?'

Reed smiled.

'Ok, so, like I said, I didn't know him. So I've been sniffing around. His father was a big noise Lieutenant General, highly decorated, Korea, Vietnam. A lifer. And Major Hayter followed in his footsteps, got into West Point and I guess that was just because of who his dad was. Graduated second lieutenant and posted to Fort Alice down in Alabama. Started working in supply and that was his career. He found his place and it suited him I guess. He was good friends with General Morgan, and served at a few bases with him. He's been at Indigo seventeen years. General Morgan was there a while back and then returned five years ago after Afghanistan, and made CO. He's at the Pentagon now.'

'General Morgan? I'm sure I know that name,' commented Warner.

'It's possible, he's a high flyer. Indigo is infantry, and he is seen as a star tactician in it. To be frank, I'm sure that was true more than ten years ago but I believe him to be a liability. I was with him in Afghanistan. Dangerous. Making decisions without good reason. But that's my opinion. He glanced at Gonzalez who shot him a warning look in return.

'I'm just saying, is all,' Reed finished lamely.

'But what about the man himself?'

'OK, well the word is he's a loner and always has been. He got married just three weeks ago. Bachelor up to then, lived in the barracks. Officer's quarters. Had a few friends around the base it seems, but not as many as seventeen years would normally make.'

'Yeah, you heard about his wife?'

'I did. Sergeant Gonzalez here broke the news to him.'

'How did that go?' Judy asked her.

Gonzalez spoke for the first time. 'Speaking plainly, as we seem to be, it was strange. He didn't really react. Just looked at me and started making coffee. They weren't living together neither. I went to see him at the barracks, soon as we got the news. He was just up, but no sign of anyone else living there, man or woman. I think he seemed real surprised she was in LA.'

They all looked at each other, digesting the information.

'They married in Vegas,' Judy said, as if thinking aloud.

Reed nodded.

'They did, and he had been spending a lot of time there. In like, maybe the last few months, he was up there pretty much every week.'

'That would make sense if he met Deanna, right?' Judy said.

'OK, so there's more. I spoke to the couple of guys said to be his buddies. They never met Deanna, knew very little about her. Hayter told them they met at the casino in The Bellagio a few weeks ago.'

Keane shrugged. 'So?'

'His buddies went up there with him a couple of times, they were real surprised to hear about The Bellagio, he stayed in a motel on East St. Louis Avenue and hung out at The Stratosphere when they were with him. Never went south at all. They said the motel was a dump, they stayed in the hotel. And it seems that he really met his wife a few weeks before he said he did. Seems she hit on him, but he wasn't interested. Word is she kept showing up at the hotel. Captain Bryant knew and told them about it, but Major Hayter gave them a different story.'

John had worked in Vegas a couple of years before, and spent a lot of his time there walking around. The Stratosphere is a long way north of the strip, nearly halfway to Freemont, which is old Vegas.

'Deanna was a stripper in a club just off East Tropicana, down in the south; long way from the Stratosphere. She wouldn't go wandering in there after her shift,' Judy told them.

'Well, she was in there looking for him. That's what Tom's telling us, no question,' Warner ventured.

'When was the last time these guys were up in Vegas with him?' John asked.

'Well, that's a good question. Not for a while, a couple of months ago they said. But I got the feeling they weren't real tight with Major Hayter. His only real buddy was with him last night, Captain Bryant.'

'We got him with us right now, we're talking to him,' Keane said.

'Right, well he is close, or was, to Hayter, is what I hear. He should be able to tell you more. But there is one thing that's come out of all this. He owed money all around, ten, twenty bucks here and there, a couple of hundred to one guy.'

'Gambling?' Warner surmised.

'Yeah I guess so. Vegas and all.' Reed shook his head.

'Can we get financial records for Major Hayter?' Keane asked. 'Will the army allow it? I'm getting them for his wife right now.'

'I can ask. I don't see why not. He died in a public bar, right?' Reed looked at Gonzalez who produced a notebook and started writing.

'So, what do we really know about Deanna Hayter?' Warner asked.

Judy dug out a file.

'OK, right, thirty-three years old, nee Clark. Born in Henderson, Nevada. Married Donald Hayter at the Happy Chapel on South Las Vegas Boulevard just over three weeks ago. Her address is shown as apartment 11d, Walt Drive, Paradise, Las Vegas, living there for six years. She's been brought in for soliciting by the South Vegas PD on several occasions, the last one was less than a year ago, never made it to court. She was also indicted for possession of cocaine when she was nineteen. Been a stripper for a while at various places, been working at the Mile High Club for about two years.'

She pushed a couple of photos across the table. One was a simple black and white mugshot showing a pale woman with greasy hair and dark rings around her eyes staring at the camera, and the other a creased colour photo of two people standing under a white painted wooden arch. Deanna was on the left, wearing a white minidress and a lot of makeup, but looking a million miles better than in the mugshot, her arm around the man on the right, who was bald, plump and pink and wearing a cheap suit. He was a good bit shorter than her, both had wide smiles on their faces.

'Wedding photo. It was in Madeline's bag.'

'That Hayter?' Keane asked.

Reed nodded. 'Yep, that's him.'

John looked closely at the two photos, trying to place the woman to the one he had stood close to on the platform but the truth was he hadn't taken a lot of notice.

'OK, so, where are we now?' Warner asked looking around at everyone.

'I think Deanna is the key, has to be something there,' John replied.

Judy nodded.

'I agree. Vegas PD have let us have what they got but it doesn't tell us much about her. I mean why was she in LA on Sunday night anyway? Louisa said she wasn't living with the major. Maybe he wasn't expecting her, or maybe he just got back from Vegas and she followed him, I guess we'll never know.'

'That's a good point, can we find out if they were together during the day?' John asked.

Keane shrugged. 'Could try I guess, ask around. We can maybe find out when she got into LA, if she drove or got the bus, or even flew. She was at the Metro station.'

'Do we know the last time the major was in Vegas?' Warner asked.

'I can tell you exactly. He didn't come back from Vegas on Sunday. He didn't go anywhere. The last time he left the base was the weekend before last. Signed out at 4.11 Friday afternoon back in at 7.19 on Sunday evening,' Gonzalez told them.

'Assuming he had been to Vegas, we need to know where he stayed, and if Deanna was with him, and if they were together in LA this weekend,' Judy said, making copious notes.

'Like I said, he didn't leave the base,' repeated Gonzalez.

'Any visitors?' Keane asked.

'I'll find out.'

'Vegas,' Keane said thoughtfully. 'We got a big question mark there.'

A mobile phone rang, and as usual everyone automatically checked theirs. Gonzalez produced a beaten-up chunky unit, and answered it. She listened for a while.

'Shit,' she said, and listened more.

'OK, we're coming back.'

She hung up, looked around at everyone then helplessly at Reed.

'Er ...'

'What is it?' he asked.

'Well, I'm not sure if I should say in the present company. Sir,' she replied primly.

'Does it concern Major Hayter?' Reed asked her carefully.

'Yes sir.'

'Then out with it.'

'Right. Well, Major Hayter's billet has been searched.'

'I know that. It was done this morning. I was there.'

'No sir, I mean as in turned over.' She glanced around the table, as if worried about what she was saying. 'As in by a third party. Like the captain says, we went through it first thing. This was done since.'

'Wow,' Reed said and looked at everyone.

'OK, so how can that happen?' asked Judy.

'Has to be a soldier, or soldiers. Nobody can just walk into the base, even the cleaners are enlisted men. We need to go, I'll get back to you as soon as I find out what's what,' Reed told them, standing up and squeezing out from the table.

They watched the two soldiers go.

'What the fuck is going on?' Warner wondered aloud.

Chapter Fourteen

Grand Marshal Yin was half listening to his assistant explaining why the operational costs on a new tank that was being trialled were spiralling out of control when there was a soulful beep from a cupboard in the corner of his office.

The assistant went quiet and looked at Yin, both men wondering where the noise was coming from.

Next a whirring sound was heard and Yin realised what it was. He sent the assistant from the room and walked across and opened the cupboard door. Inside was an old fax machine, a technology rarely used these days.

Yin had kept it because it was occasionally useful for receiving sensitive information, and that is what he was hoping for now.

Several sheets fed out from the machine and then it went quiet again.

Yin collected all the paper up, closed the cupboard door and went back to sit at his desk. The temptation was to fan out the sheets but he made himself tidy the stack and then turn them over, so the cover page was visible.

He read the text and smiled, then went through each sheet, his smile getting bigger and bigger. He read the last page and laughed, long and loud, getting tears in his eyes.

There was a knock on the door and the assistant opened it, head round the side enquiring if everything was OK.

'Yes. Everything is very ok, very,' Yin replied, still laughing.

The assistant withdrew and Yin read through the sheets again. At the bottom of the last page was the eagle wings, crown and crest of the Russian Army. He kissed it and laughed again.

He stretched and picked up his briefcase, and took out a slim folder from inside. He opened it and placed the sheets of paper reverentially on top of the pages that were already there, and then with equal reverence closed the folder.

He pressed a button on the desk and still grinning told his assistant to get his wife on the phone, they were eating out tonight.

***

Colonel General Rostov dropped the mobile phone down on the desk and stood up, turning to look out of the window. Snow was falling heavily again, across the street he could see a beggar on the corner, his head and shoulders heaped with it.

Rostov shook his head and then turned around, picked up the mobile and stood tapping it on his chin and thinking.

He was running out of time and options, he knew that.

He should never have trusted the Americans. They fucked everything up. Too busy trying to avoid doing any actual work. He had done all he could, had everything in place, but it had gone wrong.

They were stupid.

He didn't have any idea what he should do next, and this was alien to him. All his life he had succeeded, had never been beaten.

He looked out the window again, brain whirring.

Maybe, there was still time. Time to do what he should have done in the first place.

He looked at the mobile, and then dialled a number from memory, he couldn't very well save it in the phone.

There was time, he told himself. It wasn't too late. Yet.

***

Sitting opposite each other in McDonald's, Rico was elaborately telling Sal a story about a Mexican girl he had met in Washington, and was just getting to the good part when he saw the other man jump and his eyes widen. He desperately nodded out the window at Rico, who turned to see what it was that was so disturbing.

Yann Voorhees was walking down the pavement looking in at them, his bulk moving like a huge tanker among the sea of people who were hurrying on their way to wherever they needed to be that morning. He stopped and pushed the door open and squeezed his way over to their table.

'You still hungry?' he asked, looking at the wrappers strewn across it.

Both men shook their heads.

'Coffee then?'

Both men nodded.

Voorhees turned and walked across to the counter, oblivious to the stares he was getting. Rico shrugged inwardly. Fat man in McDonald's. Go figure.

The two men just sat there in stunned silence, until Voorhees came back with a tray loaded with food and coffee cups.

Rico looked at the plastic seats, no way would Voorhees fit, but the big man perched on the end of a bench next to them, making the family already sitting there move over. He delicately unwrapped a sausage muffin and took a bite.

'I'm starving,' he said. 'Busy out there right?' He nodded his head back toward the streets outside the window and took a drink of coffee.

Rico and Sal added milk and sugar to theirs and took a mouthful. This was surreal, not only had they never seen Voorhees set even a toe outside of the apartment now he was sitting here as large as life, actually a whole lot larger, casual and comfortable, making small talk.

He finished the muffin and took another.

'Eat. Please,' he told them.

Sal cautiously took a muffin off the tray so Rico did too, and all three men unwrapped them and ate.

'Thanks Yann,' Rico said when he finished.

Voorhees raised a hand.

'Not a problem. I came here to tell you Sal is quite correct.'

Sal spluttered while drinking his coffee and had a coughing fit.

Voorhees watched him solemnly, Rico wondered if he should bang Sal on the back, but he calmed down and apologised. Voorhees shook his big head patiently.

'Yes Sal, you are right. Karl Weiss was an asshole. I knew it when I was told he would be joining us. It was obvious just from the description I was given. But, we were shorthanded and when I spoke to him he made all the right noises. He was clever, said what I wanted to hear. He was only seeing dollar signs. And to be frank, I have been distracted by failure. But of course, hindsight is a wonderful thing. Wonderful. And I knew, when I talked to him, I had misgivings. But I got the call, and we had to act. There was no time to change anything. I had no choice.'

Voorhees spoke calmly and quietly.

'But actually, it gets worse. I made a call to check on the progress of the rest of the recruits who will be joining us, and I was told some very grave news.'

Sal and Rico looked at him expectantly, bad news was not what was needed that was for sure, at least he wouldn't blast their heads off in here. Probably. Maybe.

'Karl Weiss had a cellphone.'

'What?' asked Rico, genuinely aghast despite himself.

Voorhees nodded.

'He did. And of course I asked him, told him to give it to me, we would have to switch it off and lock it away, but he said he didn't have one, he told me there had been some issues and he had to get rid of it. And I accepted the lie, another failing on my behalf.'

'How the hell did you find out?' Sal asked.

And Voorhees smiled. Another first.

'Because the asshole sent a text to the guy that introduced him to us. He must have sent it when he was in the car, not your fault. He told him he was on his way, there was a hit already. Of course, the guy was very shocked, and the news that Weiss is no longer around forced his hand to come clean.'

'The cops will have the phone,' Rico said.

'Correct,' Voorhees confirmed. 'I now also know that he was shot by an off-duty cop, so there will be even more heat.'

'What does this mean Yann?' asked Sal.

'Well, we need to take action. The police can track the phone, I understand they can go back several days, maybe more. They will find out he came by train, and he was at the apartment. It will take a while, but it can be done. And I also wonder what else he might have on the phone, you know how it is; messages, contacts, pictures, could be anything.'

'Shit,' Rico swore quietly.

'Look, all we can deal with is what we know. There may be nothing on it at all. But we must assume the worst and prepare for it. I have been busy and already have alternative accommodation I think will be perfect.'

'So, we are still on?' Sal asked, confused.

'Of course. I should have been more open with you. I apologise. It is force of habit, but as you rightly said, we have been together for a while now, and you should know what we are doing. What we are after is a document. Just a few sheets of paper I understand. Now as Sal alluded to; the intelligence has not been, well, very intelligent to put it bluntly. And it was not in the briefcase. There has been some additional work by others and it is also nowhere to be found in the briefcase owner's home. But there is a theory, and we are getting a resource that should be of great help, although he is not one that I am personally comfortable with. The others will not be joining us today, I have been advised to wait until we are set up in our new premises.'

'Right. So, er ... we better pack, right?' Rico said.

'Indeed. At least that will not take long. Our destination is in fact not so far from here, but we must be careful from this point on. And we will need to get the vehicles moved, which I imagine will take some time.'

He looked down at the tray, realising that he had eaten the last of the muffins.

'Come on, let's get started.'

He smiled again, which he clearly wasn't practiced at doing, and then eased himself upright. They left together and walked back to the apartment, which both Rico and Sal were pleased to be leaving but unsure what was coming next.

Chapter Fifteen

Reed called Keane a couple of hours later. They were back in Judy's room, Warner slowly getting more information on Sung-Min Byeon. Judy and Keane were working through the women's backgrounds, while John was getting everything possible on 1-Too.

When his phone rang, Keane stood up, relieved, and rubbed his eyes.

He talked for a while, nodding and then gave the address of the hotel and room number.

'OK, Captain Reed is coming back. It seems like he belongs to us for a couple of days; the army want to make sure they aren't going to be dragged through the shit. Terrorist attack on the subway, then one of their own officers gets shot by what appears to be the same people, the press are already onto them. So Tom Reed has been told to help.'

'That's good,' said Judy.

'Handy if we have to change a lightbulb,' John said, looking up at the ceiling and smiling.

'Really useful if we have to kick the shit out of someone,' Warner agreed, giving John a high-five.

They went through what they had found out so far.

John had been told that it appears that 1-Too were born out of Beirut initially, but there had never been any arrests or even detainment of note since they first appeared close to ten years ago. Very mysterious but deadly, no real leads on the people behind it.

Warner reported that Sung-Min Byeon came from a rich family, and had an expensive education. He ran into trouble with the police at an early age, and there are several warrants out on him in Korea. It had been thought originally that he had fled to North Korea, in which case he would have to be forgotten about, not a hope in hell of getting him back to stand trial.

Judy had some good information on the women. Deanne and Madeline shared an apartment in Vegas, they both had the same address on Walt Drive in Paradise, it seemed like they had been sharing for a long time. Madeline had been in rehab on two separate occasions, both times for heroin addiction, the last time ten years ago when she was twenty-nine. Both women had made recent forays into the porn industry around five years earlier, and had appeared in at least one movie together, and it was possible that was why they could have been in LA. Judy was getting more information on that, and was still waiting for the financial reports.

She passed around her mobile phone, there was a picture of Madeline, who had long dark hair and was very striking.

Jane Elliot had no record. She was a member of her local church, and dating a teacher. She was said to be very quiet, and had only moved out from her parent's house in the past year. She was recently diagnosed with diabetes, and had been unwell over the weekend.

Keane had the statements from Captain Bryant and David Mays.

Mays who was forty-five, was suitably vague, considering his tricky relationship with the police. Hayter had been placing bets with him for some time, and had a debt that needed paying. Mays was keen to work with him to resolve it.

'Yeah, I'm sure,' added Warner.

Mays stated they had been there about an hour when the two men walked into the bar and he saw one of them had a gun. Originally, he had believed he was the target as currently quite a lot of people owe him money, but Major Hayter was shot. Mays was still very shocked and upset by what had happened, he was keen to tell all to the police. He said repeatedly he had nothing to hide. He had never met James Bryant before, he believed he was there because Hayter was a pussy and scared, but all he had wanted to do was work out how to get paid. He knew Hayter from the days when he was in the army and based at Indigo, but he had been out over ten years and they had never been exactly friends. Deanna Hayter had not been mentioned once, he had never heard of her, had no idea he was even married, in fact didn't know anything about Hayter's personal life at all. Neither Hayter or Bryant had mentioned anything, he didn't know why they had met in that particular bar, Mays believed he had never been there before; it had been Hayter's suggestion.

Captain Bryant stated he had known Hayter for about six years, ever since he had been posted to Indigo. His position with the military was also supply, but in requisition, dealing mostly with ammunition. His previous posting was in Alabama, and prior to that Germany. Bryant had seen active duty in Iraq and Afghanistan, he was thirty-nine, and been in the army sixteen years, moving into supply from infantry when posted to Indigo.

He backed up Mays' version of events, also stating they had been in the bar for about an hour but saying he had no idea why they had met up there, Hayter had just told him that's where he would be. He arrived about five minutes before Mays, and drove straight there from the base. Hayter said nothing to him at all about Deanna's death, but he seemed very quiet. He didn't know if Hayter had been anywhere else before the bar. The two men had not seen much of each other in the past week, but when he was pressed Hayter had said that he was fine. Mays had been talking about a debt, which was the reason for the meeting. Hayter had been worried, he asked Bryant to come along, it had been arranged the week before.

Bryant had become friendly with Hayter only really about three years before, as they both had an interest in online poker. He had been to Vegas with him on a couple of occasions, and had in fact been there when Deanna first appeared. She had made a beeline for him, Bryant said. They had been at a table in the Stratosphere, but both losing; Hayter by some margin. Deanna had appeared and made a 'serious play', but Hayter had shunned her. This was probably six weeks or so ago. Maybe more. The two men had returned a couple of weeks later and she had made the same move, to be knocked back again. After that Bryant didn't go to Vegas for a while, his wife had not long ago had a baby and he was needed at home, he had been busy at the base and neither man had really spoken for some time. Then out of the blue Hayter had told him that he was married, but initially said the same as he had told the others, he had just met Deanna. Bryant had gone to Vegas with him just two weeks ago and saw Deanna. He recognised her immediately and asked Hayter, who brushed it off. He knew she wasn't living on the base, which was odd, but Hayter told him they were looking at houses so he had never pursued it. He did think it was strange his friend refused to confirm that he had met Deanna previously. Then Bryant said something interesting, that Deanna always had a friend with her, dark haired, quite pretty but real unfriendly.

Bryant also told them that on many occasions he had loaned Hayter money, but had stopped when he had to be persistent to be repaid and it had got awkward. Lately, Hayter had boasted that he had some cash, which Bryant believed must have come from gambling. Presumably he would be paying what he owed to a lot of people, including Mays.

They all read the statements and looked at each other.

'It'll be interesting to see what Tom says about this,' John said, 'There isn't really much to go on.'

Keane wandered across to the window and looked out into the street.

'I know a few people who are in with Mays, I'll check in with them, see what they say,' Keane told them without looking round, still staring outside.

Warner stood up.

'Any chance we can speak to this Captain Bryant?' he asked Keane, who shrugged.

'Maybe. I'll have to check in with Hollywood PD.'

Reed arrived, immediately filling the small room. He was on his own this time and carrying a couple of folders, and looked pleased to be there.

They all said hello, and Judy offered to go out and get coffee. After all, she reasoned, she was a mum. John suggested they all go back over to the diner, there was nowhere in the room for them all to sit anyway so they walked across the street, and made themselves comfortable in the same corner they had been in earlier.

Reed put the folders down on the table.

'So, Major Hayter's billet was ransacked, somebody was looking for something. This is strange as they would have known we searched it earlier, so anything incriminating or even interesting we found would have been taken away.'

He opened a folder and spread out some photographs, they all showed a small room in disarray. Narrow bed, wardrobe, chest of drawers, footlocker and a small table and chair. All overturned, belongings everywhere.

'We believe it was rushed. These rooms are real basic, there's no place to hide anything, no floorboards or hollow walls and of course we checked all the usual places.'

'So, a waste of time then?' Warner asked.

'That's what we think. We wouldn't have missed anything, there was nothing there. Not even any porn.'

'So not a whole real point in you tearing back there then?' Keane pointed out.

Reed shrugged and continued.

'We know there were no visitors for Major Hayter over this weekend, in fact he hasn't had any on base at all in over a year. I can go back further but I'd guess it's the same story.'

'Is that normal?' John asked.

'Well, yes and no. It's common for serving soldiers to not bother having guests, they want to get off base, but not so much for officers, especially of Major Hayter's age. Then we would expect to see family, but it turns out that he doesn't have any really, just a brother he has no contact with. But guests on an army base aren't exactly free to come and go as they feel like. I guess he spent all his free time in Vegas.'

Warner and Judy explained all they had found out about Deanna, and Keane went through David Mays and Captain Bryant's statements.

'So, what can you tell us about Captain Bryant?' John asked. Reed opened another folder.

'Ah, well I know more about him. Forty-three. Career soldier, and a good one by all accounts. He's served all over, and been in action. The word is he would be further along the chain by now, but he wanted to be where the bullets are. Anyway, he got injured in Afghanistan, lost a big chunk of his left leg. He wanted to carry on so they made him a Captain and set him up in supply, probably to see how well he heals. My guess is he will be moved somewhere else in time. I have spent some time with him, he's a good guy. Liked by everyone tell the truth.'

'His statement says he's a gambler,' Keane said.

'Yeah, but that's not uncommon. Everybody seems to have laptops, tablets and whatever these days, lot of them get online; blackjack, poker, etc., it's kind of frowned upon I guess but nobody has said anything about outlawing it. Captain Bryant is real open about it, makes jokes about doing it. He never said anything about Major Hayter to me, but they worked together, so I believe that's how they became buddies. Turns out it was down to online poker. The officer who runs supply at Indigo is XO operations Colonel William Carter, Bill to his friends. I spoke to him this morning and I found out something interesting that I didn't know. He was also at West point with General Morgan and was there later doing some training and met Major Hayter, in fact it was him not Morgan that got Hayter the posting at Indigo.'

'How in the hell is that interesting?' Keane grumbled.

'Forgive him, he's been in a shitty mood all day,' Judy told Reed, waving her hand at Keane.

'Well,' Reed continued, 'it's interesting because I never once saw Colonel Carter and Major Hayter together. Not ever, and they were often in the officer's club or the mess at the same time. Colonel Carter seemed very sorry about what happened to Major Hayter, genuinely upset about it, but he was also bothered about himself. I know this sounds like bullshit, but he was saying he needs protection. I couldn't get any more information, he was going on and on, not making a whole lot of sense. I got one of my guys to get a statement, but I'm not holding out much hope. Of course, it's possible they were stealing a fortune from the stores together but I don't think so. Whole thing was weird from start to finish. And one more thing, I went over to supply, that place is huge. Anyways I spoke to the sergeants there, if you want facts, go to those guys. They know everything. And nobody had a problem with Major Hayter, but nobody really liked him neither. In fact it seems to me that nobody really knew him, and he was there all those years. The joke was he was the office boy; clock on, shuffle papers, eat lunch, shuffle more papers, clock off, leave. He was in charge of the rota, and he never worked a weekend, and even when there was some big inventory inspection on he would still just work the same hours. So, they all kind of laughed behind his back, but it was no big deal. The one thing they all said they were done loaning him money, and that all fits with what we already heard. I don't know if this is any help, but there you are.'

'So you're on the team now then?' Judy asked him with a smile.

Reed grinned back.

'Yeah. I spoke to my CO this morning, who went straight to the top. Things like this don't happen very often, thank God. I think Major Hayter's room getting spun was the last straw, so they asked me to stick with you guys for a couple of days, try to help. It happened real fast, and I never seen that before. I got back and within an hour or so ordered to pack some civvies and set up with you guys. As long as it takes.'

'What they really want, is to know first what, if anything, we find,' John said drily.

'Of course. Always out in front. But it suits me, makes a change from dragging AWOL guys back from the bus station. I checked in here, on the army's dollar. I got the room at the end.'

'It's good to have you here,' Judy told him.

'Sure. So, where are we?'

'We think that Deanna is the key, that she was the actual target. Maybe she was supposed to be carrying something which wasn't there, so next one down the line would be her husband,' Warner replied.

'OK, but target for what?' Reed asked.

'We have no idea, not a fucking clue,' Keane said, staring out the window again.

'It could be anything. Cash maybe, drugs, guns, bearer bonds, hell, literally anything,' Warner said.

'Well one thing I can say is that the stores at Indigo are one hundred percent. There ain't nothing serious missing, no weapons or ammo, no equipment. I checked on that too,' Reed told them.

'The problem is, we don't know anything about Deanna, other than she seems to have hunted Hayter down but they weren't living together,' John said morosely.

'Bryant said they had a honeymoon; two nights in the MGM Grand,' Keane interjected.

'Busman's holiday,' John said.

'What?' Keane asked.

'It's just an expression. They spent all their time in Vegas, her stripping and him at the tables then they go on holiday there.'

'Yeah, I wouldn't have been sold on that,' Judy told them. 'I went to Mauritius.'

'Hawaii for me,' Warner said.

'Alright, alright, Jesus! Let's stop with the who had the best wedding bullshit and try and box this thing off. What do we do next?' Keane blustered.

'I think we got to go to Vegas,' Warner replied.

Chapter Sixteen

Sammy was woken by her mobile phone ringing. She had left soon after the conference, and gone home for some much-needed sleep. The daytime shows were running and she would have to look her best for the evening news.

She struggled awake and picked up the phone from next to her bed. It was just after four, so she had actually been asleep over three hours, which was enough.

She didn't recognise the number but sat up and answered anyway. 'Hello?'

'Hey hot stuff. It's your guy.'

'Who?'

'Fuck's sakes. It's Jimmy.'

'Oh. Er ... hi Jimmy.'

Shit. She had wanted him to call and she really didn't at the same time.

'Listen babe, I got some info for you. We better meet,' Frost drawled down the phone.

Suddenly Sammy was awake.

'Right, yes, of course!'

'OK. I'm at the bar, or I will be real soon. Wear the short dress again ok?'

'Er ... look, I ...'

'See you soon.'

The line went dead.

Sammy shuddered and put the phone down, then went into the bathroom. She was wearing just a Colts t-shirt that had belonged to her ex-husband. She had a bunch of them that were great for sleeping in. Sammy barely made it to five-foot-two, her husband had been a big six-three, so the t-shirts were comfortable and loose, and dropped almost to her knees.

She smiled pensively at her reflection then pulled off the t-shirt and got in the shower.

Cleaned up and dressed, she sat in the kitchen with a bowl of cereal and a cup of coffee. She really didn't want to go back to that bar, but she had to know what Frost had found out. She called Simon and asked his advice, which was clear and simple.

Don't do it.

He offered to back her up and reluctantly she accepted.

She thought hard then picked up the mobile and called Frost back.

'Yeah?'

'Jimmy it's Sammy. Look, everything is crazy here right now, we're just waiting for the next thing you know? I can't get over to MacArthur Park, can you get up here? I mean, you're not on the clock, right? Listen there's a bar down the street called Mullen's, we can meet there.'

'No way. I ain't drinking down fucking town.'

'Listen Jimmy, if you really got something there's another couple of hundred for you, OK?'

'Fuck!'

'Maybe we can go for dinner soon Jimmy.'

Like hell.

'Shit. Fine, I'll be there in an hour. Don't be fucking late.'

Sammy called Simon back, who thought it sounded better but he would still be there. Sammy told him she would be sitting outside, she knew the place and there was a terrace.

She got ready to go, excited but nervous, and really hoping she wouldn't need to keep fighting Frost off, but she ought to be safer out in the open where it was busy.

Mullen's was a recently opened bar, part of a new development. The terrace was just a simple square off the front full of uniform chairs and tables, edged by low screens and looking out over a plaza with a fountain in the centre. The whole thing was actually inside, under a high glass roof, and surrounded by shops and restaurants so the immediate area was full of shoppers moving everywhere, kids running about in the fountains, people sitting around.

Sammy was waiting close to the edge with a glass of white wine, Simon was sitting a few tables across with an orange juice. They were working hard to avoid looking at each other. From the plaza Frost appeared, staring around unhappily.

Flanagan's had been dark and gloomy, and now, in the daylight, he looked even worse. In fact, he looked a lot worse. Now it was possible to see all the individual stains on his grubby clothes and the dirt under his fingernails. He sat down miserably opposite Sammy, who pushed a cold bottle of Budweiser across the table to him.

'Fuck,' he moaned, gripping the bottle.

'What?' Sammy asked him and laid her hand on the table. Folded between two fingers was a hundred-dollar bill. Frost saw it and grunted.

'I used to be the man you know. Everybody wanted a piece of me. Everybody. London were after me for the fucking Times you know,' he rasped without looking at her.

'Yeah, Jimmy, I remember. I do.'

'Yeah, well.'

He turned to face her, she was wearing a dress, but it was done right up. She wasn't giving him anything.

'Fuck,' he complained again bitterly and took a long drink.

'So ... what you got for me Jimmy?'

Frost sighed theatrically.

'Right, well you owe me. And a lot more than a hundred fucking dollars you hear me?'

'Two hundred Jimmy. If you got anything, that is.'

'Yeah, yeah. Ok, so, this English guy. You were right, he was there, on the platform.'

Frost looked serious now, and Sammy could see the light in his eyes, the actual Jimmy Frost that was in there somewhere below all this other rubbish.

'He got taken in, you know for questioning. Now this is the real shit you are getting now. Cops are saying nothing, well in public. You know what he fucking did? The guy turned the gun back on the fuckers who opened fire down there! Way I hear it, he is a hero. Grabbed the gun up and killed three of them. Stone fucking dead.'

Sammy stared at Jimmy Frost. This was massive. She didn't know what to say.

'Word is, he's been whisked away some place, and the CIA and the Feds are with him, right now.'

'Jesus. Do you know what his name is?'

'Smith, I got told. John Smith. And don't write any of this down, I'm serious. Not one fucking word.'

'Yeah ok Jimmy, I get it. Any ideas where he is?'

'No, nobody knows, and there's a lot of people at that precinct want to buy him a beer. But they say he is still in LA, and he is working with the others to track these fuckers down. My man tells me the word is he was some James Bond government guy or some shit back in England. That's what I heard, anyways.'

'I knew there was something,' Sammy said quietly, and she meant it. She had watched the footage countless times and remembered when he had spoken to her. Blood all over him, he had just been on a train platform surrounded by armed maniacs but he had been calm, really calm, and assured. But angry, that was clear. It chilled her watching it, because she could see that he would do it. He would look for them, and he would probably kill them.

'So, old Jimmy did good yeah?' Frost asked, now smiling, showing the dirty brown teeth again.

'You did Jimmy, yeah you did.'

'I still got it baby. I got the goods.'

Sammy handed him the bank note, and pushed across a second then took a drink of wine, thinking all the time. They couldn't use this information, not yet anyway. But they could do a report 'acting on information' which outlined the basics, no names, no real details. The fact that one of the people who had been innocently waiting on the platform killed three terrorists was very big news on its own.

Jimmy Frost pocketed the bank notes, eyeing Sammy all the time.

'So where are we going for dinner babe? If I got to hang round here we need to find a decent bar.'

Sammy smiled sweetly.

'I can't tonight Jimmy, I'm sorry, I got to work, you know how it is.'

Frost tried one more tack.

'We could get a hotel ...'

'I'm sorry Jimmy. Maybe next time.'

Sammy finished her wine and stood up.

'And Jimmy, please keep digging, I would love to speak to this guy ok?'

She smiled as sweetly as she could bear then turned and walked away quickly, Simon following.

***

Rico was tired, and sat at yet another set of red traffic lights yawning. It had been a long day after very little sleep, but this was the last trip.

As Voorhees had said, it hadn't taken long to pack up. But carrying the three heavy metal chests down the stairs from the apartment had nearly killed Rico and Sal, Voorhees had of course been no help at all. They had made the initial trip in the last remaining panel van, with Sal driving, Voorhees in the passenger seat and Rico in the back with all their gear, which in truth, wasn't very much at all.

The new base wasn't too far from the apartment, it was up in Hobart, but Voorhees had to go down to Long Beach first to meet someone. He had disappeared inside a rundown old house in Carroll Park for nearly two hours, Rico had banged on the inside until Sal let him out and they had sat in the back with the doors wide open and waited.

Eventually, Voorhees appeared, waddling heavily over to the van.

He held up some keys.

'OK, we got what we need. And we got new instructions, there's work to do.'

He lumbered around and climbed into the van, which they took as a signal the conversation was over and Sal shut Rico in the back again and they set off.

Their new home was an old train goods yard, vacated about five years previously. It was surrounded by a high steel mesh fence, complete with razor wire across the top. There were massive double gates to get in, and Sal pulled up outside wondering what they were doing there.

Voorhees passed him the keys.

'Get Rico out the back, we need him to let us in and lock up again.'

So Sal let Rico out and then drove through once he had opened the gates, then waited on the other side for him to lock up again. They drove forward to be stopped by another, smaller set.

'Fuck, it's like a prison,' Sal said.

Rico appeared, unlocked the new gates, and Sal drove forward, then stopped again on the other side.

The yard was massive. There were two huge part disassembled gantry cranes that spanned the whole area, with large warehouses on the left and smaller buildings on the right. On the far side it opened out to another big open space and they could see there were still many rusting shipping containers and the remains of trailers still dotted around in there.

Rico appeared at Sal's window and looked in.

'So?' he asked.

'Home sweet home,' Voorhees answered, pointing into the yard.

Rico opened the door and stood on the step as Sal drove forward, both men wondering where the hell they were going. Everywhere was dry and dusty, glowing orange in the late afternoon sun. A wide span of multiple railway tracks ran across behind the warehouses, with a long loading area set toward the rear.

'There,' Voorhees said, pointing to a building on the right.

Incredibly, for a derelict site all the glass was still present, it was clear that kids hadn't been running around this place any time recently. There was a door set in the front, an old name plate removed from over the frame. It was a tall narrow building, four storeys, and as they looked up they could see it led onto a high, narrow bridge which completely crossed the whole yard, connecting to a round crow's nest on a pillar with glass all around in the centre to end at a warehouse on the far side.

Sal drove over and pulled up near the door.

'Here?'

'Yeah.'

Rico jumped off the step and walked over to the door, finding the right key and walked in.

Inside was a small lobby with stairs to the left and a single door at the back. He looked behind him to see Sal walking in then crossed over and pushed it open to look inside. It was a locker room, lines of them all open and empty. At the back were shower stalls and toilets.

He walked back out, and with Sal following went up the stairs. First floor was just an open plan space, a few battered desks and chairs scattered around and a glass partitioned office at the rear. Next floor was pretty much the same, but had a small kitchen set into the side. They climbed the last set to the top floor, which had half a dozen mattresses leaning against the wall, plus a sofa and arm chairs, and a TV on a small table. Everything was covered in a fine layer of dust. There was a door which led up some steel steps onto a small balcony, and then the bridge. Rico opened it and walked out, and leaned on the railings looking down.

The place was huge, from here he could see back to the gates and to the far side of the end yard. In front of him were the warehouses and beyond them many lines of railway tracks. He wondered why they decided to close it down.

Sal appeared next to him, taking in the view.

'Man, Yann is never gonna deal with those fucking stairs.'

Rico smirked.

'Now that is true.'

There was shout, and they headed back downstairs. Voorhees had made it up the first flight, and was breathing hard looking around him. They told him what was upstairs, and he nodded.

'OK, so I will set up in this office. Drag down a mattress, and all the good chairs and shit to here, we'll use this space as common ground. You guys can sleep where you like. We got electric, gas, even hot water. And this is only temporary. Get the TV down here first.'

Rico and Sal looked at each other, they had heard this before. But at least there was space, if anything it was an improvement on the tiny apartment. The busied themselves doing what they were told, moving everything around, and unloading the van. They dragged the chests into a corner of the first floor, and then looked expectantly at Yann who was sitting on the sofa watching them work.

'Right. We need the vehicles, how many we got?'

'The van, and three cars,' Sal replied.

'Right, they need to go in one of the warehouses over there, we got keys for everywhere. Nobody gonna wonder what we're doing for now, we just need them out of sight. I got four new guys coming tomorrow, so make sure everything is ready. We won't be here long.'

Sal nodded and he and Rico set off back to Mount Pleasant in the van, and between them they spent the rest of the day bringing the cars over to the goods yard.

Chapter Seventeen

By six, they had made rough plans and were sitting in the diner waiting for Keane, who had disappeared straight after lunch. Reed had changed out of his uniform, now wearing tan colour jeans and a green t-shirt washed so many times it was practically white.

'You know what? You look exactly like a soldier out of uniform,' John told him smiling.

Warner laughed heartily, Reed grinned back.

'Well, that's what I am. Anyways, I had to speak to General Morgan, I've been getting messages to call but avoiding actually doing it. He wants to know what the hell I'm doing about Major Hayter. I gave him the sanitised version of events,' he told them.

'Good plan,' Warner replied. 'What was he asking?'

'Actually, not that much. He was more interested in what we were doing and what we found out. He was being all aggressive about it, weird I guess, but that's how it seemed to me anyways.'

Keane finally arrived, looking dishevelled.

'Well, I got some news,' he said. 'I heard from Vegas PD. Deanna Hayter's apartment got turned over, they wrecked it so I'm told.'

They looked at each other, none of them were surprised.

'I spoke to an officer Kirsty Casiano. She says they already looked over it, found nothing other than some coke, a small amount of cash and some sex toys and dvds, presumably their tools of the trade. Casiano works out of the Paradise precinct, and knew Madeline pretty good but not Deanna so much. But she says that they got a file on both of them.'

Judy sat up straight.

'Really? We got nothing.'

'No, that's what I said, and there's a few things we should know. Like Madeline has a daughter.'

Judy frowned, and began riffling through her notes.

'I don't have anything about that either.'

'She's fourteen, lives with her foster parents in Summerlin, which is a real nice area. Apparently, she's a smart girl, who recently wanted to meet her real mom so the state set it up a year ago. Everything went good, and they got onto unsupervised visits. But because of Madeline's history, child services and the PD were asked to keep an eye on it. Turns out two weeks ago there was a scene, some guy turned up threatening and the daughter called the police. State said she couldn't visit no more, and that's why the PD tossed the apartment.'

'Did they get anything on the guy?' Reed asked.

'Both Deanna and Madeline said it was some drunk they didn't know. They said they never seen him before. But the daughter said he was looking for someone for sure, he was white, foreign. Big. The PD asked around and got a witness, and one of the neighbours backed it up. But no, they got no ID.'

'What, maybe Madeline was the target after all? Deanna and the major were some sort of fallout?' Warner asked.

Keane shrugged.

'Could be I guess. I don't know.'

'Can it be about the kid? Who's the father?' Judy asked.

'Well, that's also a can of worms. At the time Madeline was giving out freebies to cops to let her alone. The girl's dad is apparently a cop called MacMillan, who's actually in the slammer now, some big corruption scandal in Vegas a couple of years ago. But he never had no contact. None. He was married, refused to admit to anything, wouldn't do nothing, word is he's a real piece of shit.'

'What was the scandal?' Warner asked.

John coughed.

'Er … I know about that actually. I got kind of caught up in it. It was a guy who owned a hotel, well his dad did anyway. The son was a proper scumbag into all sorts, and paying off cops on top of everything else. I met MacMillan, he interviewed me actually. FBI stepped in, Patrick sorted it,' he looked at Judy.

'Man, you get stuck in,' Reed said, impressed.

John shrugged.

'It was a missing person case. I was looking for somebody's daughter. MacMillan was just another part of the shitstorm I walked into.'

'So, can he be involved somehow?' Judy asked.

'Not sure, I can't make that fit, not with what went down at the Metro station. And why kill the major? But maybe Kyle is onto something. I suppose it could all be about Madeline. She lived with Deanna, they were friends, hell they were standing side by side at the Metro,' Keane looked at everyone.

'All the more reason to get to Vegas,' Judy said flatly.

'Yeah, I got to talk to you guys about that,' Keane said. 'Come out to the car lot.'

They filed out, and Keane showed them a big minivan, and slid open the side door.

'I figured with these two huge motherfuckers travelling in a normal car wouldn't work,' he told them nodding at Warner and Reed.

John looked inside, it was a few years old, but a sea of leather and comfort.

'Smart idea.'

'I borrowed it, we got things like this falling out of our assholes. But listen up, I got bad news on Vegas, I ain't gonna be coming with you. All sorts of pain in the ass jurisdiction issues between us and Vegas PD, no way are they gonna let me trample everywhere talking to any of their citizens.'

'Really? That can't be right,' Judy looked confused.

'I got to follow orders like everyone, and that is from the top. But I figure you probably don't really need me, you got

CIA, FBI, and Tom here is a cop, of sorts, plus you got John, if anyone gets difficult.'

'Well …' Warner started, but Keane interrupted him.

'I'm sorry. I got to sit this one out. But really, you don't need me.'

They decided to go and eat dinner in the bar, and filed back across the street in silence. John was disappointed that Keane wouldn't be going with them, but he supposed that they would be OK.

They decided they would leave for Vegas first thing in the morning, concentrate on the south end of the strip, but they would get up to The Stratosphere at some point, and check out the motel that Hayter used to stay in. Hopefully they could find someone who knew something, knew more than they did anyway.

***

Alone in the first-floor office that had become their base, Rico made a what would eventually become an important discovery. Back in the apartment Voorhees would lock himself away in the office and he and Sal would be none the wiser to what was going on, all they could make out was the odd word here and there. But now, he could hear every word that Voorhees said when he was talking on his mobile phone, something he did a great deal of.

Sal had gone out for some dinner and they had eaten, then Voorhees' phone rang. He got up and went into the office to take the call, closing the door behind him. Sal went downstairs to take a shower, so Rico was left sitting on the sofa. They were trying to make the TV work properly so he was just relishing a few minutes on his own.

He realised he could hear Voorhees talking, and glanced over. Through the glass partition he could see the big man pensively rubbing his head. He was listening intently to whoever had called him, the phone glued to his ear, and trying to speak when he could get a word in.

Voorhees spoke at last.

'*Well OK, I guess it's your call, but I got to tell you that it's out of my control if you do that,*'

Listening.

'*I don't know, I was told it was three …*'

Listening.

'*Do you need me to …*'

Listening.

'*Yes … but …*'

Listening.

'*I don't know him …*'

Listening.

'*I still think …*'

Listening and looking frustrated, trying to speak.

Then he saw Voorhees stare at the phone and drop it on the desk they had put in there for him. Whoever he was speaking to had hung up the call. Voorhees stood there, static, and Rico could see he was worried. Then he picked up the phone again and dialled.

'Vegas.'

This was the only thing he said, then hung up the call.

He walked out the office and stood in front of Rico.

'Where's Sal?'

'Shower.'

Voorhees nodded slowly.

'OK, we got to step up tomorrow, get prepared. Everything will go down this week and we need to be ready.'

'What we got to do Yann?'

'We get four new guys, tomorrow, probably late. They're a team, always work together, so we aren't just gonna get some lowlife assholes. This time. But we need to make sure we're squared away, right? I don't want no problems, no bullshit.'

'A team?' this puzzled Rico, he had always thought they were all loners, like he was.

'Yeah. Coming in from St Louis. Apparently these guys don't fuck around, so we got to show we are for real.'

'Got it.' Rico looked around the tatty, dusty room, wondering how it would look to any newcomers. But he didn't say anything.

Sal walked in drying his hair with a towel, and Voorhees repeated what he had just said to Rico.

Rico watched Sal nodding and sitting down, knowing he was thinking the same thing he was.

What now?

Chapter Eighteen

They decided to get breakfast on the road so got away early in the morning. Warner drove, as usual, with Reed sitting up front next to him. John and Judy shared the bench seat behind. There was a lot of room, and everyone was comfortable for the long drive ahead. But Judy seemed on edge, constantly chatting about nothing in particular and desperate to make progress.

Reed told them that Louisa Gonzalez had got the financial information on Major Hayter. He was in the army but basically, he had an office job, and as they already knew didn't work weekends. He lived pretty much hand to mouth, he would get paid, make a big cash withdrawal on a Friday. Maxed-out credit cards, overdrawn at the bank. Until three weeks ago. He hadn't taken a cent out since, so he was in credit. Even paid off some of the balance on his cards.

'Was he paid to marry Deanna?' Judy wondered aloud.

They stopped to eat just outside Barstow, Judy and Warner sat at the table fiddling with their mobile phones while John and Reed watched the traffic go by outside the window. John realised he'd left his own mobile back at the hotel. Not that it mattered, he wouldn't be needing it.

'You been to Vegas much?' John asked.

Reed shook his head.

'Not really. We went on a road trip when I was a kid, I don't really remember it. My brother had his bachelor party there a couple of years ago. That was a pain in the ass, I had to fly in from Japan and then back out again a couple of days after. Selfish bastard,' Reed smiled.

'I've only been there once, I thought it was OK actually. I liked it, apart from all the other crap that went on at the time,' John watched a blue Buick roll into the car park and stop, two guys inside.

'Yeah, you're some kind of badass private investigator, right?' Reed asked him.

'No, I'm a lot of things, but absolutely not that. People play me to sort out problems. That's it.'

The food arrived and they ate, Judy talking about her granddaughter and Warner about his kids, and both complaining about how they hated the time they had to spend away from their families. The food was fried but good, and they were hungry. It was nice in the diner, done out like an old-fashioned ranch house.

John's eyes kept going back out the window to the Buick. It was parked close to the car park entrance pointing toward the building, and the two Hispanic looking guys inside hadn't moved. Warner's phone chirped and he answered it, walking away from the table and Judy became engrossed in hers again.

John looked around the building and then at Reed, deciding. He set a smile on his face, just two guys having a chat.

'Tom, there's a couple of guys just pulled in. They haven't moved. I've got that feeling you know?'

Reed didn't turn to see out the window behind him, instead returned the look straight back at John.

'Oh yeah, I know that feeling.'

'It's a blue Buick, behind you. They can see right in. I'm going to go to the gents, nice and slow and obvious.'

Reed nodded, keeping the act going.

'Right, OK, so I get your back?'

'They will probably only send one in after me, so how about you go and get something from the car, be really casual about it.'

'Yeah, OK. I'll deal with the other one.'

'Keane got me a gun, it's in the car, so I'll have to do it old school, but that's OK.'

'I don't have one, it shouldn't be a thing.'

'Just keep watching this way, I'll let you know.'

'Right.'

John stood up and stretched, then eased away from the table and sauntered across the room to the toilets. Out the corner of his eye he saw both doors open on the Buick. Maybe he had been wrong, and the two men would come in. He wasn't worried, Reed was at the door and walking into the car park, he would be able to see what was going down.

He walked in, the gent's toilet was a large room, three cubicles on the right and urinals straight in front, with another door next to them, which presumably led straight into the car park. Sinks down the left wall. He quickly made his way across and stood at the urinal at the far end, waiting.

He heard the door slowly open, a pause, then footsteps. The door closed again. He didn't look over his shoulder, there were chrome fittings above the urinals and he could just about make out an unclear reflection of the room. A Hispanic man, wearing a blue suit, light shirt. He was moving gradually across the room, light on his feet, hand reaching into his jacket.

John made a show of finishing, and stepped back, coughing loudly and covering his mouth, turning toward the sinks, counting slowly 1, 2, 3, 4 in his mind. The element of surprise. The man moved closer.

John wandered over, casual, relaxed, just a guy doing what he did several times a day as he made his way toward the sinks, closing in, then shot out his left arm, and seized the man's hand in his inside pocket through the jacket, feeling the gun that was in there. He squeezed and twisted upward, unrelenting, then pulled the man toward him. The man was shorter than him, his mouth opened in shocked surprise then gasped when John wrenched the arm up further, still with the hand pointing down. He reached out and grabbed John's t-shirt, but it did no good, just took both his hands out of action.

Without letting go John punched him twice hard in the face, the first one a swing which caught the man high on his left eye, the second more accurate, smashing his nose and breaking some teeth. John pushed him back hard, he fell against the sinks and John hit him again, this time in the stomach and as he doubled over John grabbed his hair and slammed him to the floor, his head smacking heavily against the tiles.

John dug the gun out of the jacket pocket, a Ruger with a thick, long silencer. He threw it in the nearest sink.

He pulled the man up and sat him against the wall. He was dazed and bleeding, left eye closed. John laid his right hand on the floor and stamped down several times as hard as he could, covering the man's mouth to hide the scream.

'OK, so who sent you?' John asked, leaning close to the man's ear.

The man looked at him with his good eye, in a world of confusion and pain.

'It all seemed really simple, right? Guy goes for a piss, and you just pull the trigger. One down. But that didn't go to plan, so answer the question. Who sent you?'

'Costa got the call,' the man whispered.

'Who's Costa?'

The man indicated outside with his head.

'Ok. When?'

'Last night.'

'And what were you told to do?'

'Stop you going to Vegas.'

'Right, well, killing me probably wouldn't have done it. So you would have taken us all out?'

The man shrugged miserably.

John looked at him then grabbed his shirt front and hurled him back against the wall, his head bounced off it with a loud crack and he was out cold. John searched him, finding nothing other than a couple of hundred dollars which he put in his pocket, and methodically broke both the man's arms, then stood up and washed his hands.

Then with a loud bang the door next to the urinals crashed open, and a second small Hispanic man came bundling through, tumbling to the floor. He was a mess, he collapsed prostrate on his back, his face and shirt just a sea of blood. Reed walked in after, relaxed, looking as if he had just taken a pleasant stroll. He looked down at the man John had dealt with and smiled.

'Ah,' he said, 'Snap.'

'Yeah. Apparently, they got a call last night, stop us getting to Vegas,' John told him.

'This guy told me the same. Claims not to really know who called him, just some fella gives out work sometimes. I got his cell,' Reed held up a smart phone.

John looked down at the man Reed had thrown in, and stamped down hard on his hand.

'Ouch,' Reed said wincing.

'Helps to incapacitate these guys,' John explained, unembarrassed.

'Good point,' Reed said, and stamped down even harder on the other hand, then dragged him across and sat him next to his colleague. He picked up the Ruger from the sink and looked at John questioningly.

'Keep that somewhere. What did yours have?' John asked him.

Reed dug in his pocket and pulled out a wicked switchblade, easily six inches long. He pressed the button and the blade popped out, sharp, gleaming. He raised his eyebrows and pushed it back in.

'He hadn't thought it through. I got to the car and realised Kyle had locked it, and he had the keys, so I fumbled around like I was looking for them and he tried to come up behind me. I got long fucking arms,' Reed told him.

'Let's go and check the car,' John suggested and they walked out into the car park.

The Buick was unlocked, keys in the ignition. They looked over it carefully, it was a rental, collected at LAX around the same time that they had left that morning according to the paperwork inside, reserved in the name of Franks. They disregarded that, there was an obviously fake ID in the same name in the door pocket. Reed found a fat envelope in the glove box and opened it. Full of hundred-dollar bills.

'Shit, got to be fifteen grand here,' he whistled.

'Stick it in your pocket, that's Vegas paid for,' John replied with a smile.

They stood by the car looking at each other.

'You know what this means,' Reed spoke quietly.

'Yeah. Yeah, I do, unfortunately.'

'Who is it? Judy's been acting kinda weird.'

John nodded. He didn't want to think about it, but there was no choice.

'I dunno. Maybe someone at the police station, although Keane said he wasn't talking to them there.'

'Fuck.' Reed kicked at some stones.

'Look, I don't have any idea. You're right, Judy has been edgy the whole morning and Kyle never stops fiddling with his damn mobile.'

'It could be me,' Reed looked at him seriously.

John smiled. 'No Tom, one thing I do know, it ain't you. It's more likely to be me. You got thrown into this.'

'Hell it ain't you. Christ, you're the only one who seems to do anything.'

They looked at each other. Tom stuck out his hand and John shook it, then they began to walk back to the diner. John stopped and went back to the car and pulled out the keys, then caught Reed up.

'Way to take out the trash, you fucked that guy up for sure,' Reed told him.

'Same for you. Listen, don't say anything about those guys to Kyle or Judy ok? Just keep it close for now, I'm not saying it's either one but we need to keep ahead.'

'Yeah, agreed. For sure.'

A rusty pickup rumbled past, John threw the Buick keys and the phone into the back.

They walked in. Warner was tapping away on his mobile, while Judy was talking on hers, pacing up and down and gesticulating.

Reed carefully dug out a hundred-dollar bill. Warner looked up, and shook his head.

'It's done. CIA's dollar, they got enough.'

John and Reed glanced at each other and smiled, the bonus sitting in Reed's pocket.

'So let's go,' Warner said, and they filed back to the minivan with Judy in tow, still talking on her phone.

They got underway, and eventually Judy hung up and sat back, looking up at the car roof.

'You ok?' John asked.

She looked at him, and John saw for the first time the lines and bags around her eyes. She looked exhausted.

'Yeah, I guess so. Like I said, I got a case going to trial, as usual there's the same old bullshit. It's hard to be on top of everything when I'm out here. I mean I want to be doing this, but you know, I got my day job. I'm burning the midnight hours just to keep up.'

That explained why she was so jumpy.

'Sit back, we still got probably another two hours to go. Get some sleep. You could even lie down on the seat behind you.'

She looked at him gratefully and did just that. John looked back a few minutes later and she was curled up with her eyes closed.

***

Rico and Sal discovered their first drawback the following morning. They had decided to sleep up on the top floor, and when they were awake went downstairs to realise they couldn't really hang out in the communal area, as Voorhees was asleep in the office at the back, they could see his huge bulk on a mattress in the corner behind the glass partition. They had fixed a sheet across the outside window to try to nullify the daylight but he was still clear as day inside the office, and they could hear him snoring.

Rico had a shower then they picked up a set of gate keys and the two men walked out looking for breakfast. It was a good distance across the yard to the first gate, which they opened and closed and repeated for the second. Then they were out in the street looking around.

Not much to see. To their left the road curved around, with warehouses and industrial units, a tyre garage just along from where they were standing. To their right were some smaller units, which all looked closed and a short run down to a crossroads so they walked there and looked both ways along the wide main street and saw a faded, grubby hotel on the left, so decided to head there, not a lot of choice. As they neared it, they spotted a small semi-circular mall facing them across the street, so they dodged the traffic and headed over.

'Fuck it, Golden Arches again,' Sal said, looking up at the McDonald's sign high above. There wasn't a lot else, a small Starbucks, a bar and a pizza place.

Rico shrugged, he was hungry.

They sat inside to eat, Sal fidgeted around and then leaned forward seriously.

'Look Rico, I never got a chance to say nothing before, and I may be really fucking up. I sure as shit hope not. But I trust you. Maybe I shouldn't, but right now you're the nearest thing I got to a buddy.'

'What is it?' Rico asked, surprised.

'Listen, I am going way outside here.'

'Sal, fucking hell we are buddies. You sure as hell are the only person I trust. Whatever you say, I ain't never gonna repeat it.'

Sal nodded.

'OK. You know I checked the car after we had to dump it, you know, that asshole Weiss situation?'

'Yeah.'

'So ... I found the silencer like I told Yann. But I also found this.'

Sal looked around and then carefully put something heavy in Rico's lap under the table. Rico moved back and looked down. It was an old Glock 17. He checked it over; fully loaded. It had seen some action. He passed it back nervously.

'Fuck! It was in the car?'

'Yeah, under the passenger seat. And it weren't there before. We the only fucking guys who ever drive, and Yann doles out the guns right? It sure ain't mine, and I never seen you with nothing, not ever.'

Rico shook his head.

'I never seen it before.'

'Look, things have been going to shit, right? So I figure, let's keep this quiet, and keep it close. It's under my mattress, fucking Yann ain't never going up those stairs, and we put the new guys below us, move it if we have to but we both know where it is. That sound good to you?'

Rico looked at him, suddenly very grateful. He had been feeling alone and isolated for some time. He liked Sal ok, but he didn't really know him. This was good for both of them, a shared precaution. He held up his fist and Sal bumped it.

'It's very OK man. I don't know what the fuck is going to happen next, but I have sure been wishing I was someplace else. This is what we need brother. Under your mattress, sounds good to me.'

***

Warner didn't like to hang around, so it was just under two hours later when they passed the iconic 'Welcome to Las Vegas' sign as they approached from the south.

They had discussed how to proceed on the journey, and had decided to find officer Kirsty Casiano first, to get the lowdown on Madeline and hopefully some more intel on Deanna, Warner was confident he or Judy could get access to their apartment so they could take a look around. Maybe officer Casiano would be able to do some digging for them, find out if there had been any problems with Hayter in one of the casinos.

Then they would go on to the Mile High Club, and find out as much as they could about Deanna, see if she met with anyone else regularly. After that, up north to the motel Hayter used to stay at, and then The Stratosphere to see if they could add anything.

Then the drive back, it was going to be a long, long day.

They entered the bottom end of the strip, John saw the Mandalay Bay hotel and the Acropolis opposite, which brought back memories. Warner turned right at the next junction, as ever he seemed to know exactly where he was going. They travelled along for a distance, then he turned left and pulled up in front of a plain brown building with Las Vegas Police Department across the doors.

John checked his watch, just gone eleven. He gently woke Judy.

The walked into the police station and up to the counter, then asked to speak to officer Casiano.

The desk clerk looked closely at Judy's ID then tapped on her computer keyboard.

'Officer Kirsty Casiano isn't due on shift until 2pm today. Do you want me to call her in?'

Warner went to speak but Judy cut across him.

'No, that's fine. We'll be back at two, thank you.'

They walked out, Warner looking quizzically at Judy.

'Why didn't you just get her in? We need to be moving on this,' he asked grumpily.

Judy turned to look at him.

'I don't know how this works with the CIA, but we get all sorts of crap from local PD when we demand to get their guys in off shift. Seriously. They get shit off the unions, and the whole thing gets real messy. Look, we don't even know if she can tell us anything right? I'm already way, way out on a limb here. I don't need any more heat than I already got.'

'It's OK,' John said as they reached the car. 'We don't need to keep a tight schedule, we know what we've got to do. Let's find the Mile High Club.'

And then there was the next bit of bad news. They found the club easily enough, it was the ground floor of a small office block, down the road from Hooters and next to a gym. It had big plate glass windows on both sides of the doors which were thickly painted over, one which said, 'Mile High Club – Your Eyes Only' and the other had silhouettes of naked dancing women and 'Nude Live Girls' written across the bottom.

It looked closed to John, but he tried the doors anyway. Locked.

Reed was tapping the glass close to the doors.

'Place opens at five Monday to Thursdays, twelve on the other days.'

'Shit,' Warner said.

An old man holding a broom was walking round the building and he walked over to them.

'Help ya?' he asked.

'Er yeah, we need to talk to the manager?' Judy told him.

'Nope, nobody there. Deliveries Mondays and Fridays, you'd have maybe got lucky then. Else, probably gets here about four-thirty I guess.'

He stood looking at them, leaning on his broom.

'Thanks,' Reed told him, and they went back to the minivan.

'You see, I said we should have got Officer Casiano,' Warner complained.

John held up his hand.

'It's no big deal. We've got other things to do, we'll just change the order. Let's go and talk to the wedding people and find this motel.'

Chapter Nineteen

Sammy had a spring in her step and was ready to make history. She had been in a meeting that morning with a lady she had never met before called Davina, who worked at LA Plus as a research advisor, and specialised in dealing with information from law enforcement. She was no Jimmy Frost, she did not have the useful connections he did but she was helpful and knew what they could and couldn't do.

As she had already suspected, Sammy had been told by Davina that they wouldn't be able to run a story naming any names or any real details regarding the events on the platform, the police had a strict clampdown on information and were still refusing press access to the witnesses. But there was a lot they could do, and Davina was happy to go direct to the LAPD with the information they now had, and gauge the reaction. She believed that often this could force their hands, and also suggested that Sammy could at least appear to reach out to the police on her programme.

So, Sammy had presented the news, and then her follow up morning show, still focussed on the events that had occurred and clearly questioning the efforts to find the perpetrators.

'Where was the information from the LAPD?' she asked on several occasions.

She ran the all the video they had, John Smith visible at the end, frozen on the screens.

'There are so many questions, but no answers. Who is this man?' she asked. 'Can anyone help us to find him?'

On the floor, she saw Davina give her a thumbs up.

'LA Plus are eager to help the Los Angeles Police Department in any way we can, so please, if any of our viewers recognises or has seen this man, or has any information at all please call us straight away,' Sammy told her viewers earnestly, fighting the urge to smile.

***

The Happy Chapel was just north of The Stratosphere, a narrow building with the gilded white archway across the front that they had seen in the Hayter's wedding photograph. They parked up and walked in, to be met by a ludicrously bright orange couple with perfect white teeth and meticulously made up hair. Both well into their sixties. But behind the fake tan and the shiny clothes there was nothing going on in their minds but dollars and cents.

It was pretty much a one-way conversation. The couple fixed on their most helpful smiles and nodded a lot but they only vaguely remembered the Hayter's when they were shown the picture, they had done seven weddings that day. They produced their book, which was a large elaborate white faux leatherbound edition with gold edges and 'Special Memories' embossed on the front. They said it was their records but really it was just a sales pitch. Inside were glossy photographs and the names of the parties, one wedding per page. The Hayter's were there, the same wedding snap they had already seen. No witnesses listed, but they were told this was a common occurrence.

So, no help, at all. Thanks for nothing, and off to the next piece of the puzzle. Time was not on their side.

They found the motel, which was off East St Louis Avenue, roughly twenty minutes' walk to The Stratosphere. It was a beige and grey cube, on the edge of a small strip mall, its neighbours were a nail bar, convenience store, hair salon, two bail bond offices and a Chinese restaurant. None of them were busy. A sign outside said 'Supreme Cour Hotel. Stay in Wonderful Las Vegas – Twenty Dollars!!!!' Someone had unsuccessfully tried to replace the missing 't' using a marker pen. There was an office which jutted out to the left of the building, and they made their way across. Once inside they filled the tiny space, Reed had to wait outside with the door open.

Behind the counter was a furtive, dishevelled man with greasy hair and thick glasses who was looking at something on a computer. He peered out at them and without speaking pointed to the wall behind which had a sign that said 'Vacancy – $30'.

Nobody bothered mentioning the misleading sign outside.

Judy produced her ID and the file photo of Major Hayter, wearing his uniform.

'We need to talk to you about this man,' she said firmly.

The man looked at it, back at her ID, then the photo again, peering closer every time.

He shrugged.

'Maybe. Kinda familiar I guess. But I don't know him.'

'I'd think you do, he's been staying here pretty much every week for God knows how long,' Judy told him.

The man looked at her, then at Warner, then finally at Reed, who was completely filling the doorway. He dismissed John completely and looked at the photo again.

'Yeah, so what? We ain't friends. I never knew he was a soldier.'

'That's got nothing to do with it. When was the last time he was here?'

The man didn't produce a register, a legal requirement in the USA for any hotel. Instead, he looked around again, then back at the computer.

'I dunno. Couple of weeks maybe?'

'OK, so was he on his own?'

'Always. And always in the same crappy car.'

'You never saw him with anyone else?'

'Nope. Never.'

'Not even this woman?' Judy showed him the picture of Deanna.

The man looked and shrugged again.

'No, I don't know her.'

'So, what did he do when he came here, all those times?' Warner asked.

'He played the tables. The Stratosphere. Always. Every night he was here.'

'OK, did you talk to him much?'

The man sighed and reluctantly gave them his full attention.

'OK, so what the fuck has he done I got the feds breathing down my neck? Like I ain't got enough shit to do.'

'Done? He got murdered,' Warner told him, staring hard.

At this, the man's head flicked up and he looked back, alarmed.

'Murdered? Murdered when? Look, he weren't murdered here, I ain't seem him, I swear. It's the truth.'

'No, he wasn't murdered here. I imagine you'd have noticed that, or I hope to hell you would. But we're trying to work out who did kill him, and all we got is he spent a whole load of time up here and he just got married. His wife is dead too, and she lived here in the city. So now you can see why we're talking to you right?' Judy explained patiently.

'Fuck. Yeah, OK. Fuck. I don't know nothing about any of this shit. Jesus. OK, so I did talk to him sometimes. Look, he stayed here a lot, always paid cash. I asked him once why the hell he didn't stay at The Stratosphere, it would've been easier on him. It was the money, but I knew that. Sometimes he had a bundle, others he just about made it. Hell, I let him off ten bucks here and there. But he never said nothing about getting married, and he was never with anyone. But listen, there's a pit boss at The Stratosphere, guy called Aidan Connelly. He's always around, he uses this place sometimes. If he got … business. Anyways, I saw them together a couple of times. He might know more.'

John new exactly the business this Aidan Connelly would be doing at the motel.

Judy took the photos back, and looked around at the others.

'OK, so what's your name?'

'Gary.'

'OK Gary, that was kinda helpful. Will Mr Connelly be there now?

Gary shook his head.

'No way. The real pit bosses don't start till maybe nine, ten? Just be some jerkoff part-timer now most likely.'

'What time did Major Hayter usually get back here from the casino?' John asked.

Gary looked at him, surprised by the accent.

'I don't do a lot of nights if I can help it, but when I was here, I'd say about one, one-thirty. Sometimes earlier, I guess it depends how he was doing, right?'

'Did he walk?'

'Yeah, always.'

They grouped around the minivan outside, Judy fretting and fiddling with her mobile phone.

'So, it's gonna be a night in Vegas.' Warner surmised.

'Looks like it,' John agreed.

'Hell, I got to buy me some underwear,' Warner grumbled.

John said nothing, he had bought a few clothes and toiletries in a small rucksack, and noticed Reed had too.

'Shit, I better had too. So, what now?' Judy asked.

They had a couple of hours before they could meet with Officer Casiano, then another couple before they could go to the Mile High Club, and even longer again before they could do anything at The Stratosphere, But the gaps in between all depended on anything that could be discovered from the meetings they had, they hoped that these could lead onto more.

John looked at Judy.

'There's an FBI office here. Why don't you just go there and work? You could get a lot more done, right? All we will be doing is hanging around. Sort yourself a hotel, I'm sure they'll have a pet one for you.'

She looked at him gratefully.

'For real? Yeah, that is an idea. But where will you stay?'

'Don't worry about us. I'm sure Kyle will be the same as you, CIA will look after him alright. Me and Tom will be able to find somewhere. This place is nothing but hotels.'

Reed watched John carefully, conscious of their earlier conversation and realising what he was doing.

'That's a good idea,' he said.

'OK, well I'll get a cab. The office is up north from here,' Judy said. She looked around, not a cab anywhere.

'Shit! Jeez, I thought I'd step straight into one in this town.' Warner grinned.

'No biggie, I'll drop you at The Stratosphere, there'll be a line there.'

They climbed in.

'One more thing, keep it very quiet about where you're staying OK?' John said as they moved off.

Judy looked at him, questioningly.

'I just think right now we probably need to be discreet, we're going to be asking a lot of questions,' John told her, trying to sound reassuring.

They pulled into The Stratosphere and Judy got out the car, leaning in through the open door.

'Thanks for this,' she said to John warmly.

'That's fine, we'll see you at the police station about half two, that will give Office Casiano time to get settled.'

Judy nodded and disappeared.

Warner had been talking on his mobile, he hung up then turned around in his seat and looked directly at John.

'You sure about this?' he asked.

'Yeah, definitely.'

'Well OK, I need to go to The Mirage.'

'Fine, drop us there, we'll go find a hotel.'

Chapter Twenty

Ryan Gallagher was a day short of his twenty-eighth birthday. He had just woken up, having been asleep on the floor of junkie prostitute and his occasional girlfriend Angie's room in the apartment she shared with three other similar ladies. Angie was still sleeping, lying naked on her back on the grubby bed, ribs sticking out of her emaciated, pale body, angry track marks visible on her arms and feet. To an observer, she could actually be dead, something which he had thought many times before.

But not anymore, he had got used to that.

He glanced at the clock next to the bed, nearly twelve, and sat up.

He looked around the room, he had ended up here, with no other place to stay. The police had warned him against vagrancy but he had bigger problems with being out on the street, he owed a lot of money around, doing deals that didn't really exist. He couldn't even risk begging anymore, so had resorted to thieving out of cars again, but this wasn't so lucrative as it once was. He had managed to steal an iPad from a tourist's convertible in the car park behind the Wynn hotel a couple of days ago, but had made barely a hundred bucks. He checked his pockets, he had less than five left. He was fully dressed, half in and half out of a tatty, smelly sleeping bag. The room was a tip. It was tiny, just a single bed and a chest of drawers but there were dirty clothes and crap everywhere, needles and burnt foil scattered across the top of the drawers.

He hadn't met the apartment's other occupants, Angie had only been living here a week or so. He wasn't even totally sure where he was in the city, but he knew he was way north of the strip. He'd been walking for hours last night, or so it had seemed.

He sighed deeply, and pulled his feet out the bottom of the sleeping bag, staring at the holes in his socks.

Life sucked.

He'd been broke and on the street for way too long. The only positive in his life, and it had been a close call, was that he had stayed off the hard drugs. He was absurdly grateful for that, considering just how crap the last ten or more years of his life had turned out, but he knew all too well it could have ended up worse. He'd witnessed that descent many times. Angie spent pretty much every cent she earned in alleyways and on the back seats of cars all over Vegas on heroin, and always needed more, she was only just out of hospital after yet another trick beat her badly. And she looked fucking awful, but despite his meagre lifestyle, he still had his baby face and puppy fat. He stood up, and looked in the small mirror on the back of the door. He wasn't looking good either, he had to admit it, fading black eye and greasy spots. His shock of bright red hair was a curse, it was easily recognisable from a distance. He had dyed it but it never really took, so now whenever he was out he always wore a beanie.

There were too many people looking for him, way too many. All of them no good, some really bad, and the rest pure fucking evil. He'd sought out Angie down to pure desperation, with luck nobody would know where she was either. He needed to make some fucking money, that's what he needed to do.

He looked around the room again wanting nothing more than to hide away. But he couldn't stay here. He needed to sort his shit out. He looked in a couple of drawers and rooted around inside, knowing there was no point. There was no cash in this room, that was for damn sure.

He pulled on his trainers, which had maybe just weeks left until they completely disintegrated then shrugged into his jacket and with a resigned look back at Angie left the room. He was in a short narrow hallway, a door open on his left showed a small sitting room, with several people lying on the floor. The place stank. The next door was a bathroom, which he used. Then a tiny, filthy kitchen. There were two other doors on the opposite side of the hall which were closed, and he ignored them. He knew of old there was no point minesweeping this apartment, nobody here would have anything worth stealing, so he let himself out the front door.

He put on the hat and walked down two flights of worn litter-strewn steps then he was back on the street. He checked his jacket pockets and was relieved to find his cellphone, he'd managed to not try and sell that for a couple of bucks. He frowned, there was a message.

From Tibor.

Fuck. He knew exactly what that would say. He was going to spend the day hiding. Again. Fuck, he needed to raise some cash, he was never going to do it tucked away out the back of a store or a restaurant, hoping for some scraps.

But he pressed the button anyway, and was for the first time pleasantly surprised. Tibor was offering him something!

The message said '*I got a job for you. You'll see five g's once I get my three. If I was you I'd do it.*'

Five grand! Yes please!

He saw the message had been sent a couple of hours before, shit! He sent a reply with a lame excuse about his girlfriend being ill. Tibor knew Angie, so he wasn't expecting any sympathy. He got a message back immediately that said '*Be at Caesars for 2. Car park level 4.*'

That gave him a couple of hours to get down to the strip, he should be able to do that, wherever the fuck he was right now. He stood still and looked around, and spied a medical centre he knew. He's taken Angie there a couple of times, and knew it was only ten minutes to Freemont.

He set off, willing his trainers to stay together as he had quite a walk in front of him.

***

John was enjoying being in Vegas with Tom Reed. The big man seemed to be having a good time, away from Indigo, and the army, but still working. They decided to stay in the Luxor after looking around, and paid cash for rooms side by side, high up in the East Tower.

John felt reasonably anonymous, the strip and all the hotels were as busy as ever and he was confident they had not picked up a tail after Barstow, but he knew for certain that people would be looking. They ate a light lunch in the Tropicana and then decided to walk down to the police station, they had walked everywhere so far and it was easier and more forgettable than flagging down cabs. They followed the road, walking past the Mile High Club on the other side, which was still locked up tight.

They saw the minivan parked outside, and walked in through the entrance. Warner was sitting in a chair by the front windows, and had watched their progress.

'You guys walk from the strip?' he asked.

'Yeah,' Reed replied.

Warner raised his eyebrows and shook his head slowly. Any exercise was for other people. John looked at the clock, only just twenty past, so he sat down to wait for Judy. She arrived bang on 2.30, bustling through the doors, still looking stressed. She waved a quick hello and went over to the counter and talked to the man at the desk, who picked up the phone.

Five minutes later a side door opened, and a fresh-faced Hispanic policewoman with curly black hair walked over to them and introduced herself. She led them into a small room next to the lobby, inside was a round table and plastic chairs scattered around.

'So ... how can I help?' she asked.

'Deanna Hayter, you probably know her as Deanna Clark, I think you already got a call,' Judy said.

Casiano nodded.

'Yeah, that's right. LAPD. But they didn't ask a whole lot.'

Judy was confused.

'You told them about Madeline, and her daughter?'

160

Now Casiano looked lost.

'Er … I don't think so. Sorry, yeah, they asked me about Deanna, and I sent them what I had, but it wasn't a long call. They didn't ask a whole lot. I don't recall talking about Madeline. Maybe I did, sorry!'

Great, thought John. Airhead.

Warner sat down uncomfortably.

'OK Kirsty, let's say we reset. Let's assume we're discussing this for the first time. So, we understand that you knew Madeline, but not Deanna, what can you tell us about them?' he asked.

Casiano looked around at them.

'I know they are both dead, killed in that terrorist strike in the subway in LA. So you mind me asking what your interest is?

Judy took over. She was well used to dealing with local police, and knew exactly how to handle it. She produced her ID and smiled at Casiano, and asked her to sit down.

'Ok Kirsty, so here's what we know. This is John Smith, and he was down on the platform when it went off. He has given us information that leads us to believe it's not so straightforward as terrorism, but we aren't releasing this so I'd be obliged if you can keep that to yourself for now. These two big guys are Kyle Warner from our old friends the CIA, and Tom Reed, a captain in the army. Deanna recently married, did you know that?'

Casiano shook her head, eyebrows raised.

'No, I didn't.'

'Well, she did, to an army major. And he's been killed too, shot dead in a bar in Hollywood. We believe it's all connected, and the theory we are working on right now is that Deanna was being paid to hook up with the major. Why, we don't know. Who wanted it, we don't know that either. So, we're trying to work backwards, if you see what I mean, maybe we're wrong and it's possible that Madeline was the target, we can't rule that out. It could even be just the major.'

Casiano considered.

'OK, well, let me tell you what I know. I met Madeline a few years ago, we had a couple of run-ins, but I actually liked her and at one point tried to help her. In the end she trusted me and we ended up getting along, she became a kind of covert informer, she was real useful at times, she worked out of the hotels, knew everyone and we tried to look the other way for her. It works like that same in this city as everywhere. She had been with Deanna a long time, they were serious, so I got to know her too. Deanna was working the strip clubs, but she was still hooking, on and off but not enough she got any attention.'

John looked at her, surprised.

'You said she was with Deanna, they were serious. You mean like a couple?'

Casiano frowned.

'Well, yeah. Like for ever. Why, is that a problem?'

'Kind of, but this is another thing we didn't know. And she married the major,' Judy prompted.

'It's hard to believe; I don't understand that at all. I saw Madeline two weeks ago, she never said anything other than she was happy now, they had some money, she was going to get out the game, prove she could be a mom to Carrie. She was optimistic. I actually believed her.'

'Right, well that fits. That would add up to Deanna being paid to get with the major,' Warner rumbled.

'I guess so.' Judy didn't look convinced.

'So let's start with Deanna, what can you tell us?' Judy asked, producing a notepad and pen.

'This is what I know from talking to Madeline. Well, she was born in Henderson. White trash family; dad the local booze hound, earning dollars with bare knuckle fights and mom on the game. Two brothers, no contact at all with any of her family, who are incidentally still alive. She moved up to the city when she was nineteen, had some lowlife boyfriend who was a small-time coke dealer, she was carrying it around for him, got herself arrested. That's how it starts. She stayed up here, started working as a street hooker, got a real bad beating and went to the strip clubs. Madeline helped her out along the way and they got together, ten years now. She wasn't a bad person, not really.'

'OK, when was the last time you spoke to her?' Judy asked.

'Deanna? Not for a month or so. I was at the apartment, she was just leaving for work. But she seemed ok, she did say she was working on something that would be good for everyone.'

'Nothing else?'

'No, like I said, my main dealings were with Madeline.'

'Right, and what can you tell us about her?'

'She's interesting. Or was, I guess I should say. She came here when she was twenty-three, basically ran out on an abusive relationship with her pimp in Colorado. She was a heroin user, got busted for soliciting, and got in a rehab programme. Cleaned up for a year or two, but still working the streets so straight back on it. Busted again, rehab or jail, she took the rehab. But this time, she made it stick. Moved up to the hotels, I think she got lucky with a concierge someplace and got her foot in the door. She's been doing that since, but was moving around the hotels, everybody knows her, there's always work for prostitutes in this town, and she was pretty for a whore, I know I shouldn't say that but it's true. Anyway, I brought her in about six, seven years ago after one of her tricks went apeshit at the Venetian making out he's been robbed. Madeline was there with a second hooker called Marianne Glass, who is a real menace, and definitely stole the money. Nothing to do with Madeline but she ended up here. But I know Marianne all too well, so I worked it out. Me and Madeline struck a deal, and she's given me some gold over the years. Yeah, I liked her.'

'Is this Marianne still around, is she a friend of Madeline's?'

'I'd say they weren't friends, but often there's a guy who wants a couple of girls, so they probably worked together now and then. I don't know where Marianne is now for sure, we've had dealings with her over the years but she gets away with it, complaints get dropped nine times out of ten once it looks like it could get public. Madeline was at Caesars, but she told me she just switched to the MGM Grand, not sure why, Caesars was a goldmine for her.'

It was interesting stuff.

'Any chance we can see the apartment?' Warner asked.

They followed Casiano in her cruiser and she drove south and west, not far at all, then pulled up in front of a squat apartment block, the end of a group of three identical buildings.

Casiano tapped in a code at the door and they followed her up some stairs to the next floor. There was a door crossed with police tape. She pulled it free, produced a key, opened up, and they walked inside.

The place was wrecked, not a complete piece of furniture anywhere.

Judy showed them around and explained.

'So, after the call for an intruder, we got told that Carrie wasn't allowed to visit Madeline until we had cleared it, so we came by and searched the place. When it first came in a patrol came by and did their usual, but nobody had been hurt, there was no sign anyplace of the guy. I got alerted after, so back we came. We found nothing really, a tiny bit of cocaine that Deanna admitted to, some cash. That was it.'

'How much cash?' John asked.

'Getting on for five thousand, enough for us to be interested but it was Madeline's business after all. We didn't take it.'

'You didn't find any notes, letters, or anything. Any computers? Did you check their phones?'

Casiano shook her head.

'No, look, at the time, this was a domestic, and we weren't there responding to the intruder call. Nobody had been assaulted, the guy did not enter the apartment. There was no reason. We just did what we were asked, I didn't agree with it at the time I guess but it's what it was. Look, it's always the same, you know, in hindsight I wish I'd done more and now I sure mean it but then, we just took it for what it was. Carrie was real upset.'

'It's not your fault, I understand,' Judy told her.

And John did too. There was nothing more the officers could have done, they were here purely on a public safety issue and there was no crime; the guy whoever he was had disappeared days before. Nobody was to blame.

'We got a call a couple of days ago, there was a disturbance here. Routine patrol came by, and found the place like this. No sign of anyone, and no prints anywhere. Door wasn't forced neither.'

'So, they had a key,' Warner guessed.

'Oh yeah. The super here had no idea about it, he wasn't anywhere near the place. My guess is it came from inside the PD, I hate to say it but I can't see no other way.'

'Shit. So, you got yourselves an inside man,' Judy said.

'Or woman.'

'Yeah, or woman.'

'Look, I shouldn't say this, but I would really like to help. And I got to say, LAPD weren't real interested. I got no reply at all to the email I sent, and they got everything I had,' Casiano spoke earnestly. 'Now I got the FBI, CIA, and I have no real idea who the hell these two guys are asking the questions I should have been asked before, right?'

'Aaah, right, sorry, yeah I should have explained better. So yeah, Tom here is an MP, he's helping us with the major's murder. Like I said, we believe it is all connected. And like I told you, John, well John was there, in the Metro when it happened. And he's kinda worked on stuff like this before. Whatever this is,' Judy explained apologetically.

Casiano looked at John.

'I can't believe you were there. Unbelievable.'

John nodded.

'Yeah, and we are on the right track. We just desperately need some answers.'

There was nothing more to see in the apartment so they left, and followed Casiano back to the police station, but now John had the feeling that they definitely weren't wasting their time.

Chapter Twenty-One

He entered the car park through the vehicle entrance and followed the ramps up through the levels. It would have been easier to have just walked in through the hotel but as usual Ryan Gallagher had no idea who he might bump into, he wasn't a popular figure among security in the strip hotels anyway. It was busy; cars parked in long lines and he was careful to stay as much in the shadows as he could, Caesars was a hotel in particular he had to stay well away from and he was decidedly uncomfortable just being in the car park. He made it up to the fourth floor, there were a lot more empty spaces here. He walked away from the ramp, looking for Tibor. He was justifiably nervous, he'd been skating on very thin ice for a long time, and had been getting away with it purely by staying out of the way, but now he was in the open. He swallowed hard, what if this was just a trick?

He stopped dead. He couldn't believe this had just occurred to him. He farted wetly. He realised he was literally about to shit himself.

Fuck, what was he thinking? He'd walked all the fucking way here and now was in a car park on his own with Tibor for company.

He was dead. He was so fucking stupid. He deserved everything he got.

He turned, ready to run and then headlights blindingly flicked across at him. He jumped, and peered over. Low-slung sportscar; one man sitting in the driver's seat, arm hanging out the window. He walked forward cautiously. No choice at all now. Nowhere to go. Greasy cold sweat dripped down his back. He approached the car at an angle, reasoning he could see better and spotted the spiderweb tattoos on the arm.

Tibor.

But he looked to be on his own.

'Hey!' Gallagher called out, trying to keep the fear from his voice.

Tibor was watching him, a half-smile on his face. As soon as Gallagher got close Tibor leaned out the window, raised his arm and pointed across the car park, back the way that Gallagher had just come. Gallagher stopped and looked over his shoulder, confused, what the fuck now?

'Go talk to the Russian,' Tibor told him.

'What?'

But Tibor said nothing else, just pointed, so Gallagher warily turned and walked back, past the ramp, staring into the gloom and then he could just make out a man leaning against a car, right where there was hardly any light at all, impossible to see him clearly from this distance so with growing dread he continued on, every step toward his inevitable doom.

The man didn't move at all, just continued to lazily smoke a cigarette, looking at nothing. Gallagher stopped ten feet away and coughed nervously. The man bent down and picked up a small sports bag from the floor next to him and threw it across so it landed heavily at Gallagher's feet.

'Look inside,' the man said, in clipped, precise English.

So Gallagher did, and squatted down. Inside was a handgun, fat, boxy, he didn't recognise the make but he could see it had a silencer, and also an envelope and a single piece of paper. He looked up at the man, who flicked the cigarette butt away and walked over, then crouched opposite him and smiled.

The man was big, solid, with a bald head that gleamed in the half light. His teeth were sharp and broken, and he had heavy scarring around the right side of his face and head, he was wearing all black; leather jacket, jeans. Close up he smelled of Old Spice.

'This is what you do,' the man told him, reaching into the bag, removing the sheet of paper and opening it out. 'Is simple. These are four people. You kill them. Is five thousand. Each. Where the people are is written next to them, we knows only two for sure so far but soon will know all, so we will send you message, understood?'

Kill people?????? What the fuck?

'But …'

'No buts. Tibor tells me you will do this. Now understand. To me, is nothing. I just need this done. If you don't want to do it then OK, I find someone else. Plenty people. And Tibor will most likely hurt you bad you anyway. So, I don't care.'

The man stared back at him, it felt like it went straight through, and Gallagher felt a chill running deep down his spine.

'But, I never killed anyone! I never even fired a gun!' he stammered.

The man picked up the gun.

'Is simple.' He pointed to the rear of the gun. 'Is safety catch. You click here, is off. Then just point the gun and pull trigger. So make sure you close. Is full of shells, don't use them all on first one!'

The man laughed, showing more broken teeth.

'There is spare magazine in the bag. After, you dump this gun and disappear. Tibor says give you some cash now. He say you owe him money. I pay it already. So, you owe me I think. There is one thousand in the envelope, is all clear?'

Five thousand Tibor had said. But there was actually twenty being laid out in front of him. Plus the debt was paid, and Tibor was one of the worst to owe money to, that was for sure. Gallagher had been avoiding him for months, longer. And he could do this. He looked at the sheet of paper carefully. Four photographs, taken without them knowing. Three men and a woman. He didn't know any of them, and there were no names anyway. Just a hotel written next to the black man and the woman, nothing for the other two. How hard could it be? Bang, bang, bang, bang. Twenty thousand richer. That's debts paid, the deposit and a year's rent on a room right there, plus clothes, and food. He could be straight again, no more jumping at shadows. He could get living again if he had some cash. He thought about waking up on the floor that morning. Like most mornings, if he was lucky. The holes in his socks. The times he had slept in car parks like this one. But with money, it would be different. He could walk around, untroubled, free. He imagined lying on a comfortable sofa, a big TV on, a cold beer in his hand.

This was that chance.

'Ok,' he said simply.

The man stood up, towering over him so Gallagher sprang to his feet too. Not that it made much difference, he was barely five foot seven so he was still looking upward at the man, who glowered down at him and spoke softly and slowly.

'Understand me. Listen. We will be watching. We will see everything, and if you are caught, you shut the fuck up and say nothing to nobodies. You are, what is it, er … expendable! You are expendable. Disposable.'

'Yeah, sure, I get that.'

Gallagher bent down and pulled out the envelope. He opened it and saw ten crisp hundred-dollar bills.

Yep, he could do this. For dollars, right now, he could do anything.

The man patted him heavily on the head and walked off, disappearing into the shadows again. Gallagher heard a car start and watched Tibor pull away. He picked up the bag and made his way back out the car park.

***

They stood together outside the police station. Casiano had spoken with her lieutenant and afterward promised to be at their beck and call if they needed anything. Judy was anxious, distracted and Warner kept tapping away on his mobile. John looked at his watch, half past three.

'Tell you what,' he said, 'You two go back to doing whatever you're doing. Me and Tom can deal with the strip club, to be honest, we're more likely to get something out of it, keeping clear of the official involvement as it were, and we can walk over to Caesars and the MGM Grand, just keep digging. You guys get straight, and then you go to The Stratosphere later. This concierge, whatever his name is, is probably best to lean on heavily, if I know those people so the official line will be best there.'

'Aidan Connelly,' Judy replied.

John looked at Tom, who nodded.

'John's right. Listen I've had to deal with strip clubs a thousand times, there's always a soldier getting into trouble in those places. There's ways of dealing with them for sure.'

'I ain't arguing,' Warner replied.

Judy looked at the three of them.

'OK, so I won't either. But promise me you'll stay on the right side of the law. Please, this is wayward enough as it is.'

John held up his hand.

'It's a promise.'

'Definitely,' Tom told her. 'I'm as much under the microscope as you guys are.'

'I seriously doubt that,' Judy replied, 'but look, it's a kind offer. I am fighting a losing battle right now, it will give me time to straighten a lot of it out. I should be able to relax after. Well, relax isn't the right word but it'll be easier.'

'OK. But remember. Not a word about where you're staying. I'm serious,' John said.

They arranged to meet for breakfast at Caesars in the morning then got in the minivan and Warner dropped them on the strip on the corner of the MGM Grand, they watched the others disappear into the traffic heading north, then both turned and looked at the huge white hotel.

'What do you think?' Tom asked.

'May as well.'

As they walked toward the entrance John could feel his sixth sense prickling him even worse. He trusted it, it had never let him down. He slowed up, and turned, as if looking across at Excalibur on the far side of the road. And he saw it straight away. A man, ducking out of sight behind a pillar under the footbridge.

'Wait here,' he told Reed, and then set off, moving fast, the long way around and approaching the pillar from the blind side. Reed watched, confused, and then realising something was up started walking the other way toward the same spot.

The man was still there, facing away tying to peer round the corner and John grabbed his t-shirt collar and hauled him backwards and onto the ground. As soon as he did so he punched the man twice, the first straight in the mouth breaking some teeth and the second into the right eye.

Then he pulled him up so he was sitting dazedly leaning against the pillar.

Reed joined him.

'What, we had a tail?'

'Yeah.'

John crouched down. The man was staring at him, confused, scared.

'So, who told you to follow us?' John asked quietly.

'Fuck, fuck you!' the man replied, at least with an attempt to stay tough.

Reed leaned down and grabbed the man's hand and lifted it then started to twist.

'Fuck you. I'm saying shit!' The man blurted out trying to pull his arm free.

It did no good. Reed continued to twist and there was a pop as his shoulder dislocated. The man screamed shrilly. Reed let go and asked the same question again.

The man looked up, tears in his eyes. John searched him, there was a car key, nearly a hundred dollars in cash but nothing else. He pocketed the money and dropped the key down a drain.

'The Russian. The Russian told me. I work for Tibor.'

'Who's the Russian? And who's Tibor?' Reed asked.

'I just run shit for Tibor. He gave my number to the Russian. I never met him, don't know him, don't even know his fucking name. He said he got a call, you would be at the precinct. He told me to follow you.'

'When?'

'What?'

'When did he call?'

'Fuck man, I don't know. About an hour ago I guess. I went there and waited. You was inside, then you came out and I followed you. He told me I had to follow the two white guys. That was it. I had to find out where you was staying.'

'How many are you?'

The man spat thick blood onto the ground.

'Just me. Fuck. Only me. This Russian, he asked for more, but I thought it was a bullshit job. Simple.'

He looked balefully at the two men. How wrong could he be.

'And you didn't want to split the money. What's your name?' John asked.

'They call me Lucky.'

'That's a bad choice today.'

John looked around, there was a cab slowing for the junction. He hailed it and together they bundled Lucky inside. John passed the driver a twenty and told him to go to the airport. They watched as the car went off round the corner and then walked up the steps.

They entered the hotel, and up to the main floor. John saw the restaurant sign high on the wall. Hakkasan.

'Wow let's eat there later. I love that restaurant, and we got plenty of cash.'

Tom looked too, but it meant nothing.

'You remember it from before?'

'No, I didn't know it was here. But they got two I think in London. Food is great, different gear altogether.'

'Ok, yeah, let's do that.'

They went over to the bar and sat down at the counter. For once, this one wasn't right smack in the centre of a casino, but close to the entrance which led over the footbridge to Excalibur. Tom bought a couple of Budweisers and they clinked the bottles together and drank.

'I wonder who this Russian is?' Reed asked.

'I've got no idea. I'm more concerned that they knew we would be at the precinct.'

'So … who is it?' Tom asked. 'I think it's Judy.'

John shrugged ruefully.

'If it is one of them, and I'm not saying it is, then my money would be on Kyle I suppose, he hasn't been really interested all day. He could be just going through the motions. But I don't know, and I really don't want it to be either of them.'

'It sucks, it really does, we shouldn't have to worry about this crap.' Tom hunched forward, massive shoulders straining his t-shirt.

John looked at the barman and dug the photo of Madeline out his pocket.

'Say, you know this lady?'

The barman, an elderly black man looked at the picture and smiled.

'Lady? Ha ha, yeah, oh yeah I know Maddie, known her a long while.'

Tom sat up.

'Can you tell us about her? We want to know if she was with anybody new lately.'

The barman shook his head.

'Not really. I worked at Caesars before, she was always up there, then she just turned up here a while back. It was good to see her, she's a nice person. She seemed to have stuff on her mind, but she was happier, last time I saw her. But that was actually some time ago now, she hasn't been around for a couple of weeks I guess. She moved pitch, probably.'

Her death explained it better, thought John, but she wasn't working before that either. So that confirmed the money, again. Everything they were hearing confirmed it.

'Is there anyone she was friends with around here today?' Reed asked.

The barman shook his head.

'Not this early. If you're here this evening you'll maybe be able to catch someone. Depends how happy they are to talk.'

Chapter Twenty-Two

Rico and Sal had spent most of the day attempting to clean the place up, Voorhees kept mentioning they were being joined by a professional team, and they had to look good, so they had washed and swept, and gone for lunch at the bar at the mall, then come back again and continued with tidying, aware that they were just trying to keep busy while Voorhees sat in the office on the first floor. They had no idea what he had eaten, there was no chance of getting any food delivered here, and he was never going to walk to McDonald's.

They ended up working in the room outside, Voorhees visible through the glass. He had been tapping away on the crappy laptop, no idea why, there was no internet, maybe he was writing his memoirs. Now, he was on the phone, raised voices again.

He walked out and looked at the two men.

'So, I have been getting shit right? Blamed for the failures. Well, other teams are making worse fuckups, I kid you not. I'm told the endgame is nigh, and it's time for us to shine.'

Rico and Sal looked at each other.

'Now,' Voorhees continued smoothly. 'Good job on making this place look ship shape. Tonight when the boys get here they will be hungry, so I need you to get some food arranged, ok? Pizzas, whatever, but make sure all you need to do is collect it, I want everything ready.'

Sal nodded, satisfied Voorhees continued.

'I think we're going to be given a new mandate tomorrow, if things don't change we are going to have to get rid of one, maybe two people, so the focus will be on that. I'm hearing it's being dealt with but I don't believe it. Other people are making worse mistakes it seems. There is every chance you will be mobile tomorrow, I will work out the pairings when we meet the new guys tonight. But I need you to be sharp, be the best, hold your heads up. We were here first.'

'What went wrong Yann?' Rico asked.

'What?'

'You said another team fucked up. I wondered, what went wrong?'

'They dropped the ball Rico. Underestimated their targets. I wanted to deal with this problem before but was overruled, now I am back in charge. And we do it right.'

He looked at the two men, then walked back into the office, obviously pleased with himself. He stopped then turned and looked at them.

'Say, go get me something to eat, will you? I'm famished.'

He held out a twenty.

Sal walked over and took the money, and then left with Rico, headed for McDonald's. They were happy to go. It sounded like it might soon be all over.

***

At five-thirty John and Reed walked into the Mile High Club. Inside, it was a big square, an L shaped stage in the far corner complete with shiny poles and a bar along the back wall. There were booths along the remaining walls and tables dotted around the centre. Next to the stage was an archway with 'Private Invitations' written across it.

There were a few guys scattered around, some watching a girl in zebra stripe knickers do her stuff to a pop song John vaguely remembered.

There was nobody at the greeter station, it was still early but a slim middle-aged woman wearing way too much make up hurried over when she saw them entering, another one too long under the sun lamp.

'Table or booth?' she asked. 'No food until seven.'

'Table's fine, and I think we're ok for food,' replied Reed.

The woman looked up at him in wonder.

'Jeez, I'd love to take you home! I'd get some peace at last,' she muttered, and led them over to a table toward the stage.

'Thanks,' John said. 'Can we get a couple of beers, and any chance we can see the manager?'

Her eyes flicked around the room.

'Maybe. I don't know that he's in.'

'Well, do you think you could look? It is important.'

'Sure, why not.'

She tottered off on high heels, head held high, still believing she looked twenty-one.

Reed looked all around him.

'Man, these places are all the same. It doesn't matter what city, what country you're in, they're all identical.'

'Yeah. How do you want to play this?' John asked.

'How about you take the lead, and I'll chip in when I think it's needed? I meant what I said, I'm forever in these places.'

'Ok.'

The woman returned, and placed two cold bottles of Miller in front of them, condensation running down the outside. A man followed her over, older, tall, heavy build, long grey hair in a ponytail. He leaned on a chair back at the other side of the table.

'What can I do for you fellas?' he asked.

'We just need a few minutes. We need to ask you a couple of questions about Deanna,' John told him.

The man rubbed his head with both hands, and thought for a while, eyeing John and Reed carefully, then sighed and sat down, laying his arms on the table. He had a badge with 'Manager – Rob Johnson' pinned to his plaid shirt.

'What do you want to know? I guess you know what happened to her.'

'Yeah, we do. And it wasn't what the press are saying. I can't go into any details, I'm sorry, but it's a lot more than a bunch of crazies with machine guns in a subway,' John replied.

Johnson looked surprised, then leaned forward, cupping his face in his hands.

'Ok, say I buy that. Why?'

'We think that she was paid to marry an army major.'

Johnson shook his head.

'Yeah, I wondered, that wasn't really Deanna, it made no sense. She wasn't interested in men, other than the ones paying her.'

'Yeah, we've been told about that. Look, we just need some help. People are dead. Did she mention any money to you?'

Johnson looked off into the distance, clearly weighing everything up in his mind. He sighed again.

'Actually, yeah. She did. Look, I liked Deanna. She was hard work at times, her own worst enemy, but she was here a long time. I never had no problem with her.'

'What did she say?'

'About a month ago she told me her troubles were over. They needed some cash and now they had it.'

'We know all about Madeline, did you know her well?'

'Oh yeah, she would often drop in here. I liked her too. She was tough, for sure, but the money was so Maddie could make a home for her daughter. They used to talk about that all the time.'

'Did Deanna tell you about the wedding?'

Johnson frowned.

'Yeah, she did. Not much, but she told me about it.'

At last. Someone knew something.

'What did she say?'

'She told me that Maddie had been approached at Caesars, a while back. Marry this guy and get paid for it. But Maddie had some problems at Caesars, there were a couple of guys or something, some shit happened I guess and she didn't want to be around there no more. Whoever was setting this up was always there. Anyway, she took Deanna with her and she said that she would do it.'

'Caesars? What's the connection?' Reed asked.

Johnson shrugged.

'That's where Maddie was approached about doing it in the first place. She's a great looking woman, shit, was, been around a while, and a lot of people know her. But she needed to get away from the hotel, or someone there most likely, I don't know why. There was some trouble I guess. But it was cool for Deanna, so she took it on.'

'Any idea how much we're talking about?' John asked

Johnson stared back at him.

'Forty.'

Reed whistled slowly. Johnson nodded.

'Yeah, it was a lot.'

'Do you know the guy who put all this together? Did you ever see him, or maybe her?'

'It was a him, and no I never met him. But it took Deanna longer than she promised. A lot longer. The guy turned up at their apartment. Deanna called me, I said get the cops. I'm not superman, I was worried.'

John and Reed looked at each other. At last things were clicking into place.

'Any idea why they went to LA?' Reed asked.

'No, well, not really. They went a couple of times recently, Maddie had been told about somebody there, who was going to help with her daughter. Some attorney I think. But Deanna didn't really say much about it.'

Johnson looked at them levelly.

'Listen, I got no idea who you are, but you ain't cops. You ain't carrying neither. So I'm gonna take a chance, I could be really fucking up here. Go see Paul Faber at the MGM.'

'Who's he?'

'Security manager. He's a good guy, drops in here after work. Real friendly. He knew Maddie pretty good, looked out for her, he might have some idea about who you're looking for. He's another one who's been around a long time, knows everybody. If you're straight with him, he won't have a problem talking to you.'

'OK, thanks,' John told him, and raised his bottle. Reed did too.

Johnson stood up, and the three men shook hands.

'Good luck boys. If you need anything, I'll be here. I meant it; I liked Deanna. And Maddie. And if someone got to pay for what happened, then I hope they get what they deserve.'

***

Sammy had felt like she was running on empty most of the day and after stifling yet another yawn she bailed out, reasoning that with an early night and a good night's sleep she could be back working one hundred and ten percent in the morning.

After a nice Thai meal.

So she was home by six, and in the bath by six-thirty. Luxuriating with lots of bubbles and thinking about everything that was going on. Really, this could make her career, she just needed a little bit of luck. The nationals were showing an interest, and her name would definitely have come up, so she had to make sure she did everything she could to take advantage of it.

Her mobile phone chirped insistently, and she cursed. She ignored it, and it stopped. She sighed and sank back, whoever it was, they would call back.

Her phone rang again.

Shit.

She levered herself up, reached over the side and picked up the phone, then sat back looking at the display.

Jimmy Frost.

Instinctively she shrank back down under the water, making sure the bubbles covered herself and then answered.

'Hi Jimmy.'

'Hi babe.' His voice was so thick she could smell the rancid beer and tobacco stink from his filthy teeth. She shuddered making the water splash.

'Say you in the bath sweetheart?' Frost was positively oozing down the phone, she felt very sick.

'No Jimmy, somebody is washing their car,' Sammy lied.

'Shame, I would've scrubbed your back. And your front, hee hee.'

'Yeah. So, have you got news?'

She heard Jimmy taking a drag on a cigarette, there was muted background noise, a bar, somewhere, probably the same one in MacArthur Park. She wanted to shiver but managed not too, instead climbed out slowly and silently then wrapped a towel around herself.

'Yeah baby, and you owe me. Remember that. You need to be real nice to Jimmy. And that is real nice. I'm expecting breakfast after, if you can still think straight.'

She grimaced as she walked through to the living room. He would need to be put straight once this was done.

'Yeah Jimmy, of course, so what news?'

'Word is the British guy is in Santa Monica, with a couple of others. Sounds like they are hiding him away.'

Sammy drew a mental picture of LA in her mind, she believed she knew at least roughly where Santa Monica was.

'OK Jimmy that's great. Where in Santa Monica?'

'Now that, sweetheart, I don't know. But it's a start. And because you're so cute, I'll keep digging.'

'Thanks Jimmy.'

'Well just remember. This ain't free. You owe me.'

He hung up and Sammy stood still looking at the phone, she really didn't want to be in debt to Jimmy Frost.

Chapter Twenty-Three

John and Reed were back in the bar in the MGM Grand. It had got a lot busier since the afternoon, but the barman they had chatted to earlier was still working. He gave them a nod as they walked over, and Reed asked where they could find Paul Faber. The barman told them the security office was near the concierge desk, he might be there, but he was normally out and about walking around the hotel. He was certain they would be able to track him down.

They headed off to the hotel reception, and found the concierge desk at the end. It was very busy around the area, queues of people checking in and bags piled up on trolleys everywhere. Reed collared one of the bellboys and he pointed to an unobtrusive door set into the wall next to the cashier office, so they walked over and Reed knocked loudly.

The door was opened by a young man in an ill-fitting suit, behind him the room had a bunch of desks in the centre but they could see there was nobody else there.

He looked at them balefully while they asked for Paul Faber, didn't ask who they were or why they wanted him, petulantly picked up a walkie-talkie off a desk and spoke into it, then walked back to the doorway.

'He's in High Roller. He'll wait for you,' he told them, then closed the door in their faces.

John and Reed looked at each other, then made their way across into the casino. They passed through lines of slot machines, into the tables, looking up at the signs. The place was massive. The found the High Roller room eventually at the back, and walked over. There was an open doorway and discrete lighting inside, just a couple of men playing. A girl walked over and invited them in but John asked about Paul Faber and she stepped outside and pointed to a man in a dark blue blazer talking to a waitress so they moved and waited next to them.

Faber was a dapper man in his fifties, with neat hair and a tidy beard, he looked at them and finished with the waitress.

'You the guys looking for me?' he asked cheerfully.

'Yeah,' John replied, and dug out the photo of Madeline. 'We're trying to find out more about Madeline, it's really about her partner Deanna but it seems like we would be better off trying to work it from her side.'

Faber looked at them both, considering.

'Yeah, I know Maddie. I haven't seen her for a spell. What's this about?'

John glanced at Reed. Faber obviously didn't know what had happened.

'Can we sit down?' he asked.

'Yeah, sure,' Faber guided them across to a table at the edge of the VIP bar, which was right next to the High Roller's room.

'So?' Faber asked.

'Madeline's dead, she was at the Metro station shooting in Downtown LA,' Reed told Faber gently. 'I'm sorry.'

Faber looked shocked, and rubbed a hand over his face.

'Shit, I didn't know. Jesus. Poor Maddie. Fuck.'

'I'm real sorry to break it to you like this Paul, but that's why we're here. There's something else going down, and it looks like Maddie and Deanna were caught up in something that got out of control. We're just looking for some answers. We were at the Mile High Club, Rob Johnson told us you can maybe help,' Reed explained.

Faber looked at him, then at John.

'Sure. Maddie was never any trouble. I don't know what you been told about her.'

'Well, we know what she did, that's kind of why we're here,' John said.

Faber nodded.

'Jesus. I can't believe it. I liked Maddie. A lot. Ask away.'

'We heard that she started operating over here, but she was at Caesars before. It seems like she was avoiding someone, did she say anything to you?'

Faber gave a small laugh.

'Operating. Yeah, I guess that's as good a word as any. But Maddie wasn't really like that, she was different. Look, I knew Maddie pretty good. She never gave anyone any problems, we never got guests climbing the walls or nothing like that. She would move around, centre on a place, then move on. She was at Caesars. She was pretty upset about something, that's for sure. There's a guy up there called George Scott, everyone calls him Gee-Gee. He's front of house manager, and he really is a dick. I knew Maddie had a couple of run-ins with him, I guessed that was why she got out of there but look, I never asked ok? I liked her but it wasn't my business.'

'Why was Maddie different?' John asked.

Faber smiled.

'Look, prostitution, it's a real big deal round the strip. This place is full of guys all the time. They come here on bachelor parties, boy's weekends, exhibitions, conferences, you name it. Every day of the year. And a lot of them want to party. Now most of us turn a blind eye when we know the girls, because we got an understanding. No shit on our doorstep. But there are others who come and go, and cause problem after problem. Maddie got it. She was a looker, she was expensive, and she would do two, maybe three a night at the most and never once had a problem. I don't know what happened at Caesars, I avoid that prick Scott, but my guess is it likely wouldn't have been her fault.

John Looked at Reed, who nodded.

'Let's go see George Scott,' he said.

Faber stood up and shook their hands.

'Listen guys, George Scott isn't a popular guy, he is a real scumbag. He pulls all kinds of strokes but he's got protection up there; he's been at Caesars for years. My advice is lead with the big guy. That will rattle him, he thinks he's tough. I'd like to see it for myself.'

John patted Faber on the back.

'Thanks a lot Paul, and really, we are sorry to have to tell you about Madeline.'

Faber shrugged, and then walked off into the body of the casino.

Reed stood up and looked lost, John rubbed his eyes and got to his feet, unsure if things weren't just getting even more complicated.

Chapter Twenty-Four

Voorhees was in his office tapping away on his laptop keyboard while Rico and Sal were still trying to get the television to work properly in the adjoining room. Sal checked his watch.

'Man, I'm starving,' he murmured.

'Yeah me too,' Rico replied, and his stomach rumbled in agreement.

Voorhees had adamantly declared they wait for the new guys to show up and then Rico would go and pick up the pizzas so everyone would eat together. But there hadn't been any time given for this, Voorhees had eaten something in the afternoon, and it was after nine now. As usual Voorhees' word was law, they hadn't even considered not following it to the letter.

'When are these guys arriving?' Rico asked quietly.

'I got no idea. Yann just said today, maybe I should ask, what do you think?'

They both looked through the partition glass at Voorhees frowning away at the screen.

'Maybe better give it half an hour.'

They carried on messing about with the TV, which was kind of working, and just as it was becoming frustrating it suddenly flashed up clearly with an HBO movie, so they sat down to watch. As soon as they got comfortable Voorhees' mobile trilled out suddenly, both men looked across.

Voorhees was talking and nodding, then hung up and struggled his big frame out of the chair. He waddled out and into the room and stood directly in front of the TV.

'Get down to the gates and open up, take a car, we don't want to look like assholes. Then Rico you get your ass down the street and pick up the food, savvy?'

Sal and Rico jumped up, left the building then jogged across the dark yard to the big storage shed opposite where they had put the cars and climbed into the Lumina, which they hadn't really used since they picked up Weiss from the station. Sal started it up, then drove out and headed for the gates, switching on the headlights at the last minute. Rico climbed out, opened the first gate and watched Sal drive through, then closed and locked it and opened the second. Sal rolled through about halfway and stopped, Rico got back in.

They both peered out through the side windows and the windscreen. Both directions from where they were sitting were clear, a few cars moving on the main road ahead but that was it.

'Do you think Yann meant they were here already?' Sal asked.

'I got no idea, I thought that's what he meant.'

'Yeah me too.'

Frustrated Rico slammed his hand down on the dashboard in front of him.

'Fuck this man. All the fucking time it's the same old shit. Nothing gets organised properly.'

Both men were uneasy, they were out here, in the open, waiting for people they didn't know who could have another Karl Weiss with them, and also had no idea who might be watching, they were completely exposed.

'Man, I wish I bought that Glock, this sucks,' Sal spoke gloomily, as the minutes ticked by.

'Fuck it, back it up, there ain't nobody here, right? We'll tell Yann then go get the food, we can't get the blame for this bullshit.'

Sal put the car into reverse and started to roll backwards, there was a loud thump on the driver's side of the roof. Sal slammed on the brakes, and then a man with a bushy beard stared in through the window at them.

'Fuck it,' Sal said, buzzing the window down, believing it to be a tramp.

'Give us some room pal,' he said, and continued rolling backwards then stopped as another man appeared leaning on the boot, peering in through the rear window.

Rico got out the car and leaned on the roof, wishing again that Sal had brought the Glock. Fist fights weren't his thing.

'What do you want guys?'

A third man appeared out of nowhere, this one big, with a shaved head. As he got closer Rico could see a mess of scars on the side of his face that gleamed dully in the streetlights. He stood right in front of the car, Rico couldn't stop staring at him.

'I think you been expecting us,' he announced, with a thick accent.

'Er, yeah, we have,' Rico replied, thinking fast.

The man at the back of the car held up a big bag, and Sal hit the switch that opened the boot. Looking over his shoulder Rico watched as the bag was dropped in, the boot slammed shut hard and then the men started to get in the car. The big man looked at Rico.

'I ride in front.'

'Fine.'

With a loud sigh Rico watched as the car reversed in and he locked up the gate, then jogged across and opened the second set. He climbed into the rear once it was all secure and they drove back across to the building, nobody speaking. Sal stopped, popped the boot open and he and Rico got out the car. The two men from the rear seat emerged first, and stood still looking around. Both were very similar looking; bearded and thickset. The big man stayed sitting in the car, eventually swinging his legs out, staying like that for a few seconds and then standing.

Sal gestured toward the office building door.

'This way.'

They followed him into the building and everyone filed up the stairs, emerging into the common area. Voorhees was sitting in the office watching then came out of the office, his eyes never leaving the big man. He stopped and stood very still, then licked his lips.

'Leo,' he stated, still staring.

The big man, who had been casting an eye over everything glanced across indifferently.

'Yann. So, still with us then.'

End of conversation as the big man disappeared to walk up the stairs.

Voorhees angrily shook his head and turned to the other men.

'I'm Yann, I'm running the show. This is Sal, and that's Rico. Who are you guys?'

The two men were standing side by side, the left one spoke.

'I'm Gregor, Greg, and this is Rolf.'

'Pleased to meet you,' Sal spoke up and shook hands, Rico followed, and finally, reluctantly Yann.

'OK, show them where they sleep, we will do a briefing later. Rico, where the fuck is the food?' Yann was not a happy man.

'Sure Yann, I'll go right now,' Rico replied, and scurried out, just glad to be out the way, however temporary that was.

***

John was getting frustrated. They had been wandering around Caesars Palace for nearly forty-five minutes asking for George Scott, and getting the run around. It didn't help that every employee they asked would immediately look like they wanted to run away, and then give some vague idea of where the man might be. The place was vast, with a huge casino that spread out in all directions, and they had been sent literally from one corner to the next.

But they got lucky, in the end.

A man and a woman, both wearing the hotel security uniform came out of a side door into the casino right in front of them, so John stopped and asked the same question.

'Excuse me, do you have any idea where to find George Scott?'

The man immediately closed up, but the woman eyed Reed with interest.

'Now you are a big boy,' she told him, pouting.

'Thank you ma'am, but could you please answer the question? We've been looking for him all over,' Reed asked politely.

The woman looked at him, then smiled, all teeth and makeup.

'Sure. The asshole is through here.'

'Monica,' the man with her warned, but she ignored him.

'Fuck him, he is an asshole. You hear how he just spoke to me?'

She turned and swiped a card through a lock next to the door she had just emerged from and pushed it open.

'Down here, first right and then go to your left. The jerk is in there.'

They looked inside, it was a long corridor.

'Thank you,' Reed said.

'No problem honey, and you come find me afterward. I really hope you came here to break lumps off him, and I would love to buy you a beer.'

'Thanks,' John told her, and then they walked through. The door closed behind them, shutting out the racket from the casino.

The corridor was empty, and obviously led right into the bowels of the hotel. They took the first corridor on their right, and shortly after there was a long caged off section on the left, with an open door to an office just inside. There were stacks of boxes piled high with a man in overalls next to an open gate moving some off a trolley.

'Hey, is George Scott around?' asked Reed confidently.

The man spun round and stared at them.

'Who wants to know?' he asked loudly, going to close the gate.

But Reed got there first, shoving so hard the gate flew open and the man fell backwards against the boxes.

They ignored him and walked into the office, which was small, just a desk, with two men there, one counting through a small pile of crumpled dollar bills.

'You George?' John asked, standing in front of the doorway.

The two men froze and looked up.

The nearest man was wearing overalls like the one in the cage, and was young, furtive, guilty looking. The second man who was counting the cash was a lot older, in a burgundy blazer. He had elaborately coiffured grey hair and heavy jowls on a red face. He looked annoyed.

'Who the hell are you?'

Then Reed appeared behind John, and the man's face dropped, eyes wide. The young man jumped up.

'I better go Gee-Gee, I got, er … that er … thing. Yeah.'

Then he was off, squeezing past, with the other man in the cage following him rapidly away.

John walked in and stood to the side so Reed could follow and effectively fill the room. Now it was Tom's turn to show what he can do.

'We need to have a word with you George,' he said passively.

Scott looked down at the cash on the desk, then back up.

'Look, it's no big deal OK? These fucking guys, they got more money than sense, right? All I do is arrange some ….'

But Reed interrupted him.

'It ain't about whatever that bullshit is George. We don't give a shit about that. It's about Madeline.'

John produced the photo and laid it on the desk.

Scott looked nervously down then back up again, confused.

'Jesus Christ. What about that bitch? Whatever she said, it's bullshit. I looked out for her. I gave her loads of chances to make dough, she's lying. They all lie, these fucking whores.'

'She's dead,' Reed told him, folding his massive arms.

'What? When? Nah, that's bullshit.'

Reed leaned on the desk, just like he had done countless times before, and John could see it, the cowering soldier who had screwed up, ready to own up to anything to get this giant out of his face.

'Why did she quit working at Caesars?' Reed asked slowly.

'What? I don't know. She was always fucking complaining.'

Reed stood upright and glared down at Scott, who was looking at John, appealing for support. Then Reed walked around and hauled the man out of his chair and across the desk as if he weighed nothing at all, and threw him headfirst out into the caged area outside. Scott landed heavily on his side and slid across the floor. Reed walked out, and picked him up again and threw him even harder back into the office, where he crashed full pelt into the desk, sending the chairs everywhere and the cash flying all over the room. Reed stalked back in and pulled him to his feet, then pushed him across the desk so he was squashed against the wall and started banging his head against it, hard but not so hard it would knock him out.

'I don't like you George. I don't like you at all. So, either you answer our questions nice and politely, tell us the truth and play like a good boy or I'm just gonna carry on throwing you around. What do you say?'

Scott had his arms up. His nose was bleeding and one side of his face was grazed and bloody. His blazer was torn and the white shirt below it filthy.

'Ok! Ok, stop please, Jesus stop.'

Reed let Scott's head fall back, then dragged him onto the floor with a thump, and rested one big foot between his legs. Scott stared down in a panic.

'OK. Here's how it works. You answer what we ask, and every time we think you're lying to us I'm gonna really hurt you. Understand?'

'Oh shit. Oh shit. Jesus Christ. Yeah, yeah, of course.'

'Good. John?"

With a big grin all over his face John slapped Reed on the back and crouched down.

'I'll just repeat Tom's question. Why did Maddie stop working here?'

Scott looked wildly at him, and John knew he wasn't going to bullshit.

'It was the Russian. It wasn't me, it was the fucking Russian!'

The Russian. They had heard that earlier in the day. The foreigner? A pattern was emerging.

'What Russian, tell us about him.'

'Fuck. Pinsky. Leonid Pinsky. A real badass. Stays here a few times a year.'

'OK, and what's the connection with Madeline?'

'Look, I'm telling you it's nothing to do with me!'

John looked at Reed who leaned down with his foot, and Scott immediately squealed out.

'I thought we had explained George. We need you to answer our questions. Sorry if that wasn't clear, my fault I'm sure. Must be my stupid accent. I'll ask Tom to throw me around later as a punishment. So, where were we? Ah yes, the connection.'

'Fuck!!! OK, OK. Look Leonid, he always has a suite, OK? Always, and there's guys come and go. He wants things, and I sort it for him.'

'Right, by "things" you mean girls, drugs, whatever the hell he asks for, right?'

'Well … yeah I guess. They gamble and do all sorts of shit. There's always a bunch of them. Make a pile of cash for the hotel. But girls, yeah, always. Maddie is real good looking, the men love her, so I line her up, with a couple of other girls. She gets paid but she is real pissed about it, starts saying she ain't doing it again. I dunno what went on, I swear.'

'Was,' John said.

'What?'

'You said "is good looking", you should have said "was". We just told you, she's dead. But what happened next?'

'Yeah, right, I'm sorry. Well he comes back, and wants Maddie again but she ain't having it. Then Leonid says he got a special job for her, worth fifty grand. I'm like fifty grand! So, I go and tell her all about it.'

'Yeah you did. Less your ten you fucking chancer.'

'Hey look, it's the deal. I look after the girls, I get my cut.'

'Right. Twenty percent for doing fuck all. I should let Tom start breaking bones anyway.'

'Wait! Just wait! I'm answering the questions right! So, Madeline says no, and she is real pissed at me anyways, but we both know it's a lot of money and she's gonna think about it, then next day says that she got someone else who will do it, and she's got this blonde woman with her. I seen her before, cute enough I guess but not a patch on Maddie. So, I bell Leonid and he comes down and they go off and talk about it and everybody seems happy again.'

'How long ago was this?'

'Er … it was a while ago. Like months ago.'

'Then what happened?'

'Nothing. I mean it's all like it was. No sign of anyone, and Maddie ain't around neither. She ain't been here in a long time I swear. Then Leonid comes back, and he is pissed. Real pissed. Starts on at me, the fucking girls are no good, it's all my fault, I fucked it all up, but I don't know nothing about it. I ain't seen no one since, right? And Pinsky is not a guy you fuck with, he is always ready to get someone hurt, or worse. So now I am pissed, and I got to go find Maddie and tell her she got to deal with Leonid, that he wants to see her and it's fucking urgent is what it is. She just starts freaking, and she tells me to fuck off.'

'OK. So what did you tell Leonid?'

'Look, I had no choice. It's what I'm saying, you don't fuck with these guys. I gave him Maddie's address.'

'Smart. You arsehole.'

John looked at Reed who raised his eyebrows and shrugged. Scott had filled in a few details and more or less confirmed what they already knew.

'You said guys come and go to Leonid's suite, did you see any of them?'

'Well, yeah. I kinda dealt with it for him, you know, meet them and take them up. Make sure they get looked after. Part of the deal.'

'So who were they? Any soldiers? Police?'

'A couple of times, yeah. Mostly just guys, lot of Russians.'

John dug out the photo of Major Hayter.

'Ever see this guy here?'

Scott looked at it closely.

'Yeah, but only once, he was on his own, weren't wearing no uniform. But something went down, he didn't stay long. Leonid was pissed about that too.'

'Where can we find the Russian, this Pinsky? How do you contact him?'

'I don't. He comes here, but I don't never hear from him when he ain't around. We're not like, buddies, I guess.'

'Where is he now? We got to speak to him.'

'He checked out this morning. I wasn't working so didn't see him but I heard he still seemed pissed.'

John stood up, and Reed stepped back, removing his foot. Scott gingerly sat upright on the floor, looking warily at Reed.

'That it?'

'Yeah, for now. We'll be back here if you've given us one word of bullshit, you can count on it.'

John leaned down and straightened Scott's crumpled blazer then spoke quietly.

'You got one thing you have to remember Gee-gee. I know who you are. You're a bully, we can both see that, and I don't like bullies, and Tom here, well he really has a problem with them. So, if one word of our conversation gets mentioned anywhere we are straight back here, and if you're not here, we will find you. We are very good at that. So, am I clear?'

Scott nodded, even more frightened now.

'Yeah, crystal. I got it.'

Reed picked up some of the bank notes and tucked them into Scott's torn shirt pocket.

'We'll be seeing you.'

Chapter Twenty-Five

After a strained meal of mostly cold pizza, with not a great deal of notable conversation, Greg and Rolf disappeared upstairs with the big bag, to sort out their sleeping arrangements. Rico and Sal sat on the sofa, while Voorhees, perched on the only chair that he dragged out of his office picked at the remaining scraps of food. Leo stood static in the centre of the room, a half-smile on his face, hands in his black leather jacket, which made Rico and Sal even more nervous and uncomfortable, so they made some poor excuses about helping the others and stood up, but Leo stopped them.

'Is ok, I go. I think Yann needs to talk to you.'

He stalked across the room, and moved up the stairs.

The two men looked at Voorhees.

'It's not a big deal,' he said evasively, wiping his mouth.

'Ok,' Rico wanted some plain speaking, 'you said four men, but there's only three.'

'Yes, ok, ok, but it's enough for what we got to do.'

Voorhees dusted himself down and looked at the TV. It was clear that he didn't want to talk about it, which irritated both men, who wanted to know what was going on.

'And what's the deal with Leo?' Sal asked. 'You know each other, right?'

This had immediately seemed strange, and struck a chord with something Voorhees had always taken great pains to tell them, which was every team was independent. Nobody knew each other, there were never any names disclosed.

Voorhees pursed his lips and frowned, then rubbed his face with his fat hands.

'Fine. I'll tell you. But it won't help any. We didn't get four men. This is true, I only found out today, there has been some trouble with another team. They're out of action. We actually got only two. Greg and Rolf.'

Sal frowned.

'But Leo ...'

'Leo is not with us.'

'So who the hell is he? He was at the gates with the other two?' Rico asked, annoyed.

'Leonid works for our client in this matter. I was told yesterday he would be with us but I didn't think it would happen. My understanding was he was dealing with matters elsewhere. He has come here because they are not happy with our progress, or our mistakes.'

Rico slumped back on the sofa, while Sal looked behind at the stairs.

'I don't understand,' he said eventually.

Voorhees wheeled himself closer, and after checking the staircase for himself spoke very quietly.

'Right. Understand this. Leonid was originally doing the work. I believe he failed. This is why the client came to us. I met with him, and he made it clear he did not believe that we could do the job. It was a very difficult meeting. But the client said for us to proceed, Leonid was not very happy. He still believed he could get it done. I didn't know he was coming until very late, there was nothing I could do about it.'

He moved even closer, and spoke in a whisper.

'Do not trust him. He is a dangerous man.'

Then he pushed himself back, and stood up. He looked closely at the two men, tapped a meaty forefinger against the side of his nose then went back into his office, pushing the chair in front of him.

'Fuck,' Sal said quietly, and silently, Rico agreed.

***

John and Tom Reed sat in the bar in the Luxor. They had enjoyed a good dinner at Hakkasan, then made their way back. Now they had a table at the edge next to the busy casino. John was enjoying working with Reed, the big man was genuine, and dependable. He didn't get fazed. They had discussed what they now knew for sure, along with what they suspected. It felt like there was something tangible, at last.

'How fucking tall are you anyway?' John asked him, eyeing his ridiculous frame.

'Why? How tall are you?' Reed replied, grinning.

'Six foot. Boring. I wish I was you.'

Reed shook his head.

'It's not all good. At thirteen years old I was over six-two. Try explaining that in the yard. I had a bad memory as a kid, real bad. My mom tells everybody I just forgot to stop growing. I'm six-seven, as you asked.'

'Six-seven!!! That's stupid, you must be a cartoon.'

'Yeah, I know it. I got a brother, he's six-five so also big. And the really weird shit is my mom and my dad are just regular and so is everyone else in the family. Funny thing is I had a buddy at school, boy call Artie Hill, he was even taller. I ain't joking. Stands best part of seven feet now, plays for the Heat down in Miami. Not me, I was shit at basketball. I missed my calling I guess.'

'Yeah, but you're not just tall, you're the size of a house!'

Reed shrugged diffidently.

'Always have been.'

John cast his eye around the casino, he felt pretty secure. They hadn't stayed in one place anywhere for any time the whole day; dinner was probably the longest, and he was confident nobody was following them. They had paid cash for the rooms, and there were dozens of hotels right on their doorstep. He leaned forward.

'So, we let's confirm what we know, some of which we had already kind of worked out.'

Tom also moved toward him.

'Yeah, this guy Pinsky was setting up Deanna; she was being paid to get close to Major Hayter. Right now we got no idea why. But it wasn't going well, and it looks like she must have offered him some cash to marry her. Probably desperate because she knew the Russian guy, this Pinsky, was getting pissed at the lack of movement, and everybody seems terrified of that guy, plus we know Major Hayter was always short of cash down to the gambling and owed money all over.'

John nodded.

'Right. And we know that originally Madeline was lined up, but she had already met Pinsky and didn't want to touch it, even for forty grand. Plus, she didn't trust that arsehole Scott and who can blame her.'

'Ok. And we know that Madeline and Deanna had been to LA before, so there was maybe nothing special about this trip, but other than a couple of nights at the MGM Grand it doesn't look like she spent any time with Major Hayter, of course the whole honeymoon thing could be bullshit anyway.'

John took a drink of beer.

'So what we need, is to find Pinsky. That's the key. Just who in the hell is he? Does it mean something that he's Russian? I can't work out his involvement in the Metro shooting, and if I'm honest, that was a bit ragged really. No way should I have been able to just pick up the AK. But we need to find him. He is the name now, got to be central in this.'

'Well, I'm not sure there is much more for Kyle and Judy to find out at The Stratosphere. Even if this Aiden Connelly knew him, the most he could say right now is maybe he was trying to help Deanna? But even that, it doesn't seem very relevant.'

John shook his head.

'I don't think that's it, but you're right. I think we've pieced it together, as much as we are going to anyway. We should probably call Kirsty when we set off tomorrow, let her know everything. See what can be done to track down Pinsky.'

Reed tapped his glass against John's.

'I've learned a lot today. I'm not really, well what you would call an investigator. I'm an army cop. We have people that do more of that stuff, but not me.'

'You did good. You dealt with Scott perfectly, I probably wouldn't have got that much out of him. I could have hurt him, but that doesn't always get what you need.'

Reed nodded.

'Well, we'll be able to break it down for Judy and Kyle tomorrow, it'll be something to talk about on the drive back.'

'Yeah we got a lot to do. And finding Pinsky is at the very top.'

***

Ryan Gallagher walked into The Mirage through the front door.

He had already spent some of the money, he was wearing a nice new pair of trainers for a start. And a sweat shirt, and jacket. He had been able to take a shower and had slicked back his hair.

He was confident that nobody would immediately recognise him but was careful not to meet anyone's eye.

He wasn't so confident on what he was doing. He had gone out to the gun store that afternoon, and bought thirty rounds on an automatic, then stood in front of a target plugging away while someone watched to make sure he didn't do himself or anyone else some harm. The Russian was right; it was easy, laughably so. He hadn't been very accurate, but he reasoned that he had been told to get close and so it wouldn't make that much difference.

He swallowed. The target had a room on the twelfth floor. No suite for this guy. He made his way over to the elevators, there was one waiting on the ground floor; doors open.

He casually walked in and pressed the twelve button.

Nothing happened.

He pressed it again.

Still nothing.

Then he saw the slot in the panel and the sign advising a room key was required, so just as casually he sauntered out back into the casino. What to do?

He could get a room.

Now that might be nice.

No that was stupid. Mentally he slapped himself on the head. He could hardly hang around here, he needed to get away from the hotel, and fast. He turned back and watched people coming and going from the elevators.

You are an asshole, he told himself.

He wandered across, and let a couple walk into an elevator in front of him then got in just after. He made a show of going into his pocket but the guy had already put his card in, and pressed the button for twenty-one. With a smile, Gallagher hit the twelve. The light came on, and the lift started to ascend.

No going back now.

Chapter Twenty-Six

The following morning after checking out, John and Reed walked up to Caesars, then queued at the buffet for breakfast. They were a bit early, it had been agreed to meet for eight, so they found a table at the back of the room and sat down to eat, comfortably anonymous, John talking about his daughter.

Eight-thirty came and went, no sign of Kyle Warner or Judy. Nine o'clock, and still not there.

'We definitely said here right?' Reed asked, there were so many possibilities along the strip that if they had misheard it could be a very long day. John didn't have his mobile, Reed had his but he hadn't thought to give out the number.

'Yeah, definitely. Buffet at Caesars, eight o'clock,' John replied, also puzzled.

They got a coffee top up and continued to wait.

The buffet was quite big, but from their seats they could see the whole place so it wasn't possible to have missed the other two. John couldn't think how to play this, they had no idea where the others had stayed last night for a start, Kyle had gone to The Mirage but they didn't know if he had actually been given a room there. It was possible that maybe they had found something out last night and gone this morning to check it out. He decided that was the most likely and told Reed, who agreed.

But it was nearly ten o'clock and there was still no sign, and they were considering going back to the Paradise police HQ when Kirsty Casiano appeared, looking out of breath and harassed. She spotted them then rushed over and leaned on the table.

'Something's happened. Something bad. Come on, we got to go.'

John and Reed stood up, concerned.

'What's happened?' asked John.

'I'll fill you in on the way, let's go.'

She rushed out of the buffet and the two men followed her, wondering what was going on.

Her cruiser was right outside the main doors, roof lights flashing.

They climbed in; Reed in the front and John in the back and Kirsty floored it, wheels screeching as she shot out onto the strip and headed north, siren blaring, working her way steadily through the traffic. She looked at Reed and glanced at John in the mirror.

'Ok, no easy way to say this. Kyle is dead. Shot last night right outside his room at the Mirage.'

'Oh fuck!' Reed proclaimed.

'What the hell happened?' asked John.

'Right, PD have already caught the guy. He just walked up and knocked on Kyle's door. No chance at all. City are dealing with this. Perp is a local man known to us, one Ryan Gallagher, I've never had the pleasure. But nothing like this before they say, just low level street shit in his past.'

'What about Judy?' Reed asked looking at her.

'Judy is ok. She's safe. She stayed at the Wynn, Gallagher was arrested right outside. He is some kind of asshole, the whole thing was caught on camera, City PD went all out, made the connection and picked him up less than an hour later. He was walking to the front entrance.'

'So, who is he?' John asked.

'I never heard of him but City know him, he works mostly Downtown but does hit the strip. Petty theft, begging, usual shit, no violence on his record.'

'Have the police got anything on why?'

Kirsty braked hard to avoid a truck changing lane and then swerved around it, accelerating away and blasting the horn, then cutting across sharply to turn right.

'Oh yeah. He coughed alright, won't stop talking. He was put up for it by another local hood, and this one is a real piece of work, one Tyrone Bortado, known dealer, money-lender and pimp. Bad news. PD have been chasing him around for years, nothing ever sticks. Another one I don't know but these guys do; they know him real well. He can't hide, they have gone for him now. Here we are.'

She pulled up in front of another tan coloured office block, with an identical Las Vegas Police Headquarters sign across the front. She jumped out and opened the door for John and they walked in. They had to sign in, but the desk officer seemed to know what was going on. Kirsty led them through a big open plan office and then up some stairs. Judy was sitting just outside an office, her eyes red from crying. She jumped up and Reed held her tight.

She seemed lost, unable to say anything.

'It's ok,' Reed told her. 'You're safe.'

'He was coming for me,' she sobbed.

Reed rubbed her back.

'Yeah, we heard, but they got him. You're safe now.'

There was some activity from the office, and then a young lieutenant rushed out. He looked at them in surprise and paused, then half-smiled at Kirsty.

'He's downstairs,' he told her.

They followed him back down through the office and then another flight into a basement. He punched in a code by a door and walked through into the custody area, then talked to a burly sergeant behind the counter.

He walked back, smiled again.

'Ok, Bortado is being detained, they are gonna start questioning him. I'll take you through to the viewing room.'

They walked back out the door and down a short corridor, then the lieutenant pushed a door open. It was a small room, with some chairs and a window into the one next door, with a short counter underneath. A microphone fixed to it on a bendy stalk with 'Talk' next to a red button. John looked through the glass, standard stuff, square table with four chairs, everything bolted to the floor. Camera on the wall and microphones on the table.

Everything was happening so quickly he hadn't even started to try and compute the situation. Kyle Warner had been murdered by some completely random guy it seemed, and how did that fit with what they were supposed to be working on?

He sat down with his elbows on his knees and rested his head in his hands, thinking.

Kyle Warner was dead. Shot in The Mirage by one Ryan Gallagher, who had spilled the beans and was put up to do it by the guy about to be interviewed Tyrone Bortado. Where was the connection? What about Leonid Pinsky? What about 1-Too?

'You ok John?' Reed asked him quietly as he settled alongside.

John looked up.

'Yeah, I'm fine. It's just … well.'

Reed clapped him on the back.

'Yeah, I know.'

'What about this other guy, Gallagher or whatever?' Reed asked.

The lieutenant, still smiling away to himself, shrugged and explained.

'Mirage has cameras watching the elevators on every floor. Most of the Strip hotels do. They had him coming out of the elevator and getting the gun out. Eyewitness, a room service waiter walking down the corridor from the other side saw the whole thing. Gallagher banged on the door and then moved away. Kyle came out into the corridor and that was it. Three shots. PD went into overdrive, and picked him up as he was walking toward the Wynn.'

'Towards me,' Judy added shivering.

'You're ok now,' Reed told her.

'Yeah I know. But Kyle, he didn't deserve it. Gallagher knew he was done for, he gave it all up, but he'll still get life, they got the death penalty here, he should get that.'

The door opened in the room through the window, and a grizzled detective walked in, closely followed by a uniform officer who was leading a coffee coloured stocky black man in his late twenties. The officer sat him down in a seat opposite the camera and the man looked up and waved, then laid his meaty, tattooed arms across the table.

'That's Tibor,' the lieutenant said.

John looked at him.

'Sorry Tyrone Bortado. Tibor is his street name. Yeah, I know it's bullshit. He's been in that room more times than I have.'

Another man walked in, this one in his thirties wearing a suit. He shook Bortado's hand and sat down next to him, pulling out a thick notepad and pen from a briefcase at his feet. The detective watched him but didn't acknowledge either of the two men now sitting opposite.

Bortado immediately began a rant about Vegas PD and his time being wasted, the man next to him nodding sympathetically and making notes.

The detective still said nothing at all.

It was like watching a bad soap opera.

Then Bortado jumped up and stared over at the window, which would be reflective glass to him. He spread his arms out wide and smiled, beckoning.

'Hey you fucks! Come on in here, join the party!' he shouted. 'I got nothing to hide, and I don't give a shit neither!'

The cop standing by the door walked over and pushed him back onto his seat.

Still, the detective didn't move or speak.

Bortado laughed.

John frowned, then stood up and dug in his pocket. He pulled out some rumpled dollar bills, selected a ten and laid it down on the counter in front of the lieutenant.

'A tenner says you get nothing,' he said.

'What's a tenner?' asked the lieutenant. 'Oh …'

Judy, still clearly upset pursed her lips and went into her purse, then laid another ten-dollar bill on top.

'Make it twenty.'

'No,' the lieutenant said. 'These guys are the best. He'll talk.'

Reed stared hard at him, then added his own note.

'That's thirty.'

The lieutenant went to speak, then clammed up angrily, for the first time he wasn't wearing the same fixed, cheesy smile.

They saw the door open again, and a tall man walked in, smartly dressed, probably late forties. He stood next to the table and looked own at Bortado.

'Hello again Tyrone. I'd like to say it's been a while, but it hasn't.'

Bortado looked up at him and sneered.

'Detective Cooper. I thought they'd retired your skinny ass, man.'

Cooper nodded and sat down then looked expectantly across at the man sitting next to Bortado, who appeared flustered and eventually introduced himself as James Winter, attorney.

John sat up straight to watch, maybe he had been wrong. He hoped he had. Cooper seemed very assured, ready to do his job.

But it became abundantly clear within ten minutes that they weren't going to get anything out of Bortado. He was cocky and arrogant, and turned every question around, laughing as the two detectives opposite tried to get some traction. Nothing seemed to faze him, he countered everything, twisting whatever was said.

He was an expert, probably dealing with the police from very young.

Eventually the grizzled detective started to lose his temper, which really was the end of it and Cooper called time, no other option for him. Laughing Bortado was led from the room.

John looked at Judy, who was still shellshocked, desperately trying to get some sense out of what had happened.

'Let me try.'

'No way,' the lieutenant said.

John ignored him, still talking to Judy.

'We know everything Judy. Me and Tom have put it together. Bortado was involved, but it's not his idea. It's a Russian, name of Pinsky, and we have to find out where he is. Please, do whatever you can with these guys and let me and Tom deal with it. And not here. We have to act, and quick. No disrespect to anyone, but Bortado is way too comfortable here. He can play the system, he knows it inside out. It's too easy for him. But we can open him up, and we really don't know how long we have.'

'That's not going to happen,' the lieutenant's smile hadn't returned.

John looked carefully at Judy, who returned his gaze.

She nodded.

'Can I talk to you lieutenant?' she asked.

Unhappily the lieutenant stood up and they left the room.

'This is bullshit, we can break this guy,' Reed said, annoyed.

'You can Tom. He'll cave once you start, that's for sure. I've seen these guys over and over.'

'Yeah, me too.'

'Tough guys when they know nobody is going to break any rules.'

'For sure. And you're right John, we got to get on with this.'

'This is only gonna get worse if we don't. There's only one answer to all this, but not in here. Not now.'

They waited impatiently, then the door opened, and Judy walked in without making eye contact with either man, followed by the now sheepish looking lieutenant and also a captain who looked at the two men sitting in his viewing room appraisingly.

'This is an unusual request, even from the FBI,' he opened with. 'I'm Captain Day.'

'Hello Captain, I'm John Smith, this is Tom Reed. So, you know all about Kyle Warner, and you also know we are facing a race against time now. People are getting killed. We need the Russian.'

Day looked confused and looked at the lieutenant.

'Who is this Russian?'

'Leonid Pinsky. We started hearing about a Russian just yesterday and John and Tom found out who he is. He's driving this, he got Bortado to find a shooter. Ryan Gallagher won first prize,' Judy explained.

The captain looked around again.

'And you want to do what with Bortado?'

Reed stood up, and immediately both police officers stepped back without thinking about it.

'We need to frighten him. He'll talk. He'll never say nothing to you guys,' he said simply.

The lieutenant shook his head, but the captain looked up at Reed.

'So, tell me about Pinsky.'

'He's involved in the LA Metro shootings, and also the death of an army major,' Reed replied.

'And Kyle Warner,' Judy added defensively.

'We're getting close. They tried to stop us even getting here to Vegas in the first place. And there will be even more killing, and very soon if we don't find him. This guy thinks he can do whatever he wants from what we've heard,' John said.

The captain mulled it over while the lieutenant started telling everyone loudly about procedure.

'Look, Judy …OK, I never met the lady before, but she's FBI. You two I don't know. I got an MP and a, well I got no idea at all asking me, no telling me, they want to remove a detained prisoner from the precinct so they can question him about some Russian. Because apparently, we can't do that ourselves,' the captain sounded more puzzled than annoyed.

John and Reed looked at each other, well aware of how it sounded.

'We are asking Captain, not telling. But we are fighting time here, and losing, we need answers. If we get Bortado out his comfort zone he'll buckle. Listen, we've both seen this before.' Reed said.

The captain said nothing, just looked into the empty room next door. Suddenly, where they were all standing got very quiet.

'You got two hours. Not a minute longer. Lieutenant, get Bortado ready, he stays in handcuffs and I want two officers right behind them, wherever they go,' the captain announced suddenly.

'Thank you, Captain. We need a car,' John asked him.

The captain stiffened, then nodded.

The lieutenant started to speak, but stopped abruptly when Reed walked over and bent down.

'You owe us thirty bucks. Now, you got somebody in maintenance around here?' he asked brightly.

***

Sammy was feeling the screw tighten.

Moran had got on her case as soon as she had stepped into the office that morning. ABC news had interviewed a Metro worker who claimed to be at the scene, although the name didn't appear on any witness list that Sammy had seen and the police had made no mention of at all. But true or false it was news, and Moran was blaming her, saying that they were back where they started. She should have made contact with this guy, she wasn't focussed.

Even Simon was starting to lose faith, she could feel it.

In the end, out of desperation, she called Blanic.

She knew she shouldn't be doing it, this would just lead her to getting into even more problems with Moran but she had the information on Santa Monica now, and wanted to follow it up. Without support from the station it just wouldn't happen, and she would be back reporting on liquor store robberies and whoever was upset with City Hall this week. She couldn't let this go.

Blanic answered, and was surprised to hear from Sammy.

She spoke confidently, but carefully, not mentioning Moran or anyone else, just that she had information the British guy; John Smith, was currently in a hotel in Santa Monica. She just wanted to get down there for a day or two, stay one night and work the hotels, try and find him.

There was nothing that nobody else at the station couldn't handle while she was out the picture for forty-eight hours, and if it didn't work out, then at least she had tried. Better than nothing. And it probably wouldn't be that long.

Blanic listened, but said nothing.

She felt herself talking for talking's sake, and willed herself to stop.

There was silence on the end of the phone.

'Put Frank on,' Blanic told her eventually.

She stood up and shakily walked across to Moran's office, and handed the phone over. He stared at it in her hand.

'It's Costas,' she told him.

He grabbed the phone and covered the microphone.

'Oh, you fucking bitch,' he hissed, then closed the door on her.

She walked back like a robot, and sat in her chair, her eyes constantly flicking across to Moran's office. She could see him through the glass wall, hunched over his desk, phone glued to his ear. Simon watched her but when their eyes met he looked away, fast.

She may well have made a major error this time, Moran would be really going to bat on what he thought about her, and Blanic would have no option but to listen. Moran was in charge, and she had just trampled all over him, gone right over his head, and she knew that Blanic would not approve.

She watched Moran shaking his head, still looking down.

She could even be out of a job.

Then his office door crashed open and Moran stomped out. He stared at her, then walked across, his head held high, never looking away.

He dropped her phone into her lap.

'So off you go then, have fun at the beach.'

She stared at him.

'Oh yeah, make me look like an asshole, thank you for that. You got forty-eight hours, and before you book anything I want to approve it. So don't spend one cent of our money less I say so. ok?'

She nodded dumbly.

'Yes, ok Frank. Thank you. I'll hand over here, then get down to Santa Monica.'

He was still staring down at her, then he leaned forward and spoke right in her ear.

'You know what cutie? Your tits and ass ain't gonna keep on saving you from the real world. Nothing lasts for ever. And I'll be waiting.'

He spun round and headed back to his office.

Unable to help herself Sammy broke out a big smile, which Simon joined in with, and she blew Moran's retreating back a kiss.

***

The captain told them to wait in the canteen, which was on the next floor up. He insisted Judy go to his office so they could check in with the FBI before anything went ahead. He was justifiably nervous and needed to know that they would support any action like this. If there was any hesitation from their side, then Bortado was going nowhere.

John and Reed sat opposite each other at the end of a long row of tables, there were officers of all ranks dotted around, drinking coffee and eating. Reed was making small talk, but John was sitting still, stewing.

He put his rucksack on the table in front of him and looked around.

Nobody could really see what he was doing.

Carefully he drew the SIG Sauer toward him from under the clothes inside, all the time keeping it in the bag and then dismantled it, slowly and carefully until it was stripped down inside the bag …

Fuck.

Now he knew. After this morning he had started to suspect, he hadn't wanted to believe it but here was all the evidence he needed. No question at all now.

'It's Keane,' he told Reed, who looked back questioningly.

213

'Keane's the leak. It's him,' John repeated quietly.

'What? No way, it can't be. Why do you think that?'

John reassembled the gun and spun the bag around so it faced Reed.

'Take a look at this. You remember I told you Keane got me to go down to the bar with him? This is the gun I got. Check it for yourself.'

Reed frowned and then repeated the process that John had just undertaken, still in the cover of the rucksack.

He looked up. Now he knew. John was right.

'Shit. No firing pin.'

'Exactly. It was a set up. I get a gun that's no fucking use. It was convincing, I mean it's loaded, it all looks kosher, but in the event of something happening I'm done. Out of the way. I bet there's a tracker in that minivan, that's how the two guys at the diner found us. And that's how they knew where Kyle was staying, and probably Judy too as Kyle was running her around. Fuck. I can't believe it, he was the last one I suspected. Apart from you that is.'

John stood up and walked round the table to the window. He leaned forward, resting his forehead on the cool glass, watching the traffic below.

Reed stared into the rucksack.

'Fuck.'

Chapter Twenty-Seven

Sal and Rico had got up, showered, and gone straight out for breakfast.

Something was going to go down, that was for sure. Leo had been prowling around for most of the night, neither of them got a great deal of sleep because of it.

Rico was also convinced that Greg and Rolf had no more idea about Leo than they did, at least they already knew Yann reasonably well for the lot of good it did them. He and Sal had been speaking with them yesterday evening, originally on the pretext of checking they had everything they needed but successfully steering the conversation round to trying to find out just what the fuck was going to happen next.

It was obvious the two men were equally mystified, neither of them had any real idea of what they should be doing, and it was clear that being sent to an old train yard in a city they had never been to before had not been in their plans.

They had been together for a while, and were doing their thing, whatever that was when they got the call, and made their way down to LA from Reno. Rico had mentioned that he had been told there would be four men, a team, which meant nothing to them. They had worked together, but only recently really, not more than a couple of months, so similar to he and Sal, in fact not even as long.

Rico had asked about Leo but they had just looked at each other and shrugged, which pretty much mirrored his and Sal's own feelings.

Now they sat and ate, both men wondering how they could avoid going back.

The door opened, and in walked Greg and Rolf. Both groups of men looked at each other. Rico grinned.

'Come sit with us.'

Greg spoke to Rolf who went to the counter to order, then walked across and sat down next to Sal.

'So, this is breakfast then?' he asked looking around.

'Yep. Same as the last place for us. Not much choice round here, there's a family restaurant just along the street but they don't open till eleven. Always McDonald's man, always. I'd kill for a Denny's, anything different,' Sal replied.

'KFC. Jack in the Box,' Rico offered.

'Applebee's. Or Taco Bell,' Greg decided.

The three men looked at each other and grinned comfortably.

'How did you get out?' asked Sal. 'We locked up.'

'Leo gave us some keys, last night. I didn't really think about it, but I'm glad he did. We were hungry.'

Rico checked his watch.

'It's early, you guys didn't sleep too good then?'

Greg looked around again, then leaned forward.

'Nah, Leo was like, pacing around. All night it seemed. That guy's weird, something going on there,' he said quietly.

'Yeah, he does seem a bit ... intense,' Sal agreed.

'What's Yann like?' Greg asked.

'He ain't easy. Better now than he was, but he's all keyed up too. At least he tells us what's going on now, he never used to. Must be some kind of history between him and Leo,' Sal answered.

Rolf appeared, and placed a tray down on the table. He had purchased two extra coffees, which both Rico and Sal believed to be a good sign.

'Thanks a lot Rolf,' Rico said.

'No sweat, we're the workers, right? Got to stick together.'

Exactly what I was thinking thought Rico.

***

They sat in the canteen for nearly an hour, before the now decidedly unsmiling lieutenant appeared, and very reluctantly ushered them upstairs to the captain's office.

It was a big room in a corner, lots of windows and light. Judy was already inside sitting on a sofa, still clearly upset.

John stood in front of the desk with Reed behind him. The captain was on the phone, then he hung up.

'Ok, so we have been taking a good look. I'm sure you understand I got to know what I'm dealing with. Mr Reed is a serving member of our armed forces, rank of captain, and his superior officers appear to hold him in high regard. You on the other hand Mr Smith, are more of an unknown although it does seem you got a lot of support from the FBI.'

He leaned back in his chair and looked up at them with strangely staring eyes. He did this for a while, unspeaking. John believed it would work wonders when he was interviewing someone, it was like he could see right through them.

In the end, he smiled briefly and leaned forward.

'Right. You get Mr Bortado for two hours. Nobody at this precinct is going to show any interest on why you are doing this or what you plan to do. That is my courtesy to the FBI, and the CIA I guess, hopefully one day I'll get my reward. The conditions for this are real simple; one; he comes back here again alive, two; he remains in handcuffs, three; two officers travel with you. They will be in a separate vehicle and take no active part in whatever proceedings you instigate. And no, none of this negotiable.'

He looked up.

'Am I understood?'

'Perfectly,' John told him. 'Thank you.'

The captain stood.

'Well ok. I need to do some work with the custody sergeants, this ain't something I ever did before. None of us have. Let's meet in the yard in fifteen minutes. I've got you a car.'

He walked out, and they followed him. John stopped Judy.

'Stay here Judy.'

'What? No way. I need to be involved John, you can't …'

He interrupted her gently.

'Look, nobody is going to get killed. ok? But we need the answers. It's best you aren't there. Sometimes dirty is the only way, and I am sure that is not how you want to do things. So stay here, and try to pretend none of this happening. That way, you knew nothing about it, you are not involved at all and there's no reason for any more problems for you. Please Judy, stay here.'

She looked at him, and then Reed, who put his arm around her.

'John's right Judy, you know it. We're way off the programme now. This is his world. I'm just here helping is all.'

The captain was waiting in the stairwell.

Judy looked at him and then at John, then she sat down without saying anything.

They went down to the basement level, and the captain entered the custody area. There was a small office to one side, which John guessed was used by lawyers when they needed to discuss whatever level of hopelessness their current client faced, and they were shown into it.

Both men sat down on either side of a table, which was opposite a rack filled with pamphlets issued by the Vegas PD, all of which basically said don't break the law.

The office smelt of sweat and lost causes.

A young cop, big but not in direct comparison to Reed spotted them and walked over.

'I got what you need,' he told Reed, who nodded.

'Thanks.'

'No sweat, I'm on the detail, you follow us, we know a perfect place.'

'Cool, thank you.'

He walked off, John looked at Reed, who smiled briefly.

'I think I know how you want to play this John. I got a good idea what's on your mind.'

The captain appeared, and showed them out a side door into a big yard, which served the custody area. It was secure behind a solid pair of steel gates, there was a PD cruiser and a dark Chrysler sedan waiting there. The young cop was standing next to the sedan, and Reed went over. Beyond the yard was a raised car park, with police vehicles dotted around.

The door opened again, and Bortado was led out, still grinning, hands cuffed behind his back. The two officers holding his arms shoved him roughly toward the cruiser, but the young cop intercepted them and they put him in the back of the sedan, slamming the door closed. John walked across.

'Over to you, ok?' the young cop said, and set off for the cruiser.

'Don't say anything to him ok? Nothing at all,' John advised Reed, who nodded and climbed into the driver's seat of the sedan, racking the seat back hard toward Bortado who had to move out the way. John got in the passenger side, and Reed drove toward the cruiser, which turned on its roof lights and set off toward the gates. They opened slowly, and the two cars made a right turn onto a four-lane road, heading west.

Bortado leaned forward.

'Hey who the fuck are you guys? You don't look like fucking cops. Believe me, I can smell them a mile away.'

Neither man said a word, instead John started a conversation with Reed about motorbikes.

His accent clearly confused Bortado, who tried several more times to butt in, to no avail.

'Well fuck you then!' he declared, and sat back, sulking.

John was aware of the time constraint they faced, they really didn't want to be driving any further than they absolutely had to. They followed the cruiser, which made good progress, and it turned off the street onto a smaller road which ran north west. The buildings started to thin out, they passed an industrial area, then a couple of trailer parks.

John checked his watch.

Forty minutes.

They turned again, and then there was nothing, just desert scrub, a two-lane road, very little traffic. The carried on for a few miles, then turned onto a rutted track which rose up, a high dust cloud behind both cars.

Another couple of miles, and the cruiser braked.

The young cop jumped out, and leaned across the bonnet pointing.

Reed nodded, and made a sharp right onto what was little more than a trail. The car bumped and rattled across the desert, every time it went across a big rut there were loud clangs from the back of the car.

John looked at Reed.

'Exhaust?'

'Nah, don't worry about it.'

He drove on, peering forward and then stopped sharply.

John looked around, but there was nothing to see, just desert. Reed climbed out, so John did too. Bortado was straining to look all around him, cursing loudly but both men ignored him.

Reed walked around the car.

Next to them was a basin in the desert, almost perfectly round, the bottom about fifteen feet below where they were standing.

The cruiser was just visible, both cops had gotten out of their car and were leaning against the front wing, pretending not to watch.

'Perfect,' said John. 'Totally perfect.'

Reed opened the rear door and yanked Bortado out of the car. He did it with such force that Bortado fell onto his face, unable to stop himself. Roughly Reed pulled him upright.

'Oh yeah, I see, so that's how it is right? Well fuck the pair of you assholes, I don't give a fuck. You take these fucking bracelets off I'll show you, I don't care how fucking big you are, you pumped up fucking freak, I'll kill both you motherfuckers you see if I don't,' Bortado ranted.

'We'll see,' Reed said quietly, and pushed Bortado stumbling onward down into the basin. He fell, rolled over and stopped halfway, then got his knees.

'You fucking asshole. I don't know you. I never seen either of you motherfuckers. What, you police don't talk? You fucking with the wrong guy. Your buddies should have told you. I swear to God when I get out this shit I am coming for you. I don't give a shit how big you is. You better get the fuck away from this bitch. I'm fucking coming after you.'

'Shut up. We ain't the police,' Reed said mildly as he walked past, and hoisted Bortado up by the arm and shoved him the rest of the way down.

Once they were at the bottom Reed went back up to the car and returned with a tired old steel frame plastic chair. He set it down in the centre, then produced a key and unsnapped Bortado's handcuffs then stepped back next to John.

Immediately Bortado reared up and got into John's face.

'Like I need some fucking Australian motherfucker on my case. What? I'm supposed to be scared? Because you got a giant for a fucking babysitter?'

John stared back at him, their noses millimetres apart, and then with both hands shoved him back, hard, right in the middle of his chest. Bortado stumbled backward, then dropped to the ground. John ran forward and grabbed his hair and punched him three times hard in the face.

'Kyle Warner' … punch 'was a good' … punch 'man' … punch.

Then he hauled Bortado to his feet and punched him again in the stomach and as he doubled over another in the kidneys.

Bortado dropped to the ground, writhing on his side, snuffling, nose broken.

John crouched down, Bortado scrabbled away, still on his side.

'I'm not Australian, I'm English. London. Literally the other side of the world from each other you ignorant fuck.'

He stood up and kicked a load of stones at Bortado.

'Nice!' Reed announced happily, and picked Bortado up like he was nothing at all and dropped him in the chair, then went back to the car, this time returning with a long-handled shovel, a big, wicked-looking axe and the Ruger John had taken off the guy in the diner.

Bortado stared at him, he was afraid now. John could see it. The man had no idea what was going on, the bravado fading fast along with the sneer. Whatever was happening to him now, it wasn't in the rules. Suddenly everything had become very serious for him.

Reed then removed his t-shirt, and folded it neatly before laying it down on a rock.

In the flesh he was even more impressive, literally all muscle.

'I don't want to get blood on it,' he explained to John, and then walked across to Bortado, who was watching him, eyes wide with fear.

John understood, and stepped back.

It was Reed's show now, the man who had to deal with drunken, violent, trained to kill soldiers who were hellbent on putting him into the ground and doing it on a daily basis.

'So Tyrone, you mind if I call you that? Tibor makes you sound like an asshole. Which, incidentally, you are, but I'm hoping that now is the time you wise up,' Reed stood right next to Bortado who cowered away, head down.

'What the fuck is this? What's going on, man? What do you want?' he whimpered.

'We know everything Tyrone. We need to talk to Pinsky. And before you start bullshitting with a "who?" or "I don't know anyone called that" we know all about it. So, like I said, wise up. This is only going one way, and that's my way. So learn fast.'

Bortado whimpered but said nothing, looking at John for help but saw no comfort there, just a cold stare in return.

Reed slapped him round the face and twisted his head so he was looking right at the soldier.

'Ok, ok. So, wow you're a tough guy, right? That's what everyone at the precinct seems to think anyways. Now, I wouldn't have never believed it, seeing as how John here handed you your ass in a cup without him breaking a sweat, but that's where we are. It don't matter. But you are in it now. Believe it.'

Reed looked over at John, who nodded, then picked up the axe and walked over, and spoke slowly and clearly.

'You see Tyrone, we aren't here. Nobody knows about us. We can do what we like, and I know what Tom can do, I've seen it for myself, and you will too soon enough. Forget the cops we followed here, they don't know us. They are just doing their jobs. They don't care, they get paid the same as normal. Nobody gives a shit. To be frank Tyrone, you're fucked.' John laboured the last word.

'Fucked,' Reed agreed. 'And what's one more body buried in this desert anyway? Place is full of them.'

Still Bortado said nothing, just sat with his head lowered, blood dripping from his nose.

Reed tutted loudly then picked up the shovel.

'Ok, well, we gave you a chance. Like I care, let's make a start. You better get digging. You ain't going back to the precinct. Or the city, even.'

He pulled Bortado out of the chair, who squealed and tried hopelessly to resist then threw him down next to where the land began to rise up at the edge of the basin.

Bortado rolled onto his back and then sat up looking at the two men, scared and confused. Reed handed him the shovel, then removed the Ruger from the back of his trousers.

'It's simple. Dig,' he said.

Bortado stared up at him, disbelieving, tears forming in his eyes. He shook his head.

Reed racked a round into the chamber.

'You're a gangster, right? A hard man. Tough guy. You know how this works, you know what's gonna happen. Like John said, we ain't here, and you sure as hell ain't either. So, get on with it, I don't wanna waste all day.'

Bortado looked around helplessly.

'No, no, I can't be doing this. No, this ain't right, I don't know nothing.'

'You wanna talk to me about right? Fuck that. I knew Kyle Warner. Dig.'

Defeated, Bortado sobbed loudly then shook his head violently.

'Ok, ok! Fuck! Yeah, yeah, I know Leo Pinsky,' he mumbled.

John moved closer, but let Reed do his stuff, laying the axe on the floor next to the big man, obviously, so Bortado saw it.

'Yeah, we know. You ain't telling me nothing. Dig,' Reed poked him with the Ruger.

'Wait! Just, wait. Jesus. ok, I'll answer, but I don't wanna die out here man. It can't go like this man, please. You can't, they got my record, I was at the precinct man, my attorney was with me.'

'I wouldn't give that any more thought. You were never at the precinct. PD were looking for you sure, but you hid your candy ass away. And your attorney won't be back, that's dealt with.' Reed lied.

Bortado just carried on staring up at Reed.

'Fuck,' he started weeping, unable to help himself.

'I'm not asking again. Dig. Or I'll take some fingers off, maybe a foot, to start with. Axes are perfect; quick and quiet. Apart from the screaming, that is.' Reed picked up the axe and rested the head on the dusty ground, leaning forward on the handle.

'What do you want to know! I told you, I know him! Jesus!' Bortado was really tearful now.

Reed sighed and bent forward.

'Ok, so talk. Where is he?'

'LA, he went to LA. Yesterday, he was in a hurry, listen I don't know him real well, I just get him some shit sometimes, that's it, you know how it is.'

'Not really. You got our friend killed.'

'No! No way. He called me yesterday, he was pissed. I don't know why. It was in the morning. He never fucking calls in the morning. He needed somebody to take care of some people, that's all he said. Offered me ten grand to find a guy, man. I was like, yeah, ok, I can do that. And that fucking chickenshit Ryan owes me, so I thought of him. All I did was get them together, I didn't know nothing about what it was and I didn't fucking ask, I swear. But like, I hooked them up, and then he says it was four people man. I didn't know nothing about it and I didn't fucking ask. But Leo didn't have all the shit he needed or something and he was pissed about it. He rang me again, said he needed some guys to set up a tail. That's all I fucking know. So I made a call, it didn't sound like no thing, and told Leo to get in contact. Then he rang later and he was pissed, real pissed, he hadn't heard nothing. He couldn't reach my guy, and I couldn't fucking get him neither.'

'Yeah, we met Lucky. He needs to change his name,' Reed told him.

'Where the fuck is he? We never heard nothing from him.'

'He's considering a career change.'

'What's in LA?' John asked.

'Jesus, I don't fucking know. You gotta listen to me, Leo, he comes and goes, sometimes I don't see that motherfucker for months. But he's been here a while, and he got business in LA. Been back and forth, but I don't know anything about it, I don't know nothing!'

'Ok, ok, so how does he get hold of you?'

'My cell, he calls my cell.'

'And how do you get hold of him?'

'I call him.'

Bortado stared upward, realisation dawning.

'Look man, he'll fucking kill me.'

'Fuck that. You do not need to worry about that. You got way more pressing problems. Give me the number.'

'It's on my cell. The cops got it. Fuck.'

Reed looked at John.

'Got any questions?'

'Just one. Where in LA, it's a big city. He got a place there?'

Bortado wiped his mouth with the back of his hand, blood and tears dripping off his chin. It was over, he was broken.

'I don't think so. Maybe. I don't know, I never asked. We ain't buddies man, I'm serious.'

'Ok.'

Reed pulled Bortado to his feet, who stood fearfully looking from one man to the other.

'So, what now? I helped, right? I gave you everything! Please!'

'Yeah, yeah.'

Reed snapped on the handcuffs and pushed him back up the slope toward the car, grabbing his t-shirt on the way. John picked up the shovel and the axe, then looped his arm through the back of the chair and followed them.

Reed drove back to the cruiser, the cops looked in the car as they approached but said nothing about the state of Bortado, just climbed in the cruiser and the two cars headed back to the police precinct. As they pulled up John turned around in his seat to Bortado, making him flinch.

'You owe us. You get that, right? You're still breathing. But here's the clincher, if you say one word to anyone about what went down out there and who we asked you about I will hunt you down. It doesn't matter to me where you are, whatever jail you end up in I'll find you. I do not give up. And trust me, it will be painful. I will really hurt you.'

Bortado believed every word, staring back at him and moaning.

They climbed out the car and pulled Bortado from the back. One of the cops handed Reed some baby wipes who used a generous amount to clean the worst of Bortado's face, then they went back into the custody area.

The sergeant at the desk looked up.

'Oh Christ,' he started, but was interrupted by the cop with the baby wipes.

'He fell on the steps sarge, it's not as bad as it looks.'

Nobody mentioned there were no steps and Bortado was led away, John and Reed waited for the captain

He came in with Judy following.

'Well?'

'He's pretty much confirmed what we already guessed, but he has told us that Pinsky's in LA. Judy, can you authorise a trace on his mobile number? Bortado's got it stored in his phone,' John led Judy over to the counter.

'Yeah, I can do that, what's the number?'

The captain ordered for Bortado's phone to be brought out, he actually had three of them on him when he was arrested. They were in separate evidence bags, and all locked.

'No problem,' Reed said, and picked up the bags. The sergeant took him over to Bortado's cell, and a couple of minutes later he reappeared holding up a mobile. There was a number under the contact name 'Russ L'.

'What do you think?' Judy asked, writing the number down.

'It's all we got,' John told her.

'Shit. Please stop fucking saying that,' Reed pleaded.

John looked at him and shrugged.

'Well …'

Judy disappeared to make the arrangements, and John asked the captain to collect the minivan from the Mirage, and get it searched it for a tracker.

They needed to get back to LA. Fast.

Chapter Twenty-Eight

Sammy parked up just off the beach close to the pier and got out the car.

She breathed in the sea air and looked around.

So far, she liked Santa Monica. She had driven right through it, following Ocean Avenue from the south. There were a lot of hotels. Big and small, cheap and expensive. All the major brands plus many more and lots of motels too. This wasn't going to be easy.

But if John Smith was here, she would find him, she was determined.

She walked over to a taco stand and bought lunch, then sat on a wall looking out over the sea while she ate. She found herself thinking about Jason, and wondered what he was doing right now. He was probably exhausted by the twenty-three-year-old stripper, although she suspected that would be over and done with. She never thought about him much, it was the proximity of the sea she decided. They had their honeymoon in Hawaii, and had holidays in Mexico and Bali.

He probably had moved on, maybe another stripper she thought, but who knew.

And who cared. She had work to do.

She finished the taco, dropped the paper plate in a bin and stood up.

An hour later she had discovered a major flaw in her reasoning. She had anticipated her usual fresh-faced appealing approach where a receptionist would be all too eager to help was the way forward, it rarely failed.

'Sure, yes we got a Mr John Smith staying here, would you like me to call his room?'

At the start, this had worked in the smaller hotels and motels to a certain extent, some staff even recognised her, although there was no sign of Mr Smith. But for the big-name brands, nothing doing, and this had become even tougher as she made her way further into the Downtown area. Here, all she would get is a surly stare, or a smirk, wherever she went.

She would have to change tack.

She found a coffee shop where she could sit and look out at least a dozen hotels, and hoped for the best. Maybe he would even come in for a drink. She hadn't spoken to Moran yet, and had hoped for something definitive before she had to. But she hadn't known the area, had never been here before, which was a mistake for sure. She should have done all the research she could first, but all she had been able to think about was getting out to Santa Monica.

His picture was etched in her brain, she would be able to spot him she knew it.

She just needed luck to be on her side.

Since she had her fair share of it in the past, surely it wouldn't let her down now.

***

The flight from Vegas to LAX took a little over an hour, which was nothing, although it had to be a lot more for Reed who was squashed into an economy seat. John gave him the aisle but it was still way too small, although he didn't complain. There was no other seating available on the flight, which was the first they could get out the city.

They had wiped down the Ruger and the SIG Sauer carefully, then dismantled them and deposited the parts in wastebins all around the strip before they had left for the airport.

Reed had spent most of the time waiting to board talking on the phone, and now as they hustled out of the airport with only carry-on luggage they got straight into an olive green sedan being driven by Louisa Gonzalez.

'So how was Vegas?' she asked, as she moved her way into the typical LA traffic.

'Not so great, since you ask,' Reed replied, looking sideways at her from the passenger seat.

'Ok, well, I've done everything you asked. So, we headed for Santa Monica?'

'Yeah, I guess so, that all good John?'

'Yeah. I need my mobile, there's an urgent call I need to make.'

The journey was short, but took a while, stop/start pretty much all the way, but finally Louisa pulled into the car park in front of the Ocean Vista hotel.

They all got out the car and John went straight up to his room with the other two following. He checked his mobile. Seventeen missed calls.

One from Judy.

Sixteen from Ron Keane.

He showed it to Reed who shook his head.

'That motherfucker,' he rumbled.

John pressed a button and held the phone to his ear. Keane answered immediately. John told him they were back and Keane said he would head over as soon as he could.

John hung up and looked at Reed.

'Ok.'

They went back down to the ground and John took position, sitting on the low wall that ran between the car park and the pool. Reed and Louisa crossed to the opposite side and sat down against the side of the building that contained the bar and the Chinese restaurant, hidden from view when anyone pulled in. John sat patiently waiting, a slither of blue sea visible between the buildings on the other side of the wide street.

Twenty minutes passed, and then a pale blue Ford pulled into the car park, moving slowly. Two men inside, a heavy white man driving and a young Hispanic man in the passenger seat. They were looking all around, scanning the area and then settled on John, both men fixed on him.

They stopped the car about twenty feet away.

John didn't move. Out of the corner of his eye he spotted Reed moving fast around the other side of the car park and Louisa standing up.

The Hispanic man opened his door, and climbed out of the car, still looking at John.

The white man was talking on a mobile phone, and then he also got out of the car.

John sat still. Watching.

The white man made a decision. He glanced around and took out a gun from his pocket, a battered CZ 75, and held it loosely, then both men started walking forward.

John stood up.

The men stopped for a second, then continued moving toward him.

John stepped forward.

The white man raised the gun.

'Now ....'

And that was all he said. Reed grabbed him from behind, lifted him in the air by his shirt and threw him hard down on the ground. John went for the Hispanic man who was so startled he froze, then turned to run but John was on him and wrestled him backwards against the car.

The Hispanic man was wiry and strong, he grabbed hold of John's hand and started to twist but John pushed back as hard as he could and then kneed the other man hard in the groin, making him exhale loudly and double over, releasing John's hand.

John stepped back and kicked him solidly in the face, then grabbed him by the hair and slammed his head down onto the ground, finally stamping down on the fingers of both hands, crushing the bones.

He stepped back and looked over at Reed who was standing over the other man prone at his feet. Louisa appeared and shook her head.

Reed shrugged.

Together they bundled the men into the car and Louisa parked it at the back and then joined Reed who had walked over to where he had originally been.

John retook his position sitting on the wall.

Keane arrived twenty minutes later. He was on his own, and spotted John but drove right around the car park first. John could see his head twisting from one side to the other as he circled. Eventually he parked and slowly walked across. He fixed on a rueful smile as he approached John.

'Man, I heard about Kyle. What the fuck?'

'Yeah,' John looked back steadily, noticing Keane's eyes constantly flicking all around as he wandered slowly toward him, clearly looking for something. Or someone. Most likely two men.

When he stopped walking Keane wouldn't meet his eye.

'I was calling you John, couldn't raise you.'

'I know, I left my mobile here.'

Keane frowned and looked up at the hotel. Behind him Reed and Louisa were approaching fast.

'Where's Judy and Tom Reed?' he asked.

'Judy's still in Vegas. Tom's .... behind you!'

Reed grabbed hold of Keane and wrenched his right arm high up behind his back and pulled him around. Keane starting protesting and was staring wildly around; looking for help that was not there. John pulled his gun from the holster on his belt then Louisa rolled up next to them in the car and Keane was bundled onto the back seat. John climbed in next to him and Reed got in the front and they pulled out of the car park.

'What the fuck is going on?!' Keane demanded angrily rubbing his arm.

'We know Ron, we know,' John told him, passing the gun to Reed.

'Know what? What the hell do you mean?'

'What we know Ron, is that it's you.'

'What's me?'

'What's you? You're the leak. It's been you tipping them off all along.'

'What?'

The car slowed at traffic lights and Keane immediately pulled on the door handle, to no avail.

Reed twisted around to look at him.

'Child locks. I'm real surprised you tried that, you being a cop and all. This is an MP car, we're used to carrying people like you,' he said.

'Undesirables,' Louisa added.

'Yeah, good word. Undesirable.'

The car pulled away again; Louisa put her foot down and Keane leaned forward, frustrated.

'So, Ron, what was it? Money? They promise you everything you ever wanted?' Reed asked.

Keane sat back and looked at John, an expression of total innocence on his face.

'Listen, I don't know what this is, but you are wrong.'

John shook his head.

'No Ron, we're not. Me and Tom knew there had to be somebody talking for sure when two guys tried to jump us on the way to Vegas. I already suspected there was a leak. But those two were stupid, bad planning. You should have given them better advice, or maybe found a couple of guys who knew what they were doing. But what we didn't know was who. After that we were very careful, but Kyle still got killed. Only one way that could happen.'

'I was as shocked about that as anyone. I don't know what you're talking about.'

'Yeah, you do. And the SIG? That was clever, that looked good, the whole escapade in the bar. We were trying to work out who it was, and I never even considered you.'

'This is bullshit. Let me out. I'm a police officer.'

'In name only. And you're going nowhere, you've got questions to answer. Give me your mobile.'

'Fuck you. I ain't done nothing wrong.'

'Mobile.'

'Like I said, fuck you.'

John sighed deeply, then suddenly launched a powerful punch right into the side of Keane's face, making his head bounce hard off the window. In shock he raised his arms and John grabbed his hand and began twisting it, making Keane shriek out. Still holding the hand John reached into his jacket and pulled out the phone and threw it into Reed's lap, then pushed Keane backward and let go.

'Jesus Christ John! You damn near broke my fucking arm. And my fucking jaw,' Keane whimpered.

'You deserve worse. Kyle dead and Judy next. But who are you working for?'

'I'm a cop! You know that! What do I got to tell you?'

'Is it 1-Too? Or is it the Russian? Both?'

Keane stared at him, and John saw something, a flash of indecision in the man's eyes. He knew one hundred percent they were right about Keane.

The traffic thinned as they moved out of the city, Louisa sped up.

'Where the hell are you taking me?' Keane asked.

'Somewhere you'll be out the way. No chance of tipping anyone off.' John replied, knowing exactly where they were going but not at all sure how Reed had arranged it.

'You're wrong. I'm telling you, this is crazy. I done nothing!'

'Save it,' John told him, and looked out of the window.

Keane continued to protest his innocence, which fell on deaf ears and he eventually became silent, breathing heavily, an angry bruise forming on his face.

They drove on for more than half an hour, and then a huge army base came into view on their right. Louisa slowed, and turned off the main road and headed toward it. The entrance was up ahead and she stopped at the barrier under a massive 'United States Army – Fort Indigo' sign, holding up her pass, and Reed had his out too. The MP looked closely, then at the two men in the back, turned and walked into the hut which was positioned in the centre. John could see several soldiers inside.

Reed got out the car and walked around to stand by the front wing. A sergeant appeared and the two men shook hands, Reed gestured at the car and the sergeant nodded, passed over a sheet of paper and raised the barrier. Reed got back in the car and Louisa drove through.

The road they were on ran straight for a few hundred metres, pristine grass on either side and white painted kerbstones. They went straight over at a crossroads, approaching a large building with a rose garden set in an island in front. Louisa turned left, and now they could see dozens of similar looking buildings, single and multiple storeys, all in neat rows laid out in front of them down a shallow hill. There were military vehicles and soldiers moving around everywhere. Louisa turned right, and rolled to a gentle stop among more of the same olive-green sedans and a couple of Humvees.

The building they were in front of was a plain red brick building, three storeys high. The entrance was a glass door up some steps, but there were no signs anywhere to say where they were. Louisa and Reed got out the car and she opened the door for John. Reed pulled Keane out and keeping a vice-like grip on his arm, pushed him up the steps and through the door.

Inside it was a spotlessly clean lobby, with stairs rising up from the centre. There was a female MP sitting at a window set into the wall at the side looking curiously at them. She said something into the room behind her and a second face appeared, this time a fresh-faced young corporal.

'Hello sir,' he called out and disappeared, then emerged from a door just down from the window.

'What the hell am I doing here,' growled Keane nervously.

'You'll see,' Reed replied easily.

'This him?' asked the corporal.

'Yep. We ain't searched him.'

'No problem. This way.'

With Reed holding one of Keane's arms and the corporal the other John followed them across the lobby toward a heavy door standing open marked 'Detention' and down a set of stone steps he hadn't noticed when they came in. At the bottom was a steel gate which Louisa unlocked, and they went into a square room with nothing than a desk, a blackboard on the wall with a list of numbers and a pair of locked gates set in the opposite side from where they entered.

'Right,' said the corporal. 'Jacket and shoes off please.'

Reluctantly Keane did as he was asked. Louisa checked both shoes carefully and went through the jacket, producing Keane's wallet and badge along with a notebook, cigarettes, spare clip for his gun and a pager.

'Empty your pockets on the desk please, and your watch,' the corporal asked.

'Wait …' Keane began, but Reed pushed him across.

The corporal stood looking at him.

'If you don't do what he says, I'll just hold you upside down and shake all the crap you're carrying out,' Reed said mildly.

Keane sighed, and slowly took everything out of his pockets. Loose change, keys, a lighter, then removed his watch. The corporal placed everything into a plastic bag and folded the jacket neatly, placing the shoes and the bag on top. Then he expertly patted Keane down.

'Clear,' he said, stepping back.

Reed looked over at the blackboard, which was empty other than one to six written down on the left.

'Good job we didn't get rid of this down here,' he commented.

'Yeah,' replied the corporal, who walked over and wrote '*Keane R* – Captain Reed' next to the number five.

There was a buzz and a beep as the pager went off, a red light now flashing. John looked at it through the plastic bag and Reed made a note of the number that was displayed.

'It'll be a burner, but I'll ask Judy to check it anyway,' John said.

Louisa opened the left side gate and the corporal pushed Keane through into a short, wide corridor with cells on either side. Simple design, just thick bars running from floor to ceiling. All identical. A gate on the left. Bunk with two beds against the back wall, toilet with a low partition at the side in the corner.

'No fucking way. I been real patient here. But this bullshit, it ends now. Gimme my phone I've had enough of this shit, I got work to do,' Keane countered, standing stock still in the centre, looking around at everyone.

'Corporal,' Reed said in reply, and the corporal opened the gate set in cell number five, which was the last one down on the right. He stood patiently, holding it open. Reed pushed Keane hard, and he staggered forward and John shoved him into the cell. The corporal slammed the gate closed and locked it. Immediately Keane started banging on the bars and shouting to be let out.

'Let's go,' Reed said, and they filed out, through the outer room and up the stairs, Louisa locking all the gates as they passed through.

Once back in the lobby Reed produced the sheet of paper he had been given by the gate sergeant and asked John to complete a couple of details and sign at the bottom. It was an application for a temporary pass. John did so and Reed disappeared into the office.

Louisa directed John to some seats at the side, then Reed emerged with a laminated pass on a lanyard and placed it reverentially over John's head.

'Ok. Let's leave him to blow off steam, he ain't bothering nobody down there anyhow, and he can shout as loud as he wants but nobody gonna hear him. We don't never use those cells much, normally only the ones on this floor that are a lot newer. Come on, let's go get some lunch,' Reed said and the three of them left the building.

Chapter Twenty-Nine

Incredibly Yann Voorhees had made it all the way up the stairs to the top floor. To the sheer amazement of everyone who was there he was now standing on the narrow footbridge that spanned the yard, forlornly scanning the area with binoculars. Sal, Rico, Rolf and Greg were watching him with interest to one side.

Below them they could see Pinsky stalking around the expanse, looking in the warehouses and talking animatedly on his mobile phone.

Voorhees stood up straight and put down the binoculars on the railing.

'I do not like this. I do not like this at all,' he said ominously.

'What's up Yann?' asked Sal.

Voorhees produced his mobile from somewhere within the folds of his gown and looked closely at it.

'It's too quiet. This phone was always ringing. Always I was being told to this, or that, or asked questions. But ever since he got here,' he nodded down at Pinsky, 'now I don't hear nothing at all. Nobody is calling, nobody.'

'What does that mean? And what were you looking at with the binoculars?' Rico asked.

Voorhees fixed him with an icy stare.

'I'm checking the perimeter, what do you think? I'm waiting instructions but not one person has rung me. Nothing at all. Yesterday I was told everything would soon be in place, but not a word today. And I got a feeling something is not right, and

I'm wondering why. Since he got here it is all him. Something must be happening.'

He looked down at Pinsky again.

'Coincidence? I don't think so.'

He looked at Rolf and Greg.

'You arrived here with him. He say anything to you?'

The two men shook their heads

'No. I got a call when we were on the way, telling us we had to meet him. So we did, he was waiting for us. But we don't know him, and he never said nothing, just that we had to get over here,' Greg replied.

Voorhees nodded.

'Yeah, basically I got the same call. I'm not happy.'

He looked at them, frowning.

'Hey you guys don't have any other cellphones, do you?'

Again, the two men shook their heads. They had switched them off and given them to Yann as soon as they first arrived, it was expected as far as they knew.

'Good, that's good, we had some problems with that before,' Voorhees told them.

'So, what are we doing Yann?' Sal asked.

'Waiting, I guess. But I do not fucking like this at all. Anything could be said, we don't know.'

Pinsky was still talking on his mobile, which clearly angered Voorhees.

'I don't get it. Why's he getting all these calls? I ain't heard a fucking thing,' he spoke bitterly.

'Is … does this mean Leo is in charge now Yann?' Sal asked quietly, saying what they were all thinking and expecting an explosion.

But Voorhees continued staring down at Pinsky below and shrugged.

'I got no idea Sal, but this shit is fucked up, and nobody is talking to me.'

'You want me to try and find out? Like, I could kinda casually mention it, you know.'

Voorhees looked pityingly at Sal.

'What you gonna say Sal? 'Say, sorry Leo, but we was wondering. You want a coffee? By the way, you the boss now?'

Sal shrugged.

'No Yann, not like that. I'd ask him straight out what's the story? How long we gonna be here? I'd tell him, Yann ain't hearing a fucking thing so's I'm asking him. I'll tell him we got no idea what the fuck is going on. He can take it how he wants I guess.'

Voorhees pursed his lips and continued watching Pinsky.

Finally, he spoke without shifting his gaze.

'Maybe. Yeah, what the hell, yeah you do that Sal. Why don't you all go. Give it a try.'

**

John and Louisa sat in the officer's club as Reed's guests. Reed had changed into his uniform and seemed even bigger somehow. The place was busy, there were over five thousand soldiers at Fort Indigo.

John was enjoying the cheeseburger, which Reed and Louisa were also eating when suddenly they both stood up.

John wondered what was going on and looked around, realising that another officer was standing behind him. He turned and looked, another big man.

'Sir, this is John Smith, he's the man we briefed you on,' Reed said quickly.

John stood up and the two men shook hands.

'Nice to meet you John, I'm Major Alex Turner,' the man spoke quietly with a distinct southern twang.

'Major Turner is MP XO for Indigo,' Reed explained.

'Good to meet you too Major, and many thanks for all your help,' John said.

'No problem, mind if I sit?' Turner asked.

'Not at all,' John slid the chair out next to him and the big major dropped into it.

He laid his cap down on the table and looked appreciatively at the food.

'Cheeseburgers are great here ain't they?'

'They really are,' John smiled.

'So, I got to ask; what's the plan here?'

'Yeah, listen I know you're breaking a lot of rules here. A civilian being locked up and everything, you have gone the extra mile that's for sure,' John said earnestly.

The major held up his hand.

'You don't need to think about that at all. I told Tom exactly what was said to me; look after the army. If that means we got to be host to someone without a uniform for a while then so be it. Soon as Tom spoke to me it made sense, all I ask is that nothing happens I may be asked to explain later. That's it. We keep a clean unit here, and I'd like to keep it that way.'

John nodded.

'I get it. The problem is we can't risk him making contact now, and we took him by surprise so they can't know where he is. We aren't telling anyone, even the LAPD.'

'Ok, that's good. Trust nobody. You heard Major Hayter's billet got searched, right?'

'Yeah, Tom said.'

'As you can guess that is a royal pain in the ass, it means that someone here on this base is no good. Lot of people here, and no clue to where to start.'

'You got cameras anywhere?'

'Not really. There are some in the stores and the armoury, but none near the billets. All we got is who might have seen something. We are asking, but nothing so far.'

'Can I take a look?' John asked, expecting a firm 'no' in response.

Turner gave him a long look, then smiled.

'I don't see why not,' he replied.

They finished eating, and then then left the OC. Luisa went back to the MP office, so John followed Reed and Turner down the hill. The camp was huge, almost a small town. Eventually they crossed a side street and up some steps into a long building lined with small windows. They walked down a corridor with rows of identical pale blue doors on both sides and stopped next to number thirty-seven. Reed produced a key and they went inside.

It was just a basic small room, like a budget motel. Toilet with a shower. Single bed, wardrobe right in front of the door, chest of drawers, footlocker and a small desk. John looked around but there wasn't much to see, all of Hayter's belongings had been removed.

'Officer's quarters?' John asked.

Reed nodded.

'Enlisted men don't have a bathroom. Fact is not many officers above lieutenant use them. Major Hayter seemed happy enough but he had no family,' Turner told him.

'Was the door locked?'

'Yeah, it was. But the truth is the locks in these buildings are really for show only. A six-year-old could open up one of these rooms if they wanted, the same key probably fits about seventy-five percent of the doors in these buildings. But there are never that many expensive possessions in these rooms. Hayter didn't own a computer or nothing. He did his gambling on his cellphone.'

John looked under the bed and on top of the wardrobe, and then slid the drawers out.

'We checked everywhere, there really was nothing to miss. Believe me, even the toilet cistern and around the shower. He didn't seem to own hardly anything that wasn't given to him by the army. Except for his car, and we searched that too,' Reed explained.

John looked at his watch then nodded.

'Ok, you're right, nothing to see here. Let's go and talk to Ron.'

They followed the road back up to the MP station, and went inside. The corporal appeared, and they went back downstairs, through the gate and then the next one and into the corridor.

Keane was lying on the bunk, he jumped up when he saw them. Reed opened the cell gate and stood in the opening, blocking it, staring hard down at Keane, who looked around and then fixed on Turner who was standing watching.

'Right Major, I hope you have come to clear this shit up. I got work to do, I'm a police chief.'

Turner looked back impassively, and said nothing.

'Ron, you need to come clean. It's not too late but we are fast running out of time. We all know that the killing hasn't stopped, it's obvious they haven't found whatever it is they are looking for. So, you may as well start talking,' John said.

Keane walked forward and gripped the bars.

'You've cooked up this conspiracy shit and you ain't listening. One more time. I do not know what you are talking about,' Keane pronounced the sentence slowly and deliberately.

John rubbed his face.

'Oh yeah, you do. You've been with us and then feeding them from day one, it's clear as day. You can keep on denying it, while we know that it's just more lies but all the time you do you stay down here.'

'Yeah? Let's see what my attorney has to say.'

Reed laughed out loud.

'Attorney? What the hell? You know where you are, right? It's exactly like John just said, you're staying here, you go no place until we get some answers. Attorney, Jesus,' Reed snorted.

Keane's cheeks flushed angrily.

'This is bullshit, you can't keep me here. I know the law.'

Turner spoke for the first time, impassively looking at Keane.

'Law? You, of all people talking to us about the law? Right now, this is the law. Nobody has any idea you are here. You belong to me. I've heard everything, and I believe that you are guilty as charged. So my advice Mr Keane, is you do as you are asked and start talking, because you can rot down here for all anyone cares. These cells are here for dangerous prisoners, soldiers who have committed serious offences and are awaiting transfer to Leavenworth or Midwest. But they aren't used anymore, there's a whole new system in place. Army finally went digital. And that means you are on your own, and you are staying where you are.'

John glanced at Turner gratefully, it was obvious his words had an impact.

Keane turned and sat down on the bunk.

'I don't know anything. This is all horseshit. You're not listening,' he mumbled.

Reed stepped back and closed the gate, and turned the key in the lock loudly. Turner walked over and spoke through the bars.

'We'll leave you to think about this. You'll get food and water. It will be put under the gate. My officers will not talk to you. We will be back tomorrow. You're not in jail, not like you know it. There is no recreation, no yard time, no TV, no library. No nothing. Just you, in this cell. This is going to get old, and fast.'

Turner spun round smartly and led the way up and out. Once they were back upstairs in the lobby Reed looked through the window in the wall and assembled his team.

'Ok, you know this man is not in the military. This is an ongoing situation, everything is unclear right now. He is to be fed and watered as normal, but I want two taking it in every time. Leave the tray and go. No talking, don't even look at him. Nobody goes downstairs on their own, and nobody speaks. Apart from chow time the only people that go in are major Turner, me, Sergeant Gonzalez and finally this man here, John Smith. Whatever he asks for, he doesn't get. If he starts making a real fuss and it gets out of hand, call me. Do not enter into conversation at any time. And finally, if anyone shows up here that shouldn't be anywhere near this place, put them straight into a normal cell and let me know. Am I clear?'

The men and women who surrounded him agreed.

'Good. I will keep you all informed.'

He looked at John, who nodded.

'Ok Tom, let's get back to Santa Monica.'

***

It was turning into a long day, and Sammy was starting to despair. She really hadn't considered what she was hoping to achieve by coming over to Santa Monica. Had she really believed she would just wander into a hotel and he'd be sitting in the lobby?

There were so many hotels and motels, and so many people. The place was very busy, and there was no clear distinction where it started and ended. She had been based in the same location for close to four hours, and had to finally admit he might easily have walked past a hundred times and she could have missed him.

She hadn't really gone into any detail of her plans with Simon, and she realised that was a big mistake. He had lived in LA his whole life, and knew it well. He would have been able to advise her, although it would probably have been 'I think it's a waste of time, Sammy.' But he would have at least offered to come down here with her, he would have done everything he could to help.

Feeling defeated she dug her mobile out her bag and called him.

As anticipated, he listened to what her plan had been with disbelief, but it wasn't in him to criticise her.

He told her about a rooftop bar at the edge of Venice Beach, which had a good view of the area and a lot of visitors went there, but other than that he didn't really have any suggestions.

Rooftop bar? What the hell, why not? A glass of wine would go down well, she told herself. Then she would find somewhere to stay.

Simon told her he would head down there later, maybe they could get dinner. As cheerfully as she could she said that it would probably be a bad idea and hung up the phone.

She thought about Moran and the way he had looked at her, and the obvious threat in his voice when he told her that against what he believed she could go and do it. How was she going to explain this to him?

She sighed so heavily as she got out her seat that everyone around her stared, then walked slowly back down to her car. She sat there for a while watching the sea, wondering how the hell she could have been so optimistic when she had first arrived here.

She shook her head, twisted the key and the engine fired up. She rolled toward the car park exit and spotted the low fuel light was on.

Typical.

Chapter Thirty

Reed had changed back out of his uniform and they headed over to Santa Monica in his own car, a battered and faded Mustang that he was clearly very proud of. They didn't talk much on the way, both men were starting to really feel the tension in the situation. At any moment they expected to hear of some new event that had occurred, and both felt powerless to prevent anything further happening.

Reed believed Keane would crack sooner rather than later, to be locked up on his own with nothing and nobody around would do it. But privately, John wasn't so confident. Keane had completely fooled him, if it hadn't been for the gun he would never have completely believed that the man was the leak, and he wondered how long this had been planned, and how deep Keane's involvement really was. John didn't believe he would be right at the top, but he could well be a lieutenant for all they knew.

Judy had been confident but in the end struggled with the track on Pinsky's phone. It turned out that he was on record with the FBI, Homeland Security and the CIA. He was connected to the Russian consulate in Washington, and listed as an attaché to the Military, although his exact role was unclear, as was why he was spending so much time in Las Vegas and Los Angeles. He had served in the KGB, and as far as anyone could tell had no criminal record, either in the US or Russia. So, because she could not confirm any crime only suspicions Judy's request was immediately denied, which put even more pressure on John and Reed to get something out of Keane.

But Judy had kept them informed; she wasn't giving up. She was determined, doggedly looking to avenge not just Kyle Warner but also the innocent women at the Metro station so began persistently calling in favours all over the FBI, and had discovered that Pinsky had been detained as part of a raid on a house in Baltimore several years previously. The local police were watching a man suspected of people trafficking and had built up a solid case. The story was this man had thrown a party at his home, and many girls, some of them very young were seen entering the property, shepherded inside straight out the back of a van, everything being recorded by the watching surveillance team. They had seen enough, so called in reinforcements then stormed into the building armed and ready; everyone was taken away for questioning.

Pinsky was one among many others detained and had been held for some time but eventually released, mostly due to his diplomatic status but the police had found he was carrying an unlicensed Beretta handgun and a small amount of cocaine on him. He had denied all knowledge, claiming they must have been put in his jacket when the house was raided but his fingerprints had been found on both.

Baltimore PD had a dilemma; they weren't used to dealing with suspects like this. He appeared to have no connection to the target they had been working on other than being invited to the party. In fact at the time of the raid he was not found with any of the girls. Despite the weapon and the drugs he was released, but flagged as 'a person of interest'.

As soon as Judy found this out, she cranked up the pressure and eventually her own chief relented and went to bat for her.

The trace would go live later today or first thing tomorrow all being well, which was great news and both John and Reed felt their motivation returning on hearing the news, getting the call just as they entered Santa Monica.

Although neither man was particularly concerned for their own safety they had decided to get out of the Ocean Vista, but opted to stay somewhere else in the immediate area. Money was no problem, there was a massive wad burning a hole in Reed's pocket, so the first thing they did was to settle up and move along the beach to where the bigger more mainstream hotels were. They had a scout around while they were at the motel; the car the two men had arrived in was still there as was Keane's, both were unlocked so they quickly searched them, finding another mobile phone in the door pocket of Keane's car. It was an old, basic model, and they could see a lot of missed calls, from many different numbers. One of them looked familiar so John called Judy, she confirmed it was the number they were starting the trace on.

Even more confirmation to what they already knew, even more ammunition, but John knew that Keane would continue to deny everything.

He stuck the phone in his pocket then they followed the crowds and checked into a nondescript Marriot right on the seafront.

John went up to his room and stood looking out the window. His room wasn't on the shore side, his view was of the wide street, a big petrol station right opposite. He watched the traffic and considered what to do next.

The problem was obvious, they were moving too slowly. They needed a backup plan.

They had Judy and the phone trace, and they had Keane locked up, which should surely be enough to pin at least Pinsky down, and hopefully others whoever and wherever they were but what they didn't know was how long it would take and how long they actually had before something else happened. There could be any number involved anywhere in the city and once they found whatever it is they were after they would probably disappear.

The biggest issue for John was he kept coming back to Keane, and the man's refusal so far to admit anything or to talk. He would have been through this many times before, from the other side of the table. He would know all the tricks and have seen delaying and avoidance tactics over and over. The only ace they were holding was keeping him isolated and unable to contact anyone, but he was holding out so far. John couldn't help wondering if this would last, everything was taking too long. He could feel his brain slowing, becoming bogged down. There were too many uncertainties, and it felt like he was totally reliant on things he had no control over.

He turned and left the room, crossing the corridor to knock on Reed's door, who opened it looking out blearily as if he had been asleep.

'Come on,' John said, 'there's someone we can talk to. I think you might enjoy this.'

They went downstairs, and as they crossed the lobby one of the receptionists hurried across from behind the counter. John remembered her from when they had checked in, and smiled. She had gone very gooey over Tom Reed, lots of smiling and attention. If Reed had noticed he hadn't said or done anything; maybe he was used to attention like this from women. Probably, he was handsome in a clean-cut way and was of course, absolutely massive. She was young, early twenties, pretty and skinny with a mass of light brown hair. She ignored John completely, asking Reed if his room was ok, did he need anything, could she sort out dinner for him? Reed thanked her politely then they left the hotel. John led the way back up to the wide four-lane road, and then started back toward the Ocean Vista but keeping on the shore side. There were several turnings off and he checked each one carefully, before heading down and then stopping outside a dark, narrow shop front.

Reed looked closely.

'What is it?'

'It's a bar,' John replied and pushed open the door. Inside it felt even smaller than last time with Reed next to him but he made his way to the back ignoring the looks from the few customers and then down the steep stairs. At the bottom he paused and then knocked hard on the door.

'Fuck off!' was the immediate response from inside.

Reed chuckled and then shoulder barged the door so it crashed open and John stepped back into Billy Wheeler's office again. Billy was sitting on the sofa with a blonde woman who was hastily rearranging her clothes.

'Hello again Billy,' John said amiably as he stepped to one side to allow the woman to rush from the room.

'Fuck do you want?' Wheeler replied, eyes fixed on Reed who was stooped down in the low office.

'Well, we need to have a talk. And it would be best if you didn't start fucking us around. My friend Tom is getting a bit fed up of people doing that.'

Wheeler stood up, and then sat straight back down again.

'Talk? I guess so. What the fuck we got to talk about?'

'Ron Keane,' Reed replied.

'Keane? That motherfucker. I knew he was going to cause me shit, I fucking knew it. That asshole has been after me for years, he was the same with my dad. Well fuck him.'

'I was kinda hoping you'd say that,' John replied.

'What the fuck do you need?' Wheeler was just resigned to whatever was going to happen.

'I need you tell me what he asked you about the gun.'

Wheeler confirmed what they already knew, and John couldn't see the point in any violence so they left the bar and walked back up the four-lane to sit at the counter by a long window in the petrol station opposite the hotel. They were drinking, or trying to, stewed coffee that tasted like it had been brewed in the 1980s. John watched the activity on the forecourt outside, and saw a red BMW convertible pull up and an attractive woman step up to the pump and produce a credit card. She looked vaguely familiar.

I wish, he thought to himself.

He saw her insert the card, push some buttons, frown, repeat the process, frown again and put the card away then turn to walk over toward where they were sitting.

She was really cute, perfect.

She glanced over at the window as she approached, then glanced again, eyes wide.

She's spotted Tom, though John, smiling inwardly. He hadn't believed his eyes either when he first saw him.

She was standing still staring in, and John suddenly realised it was at him. Not Tom. He looked behind, but there was nobody there. She recovered, and hastened to the door, pulling it open and then she was standing next to him, still staring.

'You're ... you're John Smith!' she said breathlessly.

He looked at her, and smiled. He knew hardly anybody in Los Angeles. Maybe this was his lucky day. He didn't get many.

'I'm sorry,' he replied. 'I don't think we've met.'

'I'm Samantha King. Sammy. And yes, we have met.'

John shook his head, still smiling.

'I'm sorry, I think I would have remembered.'

Sammy tilted her head to one side, which made her look even prettier.

'Outside the Metro station. I was the woman who asked you if you had anything to say. I present news and current affairs for LA Plus.'

John stopped smiling. He recalled the crush outside the station, the press, the crowds and the police vehicles everywhere, and the camera in his face. The determined woman with the microphone, he hadn't taken a lot of notice but this could easily be her.

'Right. Yes, ok,' he said shortly. 'Nice to see you again.'

He turned back to face Tom Reed, but Sammy wasn't going to give up that easily.

'I've been looking for you John. I really want to talk to you. I heard what you did. On the platform I mean, and I know you are working with the police. Helping them.'

John looked at Reed for help, but he clearly had no idea about how to deal with this either and just wore an exasperated expression on his face.

'I suppose you just heard right?' Reed asked her.

'I know how it looks. But yeah, sometimes people talk to us. Look, we aren't saying anything we've been asked not to. I'm just interested in John.'

Sammy stepped closer.

John sighed.

'Listen Miss King. Samantha. I don't know what you've been told, but I'm just a tourist. Yes, I was in the subway and yes, I do remember saying something to a camera when I came out but thankfully that was the end of it, so now I'm just hanging out in LA with a friend of mine. Happy to be here. Enjoying the sunshine.'

John had spent many years of his working life lying and believed he had it down to a fine art but now, sitting next to Tom Reed who knew exactly what was going on his words sounded flat, unbelievable.

But Sammy nodded.

'It's just Sammy. Or Sam. Well, ok, maybe you and I could just talk about what happened? It must have been terrifying.'

'Listen Sammy, I'm not interested in being in the public eye. It doesn't suit me, I'd rather fade into the background, just be anonymous. I'm sure you do a great job, I will check out your show but that's just not me.'

Sammy smiled, a winning, heart melting smile. John could feel himself being pulled in.

She looked at him carefully. She liked what she saw, she had been desperate to find him and here he was, and he was interesting. Suddenly what Moran thought seemed even less important. She glanced at Reed.

'Wow, he's big. He your bodyguard?' she asked.

Reed raised his eyebrows.

'Round the other way, miss. It ain't me doing the protecting. People don't wanna mess with John, trust me.'

Her mind was whirring. Now she didn't need Jimmy Frost any more, which was a relief. She moved closer still.

'Alright. Maybe we can go for a drink then?'

John looked at her carefully. He knew what he wanted to say for an answer. She was a ten, easy, and she seemed lovely.

'Maybe. But no interviews, no microphones?'

She smiled wider.

'Of course. Look, I'm new in LA, just trying to make a name for myself. The whole Metro thing, it's a big deal, massive.

Nothing like that happened here before. Yeah, ok, so I want your story. But it can wait. Truthfully, I needed something to make an impact and I've been spending every waking second hoping I can find you and guess what? Now I have and of course you're just a guy, same as all of us. Right now I'm way the hell out the office and down by the ocean, and for the first time in too long I feel free.'

John nodded, and smiled in return. He would love to go out with her. But this wasn't a good idea. Unfortunately.

'I'm sorry. It's great to be asked, and any other time it would be yes. But I can't, right now. Maybe another time.'

Sammy stepped back, she wasn't used to hearing no from men. But she was a professional.

'Ok, I understand.'

She dug in her bag and passed over a business card.

'I would really appreciate a call before you leave, just to hear your side. My editor is kind of a pain in the ass, and this has been such huge news.'

John took the card and slid it in his pocket. Now he felt bad. He had been asked on a date by this crazily cute woman and turned her down. All he had to do was not say anything.

'Well, I better go. I've been told about a rooftop bar, just along from here, close to Venice Beach. I'll be there later, around seven I guess, if you change your mind,' Sammy said.

'Ok, thanks. Nice to meet you, take care.'

Sammy went to the cashier and paid, then John watched her fill her car and drive away.

Reed looked at him and shook his head.

'Man, you are crazy. She is hot.'

'Yeah, I know, but what with everything going on right now it can't be a good idea. Whatever I think or want doesn't matter. You know what I mean. I don't need my name in the papers.'

'It doesn't have to be that way John, and we can't do any more than we are doing anyhow. It won't hurt to take a couple of hours off you know.'

John sipped some awful coffee and gazed out the window.

'Maybe, I suppose,' he said finally. 'Yeah, ok, why the hell not? It's just a drink, it's not like anything's going to happen, worse luck. But you're coming too, right? Make sure I don't blunder into something.'

'Yeah, why the hell not. I'll ask Cindy.'

'Who's Cindy?' John asked, wondering if Reed knew the area. He'd never mentioned it.

'Chick from the hotel.'

'Ah, you did notice. I wondered.'

'I notice everything John. Always.

Chapter Thirty-One

After a couple of hours of walking round and round the yard with his mobile phone glued to his ear Pinsky came back in and demanded gate keys.

Rico handed his set over without a word.

'You off out then?' Voorhees asked.

Pinsky stood still and stared at him. All the men were together in the main room and every one of them apart from Pinsky wished they were somewhere else. The tension was getting worse and worse.

Unsure of himself and desperately regretting saying anything, Voorhees blinked and looked away. Pinsky was clearly annoyed about something, it had to be down to the phone calls. Something must have gone wrong, but what was it? It couldn't be Voorhees or his team, they hadn't done anything. And nothing had been said about what they were supposed to be doing next ever since Pinsky set foot in the yard.

'I am needing to ask your permission fat man?' Pinsky sneered.

'No, of course not,' Voorhees replied hurriedly. 'It's just that, I've heard nothing. Nobody is telling me nothing. I don't know what's going on. Yesterday I was told that there would be a new plan, action would be starting, and …'

'And? You? Ready for action?' Pinsky interrupted, still staring.

'Look Leo, me, Sal and Rico, we been together a long time, we've done …'

'You have done nothing!!' Pinsky snarled. 'Nothing. And I had to come here to get it done. I am the client I think. I am the customer. You work for me. All we see is mistakes, you waste money and time. It was simple. Easy. A child could do it.'

Voorhees said nothing, just stood there uselessly. Pinsky wheeled round and stalked out, stomping down the stairs. Rico walked over and looked out the window, watching the Russian move fast across the yard.

'He didn't take a car,' he commented mildly.

Voorhees breathed out slowly and sat down. He chose the old office chair which was pushed against the glass partition wall and it made a loud groan, looking as if it would topple over under the weight but just about managed to stay upright.

'I tried,' Sal said, speaking to everyone. 'I asked him, you know, if he was running things now. I said I just wanted to know, I told him that me and Rico had been here for months.'

'And what did he say?' Voorhees asked.

'It was fucking scary tell the truth. He laughed. Asked me if I wanted the job. He told me it wasn't just us fucking up, some shit went wrong yesterday that wasn't down to us. For once, he told me. Something about Vegas, I don't know what he was talking about. He asked me if that was all we were worried about, who was the boss. He said I was lucky that was all that was on my mind and that I wasn't dead like all the others, he said we were useless, he was amazed we were still here.'

'I kinda know about Vegas. But it must have got worse. And he blamed me for that, I suppose?'

'No. He didn't. He didn't say nothing about you. He said none of us knew what we were doing. That's why he came. He told me everyone was very disappointed, there are a lot of angry people. He said we had pissed off everyone. But not only us. Others had fucked up too.'

Voorhees sighed. That explained why nobody was talking to him. Whatever was said now, Pinsky would be blaming him. He was supposed to be in charge.

'I have called. But they tell me they are waiting for their contact on the inside, they need some information, they should have had it by now. So there is a problem, but they wouldn't say what. Not to me anyways. They say to wait for their call, don't contact them,' Voorhees told them almost apologetically, looking around the room as he spoke.

'He said something else,' Sal said quietly. 'Just before he came in.'

'Oh yeah? What now? Don't tell me, I'm a fat turd and it's all my fucking fault.'

'No. He said if we don't get it done in two days none of us will get paid. Or more likely, we'll all be dead.'

***

They found the rooftop bar easy enough. Cindy knew exactly where it was. When they had returned to the hotel Reed had casually asked her if she fancied going for a drink with him that evening and she had practically fainted with excitement, John was genuinely concerned for her.

'I get off at seven,' she managed to say eventually.

At a quarter to eight they set off, Cindy leading the way. She had really made an effort, she looked gorgeous, putting everyone around in the shade. Reed definitely noticed.

The bar was on a corner, four storeys up, above some shops and apartments, next door to a trendy boutique hotel. There were a couple of doormen around a street entrance with a lift inside, they took one look at Reed and stepped out of the way.

Once they reached the roof level, the lift opened out into a fabric covered square lobby area with a greeter desk opposite. There were two pretty young girls in matching violet minidresses who fixed on beaming smiles and asked if they had made a reservation.

'Er, no,' John replied.

Both women looked doubtful.

'We're very busy,' one said, but by now they could see out onto the roof itself which was covered in chairs and tables. It was pretty crowded, but they could see Sammy sitting in a corner close to the edge right above the street. She looked up, spotted them and waved.

'It's ok, we're with her,' John replied and they walked across. The managed to salvage enough chairs so they could all join her at the table, and Reed ordered for everyone from a waitress.

'I know you, I love your show, and you're so beautiful,' gushed Cindy to Sammy, who smiled and looked suitably embarrassed.

'You staying near here?' she asked John, rapidly changing the subject.

'Yeah, just down the street,' he replied, cagey as ever.

'Thanks to Google I'm booked in a place somewhere around here, I guess I'm gonna need to find it at some point, but it can wait,' she replied.

They all made small talk, and Cindy successfully commandeered Reed's attention so John and Sammy were left to chat about pretty much nothing, which suited them both.

'I wasn't at all sure you'd show up,' Sammy told him.

John shrugged.

'Well, it's not like I had a better offer! And I need a night off, truth be told. It's been a bit crazy, if I'm honest.'

Sammy looked at the still bright red slowly healing scar on his head.

'Well, at least you got something to remember LA by.'

John laughed ruefully.

'It's not that bad, but it has been full on, so I'm taking a break for the evening. We both need to.' He nodded at Reed who was leaned over, listening to Cindy who was talking excitedly to him.

Sammy glanced over.

'Now that is a big guy,' she commented.

'Yep. But he's a hundred percent. I like him a lot.'

'So you just met?'

John looked at Sammy carefully. She was a journalist, and he really hoped he wouldn't have to spend the evening dodging questions or even avoiding talking to her.

'Why did you ask that?'

Sammy blushed.

'Jeez, I'm sorry. I didn't mean it like, well you know. I just wondered.'

John held up a hand.

'Ok, ok. Yeah, we met recently. It's nothing interesting.'

'I suppose asking your line of business is not allowed?'

'I could tell you, but …'

'You'd have to kill me,' Sammy finished for him. They both laughed.

'Not quite. It's complicated, and we just met. But what about you, you're a reporter right?'

'Yeah, actually I've been in TV forever. But new here in LA. And it hasn't been a great start. I kind of banked everything on finding you, and I can't believe I just bumped into you. I'd given up. Christ knows what I was thinking.'

She smiled, and John smiled back.

They relaxed, and Sammy told him about herself. John was happy sitting there, on the roof in the warm evening with a beautiful woman, a cold beer and the sounds of the sea. They sat there for a while, just chatting, no awkward questions then went for dinner, paying way too much for not nearly enough food in a bistro, ending up in another bar right on the seafront, then back to the hotel, where keeping his distance didn't seem so important anymore for John.

Chapter Thirty-Two

Rico was woken by Sal shaking his shoulder. He opened his eyes slowly, there was very little daylight coming in through the windows so he can't have overslept.

'What? What is it?' he mumbled.

'Shhhhhh … shut the fuck up man, listen!' Sal replied urgently.

Rico sat up. He could see Greg and Rolf were also awake, and watching Sal.

Rico listened, then heard voices. Yann and Leo. Arguing.

'What time is it?' he asked.

'Nearly half-six,' Greg replied.

So that was weird straight away. Yann was never awake before ten or often eleven. Which was why they always ate breakfast so late.

Rico climbed out his sleeping bag and made his way cautiously over to the stairs, but he still couldn't hear very clearly. The other two men were two floors below and all he could really make out was Leo cursing. It was obvious Yann was being accused of something but it was impossible to tell what.

Rico pulled on some trousers and barefoot made his way silently down the stairs, with the others following. He walked across until he was immediately above the stairway down to the next floor and stopped again. Leo's voice was much clearer now.

'This is why you fail. This is why. Because you do not act. We give money, lot of money, and for what? You do nothing. Just sit around on your fat ass waiting for someone else to do it.

I said all along you were useless. I was right. I should just shoot you like a broken horse.'

Rico turned and looked at the others. What did this mean? Suddenly he felt like a weight was lifted. Surely all this was over now. They wouldn't be carrying on. Leo was ending it, and if that meant Yann was out the picture then so what? Nothing had worked out so far for Rico; he had very little money and no place to live but he would sort that out. He always did. He needed to get away. The four men grouped at the top of the stairs and as they talked in whispers about what they should do suddenly there was a noise and there was Leo, standing just below them, watching, strange smile on his face.

'Come,' he told them, and turned walking back down the stairs.

They all looked at each other and then slowly followed.

Yann was sitting in the office chair which had been pulled into the main room. The big metal trunks were lined up on the floor, all open. They were full of guns and ammo, but both Rico and Sal knew that. Next to them was a small suitcase, standing open, empty apart from a couple of stacks of hundred-dollar bills.

Leo took position behind them.

'You see?' he asked.

Everybody moved closer. Neither Rico or Sal knew about the cash, but they had no idea what they were supposed to be looking at. Rico looked over at Rolf and Greg who had never seen inside the trunks either so they would be even more confused. Rico turned to watch Yann who was sitting very still, paler than ever and sweating.

In the end Rico turned to Leo.

'Yeah, we know about these. I mean about the guns, not all that money. But we been together a long time. We been practicing a lot. All these guns work I can tell you that for sure. Sorry Leo, I ain't sure what to say.'

Leo shook his head.

'No. Is not the point. For weeks, we wait. I hear "They are not ready, they need more money, they do not have the weapons." This is what I hear when I ask what is happening. Because is a deadline, no? We have to get this done, you are being paid to deliver. And all the time, is this. It does not change. But we fight in Chechnya with lot less I promise you. So what have you been doing?'

Rico didn't know what to say, and he knew Sal wouldn't either. All they had ever done was what they were told. Yann was still just sitting silently.

Leo picked up an AK-47 from the trunk, and then bending down at the other one snapped a clip into place.

'I should just kill you all I think. But especially this fat piece of shit,' he sneered.

Rico held his hands up.

'Look Leo, we're as much in the dark as you are here ok? We didn't know anything. We were told nothing. We were cooped up in this shitty tiny apartment for months, and now here. But I got no idea what is going on.'

Leo turned to Yann.

'So, is you, which I knew anyway.'

'Leo, I just follow orders, I don't get to make the decisions. Yeah, ok, so things don't go to plan. But I was told to wait and I waited,' Yann spoke fast, bright eyes staring out.

'Bullshit. I said from the start the fat man is useless.'

'Leo, I've been doing this a long time, and I …'

Leo stepped forward and shot Yann in the head. The big man jerked back in the chair, and then seemed to hang, motionless, before sliding slowly backward making the office chair squeak on its wheels, the front set up into the air. The men all stood watching. Eventually it stopped and then toppled backwards, sending Yann slumping to the floor with a loud thud.

Leo tore down the temporary curtain and tossed it over the dead body.

'Right. Now we do it right. Let's go, we eat breakfast and then we go to work.'

**

John woke up, wondering where he was. Then he remembered and turned over quickly.

Sammy was asleep next to him.

This was not supposed to happen.

He'd had a few beers last night, normally he wasn't much of a drinker. But that was no excuse, he knew what he was doing and he liked her. He thought hard about what had been said and was confident he hadn't told her anything that he shouldn't.

But this was still dangerous. They didn't fully understand what they were up against yet and they had no idea who or how many were out there looking for them. Bringing Sammy into it should never have happened. Innocent people had been hurt before down to him.

It was nearly half-past seven. He climbed out of bed and took a shower then got dressed.

'Morning,' Sammy said sleepily looking at him with one eye open.

She was gorgeous. No other word for it.

'Morning,' he replied.

'I need to get my stuff, it's in my car,' she said.

'Ok.'

She pulled on her clothes quickly and together they walked down to where her car was parked and collected her bag, then returned to the hotel where she showered and got herself ready for the day.

John walked over and tapped on Reed's door. The big man was already up and dressed, ready for action. John glanced around the room.

'No Cindy?' he asked.

'She went about ten minutes ago. Got to get changed for work. Listen John, I made the call, Keane had a difficult night, which we both kinda suspected I guess. He wants to see us. Major Turner refused to speak to him, and he made sure nobody else has either.'

John nodded.

'Ok, good, see you downstairs in five.'

The three of them sat at a table near the window for breakfast. All very friendly but Reed was agitated, keen to get moving and desperately trying to talk about anything other than what they were doing. John could see that Sammy was wise to that and asked her what she was going to do.

'Look, it's ok. Seriously. I'm just gonna write that I met you, and you're just a guy. No names. I'm not even gonna try and explain how the hell you managed to blow those guys away.'

John considered. He liked Sammy and could appreciate the difficult position she was in. He decided to at least try and help.

'Ok. Look, this is all I'm going to say. And this is it. Nothing else. Yeah, I was there. I managed to turn one of their guns on them. I'm no hero, I just did what I could. I'd never seen them before, and I couldn't understand what they were saying. The police got there really quick. Tom is not involved at all. And please keep my name out of it. Please. But you can print that right?'

Sammy smiled.

'It's not printed, but thank you. Yes, I can say that. And yeah ok, I don't have to mention your name, although of course I want to.'

'Thank you.'

'But look, what can you tell me about yourself?'

John looked steadily at her. She had spoken openly about her life but as usual he had given away very little. This was nothing new, it was how he always was. He ate some food, drunk some coffee and thought about it.

'Ok. I was in the army. But a long time ago. I don't need to say anything else.'

Sammy pouted.

'Can I at least take your picture?'

John sighed.

'Fine. But not here. Somewhere anonymous ok?'

'Ok.'

They finished up, then collected their stuff and checked out, Cindy appeared and didn't want to let Reed go but after some carefully selected words they managed to leave eventually. Sammy took hold of John's hand as they walked down the street. They got to her car and John allowed her to take a picture on her mobile phone, the background was just the side of a red brick building. Then they said goodbye, Sammy pushing another card with several phone numbers on it into John's hand.

They watched her drive off, then Reed set off back down the street moving fast.

'Let's go talk to Keane.'

Chapter Thirty-Three

General Morgan was sitting very still in his office in the Pentagon.

He was supposed to be preparing documentation for a forthcoming budget meeting regarding a large-scale training exercise that was planned for later in the year but he had not even started it. He was permanently distracted and worried, and it was getting worse.

He knew things had gone wrong, but he wasn't able to fathom how badly.

There had been a text message late the previous night. Very simple, but very clear.

He had to make a call. Another number he had never seen before.

Which he really didn't want to, but he had, and it was spelled out for him.

The overall target was now likely to be missed, but worse than that would be the fallout. Unless he could pull the mythical rabbit from the hat, which he knew all too well he couldn't.

He was supposed to be the one giving instructions. He was in charge, he was here, in the Pentagon, the entire US army at his disposal but the reality was he was ineffective and powerless. Not for the first time he sincerely wished he had never got involved, had never agreed to be part of it but the fact was it had all gone too far.

And people were dead.

Because of him.

And now he had to get out of this. Bur he had no idea how, and the thing that was keeping him awake at night was how scared he was; terrified of the people who were supposed to be working for him.

***

Reed had his foot down, the old Mustang really moving on the way over to Indigo.

'So, Keane had a bad night, what went on? He start making a load of noise?' John asked.

Reed shrugged.

'It sounds like he was making all sorts of threats at first, then he started ranting and raving, demanding to speak to the major. But the guys are well used to assholes, they ignored it, and they didn't go down there, just as they were told. But if they were in the outer room they could hear him.'

'Doesn't sound so bad,' John said.

'No, but this morning when they took his chow in, he had been hitting his face on the bars. Got some bruises and some blood. Insisting on seeing the major.'

'What, is he claiming brutality? Who is he going to do that to?'

Reed shook his head.

'I don't know.'

'It won't make any difference anyway. It's pointless. Nobody even knows he is there, it's all deniable. We could stick him back at the motel and he could say whatever he wanted but nobody would believe him.'

'I guess, but we put him there to get some answers. If we end up having to let him go then this has all been a waste of time. Major Turner has refused to see him, but I know he is gonna have some concerns.'

'Tom, he'll know none of your guys would pull any shit like this.'

Reed sighed.

'Yeah, I know that. But how does this leave us?'

John considered, watching the scenery outside fly past in a blur, the traffic actually moving for once.

'Listen Tom, we'll go and see the major first. Then let me speak to Keane. Alone.'

They reached Indigo and drove through the gates, John's pass meant they went in without any delays. Reed made his way through the camp and pulled up among the Humvee's outside the MP building and they walked in.

The same corporal came out to meet them. He didn't look overly concerned.

'How bad is it?' Reed asked him.

'It's not much. He's banged his nose and his forehead, but my guess is he knew what he was doing and didn't really want to hurt himself too bad. Scared of the pain most likely, don't blame him for that.'

'Ok, so no sutures?'

The corporal smiled.

'No sir, nothing like that. I cleaned him up a bit. He was whining and saying he needs the hospital.'

'Yeah, I bet he was,' John said.

'Good work,' Reed told the corporal. 'He eaten since he's been in?'

'Yes sir. He ate dinner and also breakfast.'

'Can't be that bad. Jesus. ok, so we are gonna go talk to the major.'

'Yes sir.'

Reed led the way up the stairs and then stopped at a frosted glass panel door. US Army Military Police Executive Officer was stencilled across the top and below in the centre Major A. Turner. Reed tapped on the glass and waited.

'Come in.'

They walked in.

Turner was sitting behind a grey steel desk, with two beaten visitor chairs in front of it. There was a tired filing cabinet in one corner and nothing else. On the desk was a big old ancient computer monitor and a grubby keyboard, some paperwork scattered across the top and two telephones, one black and one red. Turner looked up at them, smiled and said hello.

John looked around the room. Like every military office he had ever been in. It took him back.

'Feels like I should salute,' he said.

Turner chuckled.

'No, we don't do that in here. We got other things to worry about, save that for the parade ground. So you hear about Mr Keane?'

'We heard.' Reed told him.

'I'm told it's nothing, but we got to keep it in mind. I don't want any shit being thrown at my guys downstairs.'

'Understood,' John replied. 'I'm going to talk to him.'

'John wants to go in alone,' Reed said looking at the major.

Turner pursed his lips and tapped them with a pencil, thinking, then shook his head.

'I'm sorry John. I can't allow that. Captain Reed needs to be with you at all times.'

'But …' John started but Turner interrupted him gently.

'I am sorry. But this is the only way we can do this. John you were in the military, and you have to understand that we are all way out on a limb here. I can't risk anything blowing up in our faces. So, Tom goes where you go. Look, I got no problem with any of this, and you seem like a squared-away guy to me. But it's my decision.'

There was nothing John could say. Turner was absolutely right. And saying they were out on a limb holding Keane in the cells for however long was putting it mildly.

'You're right Major. Sorry for asking. I just thought I could play the "I'm not in the army so the rules don't apply" card, maybe intimidate him. Although Tom is way more suited to scaring anybody than I am.'

Turner laughed.

'Yeah he is a big bastard alright. But a gentle giant. Lucky, nobody outside knows that, so they all think twice when he walks in the room for sure. I get what you are saying. Captain Reed will use his judgement and I trust him. If he decides to use the lavatory while discussions are taking place then that's how it is. Fair enough?'

'Definitely. And thank you Major.'

'I think we all should be thanking you. But let's get this done and go for a beer, you can get another cheeseburger. The OC is actually ok here, unlike every other base I been on.'

'Good deal.'

Turner sat back and rubbed his head with his hands and then looked at them both in turn.

'Well alright. Let's get this done.'

'Thank you sir,' Reed said and walked briskly across the room and opened the door. John nodded at Turner and followed the big man out.

'Let's get a coffee first,' Reed said. 'Keep him waiting another twenty minutes.'

'Yeah, good idea. Fuck him if he can't take a joke.'

***

Leo bought everybody breakfast in McDonald's. Nobody really knew what to say, while Yann Voorhees would not be missed, for both Rico and Sal this was now a completely new start, and it was very clear that Greg and Rolf were equally unsure of what they were doing.

They sat around a table, painfully bright sunlight streaming in through big windows.

Leo ate fussily, looking closely at the food and making disparaging remarks about everything, while the others consumed their meals silently.

Rolf picked up a discarded newspaper from the table next to theirs and started reading, anything to be distracted from the position they were now in.

He looked at the headlines on the front page.

'Police Hunt Intensifies', and the following article had quotes from senior policemen on the hunt for the metro terrorists and suspects for the murder of the army major.

Leo followed his eyes across to the paper and smirked.

'Yes, that went well I think didn't it? Good way to use resource. Or I must say good way to LOSE resource. Was waste of time. Like everything so far. All wasting time. There is nothing to show. But now it change. Now it is real, we get what we want.'

Rico looked at Sal then sat up straight.

'Look Leo, we were paid to follow orders. That's it,' he said deliberately, at least relatively safe sitting in the restaurant.

'Or not paid,' Sal interjected, feeling the same way.

Now was the time to speak, in a busy restaurant, surrounded by witnesses.

Leo wiped his mouth and sat back, sipping coffee. He looked at them steadily.

'Paid? Paid for what? You have done nothing. There is no point saying to me, I am not your employer. I am the customer.'

'What Sal is saying Leo, is that we have been here in LA a long time now. We haven't been paid, apart from a few bucks here and there. We've done everything we were told to do. Everything. And there is a lot of cash back there, we saw it. My guess is that's our wages, and it would be good to earn some money. And not just us, Greg and Rolf too,' Rico told him earnestly.

Greg nodded appreciatively. Leo would surely not start anything in a crowded McDonald's.

'I will see,' Leo replied dismissively. 'But first you have to prove yourselves. Today we start. Then maybe tomorrow, next day, we all go home, and if I get what I want then you are paid. All of you.'

He stared out across the table, eyes glittering. Rico suddenly wanted to go home straight away.

He swallowed and nodded, thank drank his own coffee slowly, hoping to stay right where he was for as long as possible.

Chapter Thirty-Four

They had coffee in a small but very busy place a couple of buildings along from the MP headquarters. It was still the army, but done out just like a high street outlet and a lot cheaper. Reed was back in his uniform. John wondered where the hell the army got his shirts.

He got the call at last from Judy.

She was excited; the trace was live, finally. They should start to get results within a couple of hours, everything had to be passed through the FBI tech team first, and she had found some solid information on Pinsky. John's phone beeped as soon as he hung up and he looked at it.

A reasonably recent picture of Leonid Pinsky along with some basic history.

Hi spun the phone round on the table and slid it across to Reed who studied it and frowned.

'Jeez, ugly bastard!'

'Yep, hopefully we will be meeting him the flesh before too long.'

This was welcome news, and now they finally had it they didn't stay long, both men wanted to get on with it and soon they were back at the MP headquarters, the corporal pulled open the door then they walked down the steps and he unlocked the gate at the bottom.

They entered the outer room, everything was quiet. John walked across so he could see into the cellblock, but there was no sign of any activity. Reed joined him and then signalled to the corporal who unlocked the gate and stood back.

John walked in first, down to the end and looked in through the bars.

Keane was sitting on the bunk, staring at the floor. When he heard the footsteps he looked up, saw it was John then dropped his head again.

Reed walked across and shook the gate.

'Morning Mr Keane,' he said brightly.

Keane stood up slowly.

He had livid bruises across his face and a cut on his forehead. He looked tired and dishevelled, and a lot older than when he had been locked up yesterday.

'So what now? This crap over? I get to go home?' he asked wearily.

John smiled.

'No Ron. You're not going home, and you're not leaving here. Not until we get answers. So you could be in here a long time, but maybe by now you've realised how serious we are. You need to understand that we know Ron, we know. Not everything, but we have put it together, and we have even more now from when we banged you up in here yesterday.'

The corporal appeared with two wooden chairs, set them down facing the cell then walked out again.

John and Reed both sat down.

'This is such bullshit,' Keane muttered, shaking his head.

'It could be I guess, it could be,' Reed replied. 'But the facts speak for themselves. Everything that happened is down to you, you were the one doing the talking. But we know that. What we don't know is to who exactly.'

Keane shook his head again.

John studied him, Keane looked away.

'Leonid Pinsky?' John asked.

Immediately Keane's eyes widened and he blinked fast.

And it's a hit, thought John. One-nil.

'You scared of him Ron? Is that what this is? You been up against him before? Payback maybe?' Reed asked.

Keane sat down heavily on the bunk.

'But he's not the only one, right?' John spoke gently.

Keane sighed, muttering something to himself, then sat very still, looking up at the ceiling.

John and Reed waited, saying nothing. This was the crucial point; Keane had been there all night and would have worked out by now that this was all there was. Nobody was going to help him. Nobody even knew where he was.

'You're wrong.' Keane said eventually, but lifelessly, no conviction.

'No Ron, we're not. And we're quite happy to say goodbye, come back tomorrow,' Reed replied.

'This is all bullshit, I swear, I've done nothing, I was right there with you, just trying to solve the damn thing,' Keane said.

'Ron, you should know. We got Pinsky's mobile number. Judy put a trace on it and it's live. She just called, so soon we will know where he is anyway. So what's best? We can just leave you here and get it from him first. Because he's got a lot more to lose, believe me. He will have no problem at all naming names, and that will change everything for you. Plus, we got your mobile from your car.'

John pulled it from his pocket and threw it on the floor in front of him. Keane stared at it. He was desperate to get his hands on it, that was obvious.

'Lot of missed calls on that thing. And several from Mr Pinsky,' John told him slowly.

Keane blinked rapidly, for a few seconds it looked as if he would burst into tears then he shook his head violently, and stared down at the floor again. He rubbed his face with both hands and whispered to himself, rocking gently from side to side. Then he stopped, sighed heavily and raised a hand.

'Ok.'

He looked up.

'Ok,' he said again.

'In your own time, talk to us,' John told him.

'If I do this, can I get out of here?'

'That depends, you know that. Once we are done I don't know what will happen, you probably got more idea. You might have to be some place where nobody can get to you, but yeah, you won't be in here,' Reed replied.

Keane drank some water from a mug on the floor.

'This was never supposed to get this far. I don't know who the main guys are.'

'Bullshit,' Reed snapped.

'No, it's true I don't. I got approached maybe two or three months ago. There is a team, here in LA. They got a job to do, supposed to be simple but getting nowhere. I don't know all the fucking details. But there's some guys in the driving seat and some hired hands to do the dirty work. Yeah, they offered me money and I took it. Look, think what you like, but you don't know. I been a cop more than thirty years and I can't afford to retire, pension or no pension. I got debts like you wouldn't believe, two ex-wives bleeding me dry and kids I don't see no more. It's all gone to shit. Back in the day there was always extra here and there but there ain't no gravy anymore. Just my shitty paycheque.'

'Start at the beginning, what did they want from you?' John asked.

'You don't know who you are dealing with. I can't believe you know about Pinsky; how did that happen? That's a dangerous fact right there. You may as well wave a flag in the air. But these guys are for real. They do not stop. I'm serious, this is way, way bigger than you think. This is just one job out of hundreds they got going on. Thousands probably. You are into something that is not going to end well for you.'

'We'll take that chance. Just answer the question,' Reed told him.

'Remember Kyle spoke about the fight? Echo Park?'

'Yeah, I remember that, we went to look at the address the guy gave. Something Perez was it?' John replied.

'That's it. I got the call then. Of course, I wasn't involved, it was all with the local guys. But they had already done their homework, somehow my name must have come up because they came to me. And I fixed it.'

'You fixed it?'

'Yeah. In the end it was just a fight, nobody got killed so all the brass want is as much shit off the books as they can get. So I made the call, told them that the guy worked for me, he was a CI, bullshit, bullshit and I needed it put away and that's what happened. Everybody's happy. Like I said, it was just a fight. And I got some cash, and they said I done good. Asked if I wanted more. And I said yes.'

'Who? Who asked?'

'I never met anyone. Not once. It was all on my cell. They change the number every call I reckon. I collect the money from a mailbox, I got sent the key.'

'But you must have a name?'

'No. Not really anyways. Sometimes I'd get a message "Call Fred on this number" or "You need to call Bill," shit like that. But it wasn't Leo Pinsky.'

'Right. Let's just say we believe you, what happened next?'

'So, I get another call. A few days later. They need something. This major based right here in LA has something they need, they been working on him but he ain't playing ball. It's some kind of big deal. There was some other guy, another soldier but he's out the picture so they need this fella.'

'Major Hayter?'

'Yeah.' Keane looked morosely around.

'Unbelievable. You had me fooled,' Reed announced.

'And me,' John said. 'What did they want you to do?'

'First, get him taken in, suspect DUI, battery, anything I could but I got to keep him away from the base. And I tried, but that didn't work, there was nothing that would stick. He got no family, no friends. Then they told me they had some lady working on it but it was no good, it was taking too long and they didn't trust her, they wanted me to keep watch. They told me the lady was in Vegas. I told them I had no jurisdiction there, but they said they were dealing with that and she would be coming to LA.'

'Deanna.'

Keane coughed.

'Yeah.'

'What did they want you to do? Arrest her?'

'No, no. Just keep an eye on her. Thinking about it I guess Pinsky was involved now, he had a different idea. Like I said, it was all taking too fucking long. They had made contact with her friend, Madeline. Made out they were working to reconcile her with her daughter, and got them to come to LA. Meet an attorney. The first time, they got caught out because the women got all excited about it and turned up the same day. So they arranged a second time, but it got fucked up again. They thought that the major would just drive them in the car from Vegas, he was always there. But for some reason he didn't go. Lucky they found out a couple of days before they would be getting the train.'

'Ok. So they set up the Metro hit.'

'Yeah. This is what they do. It's the big leagues. They staked it out then did the hit. But it went to shit, as you know. What they were looking for wasn't there and you were. So it was all a big loss. And yeah, I get the call, I got to get involved, they need all the information I can get now.'

'What is they are looking for?' Reed asked.

'I don't know. Really, I don't. I heard it was some military document or something but it was real vague.'

'Military document? What like missile codes or something?'

'No, I don't think so. I got the idea it was plans maybe.'

John looked at Reed.

'The thing is Ron, that there is a problem in all this. A big problem.'

'Yeah, there is,' Reed agreed.

'What? I'm being helpful here.'

'I've only met you a few days, but right from the start you've lied. You missed your calling, you should be in films your acting was that good. The whole time you were talking, telling them who we were and exactly what we were doing. You've lied and lied and lied. And you really set us up in Vegas.'

'Yeah, Kyle is dead and Judy is frightened half to death you fuck,' Reed growled.

John looked at him again. The big man was clenching and unclenching his massive fists. John reached over and patted him on the shoulder.

'Take it easy Tom.'

'Look,' Keane blustered. 'Look, by that point there was no way out. I was in too deep. They were pushing me real hard. I had to send the photos, but I did what I could to keep them away I swear.'

'Right. Of course. Apart from the tracker in the minivan and telling them what hotels we were in.' Reed looked about ready to snap, and if he did there would be nothing that John could do about it.

'No. no, it weren't like that. Alright, there was the tracker I admit that. But I didn't know anything about the hotels. I thought you were only there one day. Listen, they did not want you to go to Vegas. They told me to set it up with the minivan and they will deal with it. Then next day off you go and in no time at all I get the call that they failed. This was in the morning, so something had gone wrong and quick. They were in a panic about it. They asked me where you were going to be, I told them about the precinct but I didn't know you were staying overnight. I was calling you John, over and over but you didn't pick up. I spoke to Kyle in the end but that was it. They must have found the rest out themselves.'

'They didn't know where we were. But you sold out Kyle.'

'I had no choice. I didn't say nothing about Judy, I told them I didn't know where she was.'

'Bullshit!' Reed snapped, face flushing red.

'When did you speak to Leonid Pinsky?' John was starting to feel the same way as Reed, so he kept on with the questions.

'I got a message, call this number. This was later in the day, after I found out they didn't stop you going to Vegas. They never told me who, just said to do it. I called and it was Pinsky. I never spoke to him before. Or again. He asked who you were and what you were doing.'

'And you told him.'

'Well, yeah, but look I didn't go into any detail! How did you know about Pinsky anyway?'

'Tom asked somebody, who was more than happy to tell.'

Reed stood up and leaned on the bars, staring down at Keane.

'You know, when we realised it was you that was the problem, I couldn't believe it.'

'How did you know?'

'It was the gun. Kyle was dead and Judy was close to it. I was trying and trying to work it out then I looked at the Sig. No firing pin. Useless. And that was another smart play by you down in that bar. There was no way I would have suspected you. But we've been back there by the way. And Billy was really keen to fill in the gaps. So I know Ron, it was all your idea.' John told him.

Keane shrugged, unable to meet his eye.

'I don't know Ron. I should just come in there and break you into pieces. I don't know what's worse, that you're a liar, you're corrupt, you're responsible for all those innocent deaths in the Metro and Kyle, or that you're a fucking coward,' Reed said quietly, still staring through the thick steel bars.

'Or all of them,' added John, standing up.

Reed nodded his agreement grimly.

Keane at least looked ashamed.

'I never meant for Kyle to get killed. I never wanted any of you hurt, I swear. But these guys, they are like a machine and once they get going there is no stopping them.'

'Name them. Who are they?'

'1-Too. Of course. You already knew that. But you caused them a lot of problems that's why you gotta watch out. What went down in the subway caught everybody out, they want to know who the hell you are. And I can't tell them anything. So I do too, who are you?'

John ignored the question; this wasn't about him and he didn't want Keane to know anything anyway.

'What can you tell us about Pinsky? Why did he suddenly get involved?' Reed asked.

'I got no idea. He came out of the blue, I never heard of him before. All I know is that what they believed was gonna be easy has all gone to shit and there is some kind of problem with them running out of time. I meant it; I got no idea of anybody's names. I guess there is a bunch of guys pulling the strings but Pinsky? I don't know who the hell he is working for. And before you ask I don't know where he is neither.'

At that point the mobile phone on the floor started to buzz. Keane strained to see who was calling but Reed swept it up and held it to the bars.

'Important call right Ron?'

Keane stared at him.

'You just don't understand what you are doing Tom. You two got no idea who you are fucking with. Let me speak to them, I can calm it down. I can buy you some time to get away. If you don't listen to me then it's gonna be you next.'

Reed threw the phone over to John who stuck it in his pocket.

'I think we'll take the chance.'

Chapter Thirty-Five

They were back at the yard, unfortunately. Leo instructed them all to work on stripping and cleaning the guns, so that is what they were doing, pointlessly In Rico's opinion as they were well maintained anyway.

But they did, because Leo asked, and because they were afraid of him, and took their time. Each man intent on avoiding any even minor error that could bring another burst of fury to their door.

Despite his brash exterior Leo was becoming increasingly anxious, it was clear. He was constantly staring at his mobile phone and seemed to be getting more and more frustrated as the hours passed. Rico guessed he was waiting for something but had no idea what it could be.

The hours passed. Finally, he exploded, first kicking and kicking at Yann's lifeless sheet-covered body then picking up the office chair he had been killed in and hurling it out of the window in an explosion of shattered glass. The others sat watching, waiting. Leo whirled around, itching for some reaction but the four men just looked at him. Not one of them would even speak, let alone try to restrain him.

He stood there, breathing hard in and out, cheeks red which made the scarring look even worse. He pulled out a Makarov pistol and then started firing out the broken window. The others had no idea what he was shooting at. Leo emptied the clip, ejected it and snapped in another.

Rico looked at Sal.

The guns were in two large trunks, all the ammunition was in another which was open, but placed toward the centre of the room. There was no chance of getting any without Leo spotting it.

But they had the Glock.

Sal looked back then nodded upward, slowly.

'Wait,' mouthed Rico, while Leo's attention was out the window.

But as abruptly as the burst of anger started, it ended. Leo shot a couple from the new clip then stopped, raised the gun up and put it back into his jacket pocket.

'That'll be hot,' Rico thought absentmindedly as he waited for whatever onslaught came next.

But there was nothing.

Instead Leo walked over and grabbed a gun, an M16 that Rolf had been cleaning. He inspected it, worked the action a couple of times and then satisfied, handed it back.

'Beer,' he said.

'Er … pardon?' asked Sal, even more confused.

'Beer. We need to have a beer. Just one. Well, maybe two but no more. Sitting in this … whatever it is …. Is no good. We go. Have a beer. While I wait for phone call.'

Rico snapped the AK-47 he had been working on back together and stood up.

'Great idea.'

The others all got to their feet. For the first time since Leo arrived they were smiling. Leo noticed this and smiled back.

'Yes, beer is good idea. Is there bar here?'

'In the mall but it ain't great. There's a hotel down the street,' Sal told him. 'We never went in there but they probably got a bar."

'Then let's go. Is not far?'

'No, not far at all. Just the other side of the street where we had breakfast.'

'Then we walk. We do not want to be arrested. For driving drunk no!'

Leo laughed out loud. The others joined in, forced but it felt good, the tension draining.

'Right! I follow you!'

Leo grandly swept an open hand toward the stairs and they set off. Sal suddenly stopped.

'Leo, I got some money upstairs. I'd like to buy everyone a beer. You know, new beginnings and all.'

'Fine. Is kind to offer. Thank you. But be quick.'

Sal ran off upstairs.

Rico watched him go, admiration growing for his friend. He knew exactly what Sal would be getting from upstairs and he was very glad to see it. He was happy to have a beer, but then they would be back here again and things were getting rapidly more unpredictable as every second passed.

***

Major Turner sat and listened carefully, occasionally making a note on a pad in front of him but keeping quiet, taking in every word.

They were in the OC having eaten lunch, and then taken a table on their own to the side.

Turner nodded and put his pen down.

'So what do we do with him? And before either of you say anything we can't keep him shut away down there forever.' he asked.

'Turn him over to the PD. They can lock him up, and he was never here,' Reed replied and John nodded.

'Right. Look, I got to ask, before anything else happens are you both in agreement here? Is this guy telling the truth?' Turner raised the question they were asking themselves.

Reed shifted uncomfortably so John spoke up.

'I'll be honest here; I've had my fingers burnt badly with Keane and I don't trust him. I don't trust him at all. He's made an arse out of me over and over. But it does all fit, everything he has told us does line up with what's happened so far, and we were able to piece a lot of it together anyway. We know that Major Hayter loved Vegas, loved to gamble. Maybe he even had some kind of a problem with it, no idea. But he was central to all this, they want something he has. It's important to someone, whatever it is, they have been to a lot of trouble and expense. Deanna was set up to get it, whatever it is, but either failed or just didn't bother. Keane now says he thinks it's plans of some kind but we don't know.'

Turner shook his head.

'I get that, but this is where it makes no sense. Major Hayter worked in supply. He wouldn't have any documents, secrets, plans whatever. He was just a clerk really. A goddamn office boy.'

'I agree,' Reed said, 'but if we look at the facts he was the target. For sure. At first we wondered if it was Deanna, or Madeline and he was just some kind of unlucky accident. But him getting shot and his briefcase getting taken does kinda put the lid on it, and it sure dragged the army in.'

'Yeah, I know. I can see that. That's why you're there Tom. I'm not saying you're wrong I'm just trying to piece it together, if that's possible. We know why he was at the bar; he was going to pay what he owed, presumably to get this Mays off his back, now he had some cash.'

'Why did he even have a briefcase? What would have been in it?' John asked.

Turner and Reed shared a look, Reed chuckled and explained.

'Well that's another thing. Our guys spoke to the captain, the two lieutenants even the sergeants that worked under Major Hayter over in the stores. We got the story. He used to get yesterday's sandwiches from the enlisted men's mess. You can basically just take them away. He would eat them at his desk. He didn't want to use the OC. We worked that out too. He was always borrowing cash. For Vegas I guess. That meant he didn't want to go to the club because everyone would be looking for their money back. So he ate stale sandwiches at his desk just to keep out the goddamn way. Kept them in the briefcase; the sergeants told me they used to check it whenever he went to the can. See what crap he was having for lunch that day. It was obviously a big joke but there was nothing in it but his sandwiches. He must have thought he disguised it I guess. On that day, they were doing counts and he was in the uniform stores all day, then he went straight off with captain Bryant. There was no way he put anything of any interest in the case, he didn't get out of there once until he left.'

John nodded.

'Well, we know they didn't get what they were looking for anyway.'

'I just can't picture Major Hayter doing anything seriously bad. It doesn't seem likely at all. He's been here for years and years, got the dullest jacket in history. I suppose maybe he could be stealing to sell stuff on, settle his gambling debts but that isn't what this is about at all. The stores all check out, we have done two audits. There is nothing of any value unaccounted for,' Turner said.

'I'm exactly the same. I didn't know him, but he just had a day job here. He wasn't really a soldier he worked in an office, Monday to Friday. He can't have had any big military secrets, there's no way,' Reed announced.

'Right, so where do we go from here?' Turner asked, which was a good question.

John's mobile rang suddenly, loud and shrill. Most of the room turned to look. John apologised and answered it quickly. It was Judy.

The trace had come back.

John sat down again with Reed and Turner, struggling to keep the excitement from his voice.

'We know where Pinsky is. Judy got the trace. He's in some old goods yard, in a place called Hobart. Apparently it's all abandoned now.'

Turner jumped to his feet.

'Let's go.'

Back in the MP headquarters Turner walked into the office in the lobby and sat down in front of a computer in a corner. Compared with the rest dotted around this one looked almost current. He logged on, and then opened up a maps page on the internet. He did some searching and they stood behind looking over his shoulder. The yard was there, not far from a freeway with a lot of railway lines running through to one side of it. Reed got the mouse and clicked a button and then there was a picture on the screen. He moved the mouse and it panned across so they could almost see the whole space. They spent a while looking and then Reed typed in the browser and read from the screen.

'Ok, well the yard closed down nearly six years ago. Logistical improvements apparently, the transport authority got a new place further out. This has been sold, planned for development.'

They sat down at a desk.

'Nothing there but empty warehouses and only one entrance I can see,' Reed said.

'I say we get over there, take a look,' John suggested.

Reed looked at Turner who didn't look at all happy.

'This is a PD matter, you know that. We can't start kicking in doors and shit. We need to call them and let them deal with this.'

'Yeah, we do, but I think we should try and get the lie of the land. The police are going to want to get their SWAT guys there, and that doesn't happen quickly. If we are there, we can start watching.' John replied.

'He's right sir. We're not going over there armed. We can just look.' Reed told him gently.

Turner stood.

'Can I talk to you please captain? John, you wait here if you don't mind.'

Reed stood up and John watched them leave the room. Reed had to do as he was told, but John didn't so as sorry as he would definitely be to be without Tom he would go on his own. Although he had no idea how he would get there.

Chapter Thirty-Six

The hotel bar wasn't busy, it never was on weekday afternoons. Sal and Rico sat opposite Rolf and Greg while Leo headed up the table. He had pulled over a stool from the bar so he towered over them, and Rico decided he would probably feel the same even if Leo was just sitting in a normal chair.

The bar was an optimistically big space for a small hotel, with booths all the way around the edges. It was gloomy inside, done out in dark red throughout and heavy curtains around small windows. The only other customers were a couple that were sitting at a table by the door, staring at a TV on the wall and not talking.

The barman, an elderly black man with an elegant grey beard brought their drinks over on a tray.

Beers all round, in frosted glasses. To the men, this was a welcome sight, they looked great. The barman carefully set them down around the table, collected the tray and withdrew with a polite nod.

Greg grabbed his up immediately and took a long gulp, and Rolf followed. But both Rico and Sal were conscious of Leo watching their every move so waited until he had raised his glass and taken a drink. Both men had the same idea; make this beer last. Hopefully there would be a second and it was all time outside of that damned yard, Leo would surely not start anything in here.

'So, who has a story to tell?' Leo asked.

The men all looked at each other and then Sal, who was always reliable in such matters recounted a tale where he was stopped by the police in New York. He had a couple of shotguns and a pile of coke in the boot, but managed to get away with it. Rico had heard it before, it was a good story, entertaining and Sal told it well.

Leo smiled and looked surprised in the right places and Rico felt himself relaxing, if only for a short while.

***

Major Turner opened his office door and ushered Reed in, then pulled it shut.

The two big men stood in the centre of the room.

Reed knew what would be said, but stood there stoically, knowing that he would not speak out. One thing that Tom Reed did was follow the chain of command.

Turner looked at him closely.

'Look Tom, I understand. But you do know, that we can't take any civil action. We are Military Police, and that's where we start and finish. We don't get involved outside.'

Reed nodded.

'Yes sir. I do know that, of course. But I'm not suggesting we take any action. We just watch, and report anything we see.'

'Tom, you are a good officer. You'll be in my shoes and I think it could happen real soon, maybe not here at Indigo but you will be MP XO for sure. You got all the right qualities. This kind of shit could screw your career permanently and I don't want to see that.'

'Sir, I …'

'Drop the sir Tom. This ain't the army talking. It's just me and you and I'm only trying to advise.'

'Sir … Alex, you know if I don't go, John will go on his own.'

Turner sighed and leaned against his desk.

'Yeah, I do know that. I can't do nothing about that, he's a civilian and can go where he damn well pleases. And I know you like the guy.'

'It's more than that sir. We've been through a lot. I've learned a whole bunch from him. He is a good man sir, one of the best I ever met.'

'What is he going to do?'

'I think he wants to see for himself. Look, he isn't a guy to start a war. We know all about this Pinsky, he's a Russian, some kind of military attaché but seems to spend all his time either here or in Vegas. John isn't at all sure that he's part of 1-Too, and that is troubling him. He can't make the pieces fit. And we don't have any real idea how many guys he has with him, but we know they haven't got this document, plan or whatever it is and it looks like they will go to any lengths to get it. I don't want nobody else to die sir, not if I could have prevented it.'

'I understand Tom. I do. Look, I got to go up the ladder here, I can't make this decision without authorisation, I'm sorry. We got you involved to make sure that the army was clean, Major Hayter getting shot dead in a bar and his new wife getting the same the day before does not look good. Lot of men above my head were worried. And you've done a great job, hell I never had to do anything like this. But I got to make a decision, or try to I guess, and for that I need the ok. So go back downstairs, and just wait.'

'Yes sir.'

John watched Tom Reed walk back into the office. He sat down at the computer and went back to studying the map screen, and printed a couple of copies out. He collected one from the printer and together they looked closely at it.

'Not a lot around,' Reed commented.

'No, there's some industrial buildings or whatever they are on the north, then to the south a hotel, and looks like a small parade of shops. But look, it's all open in front of the gates. Nowhere to sit and wait there.'

'Yeah, and a lot of buildings on the other side of the railroad tracks. Check it out, we got apartments, offices.'

'That photo you got on the map, looks like some warehouses next to the tracks. So may not be much to see from outside anyway, they could well be holed up in one of them.'

Reed nodded thoughtfully.

'Yeah, and there's another couple of other buildings across the yard, no way of knowing where they are going to be in there I guess.'

John traced his finger along the roads.

'Looks like a freeway runs right through, and above the rail tracks, then this other road comes down here, past the yard entrance and down to those shops and the hotel. Seems like that's the only way to get there. I suppose once upon a time it would have been all trucks, good freeway access, makes sense.'

'Yeah, it would have been real busy round there once upon a time,' Reed agreed.

Major Turner appeared and gestured to the door.

'Let's go.'

Lieutenant Colonel Mathews was a cheery looking man in his fifties, red face topped by thin sandy hair.

His office was on the top floor in the big main building right at the front of the base, behind the rose garden which John had first seen when they went through the barrier. His desk was old, dark wood, and he had a furled stars and stripes flag in a corner next to the window. He was sitting comfortably, and smiled as they walked in.

'Sit down, sit down,' Mathews said.

They all took a seat, Reed dragging over a chair from one side of the large room.

'I got a couple of questions, as you may expect,' Mathews said, rifling through a small stack of papers on his desk.

'Yes sir,' Turner answered for them.

'Right. So, first, does Major Turner got to be worried?'

Reed shook his head.

'No sir. We just want to go and see the place for ourselves, watch and see what is happening, if anything is of course,' he replied emphatically.

Mathews nodded slowly, then looked across at John.

'And I got you to thank for all this am I right?'

'Well, truth be told I got caught up in it. Wrong place at the wrong time.'

John found himself wanting to say 'sir' but managed to bite the word back.

Mathews nodded again and picked up a couple of sheets of paper stapled together holding them briefly up. John's military record.

'You seen some action John. And I'm told you are a good man. And from what I've been told by Major Turner here, not that I agree completely with everything that has happened I believe you deserve respect.'

'Thank you.'

Mathews leaned forward and rested his forearms on the desk, clenching his fingers together.

'Now, I believe the LAPD will be collecting Mr Keane within the hour. So my instructions are simple. See that he is put in the car and there is no record of him anyplace, and then you and Captain Reed can make your way over to this train yard where you are to stay out the way, but some place where you are able to maintain some visibility on the area. Major Turner, you are to liaise with the LAPD from now on, please make sure that we are aware of their movements and their plans. Captain Reed, you are not to take any action that will mean questions will be asked of myself or Major Turner, understood?'

'Yes sir,' Reed said gratefully.

John smiled, he couldn't help it. He made a request.

'Colonel, Major Turner, can I suggest that you contact Chief Brady in the LAPD? He is based in the Downtown area and is fully aware of the original situation. He had his own doubts about Ron Keane I believe. I think he will be very eager to help.'

'Yeah, ok John, I will make sure I speak to him,' Turner said.

'Good. And you are to take two other MP's with you in a separate vehicle, these are to be briefed and to also stay on the perimeter. It may be necessary to have some additional verification of events at a later date, but I sincerely hope that isn't the case.' Mathews instructed.

'Yes sir,' Reed told him.

Mathews leaned back in his chair again and studied the three men in front of him, a half-smile on his face.

'Captain Reed, I have to admit I knew practically nothing about any of this until fifteen minutes ago. In fact, my only involvement was approving you to assist the law enforcement services and keep us appraised of any indications of army involvement. It was extremely important that the army was kept aware of its position. Major Turner has fully explained the situation and I would like to say that I believe you have behaved in an exemplary manner and have doubtless avoided some embarrassment to the US army. It's fair to say that some of the actions performed have not been in the rulebook and while I do not condone it, in the circumstances I believe you acted in our best interests.'

'Yes sir. Thank you, sir.'

'Major Turner, do you have anything to add to my orders?'

'No sir.'

'Well alright. Captain Reed, I suggest you take your own vehicle and that the additional MPs do not use any army transport, you are all in civvies and that you maintain contact with Major Turner at all times, am I clear?'

'Yes sir.'

'Well, good luck. And it's a real pleasure to meet with you John, maybe we can get a beer in the OC once the dust settles how does that sound?'

'It sounds perfect Colonel.'

'Good.'

Mathews stood up and John shook his hand, then the three men filed out. They returned to the MP office where Reed briefed the corporal and Louisa on what was happening and what he needed them to do.

Chapter Thirty-Seven

Colonel General Rostov slowly lowered the phone handset back into its cradle and then sat back in his chair looking at it.

He couldn't believe it.

Everything is under control they had said. Repeatedly. And as the date got closer, they had maintained the same stance. Eventually they admitted that there are problems. It is taking longer than anticipated but it will be done.

But Rostov had started to have doubts and had taken his own course of action. He was a soldier, he would do what was needed.

But now it seemed as if this had also failed, the money that had been spent was inconceivable, and he was expected to wait.

He had run out of trust.

He looked at the calendar on the wall behind him and dug out his mobile phone.

He would make a call.

Rostov did not lose.

***

Magnanimously Leo had ordered a second round of beers, much to the delight of Rico and Sal who made their first ones last as long as possible.

The elderly barman brought the fresh drinks over to the table.

'Thanks Leo, this is great,' Sal said warmly, which got a shark-like smile in return.

'Yes. I do not think that staying in that place all the time was good idea. It was feeling little bit like the prison yes?'

'Yes,' Greg agreed.

Rico and Sal did also but said nothing. Greg had only been there a day or so, they had four months stuck in the shitty apartment in Mount Pleasant to think about. Mount Pleasant? Whoever thought of that name needed shooting first.

Leo dug his mobile phone out of his jacket pocket and laid it on the table.

'I wait. For one call. I wait yesterday, and today. I am calling but am told to wait. I do not understand.'

'Er ... that's what Yann told us Leo, he said he was waiting for a call,' Rico said, unsure as soon as he finished speaking if there would be an explosion hearing it.

But Leo pursed his lips and nodded, then took a drink of his beer.

'Yann was useless. Incompetent. But yes, is possible we wait for same call. Is possible.'

'How long do you think we will be here Leo?' Rolf asked nervously.

Just as they were all thinking Leo would assume he meant the bar and as Leo went to answer the phone rang, shrill in the quiet room. Leo looked at the number on the front and snatched it up, uncoiling from the stool and stalking away listening intently with his mobile pressed against his ear.

The four men watched, each one wondering what would happen now.

Whoever Leo was speaking to was obviously somebody important, he was listening and occasionally making a comment but he was not his usual combative self, there was no arm waving or scowling.

Eventually he hung up the call and headed back over, sliding back onto the stool and taking a drink of beer.

The others waited, looking at him expectantly. He looked all around the table, for the first time he did not look at all comfortable, he seemed to be wondering what to say. Then he crossed his arms and sat up straight.

'Well, there is being a change. I am in charge. There is one more call I need. Soon I will know for sure what is happening. We drink these beers then we go back, and we make plans. Then we can all go home.'

***

The LAPD arrived at Fort Indigo less than twenty minutes after their meeting with Mathews ended, two cars with roof lights flashing plus an unmarked white SUV which followed them in.

Reed got the call and he collected Louisa then they went to the gate and escorted the police through to the MP station.

John watched as Keane was brought up from the cell. Initially he was all smiles as he walked into the lobby but then froze when he saw four policemen waiting for him.

'Wait …' he said, looking at Major Turner who impassively returned his gaze.

'What?' he asked. 'Did you think you'd walk out of here?'

'Look, I can help. But I need to be on the ground. You need me.'

Now Keane was looking pleadingly at Reed, who shook his head.

'No, we don't. We know where Pinsky is and we are acting on it, as are the LAPD. So now it's time to pay for what you've done.'

A policeman stepped forward with cuffs, Keane tried to move away but the corporal pushed him forward.

'Do you know what they did? They kept me prisoner here! I was locked up! I'm a policeman, a civilian, locked up in an army cell!' Keane shouted, to nobody in particular.

Chief Brady walked through the group of police officers, John had not noticed he was there before. He walked across to Keane and gestured to the officer to put on the cuffs, which he did briskly.

'No, they didn't Ron. None of that happened. We've just detained you at your house, I believe I am correct?' Brady announced.

The officers with him all looked at each other then nodded, and Keane was led out. John followed them and watched him being put in the back of a car and then shook Chief Brady's hand.

'It would be useful to keep the army well clear of this Chief,' John said earnestly.

Brady smiled.

'Don't worry. He was never here.'

'You suspected him, didn't you? I wish I had realised it at the time, looking back I can see you didn't trust him.'

Brady sighed.

'Well, yeah, I didn't understand why he'd get involved. It didn't make a whole lot of sense, as far as I knew he was just a pencil pusher. But there have been issues in the past. I never liked Ron Keane, things seem to get tidied away way too neatly. But of course the administration do like that, less work to do, keep the outstanding list shorter. So he was never called to task over it, but I sure ain't the only one who didn't like the guy.'

'Still, I wish I'd taken more notice. A lot of the stuff that has happened would have been avoided.'

'Hindsight John. Wonderful thing right?' Brady replied with a smile, patting him on the shoulder. 'I got to say I'm sorry that Captain Truman gave you a hard time John. He's new to the job, his predecessor was there a long time, and had a lot of respect. Big shoes to fill, but that's no excuse, I guess he was kind of an asshole. He couldn't understand who you are.'

John shrugged. Life was too short to worry about what people thought.

'Yeah, well. So Chief, are you up to speed with everything? Have you heard about Pinsky, and the rail yard?'

'Yes and that's why I came down here, I got to meet Major Turner now. We got SWAT mobilised, just waiting on the go ahead then we're going to be getting over there.'

'I am too, along with Captain Reed and another couple of MPs from here.'

Brady looked at him shrewdly.

'Not thinking about getting involved?' he asked.

'No, no,' John replied hastily. 'Just want to see what is happening, Pinsky has a lot to answer for.'

Brady passed him a business card.

'Right, well here's my cell number, stay in contact and I will let you know how it's progressing, is that ok with you?'

'Yes, thanks Chief. We'll stay out of the way.'

'No problem. I'll see you there I'm sure.'

John introduced him to Tom Reed, and then they walked upstairs to take him to Turner's office. Once he was inside they went back down and walked out of the building. The two squad cars were gone, Keane was no longer the army's problem thankfully. The corporal and Louisa were standing waiting next to the Humvees and they headed across to make sure everything was completely clear.

'Ok. Let's go,' Reed said.

Chapter Thirty-Eight

In the bar Rico was deliberately doing all he could to delay finishing his drink, all the others had downed theirs long before but he managed to keep a fifth in his glass and would occasionally sip without actually consuming anything. He was desperate to keep Leo in the bar; all the time they were not in the yard they were not in any real danger. The problem was that the glasses were small, there wasn't a size option. Rico had been in bars in New York and Boston where pints were just standard, he had been told that was all there was in Europe, and he could really do with that now.

In fact, Leo did not seem to be in any hurry. Since the call he had been telling them all about Las Vegas, and the fact that others had fucked up there, then fallen almost silent, constantly checking the display on his phone but it stayed resolutely inactive.

Sal was aware of Rico's plans and was always talking, telling stories and asking Rolf and Greg questions, but it was becoming strained. The elderly barman appeared and collected the empty glasses.

Rico winced.

'Shall I get some more beers Leo?' Sal asked brightly.

Pinsky checked his phone and looked sharply at him, and then around the bar, which had not changed. He sighed and tapped his fingers on the table.

'Yes. Why not?'

Sal jumped up, and as he moved around the table Pinsky's mobile beeped. He grabbed it and looked closely at the screen.

Rico stared at Sal and gestured toward the bar with his head.

Sal nodded and practically ran over.

Leo walked away again, talking fast but quietly into his phone.

The barman brought the drinks over and set them on the table, and they all took a drink just as Pinsky sat down again.

'Ok. Have a drink. We need to be moving soon. And we have to make security good. There is changes.'

**

Louisa seemed to know the city a lot better than Reed, and they followed her bright yellow Honda along several highways and freeways, moving fast until eventually she slowed and exited, and almost immediately they saw the yard down on their left as they passed a basic looking hotel and a short line of shops, the golden arches visible from a long way away.

They drove past the yard without obviously looking at it and turned into the car park of a bulk carpet wholesaler further down the road, well out of sight of the yard.

'Nice driving,' Reed commented to Louisa as they gathered to talk.

Louisa looked baffled and gestured at her car.

'Er ... satnav? Sir?'

Reed chuckled.

'Ok. I got to get me one of those things.'

John had walked back to the road and then joined them.

'Right. So there's a tyre place just down there, and next to it looks like a closed down restaurant maybe, and some sort of industrial unit but there's a couple of cars parked all around there. It's not busy but I don't think we would stand out there, and it's probably better if we stay in the cars right now, it won't be obvious we're there from the distance if we get spotted but we'll have a good line of sight to the gates, maybe partly into the yard.

'You want us to stay together?' the corporal asked.

'No, opposite the hotel there are a couple of small warehouses, they look a bit rundown but I'd say they are in use. I spotted them as we drove past. They are set back from the road but again, a car parked there won't stand out. Remember the police and SWAT are due here pretty soon so anonymity will be a thing of the past anyway.'

They made the decision quickly; John and Reed would wait next to the tyre place and Louisa and the corporal further down the road close to the warehouses. They got into position and settled down to wait.

From where they were parked John could see through the gates, and across the yard to some huge warehouses on the far side. He watched several trains crisscrossing behind them so he knew that was where the tracks were that they had seen on the map.

There was occasional traffic, but the area was quiet. They were parked in front of the closed down restaurant right next to the tyre shop. Through the gap between the two low buildings they could see another large open area, where there were haphazard stacks of rusting shipping containers.

'Must have been busy here, once,' John commented looking all around.

Reed nodded, joining in with viewing the area with a critical eye.

'Yeah, I guess so. Lots of trucks and all sorts of industry. Must have killed it when they shut the yard, but that's progress I guess. We don't get this shit in the army, it's getting smaller for sure but nothing ever really changes.'

John smiled, it was a long time ago for him but he suspected it was the same in every country.

They sat there for a while, and then Reed got a call to say the LAPD were on their way, so John dug out the card and called Brady, who told him that he had to wait to get the all clear from the SWAT team leader before he would be at the scene. He suggested that John make himself known, everyone was fully briefed.

The SWAT team leader was a Lieutenant Oakes, and in Brady's own apologetic terms 'a bit of a jerk.'

As he was talking Reed punched him on the shoulder, pointing out the windscreen.

Five men were walking along the road toward the yard. Immediately Reed's radio crackled and Louisa called in.

'Sir, we got movement. Five men just came out the hotel.'

'I got it Louisa, sit tight.'

John had hung up and was staring forward. The men were strung out in a line, two side by side at the back, the other three single file in front. The man in the middle of the three was who they were looking for.

'That is Leonid Pinsky. It's him.'

Reed got on the radio to alert Louisa.

'Do you know any of the others?' he asked John.

'Yeah, there was intel on a couple of guys, associates of the men I shot at the Metro station. One of them was arrested at the bar fight Keane mentioned. Perez, Ascola, or something like that. I think that's him at the back.'

He called Brady back to tell him this development, and they watched the men unlock the gates, walk through and repeat the action again at a second set inside where they walked into the yard and disappeared after making sure both sets of gates were secured.

A couple of minutes later and Louisa pulled up fast. They got out the cars and stood looking over at the yard.

'They went into a building opposite the yard from those warehouses, looks like maybe offices or something,' the corporal said.

'Ok,' John replied. 'I'm just gonna wander down the hill, and then come back on that side of the road, see if I can see anything.'

'John ...' Reed warned him.

'It's ok, don't panic. I'm not going to do anything. I'm not armed anyway, none of us are. I just want to see from the other side for myself, the LAPD will be here any minute anyway.'

Without waiting for an answer John jogged down between the two buildings and ran right across behind the restaurant and keeping well out of sight came out on the other side of the warehouses. He walked across the road and strolled casually right past the gates, head straight in front but his eyes scanning the yard. He carried on until he was obscured by the buildings on the corner, then ran back to where the others were waiting.

'Right. I saw the building. It's kind of on its own, there isn't much else on that side, just some sheds.'

'Did you see anyone?' Reed asked.

'No, it's impossible from outside. But the corporal saw them go in, and from where he was watching there's nowhere else they could have gone. There is a massive crane which looks like it's in the middle of being disassembled and I think part of it is a bridge from the offices to the warehouse. If it is, that means they could move out that way but I reckon if they did we would spot them.'

'Are we ok just standing here?' asked Louisa, leaning back against her car.

'We're fine, there is no line of sight from where they are to here, but that also means that we aren't going to see them either.'

The stood watching the yard, all unsure what to do next when an LAPD black and white followed by a SWAT van came down the road toward them. Reed waved and pointed to a space further along from where they had parked but was ignored. Both vehicles stopped in the middle of the road.

A squat, heavyset officer all in black with a flak jacket bristling with apparatus climbed out the passenger side of the cruiser and then stood, looking at them from across the bonnet.

John sighed and then set off across the road with Reed following.

As they got closer the officer held his hand up.

'Hold it there. Don't come any closer. I got to speak to a Major Reed?'

'There's no Major Reed. Not here anyways. It's Captain Reed. And that's me,' Reed told him.

The officer looked annoyed and then reached into the car snapping his fingers, without taking his eyes off them. The driver, a young black officer ferreted around on the back seat and then handed over a piece of paper, which the officer took and started scanning it.

'Jesus Christ,' John murmured as he and Reed stood there in the road.

'Ok,' the officer said eventually. 'Major Reed, walk to me.'

He looked over at both men. Reed started to walk over.

'Yeah, like I said, it's Captain Reed.'

'Who's this guy?' the officer asked nodding at John once Reed reached the car and leaned on the bonnet opposite.

'That's John Smith. I think you'll find he's kind of important in all this. I imagine it's on those notes somewhere.'

The officer started reading again, lips moving slowly.

He stared at John.

'You were there? At the goddamn Metro?'

John wandered across to join Reed.

'Er, yeah. That was kind of how all this started.'

The officer threw the piece of paper back into the car.

'Well, I'm Lieutenant Oakes. This is my team, and you got to hand over to us now. I'm running the show.'

'Right. But don't you want to know anything about who's in there?'

Oakes glanced at him as he walked toward the van.

'Yeah, yeah, I got it. Some Russian dude. Gets his kicks firing automatics in train stations. Ain't the first, won't be the last.'

He banged hard on the side of the van and then walked back and opened the boot of the car and started unloading some orange plastic bollards which he threw on the ground.

Reed scratched his head.

'Lieutenant, this is a whole lot bigger than one guy with a gun. We don't believe Pinsky, the Russian was at the Metro.'

Oakes looked at him then continued throwing more bollards. Reed walked around to the back of the car and loomed over Oakes, who finally stopped and looked up warily.

'You're not listening Lieutenant,' Reed said simply.

Behind them, eight SWAT team members had climbed from the van and were standing watching, clearly wondering what was going on. Oakes slammed the boot shut and leaned heavily on it, avoiding looking at Reed who stood to one side.

'Fine. Whatever. You guys tell me what's on your mind then we'll go do our jobs, ok?'

He beckoned to the team behind who began to slowly walk across.

'We don't know how many are in there, and we have no idea what weapons they are holding. They could have an arsenal in there for all we know. You got to understand this is real serious, I ain't at all sure we should even be standing out here in the street.' Reed told him, looking around.

'We know what we're doing, just leave it to us. They are in one building right? Three floors, lots of windows, nothing we ain't done before. So just stay out the way and we'll get it done,' Oakes replied.

'It's four floors. You even seen the building? Checked the perimeter?' John called out nervously.

Oakes scowled back at him.

'Like I said, leave it to us.'

He turned and gestured to a SWAT officer that was the closest, who walked over, then he pointed down the road toward the hotel.

'Ok. Get your ass over there. Eyes on the building. Report back what you see.'

The officer looked at him then down the road where Oakes was pointing.

'Er … sir? I'll be kind of exposed,' the officer stated.

'Yeah. He fucking will,' Reed growled, exasperated.

Oakes turned his back.

'Just do it son, then we can get back. Beer and pizza. Ok?'

The officer took his firearm off his shoulder and held it with both hands across his front then shaking his head, set off down the road.

'Wait! …' John started to move and then the shooting started.

Several shots rang out, loud, shocking. John dropped fast to the floor behind the black and white, inching backwards to the front wheel. Then a flurry of firing, different guns, set to automatic, bullets ricocheting off the road and thumping into the vehicles, glass breaking.

Then nothing.

John slowly raised his head. He was safe where he was, behind the engine, cars are just thin steel, a bullet will easily pass right through, although modern vehicles have a lot more stuff in the doors. But nothing would get through the engine. In front of him Reed had thrown himself to the floor and was lying lengthways, wedged under the vehicle.

John could see the van, and several SWAT team officers cowering behind it. He turned his head, there was no sign of Louisa or the corporal, he hoped they had been able to get out the way. The officer who had been sent to watch the building was lying in the road. Head shot. A lot of blood. His gun, a Colt M4 was next to him. Reed moved his head and looked directly at him. John pointed at the gun.

Reed nodded, and stretched out a long, long leg and hooked his foot around the strap, slowly dragging it toward him and then kicking it along to John.

More shots, again from different guns, this time seeming to be aimed toward the van.

John quickly checked the gun and then keeping his head down twisted around so his back was to the wing next to where the windscreen pillar meets the panel. He raised the weapon, which was fitted with a tactical sight and slowly edged it up then peered over the bonnet right next to the pillar, keeping as hidden as possible. He could see now there were people on the bridge, at the opposite end from the building next to the large warehouses. He could see heads ducking up and down. Guns were visible resting on the top of the sides which were steel panels. A rifle and then a head appeared, slowly looking from side to side. It was some distance away but John breathed deeply, aimed and fired. A short burst and the head shot backwards. John ducked down again.

A shout, and then nothing at all.

John slowly moved so he could see the bridge again, he saw a man stand and at the same time a large gun barrel was pushed up and pointed toward him.

'Machine gun!' he shouted, shrinking down as small as he could behind the cover, and then heavy rapid fire began, bullets hitting metal and more glass breaking. But it ended quickly, followed by a couple of random shots and then there was silence.

John stayed where he was, waiting then started counting the seconds, but there were no more shots fired. Reed raised his head and looked at him. Carefully he sighted over the bonnet again and checked the bridge.

He couldn't see anyone at all, but then heard some muted gunfire from somewhere inside a building.

There were no incoming rounds so he moved around the car, using the cover to see if he could spot any movement anywhere in the yard but there was nobody there. Reed had moved up so he was lying on his elbows next to him.

'Anything?' he asked.

'No.'

John had another sweep.

'Clear!' he called out and he and Reed stood up slowly, surveying the scene.

Chapter Thirty-Nine

It was bad, but it could definitely have been a lot worse.

There were three dead SWAT officers, including Oakes, and two injured, one of which was the young man driving the car. He had ducked into the footwell and been hit twice in the arm and the shoulder, but he would live.

The remaining officers tended to the injured and got on the radio. Louisa and the corporal hurried across, they had got behind the car as soon as the shooting started, amazingly there were no more casualties. The men working over at the tyre place had gathered at the front, staring,

Still carrying the gun John walked fast over to the gates and looked in, pulling on the chain. Reed joined him and gently pulled him away.

'You know we can't go in right John?'

John looked at him but pulled on the chain again.

'We can't do it John. This is LAPD business now. We are gonna be on the unwanted list real soon.'

Reed was right and led John away. Within minutes the cavalry arrived. Three more SWAT vans along with a massive armoured truck with heavy bull bars across the front. Several cruisers and a couple of ambulances. The SWAT officers secured the scene, parking a van across the gates and monitoring it constantly. John, Reed, Louisa and the corporal sat on the ground across the road watching.

Eventually the chain was cut and the armoured truck rolled through and parked inside. After a while officers streamed in but there was no opposition, just a lot of police everywhere. John stood up when to his dismay he saw Captain Truman stalking toward him, Chief Brady following. Truman stopped and sneered.

'Well, trouble just follows you around Mr Smith. Now I got to talk to three families, tell them their loved ones ain't coming home.'

Reed leapt to his feet indignantly and towered over Truman.

'You know what, it was fucked from the start. Your man Oakes was the biggest asshole I ever saw. He did not listen to anyone. So blaming this on John is all bullshit. We tried to stop it. But he just carried on anyway, and he had no idea what he was doing.'

Truman stared up at him speechless and was clearly relieved when Chief Brady steered him away.

'I think Dennis, that it will be me doing the talking. Why don't you go and see if we've got the all clear to go inside?'

Truman glared angrily at John then stormed off.

Brady turned to John.

'Feels like I'm forever apologising for him. But I am sorry John, he had no call to speak to you like that. None of this is your doing.'

John shrugged, he didn't want Brady to feel any worse than he would be right now, with three officer's bodies being taken away right in front of their eyes.

'I'm sorry but Tom is right Chief, I don't like to say it considering what's happened here but Oakes was just not the right man for the job.'

Brady looked sadly at him, then slowly shook his head.

'Yeah, I already heard that. But it's kinda hard to take in. These guys are supposed to be the best.'

John looked across the road, surveying the scene, watching the hive of activity

'I'm sorry for the lost men Chief. And the guys that got hurt. And I'm sorry that this keeps happening whenever I am involved. But we had no idea who was in there. We tried to make that clear. All we had was just one definite name; and we saw him with four other men go into that yard. They must have set up a lookout, I saw men on that bridge. They just started shooting,' John said.

'This is one hell of a mess. And one thing we all know for sure is they are long gone,' Brady replied.

'Yeah. And they will have got rid of the mobiles, so it's back to square one,' John told him, looking at all the police officers everywhere.

'Come on. I'll get you inside. Take a look for yourselves. But watch where you walk, there will be the CSI guys in there and they don't like it when we trample all over.'

Brady led the way, and the four of them walked into the yard. If anything, it was even bigger inside the gates, and they made their way across to a narrow brick building.

Truman was standing outside and John studiously ignored him as they approached. A young uniformed officer was watching and walked over to Brady.

'This is where they were living Chief,' he told them, gesturing at the open door.

They followed him in.

They had walked into a grubby, simple reception area, with a door open at the back behind a filthy beige counter and stairs to their left.

There were two men in white suits with masks working, examining the floors and the walls, poking into drawers. There didn't seem to be any clear distinction to where anyone could walk so John wandered over behind the counter and looked into the room. It was bathroom, with urinals, toilet cubicles and some showers. Everything looked tired and well worn and John saw a damp towel hanging on a peg just inside the door. So they had been recently used, which made sense if the men had been living here.

He walked out and then went up the stairs. Now he was in an open space, more stairs directly in front of him. There was dust everywhere, battered furniture dotted around and an old television on a table. Toward the back was a glass-partitioned wall, which looked like an office. There was more activity here, and John looked closely at some open trunks on the floor.

Guns, in two of the trunks.

Mostly assault rifles, a few handguns. Different makes and ages, none were new. They were all being carefully examined and dusted with fingerprint powder.

There was one more trunk, and this contained ammo. Boxes of a variety of shells and many magazines, which he could see were loaded.

'John!'

He looked up. Reed was standing with Brady next to something, and there were more CSIs there. He walked over.

On the floor was a body. A man. A big man. No actually a huge man. Not like Reed, this one was fat, with a massive head. His eyes were open, staring accusingly up at them. He had been shot in the head. There wasn't a lot of blood, the bullet had clearly not gone all the way through, which John found surprising. He was lying almost comically flat, hands at his side, as if he was out in the sun.

John crouched down to see if he knew the face, but he had never seen him before. He stood up and looked at Brady, who gave a small shrug.

'No ID so far. But they are still looking.'

The CSIs were meticulously going through the weird vast robe type outfit the body was wearing. He didn't envy them that task he decided. He looked at the man again. Big round face, no colour which was to be expected, thin lips. Maybe mid to late forties, but that was just a guess. Greasy light brown hair. But very distinctive.

'Anybody recognise him?' he asked Brady, who shook his head.

'Not so far. But he could be from anywhere in the world, this could take some time. They found this on him though, which we are checking right now.'

He held up an elderly mobile phone.

'Ok.'

'Not a lot else on this floor,' Brady resumed, 'other than this.'

He pointed out a suitcase, which had money in. Stacks of hundred-dollar bills, with a lot of loose notes dotted around.

'Drugs?' John asked.

Again, Brady shrugged.

They walked up to the next floor. Same layout, apart from a basic kitchen area where the office had been on the first floor. Some bits of battered furniture and not much else, but everything being examined. Then it was up another flight. This floor had mattresses dotted around, with sleeping bags here and there and a door with steps outside which led to the flat roof, and the bridge across to the warehouses. John made his way over. There was another body on the far side, which he had expected. Lying propped against the panels was a man, no more than thirty at the most, black hair and a big bushy beard. Another head shot. This was the man John had killed when he was behind the car. Reed was examining a machine gun which John had passed as he walked over.

'M60. But prehistoric. The army keeps these guns forever, but this thing must be one of the first,' Reed told him as John walked across.

The gun had been thrown to the floor, there was a bandolier of bullets still sticking out the side.

'Right shells wrong links,' Reed explained. 'We got lucky. This thing would have killed a lot more of us if it had kept firing, but this is for another gun altogether, looks Chinese. Everything looks a lot closer together, this baby must have jammed. Like I said, that was lucky.'

'I suppose this could have come from anywhere right?' John asked.

'Yeah, pretty much. They've been around a long time. Bad guys all over use these things, they turn up pretty much everywhere. Rebel armies someplace, pirates, tiny guerrilla armies in Africa, they all use them, and I guess they must be easy to find if you know where to look. I don't think these guys struggle to find weapons.'

There were three more assault rifles lying along the section of the bridge, and they looked at them all. AK-47, Steyr, M16. All the guns had 1-Too burned into the stocks.

John shook his head and looked over the bridge to the road. The van and the squad car were right there in clear sight. If Oakes had pulled up where they suggested they would have all been out of sight. Such a waste. He leaned on the railing, and Reed joined him.

'Made it real easy for them,' he commented.

John nodded and then turned, to look at the end of the bridge. There was a single rusty door which was standing open, he could see the gloom of the warehouse beyond, so he walked over and looked inside at a simple metal platform with a guard rail. They were close to the roof, and it was a long drop to the floor below. The platform ran off to the right then a long flight of steel stairs which ran all the way to the bottom. There were several police officers moving around, and he could see some vehicles parked up but other than that it was just a huge empty space. There were massive double sliding doors open, presumably into the warehouse next door. He turned and looked at Brady.

'Are we ok to go down?' he asked.

Brady nodded.

'Sure. Why not.'

They made their way over to the stairs and walked all the way down then across to the sliding doors into an identical warehouse next door, this one being completely empty. Then they crossed over through another set, into the same again but this one had massive doors open at the side so was well lit in comparison.

There were more police here, gathered around outside. They walked across and John stood in the wide-open doorway looking across a deep concrete loading bay and then a dozen railway tracks nestled close to each other. Every now and then a train would clatter across loudly in either direction. On the far side was a chain link fence and then a stretch of wasteland where more police were moving until a line of office and apartment buildings. A freeway ran across high above to the right.

Brady started talking to the officers who were here, who basically confirmed what they had already guessed. The men had run across the railway tracks and then through the fence. There were visible signs and markings which disappeared once they reached the buildings.

'So, they could be anywhere now,' Reed said flatly.

'Anywhere. It's been nearly two hours. Could be out the city by now, if they had any kind of escape plan,' John replied, staring across at the far side.

'We'll find them,' Brady told them, unconvincingly.

Chapter Forty

Rico dropped onto the bed and rubbed his head fiercely with both hands.

This was absolutely not what he had signed up for.

Sal was standing staring out the window, while Pinsky stalked around the room with the mobile phone he had just purchased glued to his ear, muttering to himself.

They were in a cheap hotel room close to Long Beach. Since leaving the hotel bar things had disintegrated into madness. They had got back to base with everything seeming exactly the same as when they had left, but Pinsky had been edgy, unsettled. He instructed Rolf to get up on the bridge and keep watch, make sure he could see as much of the road as possible and then told the others to make sure the guns were all ready.

They might have to leave in a hurry was the only explanation he gave.

They busied themselves doing as they were told, the beer buzz fading and the body of Voorhees a constant reminder of the precariousness of their position. Pinsky watched, tensely holding his mobile, which rang suddenly and he jerked it to his ear. He talked fast in Russian, and then, suddenly, he relaxed. He smiled. He hung up the call.

'Is ok. We wait, but is ok,' he said, and turned on the TV.

The others all looked at each other and then joined him watching a show which had a pretend judge admonishing a woman who hadn't paid her rent. But just as everything seemed to finally calm down there was a loud shout from Rolf, who breathlessly appeared on the stairs and told them the police were outside.

Pinsky grabbed a Steyr from a case with a couple of clips and ran fast up the stairs.

'Move! Now!' he ordered as he reached the top.

Greg picked up and AK-47 and Sal an M16 and followed. Rico looked all round, wishing he had the balls to just run out the building but instead he walked up the stairs, dread in every step.

On the bridge Pinsky was staring down, and as he crossed Rico could see a patrol car and a SWAT van. He ducked down, as all the others had. The bridge had sides of solid steel about a metre high, with a railing a few centimetres above which ran across the top.

'Get the machine gun. Now,' Pinsky hissed to Greg, who gave the AK to Rolf and keeping low ran back into the building.

Rico dared to peek over the side.

The police were talking to two men, one a huge motherfucker, presumably plain clothes. Both men were agitated, looked like they were trying to explain something. They kept looking at the gates and into the yard. Pinsky was aiming the Steyr through the gap between the railing and the side panels.

'Do it,' he ordered. 'Do it.'

Rolf did the same, and Sal also lifted his gun.

Pinsky started firing. The shots caught everyone out. Rico ducked down as low as he could and Sal did too, but Rolf joined in.

There was no return fire.

Pinsky had ducked and was now looking through the gap over the side like before, and started shooting again. His clip emptied, so he ducked down to refit another. Sal and Rico were just watching, they had no idea what they were supposed to be doing. Rolf was still firing, but short bursts, then he stopped and ducked down, looking back at the others.

'Now!' Pinsky ordered, and he and Rolf started firing again.

Greg appeared, hustling as fast as he could with the heavy M60 and trying to keep down as he crossed the bridge. Pinsky and Rolf were out of ammo and Greg slid the M60 toward Pinsky, who forced the end of the clip into the breech and slammed the cover down.

'Look, tell me what you see,' he told Rolf, grinning like a child.

He's enjoying this. Rico thought to himself. He wants to kill.

Rolf peered through the gap, moving his head around, he lifted it higher when there was a sudden burst of gunfire, and red mist sprayed from his head. He fell back with a thump. Ignoring it Pinsky pushed the M60 onto the top of the railing, angled it down and began firing blindly, but he only got a few shots loose before the gun jammed. Cursing in several languages he threw it down and then ran for the door into the warehouse, pulling it open.

'Go!' called out Sal and everyone followed the Russian as fast as they could.

The doors between the warehouses were already open which was fortunate, and the huge opening to the loading bay was secured by a heavy bar inside. They lifted it off, threw the doors wide and then ran as fast as they could, oblivious to the railroad traffic, forcing their way through the fence on the far side and across the wasteland.

Once they had reached the buildings Pinsky ran into a car park in an apartment building and they hunkered down in a corner, wild eyed.

'How?' cried out Pinsky. 'Which one is the fucking rat? Is you?' he shoved Sal hard.

'What? No, of course not. Fuck Leo we've been in this shit four fucking months!' Sal told him.

Pinsky stared at them, and then pulled the Makarov from his jacket.

'Fuck,' thought Rico to himself. He had forgotten about that. He was starting to think they should just take their chances with Leo, overpower him and get the hell away.

Pinsky stared at them all.

'Is true,' he said quietly then shot Greg in the face.

'What the fuck!' Sal exclaimed, but Pinsky was already up and moving.

'Come on. We go. Now. Move.'

And Sal and Rico, not knowing any better, unable to think for themselves any more had gone with him.

They got to the street and Pinsky had produced his mobile and started dialling furiously.

Rico stared at him, and then grabbed the phone.

'Leo. This phone. You said you were in Vegas, you said it all got fucked up. What if they got this number man? They could get a trace on it. Jesus fucking Christ. You've had this thing the whole time. And you just fucking killed Greg.'

Pinsky stared at him, angry red blotches appearing across his head.

'Fuck.'

He threw the phone on the floor and ground it with his heel, then stood up and moved fast back onto the street.

They made their way to a junction and got a cab, telling the driver they needed a hotel. Sal suggested Long Beach, it was all he could think of. They came across one on the freeway with a mall opposite and got out there, making their way over so Pinsky could buy a mobile first and then checking in.

So they were comparatively safe now.

But for how long, who knew?

Chapter Forty-One

The FBI office in Los Angeles is in Westwood, just off the 405 and not far from Beverley Hills, which was where John had been heading back to the Montage when all this started.

He was tired of being in LA, sick of the deaths and constantly coming in last. The last place he wanted to be was in a conference room listening to the FBI bitch about the police, while the police try to blame the army, who have no choice other than to sit and listen.

Judy was there, along with the local section chief, a skinny incredibly grey man called Braxton, who so far had done nothing other than to berate chief Brady about Lieutenant Oakes' failings. Brady was in the meeting with a SWAT captain called Jennings, who angrily blamed the lack of cohesive intel, and the fact that the army had been involved in the first place.

John sat silently alongside Tom Reed, while Major Turner defended them with dignity.

It had been nearly five hours since the events at the train yard, and they had been in this room for the best part of an hour while the voices got louder and they were nowhere nearer any kind of resolution.

So far he had not spoken a word, and neither had Judy or Reed. And with the exception of Major Turner they were the only ones there who actually understood anything.

Braxton was holding forth about other occasions when he had had been forced to act following a failed police action and turning an even darker grey while he did it.

'Fuck this,' John said suddenly.

Braxton stopped talking and stared at him, mouth open.

'Excuse me?' he managed eventually.

'Yeah, what did you just say?' Jennings asked angrily.

'I said; fuck this. This is all bullshit. It's been hours and you have done nothing. We have done nothing. These guys are responsible for the deaths of five innocent women in the subway, whoever they were, a good, honest CIA man and now three police officers. Who knows how many others? And all you are doing is shouting at each other. Trying to blame someone else. You know what? Who the fuck cares? You, and unfortunately that means we look ridiculous.'

He looked at Brady.

'Chief, it was nothing to do with you but Keane was one of your own. And he was in this up to his neck. So what are you going to do?'

Then he fixed his stare on Braxton.

'And I absolutely guarantee you that there are people right here in this building who are on the payroll of these guys, so you need to start thinking.'

As Braxton started to bluster, John ignored him and turned to Judy.

'Judy, we know the mobile is out of action, but we expected that. Anything else so far?'

She smiled gratefully at him.

'We have some sightings, and they are all being checked. The area all around Hobart has been searched. The cops are doing what they can, they are mobilised right through the city. But as of now we don't have anything definite.'

'Ok. And what do we know from the train yard?'

'Chief?' Judy asked, and Brady passed round some sheets of paper.

'We have evidence of six men in the yard, we can't accurately say how long they had been there but we believe only a few days. We've been in contact with the developer, he claims the keys have been stolen so we are taking a good look at him. The dead man in the building, the fat guy has been identified. He is one Yann Voorhees, who is known to us, and also the FBI.'

'Known why? For what?'

'He is not a nice guy, he has been indicted on kidnapping charges, not just in LA but also in San Francisco and Richmond. High profile people but he was unsuccessful. In all cases the charges were dropped so they never got to court. He has also been investigated by ATF and Homeland Security on gun distribution, which is pending, he dropped off the radar about a year ago. Born in Johannesburg in 1974, moved to the US when he was five. His father worked for Boeing.'

John pondered the information.

'I don't get it. What's his connection to 1-Too?'

'This actually fits with how we now believe they operate John. They recruit local cells for certain actions. Vorhees could have been with them for years or just a few months. There is no strict pattern we can ascertain, which is one of the reasons we are always behind the curve,' Judy told him.

'Right, so they just turn up in LA and set up here to find these military plans or whatever?' Brady asked.

'Keane was only brought in a couple of months ago. It would make sense,' John agreed.

'We also traced them to an apartment in Mount Pleasant. They were definitely there a lot longer, but we can only find evidence of five men there. Some of the DNA there matches to the men killed at the Metro station, and again at the yard, Voorhees was there for sure,' Brady continued.

'Can they have gone back there?' Judy asked.

Brady shook his head.

'No. Well not so far, we got a twenty-four-hour watch on the place.'

'What about the other guy? The one John hit?' Reed asked.

Brady scanned the sheet of paper.

'One Rolf Gardner. Thirty-one. Chicago know all about him. Armed robbery, he did four years in Lawrence. Last known whereabouts was St Louis, he got pulled in after a drug dealer got hit in a parking lot but was released without charge. Again, we can't find any connection to Voorhees, Pinsky or anyone here in the city.'

'Recruited. It's how they work. Probably the promise of some serious money,' Judy stated.

'And we also got another body, you don't know about this one. Gregory Tilson, twenty-nine. We found him when we followed the trail into an underground parking lot at the apartments which back onto the land that separates them from the yard. Shot in the head, and the remains of a cellphone were found close by. Judy confirmed the number is this goddamn Pinsky. Local residents heard the shot, it would have been well before we entered the yard. There have been reported sightings of three men in the street around the time, we believe they took a cab, we're trying to trace it,' Brady continued.

'Gardner? Tilson? We didn't have those names right Judy?' John asked.

Judy shook her head.

'No. I got people looking into them right now, try to find out how long they been in the city.'

'There is no trace of either of them at the apartment in Mount Pleasant,' Brady told them.

Judy made a note, as usual she had her worn notebook and a bulging folder in front of her.

'So, instead of beating each other up how about we try and get our heads together to find these assholes,' Reed said reasonably.

Braxton huffed and said nothing, Jennings nodded slowly.

'Yeah, you're right. I apologise captain. It ain't a good feeling losing men, especially when it's clear as fucking day it could have been avoided. You guys got any details on the other guys with Pinsky?'

'All I have is one Rico Perez, we weren't sure about him but John believes he saw him walking to the yard from the hotel with Pinsky this afternoon, we don't know much about him.'

Judy slid some sheets across the table, Perez's brief record.

Brady read through and looked up.

'Armed robbery, but with a toy gun. No history of violence here.'

Judy shrugged.

'This is always the problem with these guys, it's damn near impossible to piece them together. We can't connect Pinsky, Voorhees, Tilson, Gardner or Perez or the guys from the Metro station we know about. And we don't know any more about Voorhees than the LAPD. They seem to be able to recruit out of nowhere, they find these guys who fit what they are looking for somehow. If we could find out how the hell they are doing it then that would be a major step forward.'

'Well, I can make a guess,' Brady said sombrely.

Everyone looked at him.

'Cops. They are the connection. They know these guys, they are in the system, it has to be them. A simple request, right? I need a couple of guys; yeah, sure I can get you some names. So it's everywhere, it ain't just Keane here in LA, it's all over.'

Everybody stared at him as the reality of the situation set in.

'Cops? But how many?' Judy asked.

Brady shrugged.

'I got no idea. But it isn't like they will turn up with a Ferrari nobody knew about. My guess it's the same deal we get with the press, always someone happy to talk. For a couple of hundred dollars, who's to know? And it's probably no more than a chat in a bar to start with, the exact same in every city I guess. I will make a start with my precinct and I will pass it on you got my word on that.'

'Well, I want to …' Braxton started but was interrupted by Brady's mobile phone ringing. He raised his eyebrows while Brady jabbed the screen to silence it.

'I was going to say; I believe that I don't have that problem here. But I will make enquiries,' Braxton continued.

Brady's mobile rang again, and he silenced it. He shrugged and looked around apologetically.

'It makes sense. I don't like to hear it, but yeah, it does add up. I have to admit we never considered that, and it's been something we have wondered for some time. We decided they must have a database, but this is much more obvious. And simple.' Judy said, still writing in her notebook.

'But it doesn't help us now,' John said woodenly.

'So it's a waiting game?' Reed asked.

'We don't even know if they are still in the city,' Jennings admitted.

There was a knock on the door and a police officer entered. He looked embarrassed as he made his way over to Brady, holding a radio.

'Er ... sir?'

Brady looked up at him irritably.

'Can't you see I'm busy here?'

'Er ... yes, I am truly sorry sir. But it's control. And they say it's real urgent.'

Brady snatched the radio and keyed the button on the side.

'Brady here, what's so goddamn important?'

He held the radio to his ear. His face dropped. His eyes widened. He scrabbled around for a pen and started to write.

'You absolutely sure about this?' he asked tersely.

Everyone in the room could hear the raised, rushed voice from the radio.

'Ok. I'm on my way.'

He passed the radio back and stood up.

'We just got a call. Somebody called 911 name of Sal Rodriguez. And he claims to be who we are looking for. He named the train yard. He's waiting for us, at a hotel.'

Chapter Forty-Two

Sammy King watched Moran shouting and raving at another unlucky individual. Normally whenever she saw this happening she would feel grateful it wasn't her for a change but now it just made her angry. Why did Costas bother with him? Despite their recent successes morale in the office had plummeted, cliques were forming and a couple of people had resigned. Moran had become so unpopular that most of the staff actively avoided any contact with him, and who could blame them.

Simon had started to catch it too, mostly because he liked Sammy and spoke up for her. He was young, and good at his job, and would be an asset elsewhere, but he was happy here, so she would make sure Costas knew exactly why he wanted to leave if he ever made that decision.

Her show had gone well that day, she had discussed meeting the British man who was on the platform at the Metro station but had chosen her words very carefully and not gone into too many details. There would be a time for that she knew, eventually the police would have to lift the restrictions.

She thought about John Smith and smiled. She liked him, he was very interesting, she had never met anyone quite like him. She hoped she would see him again. She picked up her mobile and wondered whether to send him a text, when it suddenly started ringing. At first she thought it could be John, but then recognised the number and shuddered.

Jimmy Frost. Shit.

She swallowed, and then answered.

He spoke in an exaggerated drawl.

'Hey sweetheart, I just heard something. And I reckon you are going to be VERY nice to old Jimmy the next time you see him, I'm expecting a good time, goddamn more than giving me a hundred bucks is for sure.'

Expect all you want, she thought to herself, but replied through gritted teeth.

'Oh hi Jimmy. Of course, I'm always nice aren't I? So what did you hear?'

'Well, before I get into that, how about we fix up a date right now?'

She swallowed again. This wasn't getting any easier.

'Yeah, yeah Jimmy, but I am really pushed right now. I'm behind schedule, you know how it is.'

Frost sighed heavily down the phone, she heard him smack his lips. She did not want to think about what he was going to suggest next.

But she got lucky. This time.

'Fuck it. ok. But we meet and I am expecting a proper reward ok?'

'Sure Jimmy, sure. Please, what have you got to tell me?'

'Cops just got a call. 911. One of the guys they got in the frame for the Metro, and probably that army major who got offed too. He's turning himself in.'

What?

'Er … you sure Jimmy? Is this for real?'

'As real as what I got waiting for you baby. He's at the High Tower Hotel. It's near Long Beach, a shithole but that's where he is.'

Sammy started waving frantically at Simon.

'Ok, wow, that is massive. Thank you, Jimmy, you won't regret it, let's get together real soon. Bye.'

She hung up just as he started to make his demands, and relayed the news to Simon, and more importantly to Moran who for once in his life was speechless, but immediately started to rally a crew.

If they got moving fast LA Plus would be first on scene. Again.

***

Westwood to Long Beach was one of those journeys where if you looked at a map it looked straightforward, all freeway, nice and easy but in reality could take forever.

But not this time.

They went down in three LAPD cruisers, two SWAT vans and two FBI cars, all with lights flashing and sirens blaring. John didn't think he had ever travelled as quickly through traffic and in the dark it felt like being in a weird surreal video game. Brady and Jennings had got teams together like lightning, and they were setting up as they drove. John and Reed were in the back with a grim-faced young black officer driving and Brady in the passenger seat, his mobile glued to one ear and his radio the other.

'Ok, the local guys have it all pinned down. Hotel has been evacuated, they are holding two guys apparently, and there is a third injured,' he explained over his shoulder, holding onto the grab handle above the door as the car weaved in and out.

'What do you know about them?' Reed asked.

'Not a great deal so far, other than they are compliant. Injured guy been gut shot. I have instructed to detain them until we all get there, but the injured guy needs the ER I'm told.'

'How about the hotel? Any reason to be concerned there?'

'I don't know the place,' Brady admitted, then looked at the driver. 'Mean anything to you?'

'It's known to us yeah. Calling it a hotel is a stretch, it's a dump. There will be some players there for sure, they happy renting rooms by the hour. But the Long Beach PD will be all over it,' the driver growled in response.

They crested a rise, and then pulled off the freeway where the driver made a sharp left turn. The hotel was there, in front of them, a modern ugly four-storey beige building. The whole area was a sea of flashing red and blue lights, there were police vehicles everywhere. The driver pulled up as close as they could and they all got out. Brady made his way through the congestion and was joined by Jennings. They got into a conversation with a couple of senior officers at the hotel entrance. Everyone looked relaxed, unhurried.

Brady turned and waved at John, so he and Reed headed over. Brady was smiling.

'Let's go on in. I think you're going to like this.'

They walked into a dark, dingy lobby, empty apart from a reception desk which was a small square window set in the wall under the stairs. In the centre of the room two men were kneeling down, side by side with their hands on their heads. There were several officers watching over them.

'That's Perez,' John said quietly to Reed who nodded.

'The other one has to be this Sal Rodriguez character,' he replied.

They looked at the two men then around the small lobby.

'Where's Pinsky?' John asked, to nobody in particular.

'He's upstairs. Best be quick,' Perez replied with a glance up at him.

'Room 311,' one of the officers standing watching said. 'Medics are with him.'

They hurried up the stairs to the third floor.

The door to 311 was standing open, they could see two paramedics working and a couple of police casually leaning on the wall outside. They walked in. Pinsky was on a stretcher, in the same black leather jacket they had seen him wearing earlier walking into the yard. His t-shirt had been cut open and he had a bright red stain around a white dressing in the centre of his stomach. As they moved toward him he looked at both John and Reed then closed his eyes.

'Can he talk?' John asked the nearest paramedic, who shook his head.

'He's outta it. We gotta get him to the ER. Maybe later, see how it goes ok?' he replied, and they carried Pinsky from the room.

There was a CSI officer working next to where Pinsky had been lying, carefully placing a pair of Glock and Makarov pistols into separate bags.

Brady joined them and they watched as the paramedics carried Pinsky carefully down the stairs.

'I don't know if this makes everything easier or not,' he asked.

'I don't neither,' Reed replied.

'Well, I suppose at the least we aren't looking for anyone now. We saw five men enter the yard this afternoon. The CSI guys can account for them, all the other DNA and forensics are real old. That's everyone. Two guys dead at the scene, and another close by. That just leaves us with Pinsky and the two downstairs.'

'I guess so,' Brady sounded uncertain.

'Let's see what they tell us when they are interviewed. I'm not about to start telling you how to do your job but please get your best people on that,' John advised.

'Which one shot Pinsky?' asked Reed.

'They tell me Rodriguez admitted it, told them he done it as soon as the first responders got on scene. Says he had no choice,' Brady told them.

They went downstairs, where the huge police presence was dissipating. The two men were still where they had been before but were now handcuffed.

John walked over and studied them.

'At a guess, I'd say enough was enough, am I about right?' he asked.

Both men nodded.

'Why did you shoot him?'

Rodriguez looked upward earnestly.

'We were just soldiers. That's what we were told, all the time. Soldiers. Doing a job. But in the end, I don't got any idea what we were supposed to be.'

He looked at Rico sorrowfully.

'I didn't have no choice. I never shot no one before.'

Rico gave him a half smile.

'You did what you had to brother. You got more guts than me. I never shot nobody neither. But we're here, and we're alive.'

He looked at Brady.

'Ask your questions. I got no problem talking, we know we're going to jail. All this shit that happened? That weren't us, but we were there. So I guess we'll take what we got coming.'

Brady nodded, and then indicated to the surrounding officers to take them away. They were led out, and put in separate vans. The hotel manager, who had been a constant thorn in the police side hurried over and started remonstrating about getting his hotel back, he was losing money, he would sue, etc.

'Right. Let's get you guys home, we can all sit down tomorrow,' Brady said, ignoring the man completely, and they filed out, nothing else to say.

As John was saying goodnight to Reed and being shown a car which would take him back to Santa Monica there was a sudden burst of activity on the other side of the police cordon and a voice calling out 'John!' several times. He looked up and smiled.

Sammy was waving frantically at him, also with a big grin on her face.

He turned to his escort who was waiting by the open car door.

'Actually, I don't think I'll need that lift thank you.'

The officer was unsure.

'Look, I got told …'

John interrupted him.

'It's fine, don't worry. And at least it saves you a job.'

Chapter Forty-Three

Brady worked late to make sure everything was in place and watertight. Perez and Rodriguez were taken to different precincts, and spent the next day being interviewed.

Both men were immediately frank and open, and opted to talk freely without lawyers being present. Full statements were taken, but apart from the timeline and complete details of the assault at the Metro and the murder of Hayter they soon discovered that there wasn't really a whole lot that they hadn't already worked out.

Perez explained his recruitment into 1-Too, which even though he was keen to talk was still vague in terms of definite names. He had been living in Seattle, and had split from a girlfriend so ended up sleeping on a friend's sofa, but had been there too long and knew it.

He had no proper job, no money and no prospects, and had been scraping by working for a local underground bookmaker as a debt collector earning a few bucks here and there. He had been offered cash to drive a stolen van back from Redmond but had been pulled over on the way when a keen-eyed policeman spotted the man who had offered him the money driving the car on the way to collect it. The man had various warrants out, so they were both taken in. There was nothing obvious to charge Perez with but because of his record they kept him in and grilled him anyway.

He was released eventually, and made his way across town back home, rueing his bad luck and the fact that now he was even more skint than normal. Keen to keep out of the way as long as he could he chose to drop by a bar close by and had just sat down with a beer when a cop that he had seen hanging around earlier appeared next to him. He'd been followed, and saying very little of any substance the cop slid over a piece of paper with a cellphone number written on it and advised him to call it if he wanted to earn some cash, then had disappeared.

So Rico rang, and the conversation was short. There was money in LA. So get down there and call another number as soon as he arrives. The job would take a month or so, and he would be working for a crew.

And feeling like he had run out of options in Seattle he had done exactly as he was told.

He never had any names, he had made contact as soon as soon as he got off the train and been told to go to Mount Pleasant, which had been a huge pain in the ass, to use his own words. After a lot of hanging around and sleeping in a park he had been approached by Ji-hoon, who had been watching him. Again, he wasn't told a whole lot but he was taken to Voorhees, and given a sleeping bag in the shitty apartment. From that point on he was told he was a soldier. 1-Too was never mentioned except when Voorhees was laying the law down about something. Sal had arrived a week or two later. The stated month or so became four, and in that time they didn't actually do anything until the last week. All they did was occasionally have fun firing assault rifles out in the wilds, or just fetching and carrying around the city. The Metro station had been their first action, and that had gone wrong, but he didn't know why because he hadn't been on the platform. The information given had been poor, and he believed Voorhees and given everybody separate instructions, but his understanding has been that Ji-hoon and Sung-min were to get the bag and Pol was to keep everyone on the platform. He and Sal had to stop anyone else going downstairs, but once it was underway they were to get back to van and have it running. There had been no clear picture of Deanna, and no other detail had been given. Ji-hoon had been unhappy.

Rico was asked about all the weapons, he had no idea where they came from. He told them that Pol would take care of teaching everyone how to shoot, he was the only one with any real training. Rico said they used to enjoy going out firing at targets, apparently they got quite good at it in the end.

Weiss had killed the major, which hadn't exactly been in the script. All they had been told by Voorhees was go get the briefcase.

But what happened seemed to cause panic, and straight after they had moved to the train yard, then Pinsky had shown up with Rolf and Greg and what had already been shit went way worse fast.

Finally, both he and Sal had snapped. Voorhees had been murdered, Rolf was dead and then that motherfucker Pinsky had killed Greg just like it was nothing. Weiss had left behind a Glock which nobody knew about and Sal had shot Pinsky with it in the hotel room. He had been aiming for a leg but had rushed it because he'd been panicking. Perez admitted that at the time they both were, they had been at breaking point for hours.

He was just happy to be alive.

If anything Rodriguez's story was even more poignant. He was born in San Diego, so was a naturalised Californian. But he hadn't been there long, his mother had taken him and his three sisters off in an old car in the middle of the night. He had no memory of it, he had been less than a year old at the time. They had pitched up in Miami, which was their home for the next few years until there had been another moonlight flit, this time to Atlanta. He had never known his father, his mother was Mexican. When he was ten she was arrested for her part of a credit card scam, and with a bunch of other charges ended up going to jail. So Rodriguez and his sisters were in the system. They were split up, and Rodriguez was fostered several times until at last he was eighteen. He was living in Birmingham, and involved in all sorts of petty street crimes. He did try and find his mother, but found out she had been released a long time ago but made no effort to contact him.

He too had been approached in a bar and told to ring a number, his story virtually matched that of Perez.

Yes, he had found the Glock in a car they had been forced to dump after that asshole Weiss got himself killed. He had kept it because things were getting 'as ragged as shit' and he was glad he had. He had no remorse about shooting Pinsky, it was the end of the line and both he and Perez would have been murdered for sure. He had spoken the truth, he had never shot anyone before, never aimed a gun at anyone. In the end they were stuck in a crappy hotel while Pinsky got angrier and angrier all the time while making impossible demands and he had just pulled the trigger.

At that point Sal Rodriguez laughed.

'Man, you should have seen the look on that motherfucker's face.'

Both men's statements outlined life in the apartment identically. There were rarely any clear instructions, they never had any real idea what they were supposed to be doing. They were bored and spent most of their time either in McDonald's or hanging around in the kitchen. Voorhees would occasionally issue orders to do something but was always secretive and would lock himself away in his office on the phone. The only money they had earned was the few bucks that Voorhees would hand out every now and then.

Pinsky's wounding was serious but not fatal. He was stabilised in the emergency room and once the danger had passed was transferred to a private room.

He was not a happy man.

The doctors gave the police permission to question him but he clammed up and demanded a representative from the embassy. Suddenly his previously reasonably fluent English deserted him.

The police sensibly decided to take a step back and deferred to the FBI, who took charge and met with the official when they arrived at the hospital.

There were seven charges; the murders of Yann Voorhees and Greg Tilson, the murders of three LAPD SWAT team officers, accomplice in the murder of CIA agent Kyle Warner and accomplice in the attempted murder of FBI agent Judy Blake.

The official was in with Pinsky a long time, and when he came out the FBI were advised that due to his injuries Leonid Pinsky was unable to speak at this time, and an official statement would be released.

The official statement, when it arrived, came from the White House. It was very simple.

Under advice from Homeland Security Congress has determined that Leonid Pinsky be handed over to Moscow. He has denied all knowledge of the murder of Kyle Warner or the attempt on Judy and there is not sufficient evidence to support such charges. During the events at the train yard he admits to firing a weapon but claims to have aimed well away from the officers and vehicles. He also admitted to carrying the Makarov, stating it was for his own protection and denying murdering Greg Tilson, despite ballistics proving it and his were the only fingerprints on the weapon. He states that he has acted in the best interests of government in his actions against 1-Too agents, who are known to be involved in terrorist action globally and regarded as enemies of the United States of America as well as Russia. He is to be deported back to Russia as soon as is practical in regard to his injuries, and would be dealt with the authorities there. Homeland Security have ascertained that any conflicting statements given by the witnesses currently in police custody could not be regarded seriously as both men have criminal records. This decision is final.

It was countersigned by the office of the president.

The FBI knew when they were handcuffed, and had no choice but to pass it all over to Homeland Security. Pinsky was their problem now, for the very limited time he had left in the USA.

It meant Judy was unhappy and angry but knew there was nothing she could do. While Pinsky was now case closed, the investigation into 1-Too continued. The phone records for Keane, Voorhees and Pinsky had been checked, and any matching numbers scrutinised.

And there was one on all three phones that was interesting straight away.

Charles Edward Morgan. General, US Army, formerly commanding officer at Fort Indigo, now based at the Pentagon.

The next day three Military Policemen wearing full dress uniforms entered the Pentagon. One of them, a captain, was a very big man and towered over General Morgan as he was led away, which caused a brief flurry of interest among the staff until it was forgotten, as was Morgan himself in a very short space of time.

Morgan was taken back directly to Indigo. Once the questioning started the MP's expected trouble, they ultimately had to work alongside the FBI and the charges were very serious.

But Morgan surprised everyone. His incarceration was a relief, he was a wreck, and admitted everything almost as soon as he sat down.

Chapter Forty-Four

It had all begun four years previously. Following the G8 and G20 summits the much improved communications between previously combative governments it had been decided to have seminars across several key nations for senior military personnel. General Morgan was the one chosen, to represent the US. And he revelled in it. First class flight to Paris, three nights stay in a five-star hotel, and free flowing food and wine.

On the last night after yet another elaborate and extremely expensive dinner, he sat having brandy and cigars in a lounge overlooking the city, along with his Russian and Chinese counterparts, who of course he had never met before. So he was very surprised and interested to learn that they had been having regular conversations. The Russian; a Colonel General Rostov, who had been a keynote speaker at one of the conferences and spoke in fluent English had told him that he had already been in meetings with several of the other officers from various countries before. With a laugh, he said that they had taken part in simple war games, which so far Russia had won. Intrigued, Morgan asked more, and when Grand Marshal Yin, who was one of two Chinese officers present backed it up, Morgan was sold. He could see how much Rostov and Yin were enjoying talking about it. So when Rostov, with a twinkle in his eye, had said that he could never see the USA taking part Morgan had immediately announced that he was in.

So the game was set, between Russia, China and the USA. Rostov explained the idea. It sounded laughably simple.

The three officers would each come up with some kind of developmental weapon, which could be real, fake or just imagined. There would be plans and technical information.

Each country would attempt to steal these plans from the other two countries. The rules were simple. The name of the weapon had to be divulged within one month of the game starting, along with some kind of outline. Their own names had to be included as part of any headers or footers attached, and the schematic must always remain at the military offices or base that it originated from.

After that, there were no rules. Each country could use whatever means they had available to discover the information, and they had until the next summit, which was to be in four years' time.

On arrival back at Indigo Morgan had sat down with the senior armoury officer asking for information about any weapons that were in development, due to be tested soon or for any reason had been abandoned. Understandably confused about the request he had suggested Morgan talked to the teaching staff, as they used such examples for training. So Morgan did, and eventually came away with a twenty page document on a new mobile ground to air missile which had long since been abandoned due to cost and overall feasibility. He added in his name, rank and number then sent a copy of the cover sheet to Rostov and Yin, and the game was underway.

The only other person he discussed it with was his old friend Colonel Carter, who was as usual impressed and keen to help. He offered to assist in hiding any paperwork which Morgan was very glad about as he couldn't think of anywhere and this appeared to be key in the game unfolding.

Morgan did a presentation to the Senate on the seminar and requested that he should attend the next summit, which was agreed. For the staff involved this was a win–win, it would mean they wouldn't have to lose anybody actually useful, Morgan could do no harm there and wouldn't be missed, he would be retiring soon after anyway.

Morgan was delighted, and enjoyed telling everyone about how important the summit was, then he forgot all about it.

Until six months previously, when he had got a call on his personal mobile phone. It was from a man who did not give his name, but advised that his organisation was working for the Russians to find the plans that Morgan was hiding. He was told that they would succeed. A disbelieving Morgan argued, it was impossible. No, the man told him. His organisation could do anything.

And maybe Morgan would care to use them to find the Russian and Chinese information. The man told him he didn't care who's side he was on.

After all, it was only about winning.

Morgan admitted he didn't think very long about it, the pride of the US army; his army, was at stake. Until he got the call he hadn't taken it seriously at all, but once he realised the game was actually happening and he had so far done nothing he made the decision, one that would ultimately cause the deaths of innocent people and his own downfall.

There was not much else to ask.

Chapter Forty-Five

The cheeseburger was good again, and even better chased down with a beer. Major Turner was happy. Lieutenant Colonel Mathews was happy. The army was in the clear. Any fallout would go to no more than two individuals, there would be no impact anywhere else. They sat around a table in the corner; Turner and Reed on one side and Mathews and John on the other.

'You're welcome back here anytime John, and I mean that,' Turner said seriously.

'Thank you. I plan on keeping in touch with Tom anyway.'

'You better.' Reed clinked his bottle hard against John's.

'You know this thing is almost impossible to imagine. When we first started working on it I thought either the CIA or the FBI would take it and everyone else could forget about it. But it just got more and more complicated. It's like a bad film. General Morgan, Colonel Carter and poor old Hayter all involved in it and look how it all turned out,' John said.

'Well, General Morgan is in it now for sure, I guess he's looking at jail time and I'm guessing Carter has a lot of explaining to do. He is doing all he can right now for damage limitation. Miraculously he produced the schematics, like he just found them by chance, but there ain't nobody gonna fall for that. You know I really believe that Hayter had no idea. He was told to look after the drawings and that's what he did. But Morgan knew that 1-Too were playing both sides, he can't have told Carter everything,' Reed pondered.

'Morgan and Carter were old buddies, and the pair of them also knew Hayter pretty well. So there is a history between them, but for sure Hayter didn't have a clue what was going on. Hell, all he ever thought about was going to Vegas every weekend. The army was strictly just there for the paycheque every month. My guess is that as soon as Morgan knew he was off to the Pentagon, him and Carter panicked that the drawings could get found. After all, Morgan's name was all over the schematics, which he would never have been able to explain. So they must have wanted to stash them, and where better than with the guy that runs the stores? Tons of paperwork goes through there every year, nobody would notice. Hayter had no idea what it was, and just stashed it in an old ammo case to get rid of it. He probably forgot all about it. You know we would never have found it, Carter cracked, although he tried to make out he guessed and we got lucky there,' Turner said with a wry smile.

'It's all about money. This kind of crap always is. Always. 1-Too must have decided if the Russians wanted it that badly then so will the US. They would have made it sound easy to Morgan. But this couldn't have been cheap, and I suppose we'll never find out where the money came from. Morgan can't have got it out the army coffers surely?' John asked.

'I think I can help there. Colonel Carter's wife is rich. I mean really rich. So my guess is that is one of the reasons Morgan got him involved, it wouldn't have just been because they are buddies,' Turner explained.

'Rich? Then why the hell is he in the army?' Reed wanted to know.

'Appearances. You know how these rich guys look; son-in-law a colonel in the army, it's all good. He's a less successful clone of General Morgan, and his father, grandfather, etc. all served, all heavy hitters in the army. So they follow in the footsteps and as we all know, if you're in with the right people then that's how to get on. And that ain't just the military. It's that shit everywhere. So Colonel Carter is gonna be real uncomfortable now, my bet is he'll have some kind of a story worked out for sure and it sure as hell better be good. But he'll serve his time, retire and never have to lift a finger again,' Turner replied.

'Mind you, I guess that isn't so certain now. Morgan is up on serious charges, and he may not want to take the fall alone,' Mathews added.

'But the worst thing for me is that Hayter and his wife both ended up dead as a result of it. Yeah, Deanna was recruited we know that, but she didn't know the half of it. All she wanted was the forty thousand. And Madeline only wanted her daughter back. They really didn't deserve what they got. Hayter was just the dumb schmuck who needed the cash too,' Reed pondered sorrowfully.

'And what about Pinsky? And the general in Moscow?' asked John.

'Well, Pinsky is some kind of superman. He's had some real serious wounds over the years, but still keeps going and the word is he will walk from this. I guess it was no surprise he's gonna get disappeared, no way was he ever going to stand trial over here. We know that for damn sure. It's just like what we know about Colonel Carter, for Congress, this is all about damage limitation. Whatever gets said publicly, they are not going head to head with Moscow over one bad guy. Even after we lost a major, a CIA agent and three cops plus five members of the public. And there was no linking Pinsky to either the Metro attack or major Hayter's murder. The Russian army are denying he has any attachment, they say they lost all track of him. They released some information, which is how we found out about his previous injuries but nothing up to date. And the general, Rostov? Claims to know nothing, doesn't even remember the summit let alone General Morgan, and says he never heard of Pinsky neither. So our word against theirs, the only satisfaction we get is they spent a fortune and got nothing in return.'

'Pinsky got played by Deanna, and Madeline probably,' John commented.

'Yeah, that's for sure. She did get forty grand, I bet she probably only gave Hayter a couple to get married, and she only did that to get Pinsky off her back. And Hayter would have taken it, he just wanted the cash to stay at the tables, he had no credit left anymore at Indigo. I get the feeling he would have done anything to keep going to Vegas. But I got no idea what Pinsky thought Deanna was gonna do to get the plans, it ain't what I'd call pillow talk. He must have thought Hayter had them in his room or something. Maybe he got the idea they were gonna play happy families in Vegas. I don't know. The deaths at the Metro still make no sense, somebody must have decided she was carrying them I guess, maybe she even told Pinsky or someone she did have them just to keep them sweet,' Turner said soberly.

'Maybe it was that guy Voorhees. It sounds like he wasn't delivering,' Reed said.

'Could be. It looks like Pinsky didn't waste any time getting rid of him. Perez has been saying he was told it would be at most a month and then more than four later and still they'd done nothing. He says the Metro attack was planned in two days. Voorhees must have been feeling the pressure.'

'Two days? How did they know Deanna would be there?' John asked.

'Again, Perez and Rodriguez can't answer that. My guess is she was set up to go. Maybe promised as attorney or something to do with Madeline's daughter,' Turner pondered.

'It is unbelievable. All this for a game.' Reed shook his head.

'You got that right. Morgan should never have been at that summit in the first place. That guy makes nothing but bad decisions. You always said he was an asshole,' Turner looked at Reed with a grin.

'Yeah, I did. I probably shouldn't have but there you go.'

Turner sat back with a rueful smile.

'You know I got a call this morning. I was told that the state department made contact with Grand Marshal Yin, in Beijing. I guess that was an awkward conversation but he did confirm Morgan's story about how it all started, although his version is that General Rostov put him up to it. Make Morgan look stupid is how he put it. But one thing he did say was, he enjoyed it. And what's interesting about that is we got some intel that the Russians believe that China have got hold of information on a new fighter jet. So I wonder how they got that?'

'I have to ask, but I guess I'm not gonna like the answer. What is anyone doing about these 1-Too assholes? They seem like they need wiping off the face of the earth to me,' Mathews asked, serious for the first time.

Everyone looked at John, who shrugged.

'I don't really know how to answer that. Look, they have been chased around by law agencies all over the world for more than ten years. They came out of nowhere. They're organised, and if anyone ever does get taken nobody really knows the setup so there is never any useable information. Just like we got with Perez and Rodriguez; they don't know a damn thing. Keane doesn't either, and we can't speak to Pinsky. Maybe we could have got something out of Voorhees, who knows. You can be sure the CIA, Interpol, MI6 and many others will continue trying to track them down and hopefully there will be a breakthrough.'

'But who the hell are they?'

'Well, it is now believed they originated in Beirut, but again, nobody really knows. All anyone is sure of is they are a big organisation, and rich, a lot of power. Morgan paid a great deal of money and Rostov is likely to have shelled out the same.'

'Didn't work out for them this time,' Reed commented.

'No, they lost here. For all the secrecy, and their obvious organisation at the end of the day they are only as good as who is on the ground, and it didn't go as planned in LA. Their name will come up again, unfortunately.'

'So, do I get Tom back now? I'm positive there will be some GIs up to no good that need the crap scaring out of them somewhere on this base,' Turner asked, still smiling.

'Of course, thank you very much for the loan,' John said smiling back.

'So, what are you going to do now, John?' Reed asked.

'Now? After this I'm meeting Sammy, then we'll just see what happens. I'm off to New York at some point soon anyway, I want to see my daughter. I make sure I do that at least once a month.'

'Sammy?' Turner looked puzzled.

'Sammy King,' Reed told him.

'What, her? Off the TV?'

'Yep.'

'Wow John she is hot as hell. Hotter.' Turner looked at John in wonder.

'Yeah, she is.'

'And she likes John,' Reed said with a wide smile.

John looked at the two men.

'I just had a thought. I'm meeting her downtown. How the hell am I going to get there from way out here? Is there a cab office?'

Mathews laughed.

'You know what John? Least the army can do is get you there. I'll arrange a driver.'

***

John was late, but Sammy forgave him, and greeted him with a big kiss. They had a couple of drinks, then set off back to Santa Monica, John still had the hotel room and he had to get his stuff anyway.

'Are you still saying I don't get an interview?' Sammy teased as they made their way across LA.

'Yes, that is exactly what I'm saying.'

Sammy grinned.

'We got all we need. And your picture is front and centre. You're public property now. You know John, I told Costas all about you. He was very interested.'

'Costas?'

'Costas Blanic, he owns the channel. He's Albanian, a real fascinating guy actually. Anyway, I told him about you, what you do for a living and he wants to meet you.'

'Why?'

'He wondered if you might do some work for him.'

John's phone rang loudly, he looked at the display, he had no idea who was calling but answered it anyway, he was in a good mood.

'Hey, is that John?' A woman's voice. John had no idea.

'Yeah, who's this?'

'Oh, hey, it's Sugar. You won't remember. You came into Miss Sin once. I was your hostess.'

John thought back.

'Yeah I do remember. What can I do for you Sugar?'

'Well, it's kind of difficult but you said for me to call. Like, if I was having trouble with some guy. You know, the one that likes to get rough. Anyway, he's here, and he's making me real nervous. He always stays till we close and that's when the trouble starts. The problem is I need this job. You know. But you said you can help. I got nobody I can ask. I got nobody looking out for me, but I know you were for real I just know it. And I thought about that ever since. In case he came back. I knew he would, and he's drunk and already making trouble for me.'

'Yeah, I know I did. I'll do what I can. I'll get there, just stay away from him if you can.'

'Really? You mean that?'

'Yeah. Sit tight.'

John hung up the call and looked over at Sammy who was obviously trying to listen while appearing not to.

'Er ... Sammy. I'm not trying to be a pain in the arse but can we go via Hollywood? It won't take long.'

www.ingramcontent.com/pod-product-compliance
Lightning Source LLC
Chambersburg PA
CBHW020354260626
47156CB00007B/2098